THE UNSEEN

Katherine Webb

WINDSOR
PARAGON

First published 2011
by Orion Books
This Large Print edition published 2011
by AudioGO Ltd
by arrangement with
The Orion Publishing Group

Hardcover   ISBN: 978 1 445 85756 5
Softcover   ISBN: 978 1 445 85757 2

British Library Cataloguing in Publication Data available

Printed and bound in Great Britain by
MPG Books Group Limited

Our birth is but a sleep and a forgetting:
The Soul that rises with us, our life's Star,
Hath had elsewhere its setting,
And cometh from afar:

(William Wordsworth,
'Ode on Intimations of Immortality')

. . . if we have actually proved the existence
upon the surface of this planet of a
population which may be as numerous as the
human race, which pursues its own strange
life in its own strange way, and which is only
separated from ourselves by some difference
of vibrations . . .

(Sir Arthur Conan Doyle,
The Coming of the Fairies)

In every plant and animal, we perceive the
life-filled spiritual form in addition to the
physical form . . .

(Rudolph Steiner, *Theosophy*)

May 14th, 1911

Dearest Amelia,

It's the most glorious spring morning here, on a day of some excitement. The new maid arrives today—Cat Morley. I have to admit to feeling a touch of nerves, such is the reputation which precedes her, but then I'm sure she can't be all bad. Albert was not at all sure about the appointment, but I managed to persuade him with a two-pronged argument, thus: That it would be an act of commendable Christian charity for us to take her on when surely nobody else will; and also that because of her reputation we would be obliged to pay her very little, and she would therefore represent a sound household investment. We are doubling our household staff at virtually no increase in expense! I received a letter of introduction from the housekeeper at Broughton Street—Mrs Heddingly—giving a list of duties with which the girl is familiar, and also urging me not to let her read 'for all our sakes'. I am not sure what she means by this, but I find it generally wise to heed advice given by those in the know. She— Mrs Heddingly—also passes on a peculiar rumour about the girl. I can't think why she chooses to mention it and can only assume a love of gossip— that the identity of Cat's father is the subject of much speculation, and that it has been whispered, taking account of the dark tones of her skin and hair, that he may have been a Negro. Apparently, the other staff at Broughton Street took to calling her Black

Cat after this story got about. Well, I'm certain that the girl's mother, however low her station, would not stoop to such degradation, unless she was the victim of a most heinous crime. And that her poor daughter should go under such an ill-luck name hardly seems fair. I will not hear her called it again, I am quite resolved.

Amidst the nerves I confess I also look forward to her coming. Not least because there are balls of slut's wool beneath the beds the size of apples! It's been many months since Mrs Bell, God bless her, was able to bend down far enough to see to them. The whole house is in need of a thorough seeing to. But it will also give me great pleasure to gather up one of God's creatures who has been led astray, and who has wandered perilously close to ruin. Here she will find a Godly house, forgiveness and the chance to commend herself to the Lord with hard work and clean living. I intend to offer her every succour in this endeavour, and to take her quite under my wing—she will be my project—imagine it! The chance to truly reform a person, and set them back on quite the right path. I'm sure the girl will see how fortunate she is— to be given such a chance to redeem herself. She comes to us tarnished, and will soon be polished to a shine.

And such work is surely the perfect preparation for motherhood. For what else is a mother's job than to nurture her children into Godly, worthy and virtuous people? I see how well you do with my niece and nephew, dear Ellie and John, and I am full of admiration for your gentle, guiding way with them. Don't fret so over John and his catapult. I am sure he will grow out of this mood of violence very soon: a boy's nature is—by divine design—more warlike than

2

a girl's, and it's to be expected that he feels urges that you and I can't understand. How I look forward to having little souls of my own to grow.

Amelia—please forgive me for asking you again, but I fear your last letter has left me still quite in the dark on the subject in question. Must you be so vague, dearest? I know such things are not easily discussed, and indeed are better not spoken of at all if possible, but my need is great, and if I can't turn to my sister for help and guidance, then who, pray, can I turn to? Albert is an exemplary husband, only ever kind and affectionate towards me—each night before we retire he presses a kiss to my hair and praises me as a good wife and lovely creature, but thereafter he sleeps, and I can only lie and wonder what it is that I am doing wrong, or not doing, or indeed not even trying to do. If you would only tell me in the most specific terms how I should behave, and how our bodies might be 'conjoined', as you put it? Albert is such a wonderful husband, I can only assume that it is I who am not performing my right function as a wife, and that this is the cause of—well, of my not yet expecting a happy event. Please, dear Amelia, be specific.

All is well, then. I had better end this letter now. The sun is high, and the birds are singing fit to burst, and I shall post this on my way to visit poor Mrs Duff, who has no such problems as I and has been kept abed with a terrible infection since the birth of her sixth child—yet another boy. Then, after lunch, Cat Morley should make her appearance on the three fifteen train. Cat—such an abrupt name. I wonder if she would take to being called Kitty? Write to me soon, dearest and best of sisters.

Your loving, Hester

The first time Leah met the man who would change her life, he was lying face down on a steel table, quite oblivious to her. Odd patches of his clothing remained, the colour of mud, slick with moisture. The bottom half of a trouser leg, the shoulders of his jacket. She felt cold on his behalf, and slightly awkward faced with his nakedness. His head was turned away from her, face half pressed to the table so that all she could see were the carved dark structures of his hair, and one perfect, waxen ear. Leah's skin prickled; she felt voyeuristic. As though he was only asleep, might at any minute stir, turn his head and look at her; woken by her footsteps and the sound of her breathing in that immaculate ear.

'You're not going to throw up, are you?' Ryan's voice broke into her trance. She swallowed, shook her head. Ryan smiled mischievously.

'Who is he? Was he?' she asked, clearing her throat, folding her arms in a show of nonchalance.

'If we knew that, I wouldn't have called you all the way out to Belgium.' Ryan shrugged, airily. He was wearing a white coat, like a doctor, but it was grubby and marked, and hung open to show torn jeans, a scuffed leather belt.

'First time seeing a dead body?' Peter asked, with his calm, Gallic intonation. Peter, the head of the archaeology department.

'Yes.' Leah nodded.

'Always an odd experience. At least with one this old, there's no smell. Well, not the worst kind of

4

smell, anyway,' he said. Leah realised she'd been breathing through her mouth; shallow breaths, expecting the worst. She inhaled cautiously through her nose. There was a dank smell, almost tangy; like wet January leaves, like estuarine mud.

She fumbled in her bag, drew out her pad and pen.

'Where did you say he was found?' she asked.

'In the back garden of a house near Zonnebeke, north-east of Ypres. A Mrs Bichet was digging a grave for her dog . . .' Ryan paused, pretended to check his notes, 'her dog *Andre*, if I have it correctly.' He smiled, that curving, lopsided grin that made something pull in Leah's bones. She raised an eyebrow at him, nothing more. Under the strip lights his skin looked dull and there were shadows under his eyes. But he was still beautiful, she thought helplessly. Still beautiful. 'Digging one grave and stumbled across another. She nearly took his right arm off with the shovel—see here.' He pointed carefully to the dead man's forearm. Beige skin had parted, brown flesh protruded, fibrous like earth, like muck. Leah swallowed again, felt her head lighten.

'Isn't the War Graves Commission going to identify him? Why call me?'

'So many dead soldiers turn up every year— fifteen, twenty, twenty-five. We do our best, but if there are no regimental badges, no tags, no crucial bits of kit to go on, there just aren't the resources to pursue it further,' Peter explained.

'He'll get a nice burial, with a nice white cross, but they won't know what name to put on it,' said Ryan.

'A *nice burial*?' Leah echoed. 'You're too

5

flippant, Ryan. You always were.'

'I know. I'm impossible, right?' He smiled cheerfully again; ever one to make light of something serious.

'So . . . if there's nothing to go on, how did you think I could help?' Leah addressed the question to Peter.

'Well—' Peter began, but Ryan cut him off.

'Don't you want to meet him face to face? He's remarkably well preserved—that end of the garden is waterlogged all year round, apparently—there's a stream that runs along the bottom of it. Very pretty, by all accounts. Come on—not scared, are you? Of an archaeological find?'

'Ryan, why must you be so . . .' Leah gave up, didn't finish the sentence. She tucked her hair behind her ears, folded her arms protectively across her chest, and walked around to the other side of the table.

The dead man's face was rumpled slightly, as if he'd only lain down to sleep, pushing it resolutely into a pillow of broken ground. A crease in the lower cheek, running from eye socket to mouth. His top lip still described a long, elegant curve; a trace of stubble above it. His bottom lip and lower jaw dissolved into a scrambled mess that Leah could not look too closely at. His nose was also crushed, flattened, soft and gelatinous. It looked like she could reach out, cup her fingers, scoop it away completely. But his forehead, his eyes, were perfect. A lock of sodden hair fell forward, unruly; his brow was unlined, perhaps because of youth, perhaps because the skin was swollen, waterlogged. Handsome, he would have been. She could almost see it—could unfocus her eyes, blur

6

away the terrible injuries, the wrong colour of his skin, the inhuman smell. And around each closed eye were tiny black lashes—each one separate, discernible, neatly lined up, as they should be. As they had been, the day he'd died almost a hundred years before. The lids had a faint silvery sheen, like meat left too long. Were they completely shut? Leah leaned towards him, frowned a little. Now it looked like they were slightly open. Just a little. Like some people's remained when they slept, when they dreamed. She leaned closer, her own heartbeat loud above the whine of the lights. Could she see his eyes moving, behind the lids? Would the last thing he saw be there still? Tattooed accusingly onto his irises. She held her breath.

'Boo!' Ryan said in her ear. Leah jumped, gasped audibly.

'You prick,' she snapped at him, and marched out through the heavy swinging doors, angry at how easily she rattled.

She strode briskly up two flights of stairs and followed the smell of chips and coffee to the college's cafeteria. Pouring herself a paper cupful, she noticed that her hands were shaking. She sank into a plastic chair by the window and stared out at the landscape. Flat and grey and brown, just as England had looked when she left. A neat row of gaudy crocuses lining a pathway only highlighted the drab of everything else. Her own reflection in the glass was pale—pale skin, pale lips, pale blond hair. The dead man in the cellar had more colour, she thought ruefully. Belgium. Suddenly she yearned to be somewhere, anywhere, rather than here. Somewhere with bright sunshine to etch

7

outlines onto the landscape, and warmth to soak into her bones. Why on earth had she agreed to come? But she knew why. Because Ryan had asked her to. He walked right out of her thoughts and sat down opposite her, frowning.

'Look, I'm sorry, OK?' he said, contritely. 'Having you here isn't easy for me either, you know. You make me nervous.'

'Why am I here, Ryan?' Leah asked.

'I think there could be a great story in it for you—really. The lost soldier, anonymous and unmourned all these years . . .'

'You don't know he was unmourned.'

'True enough. Undiscovered, then. And I know you think I'm flippant about it, but I'm not. It must have been a bloody miserable way to die, and I think the guy deserves some recognition, don't you?'

Leah eyed him suspiciously, but he seemed sincere. His hair had grown since she'd last seen him. It was hanging in loose tawny curls at either side of his face, matching three or four days' growth on his chin. His eyes were the colour of dark honey. Leah tried not to look too deeply into them.

'Why me?' she asked.

'Why not you?' he countered. 'I don't know that many freelance journalists.' He looked down at his hands for a minute, picked at one ragged thumbnail where the skin was already raw. Leah's own fingers twitched, from the long habit of trying to stop him doing it.

'That's all?' she pressed.

Ryan frowned, took a short, irritable breath. 'No, that's not *all*. What do you want me to say,

8

Leah? That I wanted to see you? Fine—there you go,' he said, abruptly.

Leah smiled a small, wintry smile. 'You never were very good at saying what you're feeling. It always was like getting blood out of a stone.'

'I didn't get much chance to improve before you walked out.'

'I had a bloody good reason, and you know it,' she said.

'So why did you come, then, if I'm such a nightmare and you don't want to see me?'

'I never said . . .' Leah sighed. 'I'm not sure why I came,' she concluded. 'I haven't had a good idea for a story in ten months. I haven't written anything worth reading in I don't know how long. I thought you might actually have something for me to work on, but an unidentifiable soldier? What am I supposed to investigate—the work you're doing for the War Graves Commission? What happens to these men once you've dug them up? It's worthy, of course, but it'd be a pretty dry piece . . .'

'Well, there's not *nothing* to go on, actually,' Ryan said, leaning towards her and smiling his pleased, boyish smile again.

'What do you mean? Peter said—'

'I was going to tell you downstairs, but you stomped off.'

'Well, what is it?'

'Have dinner with me tonight and I'll show you,' he said.

'Why not just tell me now?' she suggested cautiously.

'Dinner would be far more fun.'

'No. Look, Ryan, I don't think you and I should be . . . spending too much time together. Not like

9

that.'

'Oh, come on, Leah. Where's the harm in it? We've known each other long enough . . .'

'Apparently, we didn't know each other quite as well as we thought,' she said, glancing up. Anger sharpened her gaze, and she saw him flinch.

'Just . . . have dinner with me tonight,' he said, more softly. Leah swigged the last of her coffee, grimacing at the wan, bitter taste.

'Bye, Ryan. I wish I could say it was good to see you again.' She got up to go.

'Wait, Leah! Don't you even want to know what it is that we found on him? I'll tell you—then you can decide whether or not to stay. Leah! He had letters on him—they've survived ninety-five years in the ground! Can you imagine? And these are no ordinary letters either,' Ryan called after her. Leah stopped. There it was, that tiny sparkle; the shimmer of curiosity she felt before she began to chase down a story. Slowly, she turned back towards him.

1911

Cat is so completely mesmerised by the rushing blur of the world outside the window that the journey passes quickly—all too quickly. With her head tipped against the glass, staring into the chalky sky with the green blur of fields pouring beneath it like a river, she fancies to herself that she is running faster than anyone ever has before, or perhaps even flying like a bird. The train carries on, she knows, all the way into the west, further west than she has ever been. It will carry on without her to Devon, and Cornwall, and the sea. She longs to see the sea again. The thought makes her ache with need. She's seen it only once before, when she was eight years old and her mother was still alive, and the whole household upped sticks for the day and went to Whitstable. It had been a blousy summer day; all diaphanous clouds, with a curling breeze that had caught the donkeys' tails, made them stream out behind them, and made the empty deckchairs billow. The Gentleman had bought her an oyster in its shell to eat, and a strawberry ice cream cone, and she had been sick all down her best dress. Stringy little gobbets of oyster flesh in a clinging pink sauce. But it had still been the happiest day of her life. She kept the oyster shell; had it for years in a cardboard box of everyday treasures.

As the train slows, the notion of flying evaporates, and Cat feels herself grow into flesh again, feet tied to the earth. The temptation to not alight is powerful. She could sink down in the clammy seat and keep on, keep on, until she saw the sea through the dusty window. But the train squeals to a halt, and she curls her fingers tightly, squeezes until her nails bite the palms of her hands. She'd hoped to draw strength from the gesture, but can't quite manage it. The station at Thatcham is small and simple. She and one other person, a thin man scowling above his moustache, alight; and there is a busy scene at a freight car where several huge wooden crates are manoeuvred onto a trolley. Tall banks of young nettles and buddleia lean over the wooden fence, whispering softly. Cat draws in a steady breath. She would

11

rather be anywhere else in the world, but at the same time she feels numb, devoid of all feeling as though it has been shaken out of her in the pain and violence of the past few months. At the far end of the platform stands a vastly fat woman. Cat pauses, seeks an alternative, and then walks slowly towards her.

The woman is quite as wide as she is high. Her cheeks crowd her eyes, narrowing them to creases. Her chins crowd her chest, so that the line from jaw to bosom flows quite uninterrupted. A skirt of flesh hangs down from her middle, swinging slightly beneath the light cotton of her dress, bumping her thighs. Cat feels sharp grey eyes sweep her up and down. She stares back, and does not flinch.

'Are you Sophie Bell?' she asks the woman. *Sophie Bell*. Such a pretty, tinkling name. Cat had envisaged a tall, soft woman with cornflower eyes and amber freckles.

'That's Mrs Bell, to you. And you'll be Cat Morley, I take it?' the woman replies, curtly.

'I am.'

'God help me then, for you'll be no use whatsoever,' says Sophie Bell. 'Six months I've been asking for help in the house and now I get this wraith, who looks fit to drop dead by Friday,' she mutters, turning from Cat and walking away with surprising speed. Her legs swing in wide arcs, her feet strike the ground flat. Cat blinks once, grips the handles of her carry-all, and then follows her.

Outside the station, a pony and trap is waiting. The little cart leans wildly to one side as Sophie Bell heaves herself onto the seat alongside the

12

driver. Cat looks up at him, half thinking to proffer her bag, but the man gives her the briefest of glances before turning his attention back to a motor car, all glossy and black, that has pulled up on the other side of the road.

'Well, don't just stand there like a dolt! Get in. I haven't got all day,' Mrs Bell tells her, exasperated. Awkwardly, Cat throws her bag onto the back seat and climbs up after it. Barely settled, the driver flicks the reins and the pony throws itself into the harness, pulling them away with a jolt. So it is facing backwards, with a view of the road just travelled, that Cat is towed into her new role, her new life. Something in her rejects this so strongly that her throat knots up and makes it hard to breathe.

*   *   *

The village of Cold Ash Holt lies about two miles outside Thatcham, the lane winding south and east through a tangle of lakes and reed beds, water meadows so bright with spring growth they hardly look real. Young leaves flash silver where the breeze turns them, and even the air seems to carry a green scent; one of moisture and the headiness of flowers. They startle a heron, which erupts up through the rushes and seems too slow, too weighty for flight. The sun gets caught up in its greasy grey feathers, glints on the beads of water falling from its feet. Cat stares. She does not know its name. She has never seen a bird as big before, has barely ever seen birds, other than sparrows and the uniform London pigeons that scratch a living from the dirt. She thinks of The Gentleman's

13

canary, on its little gilded swing; the way he whistled at it, crooning, coaxing it to sing. She had watched, paused with duster in hand, and admired it for refusing. Mrs Bell chats to the driver all the while, a low commentary that barely lets up, leaving the shortest of pauses from time to time in which the man grunts. Most of what she says is lost beneath the clatter of the pony's hooves, but Cat catches odd words and phrases. 'She'll be back again before the summer's out, just you mark my words' . . . 'had the nerve to suggest it wasn't done proper' . . . 'her son's gone off again, and with little more than a child' . . . 'short shrift for those that show criminal urges'. Cat glances over her shoulder, catches Mrs Bell's narrow eye upon her.

The vicarage is built of faded red brick, three storeys high and almost square in shape. Symmetrical rows of windows with bright white frames gaze out onto the world, the glass reflecting the bright sky. The surrounding gardens overflow with early flowers, sprays of colour rising from tidy beds that curve through stretches of short, neat lawn. Budding wisteria and honeysuckle scale the walls and window sills, and tall tulips march the path to the wide front door, painted bright blue and sporting a gleaming brass knocker. The house sits on the outskirts of the small village, its gardens adjoining the water meadows. In the distance a stream carves a winding path, like a silver ribbon. The driver pulls up at the far side of the house, across the gravel driveway, where mossy steps lead down to a more modest door.

'You use this door, none other,' Mrs Bell tells her curtly, as they make their way inside.

'Of course,' Cat replies, nettled. Did the woman

think she had never worked before?

'Now, pay attention while I show you around. I've not got time to keep repeating myself, and I need to get on with the tea. The mistress, Mrs Canning, wants to see you as soon as you've had a chance to tidy yourself up and get changed—'

'Get changed?'

'Yes, get changed! Or did you plan to meet her in that tatty skirt, with dirty cuffs on your blouse and your bootlaces frayed?' Mrs Bell's grey eyes are sharp indeed.

'I've a spare blouse, my best, and I can put it on, but this skirt is the only one I have,' Cat says.

'I'll not believe they let you about the place looking like that in London!'

'I had a uniform. I . . . had to give it back when I left.'

Mrs Bell puts her hands where her hips might have been. Cat gazes steadily at her, refusing to be cowed. The older woman's knuckles are cracked and red. They sink into her flesh, wedge themselves there. Her feet rock inwards, the arches long ago surrendered to the weight they carry. Her ankles look like suet dough, dimpled beneath her stockings. Cat grips her own two hands together in front of her, feeling the reassuring hardness of her bones.

'Well,' Mrs Bell says at last, 'it'll be up to the mistress whether she'll provide you with clothing. Otherwise you'll have to make do. You'll need a grey or brown dress for the morning, a black one for the evening; and something to wear to church. There's a rag sale next week in Thatcham. You might find something there that you can alter.'

15

Cat's room is in the attic. There are three rooms side by side, all with views north through small dormer windows, and accessed off a bright, south-facing corridor. As if the architect had thought the corridor more deserving of sunlight than the servants. Cat puts her bag down at the foot of the bed, surveys her new home. Plain, whitewashed walls, a small iron bed with a brass crucifix hanging above it; a bible on a woven straw chair; wash stand; threadbare curtains. There's a narrow cupboard for clothes, and a patchwork quilt folded at the foot of the bed. With quick steps, Cat crosses the room, takes the crucifix from the wall and flings it out of sight beneath the bed. It hits the pot with a musical clang. Where they touched the smooth limbs of the metal cross, Cat's fingers seem to sting. Rubbing her hands on her skirt in agitation, she shuts her eyes and fights off memories of an object so similar; of Jesus watching her solemnly from a high wall, oblivious to her torment. Then she stands at the window, looking out at the lane and a field of ginger cattle beyond. Such a wide empty space. She thinks of her friends in London, of Tess with her eager green eyes, always excited about something. The thought makes her ache. She has no address she can write to, no idea where Tess will end up. Tess might not be as fortunate as she, in finding another position. *I am lucky*, Cat tells herself, bitterly. She has been told it enough times, of late.

Behind her, the door swings itself shut, nudged by some stray breeze. Cat freezes, every muscle pulling tight. She stands ramrod straight and tries to breathe when the air seems too thick all of a sudden. *It's not locked*, she tells herself. *Just shut. Not locked*. She turns slowly to face the door, braced as if some horror waits there to be discovered. The small room's walls bow inwards around her, clinging to her like wet cloth. Her knees shake, and she totters to the door like an old woman, certain as she turns the handle that she won't be able to get out. The metal knob rattles in her hand as she turns it, and as she pulls the door open a few precious inches, she knows that it is her shivering that makes the handle shake. Her heartbeat tumbles like a waterfall, and she leans her face against the pitted wood of the door, waiting to feel calm. *Never again,* she thinks. *Never, never, never.*

*   *   *

Hester arranges herself at the walnut desk in the front parlour, with the household ledger open in front of her. It's the position she adopts for her weekly meeting with Mrs Bell to discuss menus and household accounts and the arranging of chimney sweeps, grocery deliveries and bicycle repair men. And she fancies it gives the right impression— feminine but businesslike; commanding yet approachable. The afternoon sun lies pooled and yellow on the oak floor, showing up the lazy dance of dust motes and houseflies. Hester flaps a hand irritably at a fly that comes too close. She finds their hairy bodies indecent, and hates the way they go dry and hard after death, lying down on the window sills in their final moments, crossing their bristly legs as if they expect to receive a last

17

blessing. She is immensely relieved that she won't have to sweep them up from now on. Mrs Bell has been hard pushed to keep up with the cleaning and the cooking both—heaven knows the woman can hardly be expected to work at speed. She wishes Mrs Bell wasn't quite so very fat. The squeaking protest of the floor gave away her approach as soon as she left the more robust stones of the basement, and she is hardly an elegant sight. A woman should be soft, of course, her outline one of curves rather than angles, but one had to draw the line somewhere. There is little point in Mrs Bell trying to keep it all in with a corset. Years ago she wore one, and it merely squeezed her flesh up and down from the middle, so that she could scarcely sit or turn her neck. Watching her manoeuvre had been both horrifying and impossible to resist.

Hester can hear her now—creaking and thumping her way from the kitchen. She sits straighter in her chair, and arranges her face into a mild, genteel smile. She worries momentarily that she will suffer in comparison with Cat Morley's more cosmopolitan former employer. Then she remembers that the girl is a pariah and relaxes, slightly ashamed of her own anxiety when her role is to mother, and to correct.

'The new girl, madam,' Mrs Bell announces, after a short knock.

'Thank you, Mrs Bell. Do come in, Cat,' Hester says, warmly; then hesitates. Cat Morley looks little more than a child. For a second, Hester thinks there's been a mistake. The girl is barely five feet tall, and has the fragile, bony look of a bird. Her shoulders are narrow, her hands and feet

18

tiny. Her hair, which is almost true black, has been cut off short. It grazes her ears in a most unladylike fashion. Cat has pinned the front of it back from her forehead, which only makes her look more like a schoolgirl. But as the girl approaches the desk, Hester sees that there is no mistake. Her face is narrow, the chin pointed and sharp, but there are smudges beneath her eyes, and a crease between her brows that speaks of experience. Cat regards Hester with such a level stare, her brown eyes unflinching, that Hester feels uncomfortable, almost embarrassed. She glances at Mrs Bell as the housekeeper leaves the room, and understands from her pinched lips exactly what the woman thinks of this new appointment.

'Well,' Hester says, flustered. 'Well, do sit down, Cat.' The girl perches on the edge of the carved chair opposite her as though she might fly away at any moment. 'I'm very pleased you've made the journey safely.' She had prepared, in her head, what she would say to the girl to put her at her ease, and to show what a kind and calm and Godly household she had found herself in, but it has got scattered in her head by the shock of the girl's appearance, and now she can't think what she wanted to say. 'I'm sure you'll be very happy here,' she tries. Cat blinks, and although her face does not move, and she does not speak, Hester gets the distinct impression that the girl doubts this last statement. 'Gracious! I have never seen hair cut in such a style as yours! Is it all the fashion, in London? Am I terribly behind the times?' Hester bursts out. Her own hair is her crowning glory. It is light and full and soft, and gathers into a bouffant high on her head each morning as if it knows

19

exactly what it is doing.

'No, madam,' Cat says quietly, never once breaking off her gaze. 'My hair was always long, before. I was forced to cut if off after my time . . . my time of incarceration. It became terribly infested with lice.'

'Oh! Lice! How dreadful!' Hester exclaims, horrified. Her hands fly to her scalp as if to protect it, and she leans away from the desk involuntarily.

'They are quite gone now, I assure you,' Cat says, the hint of a smile ghosting across her lips.

'Well, that's good. Yes. Well, now. I am sure Mrs Bell has told you your duties, and do please look to her for guidance in all matters regarding your work. You will be expected to rise at half past six and be ready to start work at seven, but you probably won't be the first person about—my husband has a great love of walking and nature, which he is particularly able to indulge at sunrise. He will often have risen and gone out before you come down, so don't be alarmed if you encounter him very early in the day. He does not expect breakfast to be ready before his walks. You may consider yourself at liberty between the hours of three and five o'clock in the afternoon, with the exception of the tea, provided that all your duties have been carried out to Mrs Bell's satisfaction.' Hester pauses, and looks up at Cat Morley. The girl's level gaze is unnerving. There is something behind her dark eyes that Hester has never seen before, and can't decipher. The shifting outline of something strange, something unpredictable.

'Yes, madam,' Cat says, eventually, and quite tonelessly.

'Cat—your proper name is Catherine, isn't it? I

20

wonder that you mightn't like to be called Kitty? A new name for a new start? I think it would suit you very well.' Hester smiles.

'I have always been Cat, never Kitty,' Cat says, puzzled.

'Yes, I see; but don't you think Kitty would be better? What I mean to say is, you can leave all that old trouble behind with the old name? Do you see?' Hester explains. Cat seems to consider this, and her eyes grow hard.

'I have always been Cat,' she insists.

'Very well, then!' Hester cries, at a loss. 'Is there anything you would like to ask me?'

'Only to say, madam, that I am not able to wear corsets. The doctor has told me, after my illness, that it would put too great a strain on my chest.'

'Really? That is a terrible shame. Of course, you must do what is best for your health, even if some might consider it improper. Is the condition likely to improve? Do you think you'll be able to wear them at some time in the future?'

'I cannot tell you,' Cat replies.

'Well, we shall see when the time comes. Cat, I want you to know . . .' Hester hesitates. Somehow the words she had prepared seem almost silly now that she is face to face with the girl. 'I want to tell you that it won't be held against you, here. Your . . . past troubles. In this house you have the chance to start afresh, and live a clean, Godly life. My husband and I have always said that charity is the greatest of virtues, and begins at home. I hope you will find us true to our philosophy.' Again, that disconcerting pause, that immobile expression. A small shiver runs down Hester's spine, and the skin of her scalp tingles unpleasantly—just like it does

21

when she finds a black spider hiding in the folds of her bedroom curtains.

'Thank you, madam,' Cat says.

*　　　*　　　*

Hester feels considerably more at ease once Cat Morley has gone back below stairs to help Mrs Bell prepare the tea. The girl had an odd air about her, as though she were distracted by something, some unnatural urge perhaps. Hester assures herself that this is unlikely, but she can't quite shake the feeling. Cat did not drop her gaze as she ought. Well, not as she *ought*, precisely, but as one might expect her to. She was so tiny and weak looking, it was easy to imagine her frightened of the least little thing. Hester takes up her needlepoint bag, and the fresh frame she stretched only yesterday, ready to begin a new piece. She thinks for a moment, and then smiles. A gift, for the girl who insists on being called Cat. What could better demonstrate her good will? She rummages through her bag and chooses threads of green, blue and saffron yellow. Fresh colours for a fresh new season. Hester hums happily as she begins to prick out her design, and when Cat Morley brings in the tea tray she thanks her kindly, and tries not to notice the way the sinews stand raw and proud beneath the skin on the back of Cat's hands.

*　　　*　　　*

'You don't talk much, do you?' Mrs Bell observes, as Cat finishes wiping the last of the tea crockery, and spreads the towel to dry over the range. The

22

housekeeper stands with her knees together but her ankles apart, leaning her wide behind against the heavy work table, watching Cat's every move. The kitchen is half-submerged below ground, the view from the spotted windows one of sky and tree tops.

'When I've something to say.' Cat shrugs. Mrs Bell grunts.

'Better that way, I suppose, than some young chit gabbling on all the live-long day.' Mrs Bell studies Cat a moment more. 'You don't talk like a Londoner. I've heard some Londoners, when they come down selling and making speeches in town and the like.'

'My mother spoke very properly. The Gentleman preferred all his staff to do so,' Cat replies stiffly. She does not want to speak of her mother. She does not want to speak of London, of the past. Mrs Bell grunts again.

'Well, don't go giving yourself airs and graces, not now you're here. You're the bottom of the pile now, my girl, and one word from me'll be enough to send you packing again.'

'How kind of you to say so,' Cat mutters, darkly.

'Don't get lippy with me, miss.' Mrs Bell pauses, seems to check her own tongue. 'You done any cooking?'

'I used to help prepare the staff food, sometimes. Never for the family though.'

'Prepping vegetables, and the like? Can you make pastry?'

'No.' Cat shakes her head, reaches behind her back to untie her apron.

'Not so fast, if you please! There's four pigeons to pluck for supper tonight—you'll find them in

23

the cold store.' Cat reties her apron, turns to leave the room. 'And take them out into the courtyard, or you'll be chasing feathers around for days!' Sophie Bell calls after her.

The courtyard is a small area to the west of the house surrounded by a high brick wall, and paved with the same red bricks. The evening sun shines warmly on the top of Cat's head as she works, surrounded by tender green plants as they begin their steady growth up from crevices in the mortar. *In the midst of life, we are in death*, Cat thinks, as her fingers catch up the soft feathers of the birds, ripping them sharply from the slack skin. She has always hated the tearing noise it makes, always avoided the job at all costs. In London the servants were many, and their roles well defined. Only in times of panic would a parlourmaid be called upon to pluck birds for a meal. There were kitchen-maids for that. There was Tess. Smears of fat on her apron, fingernails stained brown by potato skins, smudges of flour on her smiling cheeks. The dead birds smell sticky, slightly sweet; their heads loll and flop as she works, cracks in the dry skin around their beaks. Cat thinks of dried blood around Tess's mouth; the way it had smeared her gums, drawing dark outlines around her teeth. She thinks of this same sickly smell, coming from stains that bloomed through rough clothing. Cat longs for a cigarette.

*　　　*　　　*

Towards five, a rattle and the whirr of spokes announces the return of the Reverend Albert Canning. Hester puts down her needlework and

24

goes into the hallway to greet him. He opens the door as the clock strikes the hour and smiles at his wife, who takes his hat and bag while he removes the heavy binoculars from around his neck and doffs his coat. Albert is tall and slender, his fair hair fine and downy, and just starting to thin across the crown—a development that does not age him in the slightest, and conversely seems to emphasise his youth. There is colour high in cheeks from the exertion of cycling back from town; wide blue eyes, with that look of innocence that had so captured Hester's heart from the very first; his skin soft and smooth. One arm gets caught in the sleeve of his coat, and Hester tries to help him but is hampered by his heavy leather satchel. They tussle with it for a moment, catch each other's eye, and laugh.

'How was your afternoon, Bertie?' Hester asks, as she settles into a chair once more.

'Very pleasant, thank you, Hetty. I managed to call upon everyone who had asked for me, and was able to help in some small matter or another in all but one instance, and on my way home I saw the most splendid peacock butterfly—the first I've seen this year.'

'And did you catch it?' Hester asks. Albert keeps a fine silk net and a collecting jar in his bag, in case of rare sightings.

'No, I thought it a trifle unfair, so early in the year. Besides, the peacock is hardly an exotic species,' Albert says, bending forward to release his trousers from his bicycle clips. He draws his journal from his satchel and flips it open with one long finger.

'No, of course,' Hester agrees.

'And how about you, my dear? What news?'

25

'Well, I fear we shall have to keep on sending the laundry out.'

'Oh? What of the new maid—can't she see to it?' Albert asks, looking up from his journal. In the rhododendrons outside the window, a blackbird pours out its liquid song.

'I really don't think so. The girl is quite stunted in her growth, and . . . well, I just don't think she can have the strength in her arms for it. And she has been unwell, too.'

'Oh dear. Well, if you say so, my dear.' Hester studies her husband, and finds nothing wanting. He wears his sideburns long, framing his face like lovingly cupped hands. The style is a little grave for such a young face, Hester has always thought—she knows Albert grew the whiskers to lend himself gravity in the pulpit. The sun is making them look gold, but when wet, they are quite dark. Albert feels her scrutiny, and smiles at her. 'What is it, darling?' he asks.

'I was just thinking what a fine figure of a man it is I wed,' Hester says, shyly. 'Almost a year ago now.' Albert takes her hand. He sits in his habitual pose, with his legs crossed at the knee so that his trousers ride up a little, and she can see an inch of white skin above his socks. It makes him look vulnerable, somehow.

'It is I who have been luckiest,' he says. Hester smiles and blushes a little.

'I went to see Mrs Duff this afternoon,' she says.

'And how is she?'

'A little better. I took her some of my lemon cordial, the sweet one she's so fond of.'

'That was kind of you, dear.'

'Her newest son is a fine little chap, and he

doesn't cry at all when I hold him. In fact, he studies me with such a calm scrutiny! As if he's thinking terribly important thoughts about me all the time, and coming to very weighty conclusions,' Hester laughs.

'I'm sure that can't be true of one so young,' Albert murmurs.

'No. No, I suppose not,' Hester agrees. Albert returns to his journal. She waits a little, her heart suddenly high in her throat. Then she gathers her courage. 'How I do long for the day when we will have a son of our own! Or a daughter, of course. I know you will be the most wonderful father,' she says, brightly, watching her husband expectantly. When he does not reply, she feels her cheeks begin to redden. Albert still stares at his journal, but Hester sees that he is frowning, and his pen has gone still. The nib has halted in the middle of a word, pressing into the paper, and an ink spot blooms from its tip. Clearing his throat quietly, Albert glances up at last. He gives a vague smile in her direction, but does not meet her eye; and he says nothing.

*   *   *

Late in the evening, Cat lies awake. The thin mattress is lumpy, horsehair sticking up through the worn ticking. She has propped the door open with the bible that was left by the bed. She likes to see the holy book lying on the floor like this, shown no more deference than a bag of sand. The words inside just as lifeless, just as heavy. Through the crack in the door the moon shines coldly, calmly. Cat lies still, listening to Mrs Bell snoring in the

27

room at the end of the corridor. In, out; in, out. She can hear the rattling wattle of the woman's neck. Carefully, Cat breathes all the way in. *There*. It is still there, at the very bottom of her lungs— the little wet bubble that will not dry out. Cat releases the breath, tries not to cough. All the bloody coughing, in prison—all night long, from every cell, as their lungs got clogged and muddied by the damp, the spores, the doctor's foul mixture. She runs her thumbs over the ticking, counts the little bristles, one for each second, as the night ticks by and her eyes stay open. Cat can't remember what it feels like to lie down and sleep. That peaceful surrendering of control, of power. She can't do it any more. Now, surrender feels like death, as though the very air in the room can't be trusted, as if the walls themselves will turn on her if she dares to shut her eyes; the shadows come alive to consume her.

*   *   *

In a very different room, on the floor below, Hester examines Albert's outline in the near dark. He lies on his back, his eyes shut and his face so resolutely relaxed that Hester guesses he is still awake. The beauty of his face disarms her. That valley between forehead and bridge of nose, the slight pout of his bottom lip. His face gives her an aching sensation she can't name, as though there is some sprain, some nerve inside her under pressure, in need of release. She reaches out an arm to him, laces her fingers into the hand that lies across his chest. There it is—that subtle change in the rhythm of his breathing, that slight tautening of his frame.

'Bertie? Are you awake, my love?' she whispers. He does not reply. *Once he holds you in his arms, and kisses you, and he is aware of your love and passion for him, then his passion will also rise, and your bodies may conjoin;* so her sister had written. Hester is aware of her own body moving beneath her nightdress, brushing against the cotton fabric, freed from the corsets that confine it all day long. Her hair drapes over her shoulder in a soft, caressing wave. 'I do so wish you would hold me,' Hester says, her voice trembling a little. Albert does not open his eyes, but he says:

'It has been a very long day, my love. I am so very tired.' Hester often hears these very words from her husband. She heard them even on their wedding night.

'Of course. Sleep, darling Bertie,' she says.

2

2011

Leah read the soldier's letter, a frown creasing the skin between her brows. Ryan stretched out his hand, smoothed the line away with his thumb, making her jump.

'Don't!' she gasped, snatching her head away from him.

'Touchy,' Ryan sighed. He smiled as he leant away, but Leah could tell he was annoyed. She felt a quick flash of triumph, and was instantly irritated with herself.

'But this can't be the original?' she asked.

'Of course not—it's been transcribed. The original paper is incredibly fragile. Where water has got in—and there wasn't much, he did a great job of sealing the tin—it's destroyed the envelope. In other words, the name of the person it was addressed to. Our mysterious soldier.'

'And she calls him "Dear sir". Not very helpful,' Leah murmured.

'No, but then I wouldn't need you if she'd given us his name.' Leah raised her gaze at his choice of words. 'Intriguing though, isn't it?' Ryan said.

'That it is,' she agreed. 'How had he sealed the tin?'

'With candle wax, it looks like. Melted and rubbed smooth all the way around.'

'So, would that have been easy to do? Something he would do every day, or did he only take the letter out to read once in a while?'

'Who can say? I think it was a thorough job, probably quite time consuming. I don't think he would have opened and resealed it every day.' Ryan shrugged.

'So it was special, this letter?'

'I would say so, yes. Read it out, so I can hear it again,' he suggested.

The Rectory,
Cold Ash Holt

Dear sir,

I scarcely know how to begin this letter, since I have sent so many, and received so little answer to any of

30

them prior to now. So little, I say—when I should say none at all. I can't imagine the situation in which you now find yourself, and can only assume that, when I had thought such would be impossible, it is indeed worse than the situation you left behind. The thought of your constant peril is most dreadful—you and your comrades. Please do try to keep yourself safe, if safe is a word that has any meaning on the battlefield. I discovered your departure to the front only recently, and only by chance—the casual mentioning by an acquaintance of the deployment of men such as yourself. I know that you and I parted on strange terms, and our time together was not the easiest; but even though you did not reply to any of my letters when you were relatively close by, I still feel worse knowing that you are no longer on English soil.

So, what can I write? What can I write that I have not written already? I do not understand. I live in fear. I am wretched and ignorant and you are my only hope of coming out of this fog. But you cannot or will not help me, nor break your silence. What can I do? I am but a woman. Such a feeble statement but, alone, I have neither the strength nor the courage to effect a change of any kind. I am quite trapped. How pathetic I must sound, to you who have been through so much since we parted, and who has had to endure things I can't imagine.

My son thrives. This, then, is some good news I can impart. He thrives. He will soon be three years old—where has the time gone? Close to four dark years have passed, and Thomas the only ray of light in all of it. He runs around the house and garden like a little dervish. He is not tall for his age, I am told, but his legs and body are sturdy, and his constitution good. He has yet to suffer seriously from any infection or childhood affliction. He has brown hair that curls a little, and brown eyes. Light brown eyes. I let his hair grow too long because I love brushing it so! My sister says he is too old for the style, and people will take him for a little girl, but I intend to leave it a while yet. He has started counting, and can memorise songs and rhymes in an instant—his mind is quick, quicker than mine, I dare say. I hope it gladdens you, to hear about Thomas.

I can't think what else to write. Everything has been so strange and dark since that summer. I wish I could make better sense of it, but then I think I would be too afraid to do anything if my suspicions were confirmed to be true. Too afraid to stay in my home another second, and where would that leave me? My sister might have me for a while, I know. But she could not have me for ever—she and her husband have four children now, and there simply isn't the room for Thomas and I. Will you please write to me? Tell me what you know about what happened that summer—I beg of you! Even if you think your answers will not bring me ease, I must know. To live in fear and suspicion is intolerable, though I have borne it these four years. I have written to you before of what I found, in the library that morning. The things I found. I am sure I wrote of them to you, although my mind was badly shaken at the time. It was all like the worst kind of dream. I would wake, in the days afterwards, and be happy for two heartbeats, but then I would remember it all, and it seemed as though the very sun grew dimmer. Does hiding what I found make me complicit in the crime? I fear it does, but I'm sure there are few who would have done differently. Perhaps this is not true.

32

Perhaps I am weak and fearful and lacking in moral courage. What then of you, and your *silence? Write to me, I beg you. Do not leave me here with only guesses and secrets, dogging my very steps each day.*

With warm regards,
H. Canning

They were sitting in a restaurant in the village of Watou, a fair drive from Poperinge where Leah was staying, and Ryan was based. *It's worth the trip,* he'd said, to her questioning glance as they drove out of town. He was right. The food was delicious, the ambience quiet but with a low buzz of chatter from a steady stream of locals turning up for their evening meal. Outside, rain pounded the deserted road, fizzing in the flooded gutters, scattering the street light across the window pane.

'Don't you just long for summer?' Leah sighed, staring out at it.

'I like it like this, remember? I like the dark months,' Ryan replied, pouring more red wine into her glass.

'That's right. I'd forgotten.'

'Forgetting me already.' Ryan shook his head. Leah said nothing. They both knew that would be impossible. To forget. She looked up at him, face lit by the candle on the table between them. What was it inside her that pulled her towards him? Something inexorable, like gravity. It would be so much easier to give in to it, in much the same way, she told herself firmly, as it would be easier to let go and fall off a cliff than it would be to haul oneself back onto solid ground. So much easier. The wine was warming her blood, she felt it colour her cheeks. 'You look half cut,' Ryan said. His smile mocked her gently, familiarity and tenderness softening his expression, blurring away the bad memories.

'Wasn't that your intention?' Leah asked. Ryan shook his head.

'You've always known your own mind. I've never relied on alcohol to change it for me.'

'Liar.' She smiled; and Ryan grinned.

'It's really good to see you, Leah. I don't think I got around to telling you that yet.' He put out a hand, fiddled with the wax drips on the candle shaft, frowning slightly as if gripped by deep and troubling thoughts. *Oh, you were always good at this game*, Leah thought. Always good at making her come forward, making her take a closer look.

'I'm not going to sleep with you,' she said, flatly; more abruptly than she'd intended.

Ryan snatched his hand back from the candle as if he'd been burnt. 'I don't remember asking you to,' he countered, seemingly unruffled.

They talked as their plates were cleared and they ordered dessert; but the more they spoke, the more obvious it became that there were things they could not speak about, and they drifted into silence, odd and uncomfortable.

'I wonder why he kept that letter? She says she wrote him lots, before he came over to the continent. Why that one in particular? It's not much of a love letter after all,' Leah said at last. The waiter brought their desserts—profiteroles, drenched in a slick of glossy Suchard sauce. He put the bowls down with a flourish, turning each one just so with the tips of his fingers, as if the exact position of them was of the utmost importance.

Leah caught his eye and smiled fleetingly.

'I think our *garçon* fancies you,' Ryan said.

'I think you're imagining it. You always did.'

'Except in Turkey.'

'OK, I'll give you Turkey. But it wasn't me that got to them—it was the blue eyes and the yellow hair.'

'I could have been rich. One of them offered me his house for you,' Ryan grinned.

'I wasn't yours to sell,' she retorted. 'Besides, he was about sixteen. Probably still lived at home with his mama.'

'That wasn't the only one,' Ryan said, putting a whole profiterole into his mouth, which would barely close. Leah couldn't help but laugh.

'You pig! You've got chocolate on your chin. What wasn't the only one?'

Ryan chewed for a long time before answering. 'That wasn't the only letter, in our soldier's tin. There was another one.'

'Really? Why didn't you bring it? What does it say?'

'It's a lot shorter than the one I've shown you. And obviously written earlier—fairly soon after whatever it was happened, would be my guess. It's a bit confused,' he explained.

'Well, where is it?' Leah asked, dipping her little finger in the hot sauce and sucking it clean. Only with Ryan would she have done something so childish. It was treacherously easy to fall back into old habits of being, old habits of feeling.

'It's in my room,' Ryan said, quietly.

The Rectory,
Cold Ash Holt

Dear sir,

The child is due any day now, and I am full of fear. How can I do this? You know of what I speak—I am sure you do. I might as well be alone in this house, surrounded only by ghosts. Do you see what you have done? Half of me wishes I had never known you. More than half of me, some of the time. I find myself trying to picture you now, trying to picture what you might look like without your usual clothes, without your books and your smile. All of those little icons that made you up—your 'divine truth'. What of that now? Is it all abandoned, as I am?

Everything is ruined. I can't even take pleasure in teaching any more, in the children, because as I stand on the floor before them, I know what lies beneath my feet. I told you what I did, didn't I? I can scarce remember. I'd thought it would be only temporary, a place where nobody would think to look. Trying to find what I had already found, what I picked up from the library floor that morning. I was going to destroy it all, you see. Every last thing, but then I thought perhaps you might one day have need of it to offer proof, to offer mitigation. So there it stays, beneath the floor. I can scarce think of it without such a storm of dread arising in my heart that it leaves me weak, and shivering; let alone dare to move it, to touch it.

I think this child must be a boy, and a big one. I am quite unrecognisable, I am vast. The creature has taken over my body. He's too big now to even move around and kick me like he did these last few months. He's tight packed in, like the air in a balloon. How I wish he would stay there! I don't

36

know where I will find the strength to raise him with a pure heart, happy and carefree, when I labour under such shadows. Enough now. I am tired. Even writing a letter is enough to tire me out; and especially a letter to you, sir, when I come to know that I shall have no reply. Still I hope for it, and that tires me even more.

Wishing this letter brings you some comfort, in the cruel place where you are,

H. Canning

Again, Leah read, and reread. She read the letter a third time, but only because she did not trust herself to look up, to look at Ryan and to speak to him. How did it always come to this? She cursed inwardly. That liquid feeling, hot in the marrow of her bones, as though her resolve was an actual substance that could melt under pressure, rush off into her bloodstream and be quite lost. Ryan was not even that close to her. He was perched on the window sill opposite, and she was sitting on the edge of the bed, one hand holding back her hair as she read. He stood up so suddenly that Leah jumped.

'More coffee?' he offered, voice so casual that Leah doubted herself, doubted that he had feelings anything like her own.

'No thanks.' She didn't look up.

'Sounds like she was in a right pickle, doesn't it?' he asked, pouring hot water onto a fresh scattering of instant granules. 'What do you make of it?'

'I hardly know. Something dire happened. She was left to deal with the aftermath by herself, our guy buggered off somewhere, and then to the war. She thinks he knows something about what

37

happened,' Leah said. Now she looked up at him. His back was turned, it was safer. The long, loose shape of his spine, the broad spread of his shoulders beneath his shirt. Just flesh and skin and bone, no more than she; but still magic, somehow.

'But they weren't lovers?' he said.

'I don't think so, no. She'd hardly call him "Dear sir" if they were, would she? Not even a hundred years ago. It's a bit cold and formal.'

'The content of the letters isn't though, is it? Cold or formal, I mean,' Ryan pointed out. He sat down next to her, too close, touching at thigh, hip, elbow. Leah felt a sinking inside, the pulling open of old wounds. It was an odd pain, almost satisfying; like tugging at a loose tooth, pressing a bruise. A bruise that went right the way through. She remembered his treachery, the flying apart of everything she thought she knew.

'It is and then it isn't. Very odd. It's as though she's trying to be proper about it all, but there's no way to reconcile what she needs to say with that. And the way she's so vague—it's almost like she half expected someone else to get hold of the letters and read them, and she didn't want to give too much away . . .' Leah trailed off. Ryan had tucked her hair behind her ear for her, left his fingers to brush her cheek with a touch softer than snowflakes. Mutely, she met his eye.

'So you'll look into it then? Try to find out who he was?' Ryan said. Leah nodded. 'It's like old times, watching you get stuck into a mystery. An . . . unexpected bonus.'

'What do you mean? Didn't you think I'd do it?'

'No, I thought you'd deliberately avoid doing it just because I'd asked you to.' He smiled.

38

'I did think of that,' she admitted. 'I . . . part of the reason I came out here was for the chance to say no to you. To refuse you something.' Tears blurred into her eyes and she wiped them away angrily.

'You fell at the first hurdle,' he said, softly. 'You came out here in the first place. When I asked you to.'

'I know. Not very good at this, am I?'

'I don't know. You've made me wait five months to see you. You made me come to Belgium to try to forget you.'

'That's a lie. You always wanted to come and work with the War Graves Commission,' she said, struggling to find a toehold, something to grasp as she slipped further and further over the cliff edge.

'Leah, I've missed you so much,' Ryan whispered, his lips in her hair, words touching her skin like butterflies. In silence, Leah gave in.

* * *

When she woke it was to the sound of more rain, flecked with hail, tapping at the window pane. The little room was dark and gloomy, the bed crowded. Ryan was turned to the wall, his back to her, deeply asleep. Without moving a muscle, Leah scanned the room, made note of each item of her clothing, cast off the night before. For a second, she tried to find a way to undo what she'd done, knowing it was utterly futile. She shut her eyes and let despair wash through her. It was like being underground, being smothered, seeing no way out. *I will never be free.*

But then, scribbled across the red-black of her

eyelids, came the words of the Canning woman's letters. *Everything is ruined. I was going to destroy it all . . . there it stays, beneath the floor; I labour under such shadows!* There was something there to be discovered, some hidden story, some truth. Not just the identity of the dead soldier, but whatever it was that had caused this woman such anguish, such nightmares. And why it was that the man she wrote to never wrote back to her; and why it was that he kept only these two of her letters; and why it was that she thought he might one day have had something to prove, to mitigate, as she put it.

Like a lifeline, something to cling to, the loose threads of the story wound their way down to her. She could just about reach them, concentrating hard, bending all her will to it. The first thing she had to do was leave. Not even wake Ryan, or speak to him, or tell him goodbye; never mind that the smell of him was in her hair and on her fingers and in her mouth, like traces of some pernicious drug that fed her as it wasted her. On soft feet she rose, dressed, picked up the copies of the letters from the floor and folded them into her bag. She did not look at the bed; she did not leave a note. As she left the room she thought she saw a gleam with the corner of her eye, a shard of light reflected from the dark form tangled up in the pillows and sheets. As if Ryan's eyes were open as she slipped from the room.

In the mornings, the house is cool and quiet, full of bright sunshine that glints on every speck of dust swirling in the still air, settling slowly onto the furniture. As Cat sweeps the hearths and rugs, clouds of it billow around her, resettle all around to be wiped off minutes later, back into the air, on to the floor. She is glad Hester is never up in time to see how futile trying to be rid of it is. People are made of dust. Houses are made of it. Cat brushes her fingers on her apron, again and again, not liking the thought of it clinging to her skin. She cleans the downstairs rooms and lays the table for breakfast before Hester comes down. Sometimes, she is called upstairs to help Hester dress. Then, when the vicar is back from his morning jaunt, he and Hester eat breakfast while Cat goes upstairs, gathers the dirty laundry and mending, makes the bed, cleans the bedroom and bathroom, the upstairs corridor. She airs guest rooms that she has yet to see any guests use; opens shutters in rooms nobody will enter all day, shuts them again when the sun begins to set. She persecutes flies endlessly, swatting at them; watching those that fly too high, out of reach, waiting for them to tire and die.

All the time, the quiet resounds in her ears. In London there was the steady hum of the city, even on exclusive Broughton Street. As each set of shutters was opened, a low sound of lives being lived would greet the ears. Cab horses would clatter by, steel feet striking sparks at the end of gaunt, sinewy legs; and motor cars, their engines throbbing like panting dogs. Boys on bicycles, delivery wagons, the ponderous clop of the dray's hooves. Pedestrians too, mingling voices. The servants could grab a look at passers-by, could keep tabs on the fashions of the day. Now when she opens the shutters Cat is greeted by swathes of green—a landscape, on three sides of the house, unbroken by any sign of human endeavour. The sky is wide and high and the sound is of birdsong, almost exclusively. Now and then a cart passing; now and then a dog barking. It's unnerving but she can't resist it, and finds herself hung, pausing at the windows she is meant to be cleaning, her gaze softening, reaching out into this new, quiet distance. And her body needs these rests, like it never has before. She has worked since she was twelve, her muscles made hard by it. But Holloway has made her weak, has made her legs tremble by the time she has climbed from the cellar to the attic.

At breakfast, she sits with Mrs Bell at the wooden table in the kitchen. The cook's chair creaks ominously underneath her, all but obscured by her bulk. Only spindly wooden legs are visible, chafing against the flagstones and wobbling with the strain. One day they will snap, Cat thinks. She will not be able to keep from laughing when it happens. She runs the scene in her mind—Mrs Bell, flailing on the floor like a beetle on its back, unable to rise.

'What are you smirking at?' Mrs Bell asks suspiciously.

'I was picturing you rolling on the floor if your chair broke,' Cat replies, quite honestly.

42

'Why, you cheeky minx!' Mrs Bell gasps, staring, her eyes stretched wide for once; but she can't seem to find any other riposte, so Cat goes back to eating her porridge. She has to concentrate on eating, in an odd way. She has to concentrate on *not* noticing she is doing it. If she notices it too much, the flavour of it, the texture, the brief choking sensation of swallowing . . . then panic rises and makes it impossible.

'I'd been wondering what they locked you up for,' Mrs Bell manages at last, 'but like as not it was for impertinence when you should've held your tongue! Who was it you gave back-chat to?' she asks, trying to sound angry but unable to hide the curiosity in her voice.

But Cat can't answer. At the mention of prison her throat has closed, her mouthful of porridge has nowhere to go. She can feel it clogging her up, sticking to the back of her throat. She rushes to the sink, coughs and gags it all out.

'Saints preserve us! What is the matter with you?' Mrs Bell exclaims, blood mottling her cheeks. 'No wonder you're such a sparrow! The mistress will hear of this.'

'It can only be good economy for her, if I don't eat,' Cat gasps, wiping her chin with the back of her hand. Mrs Bell grunts dismissively as Cat returns to the table and pushes the bowl of porridge away.

'Well don't waste it! Hand it to me,' Mrs Bell says, and dips her spoon into the bowl. She flicks her eyes at Cat again. 'What's that badge you wear?' She points a finger at the little silver and enamel portcullis pinned to Cat's collar.

'My Holloway medal. Given to me by my

43

friends, to show that I have been to gaol for the cause,' Cat says, her fingers drifting up to touch it.

'I hardly think it's something to be proud of,' the housekeeper says scathingly.

'You're wrong.'

'Well, you shouldn't be wearing it on show like that. Under your clothes if you must, but I don't want to see it again,' Mrs Bell tells her, with a curt nod of her chin. Cat glowers, but does as she is told.

*　　*　　*

Cat is called into the drawing room after lunch, when she had been on her way to her room, to rest for a while. Her hands are red and puckered from the washing-up suds, the nails that grew long in the week before she arrived have all snapped off again. The vicar's wife is dressed in white muslin, with frills at her collar and cuffs and hem. Her corsets cinch her in at the middle, but she is still broad, soft looking. Her breasts pile up above the whalebone, pushing outwards slightly, into her armpits. Her face looks like this too—broad, soft, accommodating. By contrast her hands are small and fine, the fingers tapering to shiny pink nails. Her feet are tiny. In high-heeled shoes, she half resembles a spinning top.

'Ah, Cat.' Hester smiles. 'I wonder if you would be so good as to take this along to the post office and send it for me? Thank you, child. And perhaps a few madeleines for tea? There is an excellent baker on The Broadway. Mrs Bell won't like it, but until she can raise a light sponge, she leaves me no choice!' Hester laughs a little as she says this. Cat

44

takes the letter, and the coins Hester proffers, hating to be called *child* by a woman only a few years older than herself.

'Very good, madam,' she says quietly. Hester's face falls a little. Cat notices that the woman's gaze darts past her and around her, and down at the letter. As if she fears to make eye contact with her new servant.

'You know the way to Thatcham, do you?' Hester asks.

'No, madam,' Cat admits. She had not thought to ask. Would have quite happily set off from the house directionless.

'Well, the quickest way on a fine day like today is to take the footpath opposite the house—there's a little stile you must climb—then follow that across the river at the footbridge until you reach the canal, which won't take you ten minutes. Turn left and follow the towpath for two miles and there you shall find Thatcham. It's a charming town. Please consider yourself at leisure to take a little extra time to look around. It will be useful in future for you to be familiar with the location of the butchers and the grocers and the like,' Hester says. Cat's heart lifts at the thought of the excursion.

'Thank you, madam,' she says, with more feeling, and Hester's smile widens.

*   *   *

Unhindered by corsets, Cat swings easily over the stile and sets off across the field. She steps lightly around the cow pats, examines the new oddness of the turf beneath her feet. She has never walked on grass so long, on ground so unmade. In London

45

the garden had a lawn, but servants were not allowed to walk on it. The Gentleman was quite specific about this—there were paths to be kept to, neatly laid flagstones, or raked gravel hemmed with miniature box hedges. Here there is long ragged grass and other plants too, things she has not seen before. Wild flowers. Tiny blue ones the colour of the summer sky; purples, yellows, spiky white clouds of something she cannot name. In the bright sunlight she feels the day's warmth seep into her skin, chasing out the lingering chill of the prison cell. She carries Hester's letter and the coins for the cakes in a purse on a string loaned to her, grudgingly, by Mrs Bell. Dangling it from her fingers, she swings it to and fro, twirls it around, makes it whoosh through the air. A skinny black-haired girl, walking a meandering path across a meadow.

The canal is a wide, lazy channel of murky water, crowded in by weeping willows. Boughs of young elder lean out over the far bank, flowering with acrid enthusiasm. Clouds of midges careen across the surface, and they soon come to crowd infuriatingly around Cat's face; to nip at the backs of her hands. Cat reaches the towpath, and looks right. All the way to London, this path leads. She could follow it; walk until her feet were ragged and bloody. How long would it take? She has no idea. And what would she do when she got there? Nowhere is home any more. But she could look for Tess. She could make sure Tess was all right, she could bring her here. To this alien place, so green and quiet and different. But Cat turns left and starts walking, more slowly now, swatting at the midges and dodging the piles of muck left by the

46

barge horses.

Soon, buildings come into view. Warehouses, small boatyards. She passes two locks, watches a boat pass through one of them, fascinated by the workings of it. As water foams through the sodden beams, it sends up clouds of scent: moist, rank, somehow alive. The breeze ripples the water's surface, makes it appear to flow. Experimentally, Cat picks up a stick to test whether this is so. She throws it into the water, but the purse string comes loose from her wrist and flies in after it.

'Damn and blast it!' she mutters, looking around her. The canal banks are steep and the water looks deep. There's a long, wide boat moored nearby, and even though it looks empty she daren't trespass on it. She casts her eyes around, picks up a fallen sycamore branch and reaches out to the purse, which, mercifully, is floating. She struggles to balance, to hold the branch steady, hook a twig around the purse string and begin to tow it towards her. It works for a moment but then she over-balances, has to drop the branch to steady herself. The purse swirls gently in a circle. Cat edges down the bank, crouches precariously, reaches her fingers for it. It is two inches beyond her fingertips. Two inches, no more, but no matter how she stretches she cannot reach it. 'Why, you stinking, cursed sprog of a pox-addled whore!' she shouts at it, standing up in a fury.

A laugh startles her, makes her step back and stumble.

'Whoa, steady there, miss. You don't want to follow it in now, do you?' a man says. He is half emerged from a hatch in the deck of the barge moored beside her. Cat gets an instant impression

47

of tawny brown, of warmth. Weathered skin the colour of the scrubbed boards of the boat; rough hair, undyed clothes.

'Who are you?' she demands, suspiciously.

'George Hobson. And more importantly, I'm in possession of a grappling hook, should you have need of one.'

'What's a grappling hook and why should I need one?' Cat snaps, feeling that she is being laughed at.

'This is the item, and I'll fetch that bag out for you if you'll give me your name,' the man offers, picking up an evil-looking metal claw attached to a long pole from the deck of the boat.

Cat frowns at him and thinks for a moment, then says: 'I'm Cat Morley, then. Do fetch it, will you, before the letter inside is soaked completely.'

The brown man comes all the way out of the hatch, crouches on the edge of the deck and sweeps the purse, drizzling water, out of the canal. He shakes it a little, folds the string into a neat bundle in his palm and squeezes it. His hands are like shovels, wide and square, the knuckles lividly bruised, ridged with scars. He jumps onto the bank and approaches her, and Cat squares her shoulders, stands up to him although she does not meet his shoulder height. He has more than twice her width; the solid look of a tree trunk.

'I'd thought you a lad in a long shirt, until you spoke up,' he says.

'Thank *you*, sir,' Cat says, sarcastically.

'Now, I meant no offence by that. Only the lasses round here, and I can hear you're not one of them, they all wear their hair long,' he explains. Cat says nothing. She holds out a hand for the

48

purse, but when he keeps hold of it she folds her arms, eyes him calmly. 'And I never heard a lass round here curse like you just did, miss. No, I never heard that,' he laughs.

'May I have that back, please?' Cat asks at last.

'You may.' George nods, passing it to her.

Cat scrabbles it open, tips out water, weed, coins and the letter, which she blots hurriedly against the front of her skirt. 'Oh, blast it. You can scarce read the address it's to go to. The ink is quite washed away,' she murmurs, half to herself. 'Perhaps there's hope—I could write over it, perhaps, if somebody would lend me a pen. Here—do you think it's readable, still? Can you make out the name?' she asks, holding out the letter to George Hobson. The big man flushes, looks at the letter with a frown of bafflement.

'I don't rightly know, Miss Morley,' he mutters.

'Is it ruined?' she asks. George shrugs one shoulder, non-committal, and Cat understands him. 'Can't you read?' she asks, incredulously. George hands the letter back, shrugs again, frowns at the look on Cat's face.

'Not much call for a bargeman to read,' he says. 'I'll bid you good day, then.' He turns back to his boat, is aboard in one wide, assured stride.

'Well now, you can laugh at me but I can't laugh at you, is that the way of it?' Cat calls to him from the bank.

George pauses, smiles a little. 'Well, you have me there, Miss Morley,' he admits.

'My name is Cat,' she tells him. 'Nobody calls me Miss Morley except—' She breaks off. Except the policemen who took her, the judge who tried her. She shrugs. 'Nobody does.'

'You'll be about town, will you, Cat?'

'Now and then, I dare say.'

'Then I shall look out for you. And that sharp tongue of yours.' He smiles. Cat eyes him, tips her head to one side. She likes the sparkle in his eyes, the way she abashed him like a schoolboy. With a quick smile, she walks on into town. After the post office she buys the madeleines, which she carries carefully, still warm and sticky; the scent of vanilla oozing from the paper wrapper. She buys herself some cigarettes, and a copy of *Votes for Women* for a penny from Menzies. She will hide it under her skirt when she gets back, spirit it up to her room, and read it after hours.

*   *   *

One Thursday, Hester and Albert eat an early supper of lamb steaks as evening falls outside and bats replace the birds, wheeling across the lawn. Cat serves them, walking from one end of the table to the other with the soup tureen, then the plate of meat, then the vegetables. In London she was to be silent, invisible; servants were not acknowledged at table. But each time she puts something on Hester's plate, Hester smiles and thanks her softly. Cat was startled the first few times this happened, and did not know how to respond. Now she murmurs 'madam' softly, each and every time, like a gentle echo after Hester speaks. Albert seems not to notice any of this, eating his dinner with a diffuse, faraway look punctuated now and then by traces of a frown, or a smile, or an incredulous lift of his eyebrows. He is quite captivated by his own thoughts, and Hester watches him fondly as they proceed across his face.

'What is the subject of tonight's lecture, my dear?' Hester asks, once Cat has withdrawn. 'Albert?' she prompts him, when he does not reply.

'I do beg your pardon, my dear?'

'Tonight's lecture. I was wondering what it was about?' There are lectures once or twice a week in Newbury, and Albert tries to attend at least one of them, especially if they deal with matters philosophical, biological or spiritual.

'Ah—it should be a most interesting one. The title is "Nature Spirits and their place in the Wisdom Religion". The speaker is a rising star in theosophical circles—Durrant, I believe his name is. He hails from Reading, if I remember correctly.'

'*Nature* spirits? What can he mean?' Hester asks, puzzled. She doesn't ask the meaning of *theosophical*—is unsure that she could pronounce it right.

'Well, dear Hetty, that is what I intend to discover,' Albert says.

'Does he mean hobgoblins and the like?' She laughs a little, but stops when Albert frowns slightly.

'It does not do to laugh simply because we do not understand, Hetty. Why shouldn't the figures of childhood stories and myth have some basis in reality, upon some level or another?'

'Well, of course, I didn't mean—'

'After all, we all know the human soul exists, and what is a ghost but the disembodied spirit of a human soul? Surely none could argue against the wealth of evidence for *their* existence?'

'Indeed not, Bertie,' Hester agrees.

'The conjecture, I believe, is that plants, too,

51

have spirits, of a kind—guardians to tend them and guide them in their growth and propagation,' Albert goes on.

'Yes, of course, I see,' Hester says, quite seriously now.

They pause for a moment, silent but for the clink of their cutlery, the sounds of their own eating.

'And you are off to Mrs Avery's, for a game of bridge? What time shall I see you back here again?' Albert asks at length.

'Oh, I expect I will be back before you, dear. We shall only play until about ten,' Hester says hurriedly, knowing that Albert does not approve of her playing bridge, and wanting to move on from the subject as quickly as possible.

'And will Mrs Dunthorpe be joining the party?' Albert asks evenly, and that small frown of disapproval that Hester can't bear puckers his brow again.

'I . . . I really don't know, Albert. I doubt it, as she didn't come the last time . . .'

'She really is not the right kind . . .'

'I know, dear; I do know. But even if she does come along, I can assure you that we'll only be playing for matchsticks, nothing more,' Hester assures him. Mrs Dunthorpe's love of gambling is widely renowned. Over Christmas last, she lost so much in a hand of poker that her husband was forced to sell his horse.

'It's not only that which troubles me—'

'Oh, don't be troubled, Bertie! Mrs Avery's character is unimpeachable, after all—and I hope you have some faith in my own mettle?'

'Of course I do, dear Hester.' Albert smiles.

52

'You above all people have proved the uncorrupted nature of your soul to me.' A telltale blush creeps up from the neckline of Hester's dress.

*   *   *

She hasn't actually lied about anything, Hester reassures herself, as she waves Albert off on his bicycle. He is to pedal the two miles to Thatcham, then catch a train into Newbury for the lecture. With him safely out of sight, she wraps herself in a lightweight coat and fastens her hat with the pins Cat hands her, patting her hair into place all around it.

'I'll be back by half past ten, when a little cocoa will go down a treat,' Hester says brightly, eager to be away.

'Very good, madam,' Cat mutters. Hester notes the dark circles under Cat's eyes, the fact that she has not yet, many days after her arrival, filled out at all. She makes a mental note to talk to Sophie Bell about it as she sets off along the garden path. There are angry purple and black clouds on the northern horizon, bulging up towards heaven like vast and ominous trees. Hester doubles back for an umbrella.

Albert's real objection to Mrs Dunthorpe lies less in her gambling, though that is bad enough, and more in the fact that she is a medium, and has more than once led a seance on a night that had begun as a game of bridge. And however much Hester tells herself that she doesn't know for *sure*, the fact remains that she spoke to her friend Claire Higgins after the service the previous Sunday, and

Claire had hinted in the strongest possible terms that tonight might be just such a night. Hester feels a thrill of anticipation.

Mrs Avery's house is the largest in the village, and well appointed, as a rich widow's should be. Her husband had invested heavily in the railways, had seen his money grow tenfold, and had then been cut down by the very thing that made him, when his cab was struck by a train as it crossed the tracks late one night. The driver had fallen asleep at the reins, and his passenger, by all accounts, had drunk himself to falling down. He left Mrs Avery very well off and very bored, so that the widow has become the centre of society in the village, and indeed in the whole district of Thatcham—outside the realm of the truly grand houses, of course. She spends a lot of time visiting friends and family in London, is always quite on top of the latest fashions; and Hester finds her more than a little frightening. But, as the vicar's wife, it would not do to be excluded from Mrs Avery's company, and so she makes every effort to maintain her good standing with her. On nights when Mrs Dunthorpe is present, it is no chore.

Mrs Dunthorpe is thickset and well-bosomed. Her hair is a faded chestnut colour, her eyes a faded blue. Aged about fifty, she has come lately to wealth; so lately that she speaks with a Thatcham twang that she can't be rid of, however hard she tries. Were it not for her extraordinary powers, perhaps she might not have been such a regular guest in Mrs Avery's drawing room. As it is, she sits proudly on a damask chair as the other guests arrive, to be greeted by each of them perhaps with less deference, but with more enthusiasm, than they show their hostess.

'Mrs Dunthorpe . . . I had *so* hoped you would be here! Will you lead us in a circle tonight? Will we hear from the spirits at all?' asks tiny Esme Bullington, her reedy voice little more than a whisper as she grips the older woman's hands.

Mrs Dunthorpe smiles with a hint of reserved mystery. 'Well, my dear; that does depend upon the wishes of our charming hostess, of course. But, should she assent, and it be the will of the party, I could of course lead a foray into the unseen world,' she says, loudly enough for all to hear, and for Mrs Avery to scowl.

'Perhaps we might wait at least until we are all assembled, and have taken a glass of sherry?' Mrs Avery suggests, rather coolly. Mrs Dunthorpe seems quite oblivious to the rebuke, but Esme Bullington retreats from the medium with two spots of colour high in her cheeks.

Hester makes a polite tour of the room before returning to stand beside her particular friend, Claire Higgins, the wife of one of Cold Ash Holt's prominent farmers. There are thirteen ladies altogether: an auspicious and carefully engineered number. They sip sherry from crystal glasses, and soon their faces are flushed beneath the pale powder, and they laugh more easily, and the lights seem to shimmer and blur the room, setting satin ribbons and skin and eyes shining. The rising anticipation is like a low humming sound; impossible to pinpoint the source of it, and impossible to ignore it. At last, when Mrs Avery deems that they have all been acceptably sociable, and have shown that her society and good graces were what matters above all, their indomitable hostess clears her throat.

'Mrs Dunthorpe. How do you feel? Are you quite up to an attempt at communion with the spirits?' she asks. The other women all fall silent at once, and watch matronly Mrs Dunthorpe closely as she seems to consider with great care.

'I believe we may have a good deal of success this evening,' she says at last, to an excited murmur and a squeak of joy from Esme Bullington.

With intent expressions, they hurry to a grand, circular table at the far end of the room, around which thirteen plush red chairs have been arranged. Mrs Dunthorpe bids them sit close to the table, their forearms resting upon it and their hands clasped firmly. Hester has Esme Bullington's tiny paw in one hand and the dry, creased fingers of old Mrs Ship in the other. Whilst they have been talking and drinking the wind has risen outside, and blows fitfully with a sound like distant whispering voices. It makes the budding branches of the wisteria patter and scrape at the window glass; sounding for all the world like the questing fingertips of someone trying to get in. As the day was so warm, the curtains have been left open and the bottom inch of the window raised to allow air into the room. But the temperature has dropped, and the breeze that is creeping in has a chilly touch. It is not yet fully dark outside, but all that's visible beyond the reflections in the window glass is the dark grey sky, bloated with cloud, and the gnarled branches of the old medlar tree in the garden. Hester shivers involuntarily, and feels Esme's hand tighten around hers.

A servant turns off all the lamps and lights a single candle, which she sets in the middle of the

56

table before withdrawing, eyes cast down. The candle kindles fire in the gemstones on Mrs Avery's knuckles, at her neck and ears. Albert would not approve of such a show for a simple assembly of ladies. Hester suppresses a spasm of guilt. There is little Albert would approve of about her evening, but these gatherings are utterly compelling to her. Silence falls around the table as the women stop shuffling their skirts and their positions, and grow still. Hester takes a deep breath to steady her capering nerves.

'I bid you all to turn your thoughts to the world of spirit, and away from that which you see and hear around you,' Mrs Dunthorpe begins. She is wearing a shawl of bright emerald green, iridescent like a starling's wing. 'Close your eyes, to keep from distraction, and bend your mind to it with all the force of your will. Send out an invitation, and a welcome, to those travellers on the roads of the spirit world who might hear, and grant us their presence.' Her voice grows deeper and more sonorous. Hester, so alive with expectation that she can hardly sit still, opens one eye and glances around the table. She is flanked by the shuttered faces of her companions, each one arranged into some expression of entreaty or thrall. Mrs Dunthorpe has thrown back her head, and her lips move soundlessly. 'There is one amongst us who disrupts the energy,' the medium snaps. Hester jumps guiltily and glances at her, but Mrs Dunthorpe's eyes remain closed. 'The circle of thought must be complete, or none may come forth,' she continues, testily. Hurriedly, Hester closes her eyes tightly, and tries to concentrate.

There is a long and steady silence. Just the

sound of shallow breathing, and the low moan of the wind as it scrolls around the corners of the house. Hester can feel Esme trembling slightly beside her, as if poised for flight like a startled deer. 'Will you not come forth? I can almost hear you,' Mrs Dunthorpe whispers, the words barely audible. Hester strains her senses. She pictures the spirit world as a vast and heavy black door, beyond which lies a stormy sea of souls too lost or confused to have found either heaven or hell. As Mrs Dunthorpe speaks, she imagines ghostly fingers curling around that door and pushing, inching it wider and wider, following the compelling voice and allowing the living a glimpse of the cold and unearthly realm beyond. Her heart beats so hard she fears it will be heard; pressure builds between her temples, as though invisible hands grip her skull. Esme has stopped trembling; her hand has gone as limp as a dead fish, and just as cold. Hester's skin crawls away from it, but she dare not open her eyes, or turn her head to look. For what if they have strayed too close to that black door; what if they themselves have trespassed into the spirit world? What if little Esme has gone, and in her place Hester holds the hand of a ghost—the cold, dead hand of a corpse? She can't move a muscle, she can scarcely breathe.

'Someone speaks to me!' Mrs Dunthorpe says suddenly, her voice taut with exhilaration. 'Yes! Yes, I can hear you! Tell me your name . . .' she asks hoarsely. Hester holds her breath, straining her ears for the voice the medium hears. 'The spirit comes with a warning . . . a warning for one of us in this very room! It says dark times are coming . . . that an evil force has entered one of

58

our houses, though we are none the wiser,' she says, her voice ranging from a vibrant blare to a heavy whisper. Hester hears someone gasp, but can't tell who it is. 'Tell us more, dear spirit . . . who is this intruder? What do they plan? How do you come to know of it—are you a relative of somebody in this room? Or a friend? We welcome your wisdom!' There is a long silence, and in the blameless wind Hester hears voices crying out in fear and pain. 'Oh! It is very afraid of what is to come! It wishes to warn us . . . The voice is growing faint . . . Come back, please, spirit! I'm losing you, I can't hear what you're saying,' the medium says; then she pauses with a loud and frightening gasp. 'Oh, saints preserve us!'

Suddenly there is a loud bang, a crash that shakes the table, lifts it up violently and clatters it back to the floor. As one the women cry out in alarm, break the circle and clasp their hands to their mouths, muffling little shrieks of terror and excitement. Then they all chatter at once, like a hedge full of sparrows.

'Oh, what was that?'

'Did you feel it? Did you see anything?'

'Dear Lord, I thought I would faint quite away!' Mrs Dunthorpe is the last to re-enter the room. Her hands remain extended to either side of her, though nobody holds them any more. Slowly, her head rocks forwards, her mouth closes, her breathing quietens. The women all watch her powdered eyelids, transfixed, as they flutter open. 'I can do no more tonight. Our visitor was frightened off by another spirit, one much troubled by grief and rage at its own passing. It is a shame that I couldn't glean anything more from the first voice that came through, since it clearly had information that would have been of great value to one of us. Such a negative experience has quite drained me, and we are lucky that this darker spirit has passed further along the road again, and will not stay to trouble us,' the medium declares.

Murmurs of consternation chase around the room. Hester shudders at the thought—that they might have opened the door to a vengeful ghoul, only to then be haunted by it, chased and hounded by it. Esme has gone as white as a ghost herself.

'Are you all right, Esme dear?' Hester asks.

'I could feel it. I could feel the last spirit—the hurt and the pain!' the girl whispers.

Mrs Avery grunts a little gracelessly, and rings a silver bell. 'Bring some brandy for Mrs Bullington. In fact for us all, please, Sandy,' she bids the servant who appears.

'You say "it", Mrs Dunthorpe—can you tell us if it was a man or woman? A child or a grown adult?' Sarah Vickers asks. 'Can you tell us why the spirit was so troubled? Was he—or she—perhaps . . . murdered?'

'Such brief encounters give more an impression of emotion, of feeling, than a coherent conversation,' Mrs Dunthorpe replies. 'I was not able to calm the spirit sufficiently to ask such rational questions as you pose.'

'But, if you heard it, surely you could determine the sex, at least?' Sarah Vickers presses. There is the hint of a challenge in her tone, which Mrs Dunthorpe is wise to in an instant.

'Spiritual noise is quite different to that of the human voice, I assure you, Miss Vickers; but if I were to hazard a guess from its tone, I would say it was male. An adult man.'

'Ah. Well. A pity he stayed only long enough to kick the table, and not to give account of himself. Perhaps we might have caught his murderer for him!' Sarah smiles.

'Indeed,' Mrs Dunthorpe agrees frostily. The two women glare at one another.

'But what of the first voice who spoke, Mrs Dunthorpe?' Claire Higgins asks, hastily filling the uneasy silence. 'Was there anything else you could discern about him—or . . . it?'

'That was a kindly spirit, a woman, I believe. She was so determined to convey her warning to us, I could not persuade her to give me much information about herself. I sensed great age and wisdom about her, and that she was a woman of refined culture and manners.'

'Well, if she had been a relation of one of us, I should say she would have had good breeding,' says Mrs Avery thoughtfully. 'My own mother died some years ago,' she adds. Esme Bullington gasps.

'Do you think it was your mother who spoke? Do you think the warning was for you, Mrs Avery?' she whispers, eyes wide in her face.

'I shall certainly be on my guard if I receive any unexpected house guests.'

'I think we all owe Mrs Dunthorpe our thanks for such a compelling display of her psychic abilities,' Hester says, suddenly desperate for the lights to be switched back on and the shadows chased from the corners of the room.

'Oh, yes! It was quite remarkable!' Esme agrees, her colour returning.

Gradually, the atmosphere in the room eases, and conversation rises again as each compares her experience of the visitation with her neighbour. They sip their brandy and eat crystallised fruit, and swap polite gossip.

'Mrs Canning, I hear tell you have a new maid of all work, come down from London,' says Mrs Avery, cutting across the circle to Hester. It is not a question.

'That's correct, Mrs Avery. Cat Morley is her name. She's beginning to settle in, although she's not quite as quick about her work as I would have expected for one trained in a grand house,' Hester replies.

'I heard that she had been *imprisoned* until lately. Is this true?' their hostess asks, her face pressed into flat lines of disapproval. Hester feels the blood rush to her cheeks. How on earth has it got about? Only from Sophie Bell, and Hester asked her most explicitly not to speak of it to anyone.

'Well, I . . . ah . . .' Hester stammers.

'Well, was she or wasn't she?'

'Indeed, most unfortunately, she was, it is true . . . not for very long, I understand . . . a short sentence . . .'

'And you are happy to have a felon living under your own roof with you? Is that *wise*?' Mrs Avery asks, peering along her nose, pinning Hester with the question.

'My . . . my husband and I thought it an act of charity to give the girl a livelihood, and a chance to regain a place in society . . . After all, she has repaid her debt, in the eyes of the law,' Hester manages.

Mrs Avery grunts, twitches the ends of her shawl into a neater shape, tucks her chin into her chest.

The light shines from the iron-grey swathe of her hair. 'Indeed. That may be the case. Very commendable, I am sure; and the least one should expect from the household of a clergyman, I suppose. Tell me, what was her crime?' she asks.

'That . . . that is . . . the details are known only to the girl . . . to Cat Morley. I have not pressed her for the particulars. I thought it better to let—'

'Oh, come now! I won't have it—you must have known what crime she committed before you took her on! No one but a fool would not have found it out! What if she were a murderer?'

'If she was a murderer, her sentence would have been very long indeed, and she would hardly have come out of it still young enough to come here to the vicar's house,' says Sarah Vickers, sensing Hester's unease.

'I . . . I have undertaken not to speak of it. I do apologise, Mrs Avery,' Hester says, her pulse racing and her cheeks flaming crimson. She squirms a little, longing for the woman's spotlight glare to move away from her. 'Whatever she did, it is between her and God. I hope that . . . by coming here she is able to leave it all behind her.'

Mrs Avery's eyebrows arch coldly, her mouth flattens even further. 'Commendable discretion, I'm sure,' she says, the words like a whip cracking.

Suddenly, Esme Bullington gasps, her hand flying to her mouth.

'Mrs Canning! What if the warning was for you? What if this new girl of yours is the one the spirit meant—the source of evil that has entered your home?' she asks, grasping Hester's arm with her short, bony fingers.

'Oh! Surely not . . . I'm sure the spirit can't have

63

meant Cat . . .' Hester smiles uneasily.

'Have you any elderly female relatives, recently crossed over?' Mrs Dunthorpe asks her seriously. The eyes of all twelve women fix upon Hester.

'Well . . . my great aunt Eliza, I suppose . . . She passed away four years ago, of the palsy,' Hester admits.

'That's it, then! That was her—it must have been!' Esme cries. 'Oh, Mrs Canning! Do be careful—do heed what was said, won't you? That a source of evil has entered your house, and will bring dark times upon you . . . Poor Mrs Canning! Do be careful!'

'Now, now, Esme. Calm yourself,' Mrs Avery admonishes the woman, who is dabbing at her eyes with the corner of her handkerchief. 'I am quite sure that nothing truly evil would take root in the house of a man of God. Isn't that right, Mrs Canning?'

'Yes, of course,' Hester says. For the rest of the evening she feels glances aimed in her direction, and catches expressions of pity and wonder on the faces of her peers. She smiles more often than she might usually, to make light of it, but the party is ruined; and beneath her façade lies a kernel of deep unease. She thinks of Cat Morley's black gaze, and the way her shadowy thoughts stay so well hidden behind it; the smudges under her eyes and the painful thinness of her body, as though some blight is indeed eating her away from the inside.

*   *   *

As Hester walks home, she wonders anxiously if

she will ever be asked back to Mrs Avery's. Twice she has lied, in one evening—but surely this second time it was the right thing to do? She had decided not to divulge details of Cat's past—and she does know more than she said, although not much more—and she stayed true to her vow. Thunder is thudding across the sky, sounding like heavy stones rolling, and the wind comes in powerful gusts, making the late spring branches flail, dashing pollen from the blossoms, sending petals flying into the air. A spattering of rain begins to fall. Hester pulls her coat tighter, and struggles with her umbrella for a while before giving up when the wind threatens to tear it.

With the sky so heavy and low, the road is near invisible. Only the faint yellow glow from the windows of houses lights her way as she passes, and this dwindles to nothing as she comes to the far end of the village, and walks the last stretch to the vicarage. Hester finds herself peering into the darkness beneath the trees and hedges, straining her eyes as she had strained all her senses at the seance. The black depths seem watchful, the wind seems to carry voices, whispered words. Shivering, Hester pauses. Her knees feel weak and unsteady. The wind curls around her, unpins her hair, threatens to carry off her hat; she clamps one hand upon it, eyes screwed up against the onslaught and the stinging rain. There is a large horse chestnut tree just outside the garden wall of the vicarage, its leaves already full out, broad and young and softly green by daylight. A flicker of lightning lights the tree with the grey tones of the underworld, and there, against the trunk, a figure stands quite still. Hester catches her breath in a gasp. No more than a black shape, a motionless outline, but quite definitely watching her with an implacable patience. Hester tries to cry out but her voice is strangled. She stands frozen, thinking of the violently angry spirit they had conjured that night, and the dire warning of evil which might have been for her. For a moment she can't think or move, and is wholly seized by a spasm of shock. Then, with a small cry of fear, she bolts for the safety of home, heart beating fit to burst.

* * *

Cat waits until she hears the front door slam shut before she relaxes again. She pictures Hester with her back to the door, eyes shut, panting; and she smiles. From behind her back she lifts her cigarette to her lips, takes a long pull. The smoke makes her lungs burn, and she coughs, but perseveres. The doctor whom The Gentleman took her to see upon her release encouraged her in the habit, told her that the hot smoke would help to dry out her lungs. The first taste of tobacco in weeks. She came outside to smoke it to be away from Mrs Bell, and to watch the storm. Never before has she stood beneath a tree whilst the wind throws it about with such violence. Never before has she heard the terrific roar that it makes—a hissing, rushing sound like waves crashing ashore. She shuts her eyes and listens, lets the sound swirl around her, until she feels like one more leaf on the tree, one more helpless, insignificant thing. Like she might fly away in the next second. When thunder hammers out, right over her head, Cat smiles in the dark.

'Where the bloody hell have you been?' Mrs Bell snaps at her when she returns to the kitchen. 'I've got the mistress clamouring for a hot water bottle and cocoa and her wool bedjacket unpacked from the winter trunk, and you nowhere to be found!'

'It's a thunderstorm, not a blizzard. She hardly needs a bedjacket,' Cat says, fetching milk from the cold store and pouring it into a copper pan. The white liquid looks gorgeous against the bright metal, and she swirls it around as she sets it on the stove.

'Whether or not she needs it, she wants it, and who are you to argue, girl?' Mrs Bell grumbles. 'You go and find it—it'll be in the trunk on the far landing—and be sure to find all the mothballs from it before you give it her. I'll do that—move away before you scald the milk!'

'Yes, Mrs Bell,' Cat sighs.

'Don't you "yes, Mrs Bell" me . . .' Mrs Bell says, but can't quite put her objection into words. She falls silent, whisking the milk vigorously and shaking her head. The whisking shakes other things too—sets up a wobble that shifts her from bosom to thigh. 'Take a lamp with you—he doesn't like the lights on upstairs after she's retired,' she calls after Cat.

'I don't need a lamp,' Cat calls back, as she makes for the stairs. Within a few paces of the kitchen, her eyes have adjusted to the dark.

*   *   *

Hester sits shivering in bed, her toes and fingers tingling as the blood returns to them. Her head is aching after the frights of the evening. In spite of the lamps filling the room with yellow light, she thinks she can still see shadows, lurking figures in the corners of the room that vanish when she looks full at them. *An evil force has entered one of our houses* . . . Hester longs for Albert to come home and banish her fears with his calm faith and soothing presence. Gradually, she begins to relax, and has just picked up a book of homilies when a soft thump outside the room makes the breath freeze in her lungs. She waits, ears tuned for the noise to come again. And come again it does—a scuffle, a slight thudding. Hester berates herself for her fears, for believing that anything ghostly has followed her home from the seance.

'It's probably one of the cats, you silly girl,' she tells herself aloud, and the very ordinariness of her own voice gives her courage. To prove that she is rational and not afraid, she gets up and crosses to the door. But with her hand on the latch she pauses, and swallows. Her throat is entirely dry. She opens the door as quietly as she can. Outside the room, the corridor is in complete darkness, and a noticeable draught noses along it, east to west. Hester makes a show of looking to either side, though her eyes see nothing but pitch blackness, an emptiness from which anything might spring. Her skin crawls and she turns to go back inside, and as she does, a figure appears right by her elbow. Hester screams, then sees the glint of dark eyes and dark hair in the light from her bedroom door. 'Cat! Why, you scared me half to death!' She laughs nervously.

'Sorry, madam; I didn't mean to. I've brought you your bedjacket,' Cat says, holding out a knitted cardigan ripe with the stink of camphor.

'Thank you, Cat,' Hester says, her pulse still racing. Cat stands still, watching her. Hester glances at her, and again feels a rush of unease. 'What were you doing out here in the dark? Why didn't you bring a lamp, or put the lights on?' she asks. Cat blinks, and regards her steadily.

'I can see quite well in the dark,' she replies.

'"Black Cat",' Hester murmurs, the nickname coming unbidden to her lips. She sees Cat stiffen.

'Where have you heard that?' the girl asks abruptly. Hester swallows nervously.

'Oh, nowhere . . . sorry, Cat. I didn't mean to . . . Thank you for bringing me this. Please do go to bed yourself now. I won't need anything else,' she says hurriedly.

'I'll bring you the cocoa you asked for as soon as it's ready,' Cat contradicts her.

'Oh, yes, of course. Of course. Thank you, Cat. Sorry.' Hester retreats back into her room, unsure what she is apologising for. Cat is still standing in the dark corridor when she shuts the bedroom door behind her.

*   *   *

Albert returns not long afterwards, with a distracted look on his face. He pats Hester's shoulders uncertainly when she flies into his arms the second he enters the room.

'Albert! I'm so pleased to see you,' she murmurs into his chest.

'Are you all right, Hetty?'

'Oh, yes. It's just . . . the storm. It startled me as I walked home, that's all,' she says breathlessly. 'I

69

had to drink some cocoa to warm up again.'

'Come now, there's nothing to be frightened of. As Saint Paul said: "God makes His angels spirits—that is, winds—and His ministers a flaming fire." In the wind that blows, there are living spirits; God's angels guide the thunderclouds, and the mighty thunderclap may be a shock vibration of the air, as today's men of science tell us, but it is also *more* than that—it is the voice of God Himself!' Albert smiles, his eyes alight. Hester smiles back at him, unsure how to respond.

'Let's get into bed. It's chilly tonight,' she says.

'Very well. It is rather late—I shan't read for long.' His habit is to read scripture for at least half an hour every night; with quiet concentration, like a pupil who knows he will be tested.

When at last Albert closes his book, lays his spectacles upon it and places both on the bedside table, Hester smiles. He turns out his lamp, slides lower in the bed, meshes his fingers across his chest. But his eyes stay open. Hester leaves her lamp on, and lies facing him. The storm is abating, but still the wind blows, and throws rain hard against the window pane. The room, with Hester's lamp the only light, seems like a close cocoon, shielding them from the wild night. Perhaps it is this, perhaps it is the fright she had earlier in the evening, but Hester feels a powerful need for comfort. She yearns to be touched, to be held by her husband. She looks at his smooth face, at the warm glow of his skin, coloured from all the time he spends out of doors.

They have never even lain naked together, he on top of her or vice versa. She has never felt the press of his skin against her chest, and thinking of

70

this makes Hester's throat dry, makes her heart rise up and half choke her. Without a word, she moves closer to Albert, until she can lay her cheek on his shoulder. He does not move, or speak. He can't claim to be tired when clearly his mind is oddly alert tonight. After a minute, when there is no protest at her touch, Hester raises her face again. Albert is so close she can't focus her eyes on him properly. He is a creamy-coloured blur, soft shades of gold and brown and milky white in the half light. The smell of him fills her nose. The soap he uses to shave with, the gentle tang of his skin underneath it.

'Oh, Albert,' she breathes, and all her love and desire for him rush into those two words, making her voice deeper, more resonant. She lets her hands run over his chest, pressing them into the cloth of his shirt, seeking the heat of the skin underneath, the slight resistance of the sparse hair growing there. Reaching up, she presses her mouth to his, feels the wonderful warmth of his lips, the softness of them, just for an instant, before he pushes her away.

'Hetty . . .' he begins, looking at her with something like despair, something almost fearful.

'Oh, Albert!' Hester whispers desperately. 'Why do you always push me away? Don't you love me? It is no sin, for man and wife to touch each other, to lie in each other's arms . . .'

'No, no; it is no sin, dear Hetty,' Albert replies.

'What then? You do not love me?' she asks, stricken.

'Of course I do, silly thing! Who could not love such a sweet wife as you?' He releases her arms, clasps his hands across his chest again in a seemingly casual manner; but it is a guarded gesture, putting a barrier between them.

'I'm not silly, Albert; I . . . I don't understand. Are we husband and wife in name alone?'

'We are husband and wife in God's eyes, and that is a sacred thing, an unbreakable thing,' Albert says, his voice almost fearful. His eyes roam the room, as though he longs to escape it.

'I know it, and I'm glad of it; but . . . our union is not consummated. And what of children, Albert?'

'I . . .' Albert shuts his eyes, turns his head away slightly. 'A family . . . a family is what I want. Of course it is, Hester . . .'

'Well, though I do not pretend to know a great deal about these things, I know we shall never have one while you will not touch me, or kiss or hold me.' Without meaning to, Hester bursts into tears. They are hot on her cheeks, and make her eyes burn.

'There, there now; stop that, Hetty! We shall have a family, all in good time! We're young yet, and . . . perhaps we are too young. Perhaps it would be better to wait a while longer, until we are both more tutored in the ways of the world . . .'

'I am twenty-six on my next birthday, Albert. You will be twenty-five. Many women younger than I are mothers thrice over already!' She sniffs, blotting at her eyes with the cuff of her nightdress. 'But it is not just that—not only that! I need . . . I need *tenderness* from you, Albert!'

'Hetty, please. Calm yourself,' Albert begs, and he looks so strained, so trapped and awkward that Hester relents.

'I don't mean to make you unhappy,' she says, swallowing her sobs.

72

'How could you? Dear Hester,' he says, and in his eyes is a look of helpless anguish. He watches her cry for a moment, and then rolls onto his side, towards her, and brushes her cheek with his fingers. He seems to come to a decision. 'Very well. Will you turn out the light?' he says, and Hester is shocked to hear his voice shaking. Mutely, she complies.

In the darkness, Hester waits. Albert moves closer still, so that the length of his body presses into her side. She turns her face towards him, and can feel his proximity, the way her own breath hits his skin and bounces back to warm her. When he kisses her she leans into him, crushing their mouths together. She can't seem to catch her breath. The room spins and it is wonderful, intoxicating. She puts her arms around him, fingers splayed to touch as much of him as she can. She gathers up his shirt, bunching it with her fists until she finds the skin underneath, and runs her hands along it, delighting in the heat of it, the smooth texture. Albert shivers at her touch. Gently, she pulls him closer and closer, so that he loses his balance and has no choice but to lie on top of her. Holding him tightly, feeling the weight of him squeezing the air from her lungs, a strong surge of joy shoots through her. She smiles in the dark, and kisses him again.

'My Albert . . . I love you so much,' she breathes. His kiss is firm, lips clamped together. Hesitantly, Hester opens her mouth; just a little, but Albert pulls back. 'I'm sorry,' she says quickly.

'No, no. I . . .' Albert whispers, but doesn't finish the sentence. His hands are at either side of her face, lightly holding her head and stroking her hair.

Hester wriggles a little, desperate to feel his hands move lower, to feel his touch on her breasts and stomach and hips. On instinct she moves her knees apart, a fraction at a time, so it seems as if it is his weight that pushes them open. He comes to rest against her pelvis and Hester moves her hands to his hips, to hold him tighter to her. The feeling is irresistible, compulsive. There is a delicious ache in the pit of her stomach, butterflies of anticipation making her shudder. She lets her hands stray to his buttocks, and pulls him closer. Albert freezes. His face pulls back from hers and she can hear his breathing, fast and almost panicky.

'Albert, what's wrong?' she asks, craning her head up to be kissed again. But Albert pulls further away. He swallows audibly, and carefully climbs off her, to lie on his side of the bed, not even touching her. 'Albert, please! Tell me what's the matter!' Hester whispers, the sting of this rejection all too sharp.

'I'm so sorry, Hetty,' he says, meek and desolate. Hester's heart aches for him, and she bites her lip to keep from crying. But try as she might, she can find no words to comfort him, no way to say that it doesn't matter. Because at that moment it matters more than anything else in the world. She lies silent for a long time, too upset to sleep; she can tell from his breathing and his stillness that Albert is also awake. They lie there inches from each other, but it seems to Hester that a wide gulf stretches between them.

*   *   *

In her attic room, Cat begins a letter to Tess. *The*

74

hardest thing for me, in that rotten cell, was knowing that you were somewhere nearby, in just such a cell, but still I could not see you or speak to you, she writes, the candle's flicker making the shadow of her pen leap and stagger. This is not true, though. The hardest thing had been waiting in the morning's pale, cold light, which woke her early, as she heard the trolley and the footsteps come down the corridor towards her. She heard it stop, heard doors open and close, heard the screams and scuffles behind them, the choking sounds, the retching and coughing, the swearing of the wardens. All the while it came nearer and nearer, all the while she knew she would be next. Her turn was coming. The waiting for it was the worst, the fear of it debilitating. In a haze of hunger and dread, she had lain for an hour, some mornings, listening to that trolley squeal and rattle its way towards her. The sound of it pushed a bow wave of horror into every cell along the row, so strong it was almost palpable. The few simple items aboard that small vehicle were enough to cause strong hearts to falter, and tears of sheer terror to well in Cat's eyes.

I'm going to send this to Broughton Street in case you have been in touch there, in case you've left word of your whereabouts, she continues. She pauses, grips the end of her pen between her teeth. How can she not think what to write, to her best friend? To the person she thinks of most often? *I do miss you, Tess. Here is not such a bad place, I can see that with my waking eyes, but all the while I feel trapped. I feel like I am still in prison. Do you feel it too? Ever since you and I made our escape from the house to that first meeting—that was when we were free, Tess!*

75

For the very first time. I didn't think it would end up this way. Cat stares at her own scant shadow on the wall, falling into the memory of it. They weren't even supposed to be friends, a parlourmaid and a kitchen-maid. Cat ranked higher, and was not supposed to talk to the lower servants, not even at mealtimes at the long table in the servants' quarters where they all met, three times a day. Tess shared a cellar room with the scullery-maid, Ellen, at first. But then the room, which was below ground level, was flooded out one night, and took weeks to dry. Mildew furred the walls, damp put a stiff chill in the air. So Ellen was given a truckle bed in with the first kitchen-maid, and Tess joined Cat in the attic.

Tess was only sixteen, little more than a child. Cat taught her to read a little, told her of faraway places, read to her from Byron and Milton and Keats. Tess's eyes would light up at each twist and turn in the story, at each horror and wonder. When the Mariner killed the albatross, when Isabella planted her lover's head in a flowerpot.

It was Tess's idea to sneak out, the first time. Until then, Cat had not considered the idea. She had been raised in obedience, and deference; she had been raised to love and fear The Gentleman. But Tess read the leaflet that was brought to the servants' quarters, and showed it to Cat. Waving it under her nose in a quiet corner of the corridor, tucked into the recess by the scullery doorway where they could not be seen from the butler's pantry or the housekeeper's room. 'Let's go along to it, Cat! I dare you! Oh, do let's go!' On Sunday afternoon, their only free time, they put on their best clothes and went. And it lit a fire in Cat. For there to be life, outside the house. For there to be a roomful of people, all gathered together of their own free will, and for her to be one of them. Tess's cheeks were pink at the thrill of it, and Cat was all but struck dumb. It was like the world had started over, and would never go back to its old, drab turning.

The local meeting hall had been decked out in purple, white and green; from the sashes, flags and swags of bunting that hung from every banister and balustrade, to the sprays of flowers in vases that stood all around, dousing the air with their scent. Huge banners wafted gently overhead. One proclaimed: *Who Would Be Free Themselves Must Strike the Blow!* Another bore the graceful likeness of Emmeline Pankhurst, and praised her *Daring Rectitude*, calling her a *Champion of Womanhood*. There was a bustle and a hum of excitement, and Cat and Tess stayed on their feet at the back, overawed by the grandness of the ladies seated towards the front, who seemed to know each other well. Never before had they been in the same room as upper- and middle-class women, and yet been on the same footing as them. For Tess, that was enough. It was enough to be counted as a person, to count for something for a while. But for Cat, it was the words that were spoken, the arguments she heard that night from the various speakers, that shook her to her very core; seemed to shake her awake for the first time in her life.

'A man may be drunk, or mad, or a convicted criminal; he may be lame, unfit for military service, or a keeper of white slaves, and yet he may vote! A woman may be mayor, or nurse, or mother; she may be learned in medicine, and be a doctor or a

77

teacher; she may work and support herself and her family in industrial factories, and yet she may not vote! A soiled dove may be taken, if she is found to be infected by venereal disease, and kept against her will for many months until the infection has been treated, and yet there is no penalty for the men who have frequented and infected her! A husband may beat his wife, and indulge all his many urges upon her body, and she has no recourse to refuse him. A man may philander before he weds, and try himself with several female partners, and still he may go on to make an honourable partnership—and yet these women he has known are cast out by society!'

At this Tess had giggled, and coloured up, and Cat shushed her, gripping her hands to still her.

'While only men can vote, only men's economic grievances will be addressed by the government of this country. Our opponents point out that we have not the earning power of men: well, how can we have when all the most lucrative and important positions are barred to us—by men? As long as a woman has no political power, then she will have no economic power, and will remain at the bottom of the ladder when it comes to earnings. Until parliament is made responsible to us as voters, none of these inequalities, none of these imbalances will be addressed! They say that if we have the vote, women will no longer listen to men, and all will descend into chaos. We say, why should men not listen to women for once? Comrades! Spread the word! Give up your time; give up your money if you can. Raise up your voices and make yourselves heard!'

There was enthusiastic applause, and then the

presentation of a medal to a frail lady, whose brown dress matched the brown hollows under her eyes, and who had recently come out of prison for disrupting a Liberal Party meeting. The woman pinned the medal to her dress, then spoke in a reedy voice of her ordeal, thanking her sisters for all their support, and vowing to fight on. She was given a standing ovation.

'Let's go, Cat—we'd better. It's almost four o'clock,' Tess whispered urgently, as the speaker stepped down.

'Not yet. I want to ask what we can do!'

'What do you mean, Cat? Do about what?'

'Did you mean for this to be our first and last outing, then? Don't you want to help them? Be one of them?' Cat asked incredulously.

'Be one of them?' Tess echoed, with a startled smile.

'You heard what she said! Why shouldn't we have the vote? Why should I earn less than the hall boy, when I am older and have worked longer and hold a higher position than he?'

'But . . . it's not for the likes of us—we've got duties to attend to. Look at all those rich women! They've the time and money to take part. What have we got?'

'And we'll always have no time, and no money, and duties to attend to, if we never do anything about it. Don't you want to be *part* of something?' Cat demanded, giving Tess a little shake. Tess's eyes were wide, and she swallowed, but in the end she nodded.

'I do, Cat. If you'll be there with me. I do want to be part of it,' she said, looking up at Cat with gentle wonder.

79

'Good.' Cat smiled. 'Come on. Let's ask what we can do.' They gathered leaflets, and paid a penny for a copy of *Votes for Women*, and learnt the whereabouts of their local WSPU office, where they could go and pay a shilling to join, and sign the declaration of allegiance.

In the weeks that followed, they went to the Women's Press Shop on Charing Cross Road to buy the colours—all manner of accessories in white, purple and green were on sale, from hat pins to bicycles—and volunteered their time filling envelopes, handing out leaflets, and advertising meetings and fundraising events. And they went, from then on, each Sunday afternoon, even though their feet were throbbing and their backs aching, and they could have spent the time lying down or drinking in the pub, or meeting with a sweetheart. They wore their WSPU badges pinned to their underwear all week, where they would not be seen and confiscated; and from then on they were not merely servants, they were suffragettes.

It was a game at first, Cat thinks. A game in which she dictated the rules and Tess played along. Cat shuts her eyes in anguish, the letter lying unfinished in front of her. How can she write something as insufficient as a letter about it all? How can she hope to make amends? Sweet, trusting Tess; little more than a child and besotted with Cat, willing to do whatever Cat asked of her. And what Cat asked of her would come to ruin her. It would end with her blood staining the ground around her, and her spirit beaten down. It would end in her violent devastation. Cat signs off with two bleak little words. *Forgive me*. She presses the letter to her chest, as if it will absorb some of the remorse from her heart, and carry it to Tess.

3

The Rev. Albert Canning—from his journal

FRIDAY, JUNE 2ND, 1911

I heard the most remarkable speaker in Newbury last night, one Robin Durrant. A young man, and yet clearly advanced beyond his years in intellect and understanding. He spoke most eloquently upon the basic tenets of the wisdom religion, aka theosophy; keeping all in the auditorium quite captivated. Particular emphasis was laid on nature spirits, the evidence for their existence, methods of detecting them, and the reasons how and why they may choose to reveal—or indeed not to reveal—themselves, at will, to their human neighbours. He spoke to me most compellingly after the lecture was given, regarding the reconciliation of theosophy with the Anglican faith.

I returned from the lecture during a terrific electric storm. What controls such things, such startling things, if not God, if not the higher order? Exceedingly well timed to coincide with my sermon on this very point. Hester much troubled by the storm, it seeming to leave her emotionally weakened and needy. I found some scripture regarding the presence of God in such things to comfort her, but at times she is inconsolable by words. Women are like children, sometimes, in their simple fears and misunderstandings.

We spoke again on the subject of a family, and at her insistence we fell into an embrace to this end, which eventually culminated in my withdrawal. Her tears, which I am certain are not designed to persuade me, nevertheless compel me into these situations. But she is right, and it is the duty of a husband to lie with his wife in a discreet manner, for the begetting of children. I cannot explain my reluctance to her. I cannot sufficiently explain it to myself. But something stops me; something forces me to retreat from the act. I can only think that God has some other plan for me—for us—that He has not yet chosen to reveal. I dare not say such a thing to Hester, who has her heart quite set upon children of her own, and who also seems to need these physical expressions of emotion in a way I do not. But we are made and designed by God, and He guides our hand, if we let Him; so I must heed to my instincts. I pray that Hetty may come to accept this. I hate to think that she may be unhappy.

1911

On Monday evening Hester comes downstairs from an afternoon nap, drifting through the house on steady feet in search of her husband. She follows the soft sounds of his fingers upon ivory keys to the library, where the upright piano that was a wedding present from her uncle stands amidst piles of papers and hymn books and musical scores. She leans against the door jamb and watches him for a moment, listening to the light notes he plays—odd little phrases, over and over with tiny variations here and there. His head is studiously bowed, exposing the back of his neck, the little hairs there lit golden in the afternoon light. She is suddenly nervous about interrupting him, displeasing him. Since the night of the thunderstorm there has been some unspoken awkwardness between them which makes her hesitate. A moment later, he seems to sense her presence and straightens up, glancing over his shoulder. Hester smiles.

'I'm sorry, my darling. I didn't mean to wake you,' he says, as she crosses to sit beside him.

'You didn't,' Hester assures him, relieved that he seems quite relaxed. 'I was awake anyway, and ready to rise. Are you writing another hymn?'

'Alas, I am still writing the same hymn,' Albert sighs. 'The same one as for the last three weeks! I can't seem to get the tune to fit the words . . . it's vexing me terribly.'

'You need a rest, my love,' she suggests.

'I can't. Not until I've unknotted it some.'

'Play it for me. Perhaps I can help.' Hester sits on the stool beside him, facing the keys.

'Very well, but it's nowhere near ready for an audience,' Albert warns her sheepishly.

'I'm not an audience. I'm your wife.' Hester smiles, gently looping her arm through his, loosely so as not to hamper his movements. Albert plays an opening chord to find the key.

'Oh! Lord God, our father, all around us we see; the fruits of Thy bounty, Thy gifts heavenly! In the crash of the waves and the singing of the birds, we hear Thy true voice and harken to Thy words . . .'

Albert sings softly, his voice jolting up and down between notes like a child at hopscotch. 'There!' He breaks off in frustration. 'I can't make that line lie happily within the melody!' Hester reaches out her hand and plays the last few notes. She hums along a little, letting the tune move to its own rhythm.

'How about this.' She clears her throat. 'In the crash of the waves and the bright song of birds, we hear Thy true voice and harken to Thy words,' she sings.

Albert smiles fondly at her. 'Darling, you have a gift for music that I envy, I truly do. You should be composing hymns, not I! Thank you.' He kisses her forehead, his face bright and open. Hester's breath gets hitched in her chest, and she does not trust herself to speak, so she smiles, and plays the simple tune again; and there they sit in the hazy sunlight, arm in arm, humming and singing and softly playing.

*　　　*　　　*

The household is all darkness and silence by eleven o'clock. The night is still and balmy mild—unseasonably so, perhaps. On soft feet, Cat leaves her room, goes along the corridor and down the back stairs. Already, her feet know which boards to avoid, how to tread so as not to make a sound. Not that much could wake a household grown accustomed to sleeping through the cavernous snoring of Sophie Bell, she thinks. Outside in the courtyard Cat smokes a cigarette, leaning her back against the warm brick wall, watching the bright red flare each time she inhales. When it fades, it draws patterns in front of her eyes against the darkness. To either side of the house, owls are calling, talking in childlike whistles and squeaks. The sky is an inky velvet blue, and she watches the little bats against it, wheeling and diving, mesmerised by the silence of their flight. Suddenly, there is no thought of her going back inside, of going to bed, lying down in this new, genteel prison she has been sent to. There is too much life, humming in the night air like a static charge. Cat sets off across the meadow, with dew from the feathered grasses soaking into her shoes.

Her eyes grow ever more accustomed to the dark, and she makes her way to the canal, turning left to follow the towpath towards Thatcham. Her heart is beating faster now, with that same excitement as when she and Tess walked to their first public meeting. Only eighteen months ago. It seems like a lifetime. It seems like another world. There is such a thrill of emotion, something she can't name—almost fearful, something she almost wants to turn away from, but at the same time can't resist. It causes a rushing in her bloodstream, causes the tips of her fingers to tingle. Where the warehouses and buildings coalesce into the town, a group of men are sitting on the bridge, smoking and talking and laughing. Another girl might see danger, but Cat is not afraid of them.

'Well, what have we here?' says one of them, as she walks right up to them, climbs up onto the bridge from the canal side and stands with her arms folded across her chest. She can't see their faces, just shadows and outlines. The smell of them is in the air all around—sweat, the rank odour of working men at the end of a long, hot day. Beer, smoke, rough canvas clothes.

'Are you lost, little girl?' another asks her.

'I'm neither—lost, nor a little girl. I'm looking for George Hobson,' she says, the name coming easily into her mouth, although she hadn't known it was waiting there.

'Good grief, he's a lucky bugger then—secret assignation is it?' the first man asks, with a leer that makes the others laugh.

'It's none of your business. Do you know where I can find him, or not?'

'Oh, she's a feisty one! That's a quick tongue you've got, miss. I'm not sure how lucky George is after all!'

'He'll be along at The Ploughman—in the back room, most likely,' one of the younger men tells her, speaking for the first time. 'Do you know where that is? Go on a bit further, and at the next bridge turn right, up to the London road. You'll find it soon enough.'

'Thank you.' Cat walks away to a variety of good-natured catcalls and hisses.

Only at the entrance to The Ploughman does she hesitate, because the doorway is low and the room inside dark and crowded, even though it's after hours. For a moment, she feels that clawing inside when she is shut in, when there is a chance she could be trapped. But she steels herself, slipping through the crowd in a way a larger person couldn't. There are a few other women in the pub, but only a few; their blouses tight, the top buttons undone, beer in their hands and red on their cheeks and kisses all over their mouths. *In the back room*, the young man had said. There is a rough wooden door, shut and latched at the far end of

86

the room. Cat makes for it. When her fingers touch the latch, she jumps. A huge roar goes up from the other side, of a hundred deep male voices booming as one. Unease slows Cat's progress, makes her pause. It sounds like a large and violent crowd is waiting behind the door, and she knows enough of such things to fear them. A hand clasps her wrist and pulls it firmly from the latch.

'Now, where might you be going, young lady?' asks a whiskery old man. His skin on her wrist is like a leathery bark, and she twists herself free.

'Take your hands off me!' she snaps, her heart lurching.

'All right, all right, nobody's trying to interfere with you! I asked a question, that's all.' He slurs his words slightly but his eyes are bright and if he wanted to stop her, Cat sees, he could.

'I'm here to see George. George Hobson,' she says, tipping her chin defiantly. 'He's in there, isn't he?'

'What are you? His woman? Daughter? I thought he had none,' the man asks curiously.

'What I am to him is my business. Are you going to let me through or not?' The man studies her for a moment, chewing thoughtfully on the bedraggled remnants of a cigarette.

'You know what this is, do you?' He eyes her dubiously and hooks his thumb at the door. Another roar goes up from beyond it. Cat's heart beats faster. She clamps her mouth shut, nods briskly though she can't think what she will find in this restricted room. 'Go on then, but you'll not make a scene or I'll have you out on your ear, got that?' He leans over, lifts the latch and presses the door open, just wide enough for Cat to squeeze

87

through. Biting her lip, her hands in fists, she does so.

The room is blue with smoke, airlessly hot, and the ceiling even lower and all of wood, like the walls. Cat's view is barred by ranks of men, their backs turned to her, all jostling and cheering and stamping and wincing, waving their arms, their fists, their pocketbooks. Cat skirts the edge of this crowd until she spots an opening, worming her way, unnoticed, to the front. She does not recognise him at first, the smiling man who blushed when she discovered that he couldn't read. Now he is stripped to the waist, his thick torso slick with sweat and blood. Light shines from the curves and contours of his body. His hair is plastered to his head, and blood comes freely from a cut above his left eye, drawing a bright line down to his chin. But his opponent looks in worse shape. This other man is taller than George, but does not have his solid build. His long arms are thinner, though the muscles stand out along them like knots in rope. Both of them have made their knuckles bloody red and ragged.

When his opponent lands a punch, George absorbs it with an outward rush of breath, and does not falter. He moves smoothly, weaving like a cat, ducking his head like a bird, more graceful than a man of his size should be. Cat watches him, quite mesmerised. She has never seen anybody look so alive. She breathes deeply, catching the salt of sweat on her tongue; hears the smack of bone on flesh, of knuckles sinking deep somewhere giving, and a collective groan from the crowd in sympathetic pain. Cat presses up against the ropes of the makeshift ring, grasping the rough hemp tightly in her hands as she yells out her support. How different, how powerfully real he seems, compared to the fat policemen in London; the cherubic vicar; her own thin and bony self.

Another punch and George begins to bleed from one nostril, sweat flying as his head snaps to the side. His shoulders slump and blood vessels stand proud along the muscles of his arms. Ugly pink bruises are blossoming around his ribs. But his expression is calm, one of steady deliberation. He knows, Cat senses, exactly what he is doing. What he should do next, what he has doubtless done before; all oblivious to the strain of it and the fatigue and the pain he must feel. His opponent's face is fixed into a grimace of effort and aggression. George is waiting, she sees. Using the other man's aggression against him. Making him feel frustrated and eager to wade in, to get the job done. Letting him land a few big punches, letting him see the path to victory, making him impatient for it, making him careless. George waits, he weaves; he blocks a blow that would have closed his right eye—just in time, letting it glance from his face as if next time he might not be fast enough. It works. The other man steps in, drops his guard, pulls back a swing that he means to be the final punch of the night. He takes a fraction of a second to wind up, to twist his whole body behind the blow. When George strikes, his arm moves so fast it's hard for the eye to follow; an upper cut that hits the taller man under the chin with a force that snaps his head back on his neck. The man drops abruptly, stunned, and lies propped upon his elbows, all bewildered.

George stands poised, but his opponent sinks

slowly onto his back, and out of consciousness. The roar goes up again, deafening, shutting out thought; and without realising it, Cat adds her voice to it, a triumphant yell for George's victory. Money changes hands, men shake their heads, George is passed a mug of beer, is clapped on the back; somebody throws a blanket over his shoulders which he shrugs off at once, accepting instead a stool to sit down on and a tatty piece of muslin with which to wipe his face. Cat makes her way towards him, wide eyed and inexorable.

'And I thought you such a gentle soul, when I first met you,' she tells him, without preamble. George frowns at her for a second, then smiles, recognition flooding his face.

'Cat Morley, who speaks so well and cusses even better,' he says, wiping his mouth with the back of his hand. Though he is tired and bruised, there's a gleam in his eye, and Cat recognises it. The same gleam that sent her sneaking out of The Rectory in the dark. 'I didn't think to see you here.'

'There's precious little entertainment in this town, it seems,' she says, wryly.

'True enough. I'd have thought you'd be kept in of an evening though, saying your prayers with the vicar and his wife?'

'Have you been asking about me?' Cat demands.

'Maybe I have, and what of it? It's you that's come and sought me out, after all.' George smiles.

'True enough.' Cat echoes him. She smiles, a quick flash of her small, white teeth. 'Do you always win?'

'Not always. Most of the time, though I say it myself. There's few around here who would bet against it, but every few weeks a fellow comes

90

along who thinks he can knock me down.' George gestures at the loser of the fight, still lying where he went down, and apparently forgotten.

'Won't somebody take care of him?'

'His people are somewhere hereabouts. They'll pick him up by and by, if they've not fallen down themselves,' George assures her.

'So why do you usually win? That man had longer arms than you, and he was taller. But you beat him easily.'

'Not that easily.' George dabs at the cut on his brow, the muslin staining red. 'What these other fellows don't seem to know, you see, is that it's not how hard you can hit that'll win you the fight, it's how hard you can *be* hit.'

'And you can be hit hard, can you?'

'My father saw to it. He trained me from an early age,' George says, still smiling but the gleam fading from his eyes.

'Well, my father was always kind to me, and somehow that was worse,' Cat says, folding her arms.

'I heard something said about your father,' George admits.

'Whatever it was, it was wrong, I promise you that.' She stands in front of him, only a fraction taller even though he is sitting down. 'So, will you buy me a drink with your winnings, or won't you?'

'I will, Cat Morley. I will,' George tells her.

'You might put your shirt back on,' she suggests, archly.

*   *   *

With the fight over the pub begins to empty, men

91

straggling off to their homes and their unforgiving spouses. Cat and George walk along to the bridge. The night has darkened to black, and Cat stares blindly along the towpath when they reach it, suddenly loath to set out along it, to return to her cramped attic room and Mrs Bell's noisy sleep.

'Let me walk you. Have you not brought a light with you?' George asks, mistaking her reluctance for a fear of the dark.

'No. You needn't, I'll be fine. The path is simple enough,' Cat says. They stop walking, turn towards each other, faces blurred by the darkness.

'Aren't you afraid, Cat?' he asks, puzzled.

'Afraid of what?'

'To be walking out with me, when you hardly know me. To be seen with me.'

'I don't think you mean me harm, but if I'm wrong it's my own fault. And as for being seen with you—surely if you've asked about me you'll have been told that I'm a sullied outcast, and a criminal, and quite possibly a killer. These are some of the whispers I've heard. My reputation can't be made worse than it is. So, aren't *you* afraid to be seen with me, instead?' She smiles, mischievously. George laughs softly, and she likes the sound. A low, bouncing chuckle.

'I mean you no harm, you have that right. As for the rest of it, I scarce gave it any credit until you came marching into the fight tonight. Now I think, a girl who'll do that, unescorted and unafraid, might just have done some of the things I heard about!'

'I did . . . I did do something. And I have been in prison for it—that part is true. And what was done to me and others like me was far worse than we

92

deserved, far worse than our crime, if crime it was. And after it, I find I'm not afraid. Not of gossip and rumours, or the wretched, petty hags who put them about either,' Cat says, angrily. 'And now you will ask me what I did, and what happened thereafter,' she sighs. Such questions seem to dog her, hanging from her neck like dead weights.

'No, I won't. If you want to tell it, I'll listen; but it's not my business,' George says, hurriedly. Cat stares along the water again to where it is swallowed whole by the night. There is a nip in the air now, and she shivers. 'I'll walk you back. Not all the way to the door, if you're worried about being seen. I'll bet you can move with the stealth of a ghost, when you need to,' George says.

'Black Cat, they used to call me—in London. For that very reason.' She smiles. 'It's two miles to the village, that's four for you to walk, and after you've fought tonight. Stay here on your boat, and rest. Don't feel obliged to play the gentleman this evening,' she argues. George clears his throat, folds his arms to mirror her.

'I would walk those four miles to keep talking to you, Cat Morley. How's that for a reason?'

Cat studies him for a moment, and thinks about insisting. But then she relents. 'Very well, then.'

A small, high moon sits in the sky like a farthing, and casts a weak light onto the towpath. In places the path is overhung by branches, made narrow by thick borders of yellow flag and willow herb. George insists on taking the lead, although he is tall enough to catch every branch, and send them swinging back for Cat to dodge. He mutters and curses beneath his breath.

'Perhaps I should lead? I can see quite well,' Cat

says.

George pauses in a patch of open moonlight, and turns to her. 'Truly like a cat, then?' he says. In the colourless night he is grey and black, his eyes empty hollows, his expression lost. For a second he seems not-human, some creature made of stone and shadow rather than flesh. But then he puts out one hand and touches her chin, and his skin is warm and dry. 'You look more like a gypsy by this light,' he says quietly.

'My mother told me once that her grandmother was a Spaniard. She was dark like me, my mother, and people always said that I take after her.' His touch feels strange, unsettling; like an intrusion, but one she finds she does not mind. She reaches up for his hand and keeps hold of it, and even in the dark she can see how avidly he watches her, how rapt his expression.

*   *   *

The house is so quiet when Cat returns to her room that she thinks she is discovered. It feels as though all is poised, tensed and ready to spring shut around her like a steel trap. Even Mrs Bell's snoring is absent. Cat strips off her clothes and hangs them by the open window to air, to rid them of the telltale smell of beer and cigarettes. Then she lies still on the bed and hardly breathes, and though her heart hammers she feels ready to fight, to spring up and lay about her with her fists, if needs be. If they put hands on her, hold her down, force her. She will not let them again. But these are memories, half brought on by the beer she drank and the sleep she hasn't had, and slowly she

94

grows calm, and shuts her eyes, and wonders if George is still out in the meadow where she left him, waiting with his cut and bruised face turned up to the attic windows, in case she were to look out and wave. The thought soothes her, lets her breathing slow and deepen; lets her sleep.

*   *   *

In the morning, Hester, her stomach hot and empty, waits impatiently for Albert to return from his early walk so that they can sit down to breakfast. She abandons the book she's been reading and drifts into the dining room where the table is set for two. Empty plates waiting, the cutlery laid beautifully straight. In the quiet room, her stomach growls audibly. It is not like Albert to be so late. *How long can a person spend communing with nature?* she wonders, hunger making her anxious.

Suddenly Hester hears the rattle of Albert's bicycle, and leaps up with unseemly haste to greet him. The front door is ajar, where Cat is polishing the brass letter plate with a piece of soft leather. The vicar bowls through the door at such speed that he runs right into her, grasping her by the upper arms to steady himself.

'My word, it was extraordinary!' he bursts out, as if continuing a discussion they'd been having all morning. To Hester's surprise, Cat lets out a shriek of protest, and fights her way free of Albert's grasp, scuttling backwards until she hits the wall, and glaring at him with livid eyes. Albert blinks and stares at her as though she's turned into a snake.

'Cat! Really, child! Calm yourself,' Hester exclaims, shocked by the girl's excessive reaction, the way she seems unable to tolerate his touch. The touch of an ordained man. 'It's only Mr Canning! There's no need to . . . take fright,' she admonishes, uneasily. Cat relaxes, and looks at Hester with that odd blankness. It falls like a mask over her actual expression, Hester sees; hiding the girl's thoughts, leaving her true nature unseen. Hester recoils a little from the baleful stare.

'Sorry, madam. He startled me, that's all,' Cat says, quietly.

'We'll have breakfast now, thank you, Cat,' Hester says, stiffly, hurrying the girl away with little shooing motions of her fingers.

'Breakfast! Oh, no—I couldn't eat anything! Oh, Hester! I have had the most marvellous experience! The most wonderful thing has happened!' Albert exclaims, hurrying forward again and taking her hands, squeezing them tightly. His face is flushed pink with pleasure, his eyes glistening with excitement; even his hair seems affected, standing out from his head at rakish angles.

'What is it, my darling? What's happened?' she asks, her voice high with anxiety.

'I . . . I hardly know where to start . . . how to explain . . .' Albert's gaze slips past her face, falling out of focus into the middle distance. 'Suddenly words seem . . . inadequate . . .' he says, softly. Hester waits for a moment, then squeezes his fingers to rouse him.

'Come and sit down, Bertie dear, and tell me everything.'

Albert allows himself to be led into the dining

96

room, and to be manoeuvred into a chair just as Cat comes in with the first plate of eggs and chops, and a basket of bread. Hester takes her seat opposite Albert, helps herself to some bread with what she hopes is not over-eagerness, and begins to spread it with butter.

'I'm all ears, my dear,' she says, when Albert does not speak. He looks up at her as she begins to eat, then bursts up from his chair again and paces to the window. Bewildered, Hester chews slowly.

'I was out walking in the meadows, up by the river, just on one of my usual jaunts. There is a place to the east of here, I don't know if you have ever seen it, where the river is shallow and shaded from the north bank by willow and elder trees, and the bulrushes are as high as my eyes in places, and the whole of it is sprinkled with wild flowers like a carpet of jewels . . . The ground forms a hollow there; a wide, shallow hollow where in times of rain a swampy puddle forms, but now in summer it is lush with long meadow grasses and horsetails and buttercups and figwort . . . The mist seems to linger slightly longer in that hollow. I was watching it clear, watching its slow rising, and the way it glowed where the sun touched it and I saw . . . I saw . . .'

'What, Albert?' Hester asks, almost alarmed by the way her husband is talking. Albert turns to her, his face breaking into an incredulous smile of joy.

'Spirits, Hester! Nature spirits! The very elemental beings that God sends to tend the wildlife and the flowers, to drive all the many workings of his natural world! I saw them at play, as clearly as I see you now!' Albert cries, his voice dense with emotion. Cat pauses in the act of

97

placing a pot of coffee on the table, glancing from Albert to Hester and back again with an incredulous look on her face.

'Thank you, Cat,' Hester says, pointedly. 'Albert, that's . . . quite astonishing! Are you sure?'

'Sure? Of course I'm sure! I saw them with my own eyes, as clear as day! As exquisite as wild orchids . . . each of them . . .'

'But, what did they look like, Albert? What were they doing?'

'They were the colour of wild rose petals— white, if you did not look closely enough, but touched with gold and pink and pearly silver if you did, and each of them slender like a willow branch, dressed in some kind of robes . . . I could not clearly make out the fabric, but that it was pale and floated about them as if it weighed less than the very air; and they were dancing, Hetty! Dancing slowly and gracefully, the way the frond of a plant moves under water—easily and with never a sudden change, their arms first rising and then falling . . . Oh, Hester! I feel as though I have borne witness to a miracle! I feel like I have been favoured by God with this glimpse at what is usually hidden from man!'

'Albert . . . this is remarkable. I mean . . .' Hester flounders. Albert is beaming at her, clearly intoxicated by his experience. She frowns at the thought, looking at him closely, and finds herself leaning slightly towards him, inhaling as subtly as she can. But there is no hint of brandy or wine, or anything of the sort. Hester smiles uncertainly. 'Quite . . . unprecedented,' she says, lamely. 'And you truly believe that these creatures—'

'No, no—do not call them creatures, dear heart!

They are not of the same ilk as the rabbits and the birds . . . these are *Godly* things, sacred beings much higher than us. Compared to them we are but cloddish clay figures!' he says, triumphantly. Hester can't think what else to say. Albert seems so strange and passionate—she hardly knows him at all.

'But . . . don't you understand what this means?' Albert demands, turning to Hester and seeming suddenly to notice her hesitancy. Hester smiles as best she can, and opens her eyes brightly to show that she is ready to hear what it means, ready to accept what she is told; but this empty anticipation seems to disappoint Albert, and he slumps a little, his face falling. In the steady pause that follows, Hester fingers her cutlery, longing to cut open the chop on her plate but sensing that to do so would spoil the impression of avid attention. 'I must write at once to Robin Durrant, the theosophist,' Albert declares, collapsing back into his chair.

*   *   *

Cat goes back to the kitchen and slaps the empty breakfast tray onto the table top.

'The vicar's seeing fairies,' she announces blandly. Mrs Bell's head comes up from the bread oven, sweaty and red.

'What's that now?' she asks. Cat throws her hands up, at a loss.

Leah went to meet her best friend, Sam, in a café not far from where she worked. She chose a table in a far corner, away from the window, and sat down to wait. It was mid-morning on a grey Tuesday in early March; Leah had been back from Belgium for a week and she still felt shaken, oddly seasick, after the trip; after seeing Ryan, and the body of the dead soldier. Both of them unsettling, compelling, frightening. Leah ordered coffee and sipped it scalding hot when it arrived. It steadied her a little, and moments later Sam burst in through the door, moving with her customary haste, all elbows and knees, and shaking her head in pre-emptive apology when she saw Leah.

'I'm so sorry I'm late! I couldn't get away— Abigail is being a prize bitch this week and really putting the boot in . . . everyone knows the real reason but we can hardly say so. She's pretending it's because she's seen our interim figures for this quarter, and they're not good enough. Sorry. Sorry!' she said breathlessly, kissing Leah on the cheek and squeezing her into a quick hug.

'Stop apologising!' said Leah. 'I expect nothing less. And you know I've never minded sitting and people-watching.' She had known Sam since the first year of school, and Sam had never once made it to an appointment on time.

'So, what's this big announcement of yours—I'm dying to hear,' Sam said, tucking a swathe of shiny hair behind her ear and lacing her fingers in front of her. Her expression was open but her eyes darted over Leah's face, never quite alighting, constantly distracted.

'Well, I've probably over-hyped it now. It's not much of an announcement, really,' said Leah, taking a deep breath. The decision had seemed a lot bigger in her mind, when she'd made it. It had just been so long since she'd felt enthusiasm for anything—real enthusiasm, the urge to work and write. Now, speaking it aloud, it sounded feeble. 'I'm going out of town, for a bit. Just a couple of weeks. I'm chasing down a story.' She saw this register with some disappointment on Sam's face, and smiled apologetically. 'I knew I'd over-hyped it.'

'No! I just . . . I thought it might be about something else. I thought maybe you'd met . . . somebody,' Sam said, then flapped her hand at Leah's crestfallen expression. 'Forget I said it. No, I think it's great news. Good for you—it's high time you got your mojo back, God only knows. So, what's the story?'

'It's . . . ah . . . the identity of a soldier of the First World War. He's just been discovered over in Belgium. Only there's more to it than that. I'm sure of it.'

'More to him being discovered?' Sam asked, puzzled.

'No—more to who he is, to what he was doing in the war. To what he did in his life before it, especially. He had two letters on him which have survived—which is amazing in itself. They're very odd letters. Perhaps you'd better read them?' she suggested, fishing the rumpled pages from her bag.

She herself had read and reread them many times since leaving Ryan lying in the dark of his poky room, in bed sheets that smelled of her. There was something so vivid about them—she could almost feel the woman's fear and desperation, rising like a scent from the elegant lettering; her confusion, and the frustration of being able to change nothing and discover nothing. And the odd tone of them puzzled her—clearly the pair had both been party to something very unusual, something deeply upsetting: this *crime*, in which the woman felt complicit by her silence. And yet, she wrote to him as if he were almost a formal acquaintance. She did not write as to a close friend or a family member. The imploring way in which she begged for an explanation, for information . . . Leah had started to feel tremors of sympathetic panic each time she picked the letters up. And why should the soldier have kept these two letters in particular, when it sounded as though there had been many others? She'd tried to find something that the two had in common, but failed—apart from the pleading, of course, the cries for help. But surely any other letters she'd sent would also have included these?

'You might be reading too much into that,' said Sam, as Leah outlined her curiosity. 'It might just be the case that he lost the others, or they were destroyed by accident, or he never got them,' she pointed out. 'Who knows?'

'True.' Leah frowned. 'I don't know, though. He was so careful with these ones. He sealed them so meticulously, and kept them on him even when he was fighting. It makes me doubt that he'd have accidentally lost or damaged a lot of others.'

'Where *did* you come across all this, anyway?' Sam asked.

Leah swirled her coffee dregs in the bottom of the cup, and neatly evaded the question. 'So you think there's a story in it?' she asked instead.

'God, yes! If you can find out what crime was committed, and even by who; and who this fella was and who the woman was . . . for sure there's a story there. How did you find it, Leah?'

'I went out to Belgium last week—that's where I was. Someone at the Commonwealth War Graves Commission put me on to it—they're holding his body for a while to see if I can get an ID before he's reburied,' she said, as casually as she could.

'The War Graves Commission? Not Ryan? Leah—you've not been over to see Ryan, have you?' Sam said, seriously. She fixed Leah with a stern stare and would not let her go.

'Not to see him! Not specifically! He did contact me about the story, and they do want to find out who the soldier was.' Leah tried to defend herself; but Sam's arms were folded, her lips pressed together.

'Tell me you didn't sleep with him. At least tell me that,' she said; and when Leah didn't answer, and could not look at her, her face fell into lines of utter dismay. 'Oh, *Leah*! What were you *thinking*?'

'I wasn't,' Leah said, twisting her paper napkin till it tore. 'I wasn't thinking at all. I can't seem to think, where he's concerned. I just get . . . scrambled up. I'm like a mobile phone too close to a bloody microwave!' she said, with quiet despair.

'Which is why I thought we'd established you weren't going to see him again. For at least a year or two. Leah—every time you see him any little bit of healing gets undone! Look at you, you look knackered.'

103

'Thanks. You're really not telling me anything I don't know.'

'Then why do I have to keep saying it? Leah, seriously. Ryan's a no-go area. He cocked up big time. I mean . . . *big* time.' Sam held her hands wide apart.

'It's not that easy. You make it sound so childish,' Leah muttered.

'I don't mean to. I know how difficult it is—you know I do. And I was around to help you pick up the pieces, wasn't I? I just . . . don't want to have to do it again.'

'I'm fine. Really, I am. I've got this story to work on now—'

'Are you going to be working with Ryan on this? Are you going to be in touch?' Sam interrupted.

'No. No, not at all. I left without even saying goodbye. I've emailed him to say I'll try to find out what I can, but that's it. No progress reports, even. Either I'll be able to find something out in the next few weeks, or I won't. And whatever I find out can go in an email. I don't need to see him again.'

'Well, I hope you're convincing yourself, because you sure as hell aren't convincing me.'

'Sam, come on. It's the story I came to tell you about—really it was. It's already more important to me than . . . what happened in Belgium. You don't need to punish me for seeing him. For sleeping with him. Doing it was punishment enough, OK? OK?'

'OK! Not another word. So you're going to . . . where was it? Cold Arse?'

'Cold Ash Holt.'

'Sounds positively bucolic.'

'Yes. It's somewhere in Berkshire. Not quite the

back of beyond, but it'll get me out of London. A change of scene, you know. New project,' said Leah.

'How was he? How's he doing?' Sam asked, curiosity getting the better of her.

'Unchanged. On fine form. Positively blooming.' Leah shrugged, unhappily.

'Where are you going to start? With the story, I mean.'

'At The Rectory, I guess. There's no date on the letters, but she wrote the second one once she'd found out he had gone off to fight in the war, so that's sometime between 1914 and 1918; and the first one about three or four years before that, from what she says. So I just need to find out who was living there then, and if there were any young men of fighting age, and . . . whatever else I can.' She shrugged. 'The CWGC have already established that there were no soldiers *registered* as living there, but somebody might know something.'

If she could have got up and left right then, she would have. Talking about it made her desperate to get started, to discover what the letters' author was so afraid of, what she could not find out. It struck Leah then that the tight despair, the desire to surrender that was captured in the letters reminded her strongly of how she felt about Ryan. She could not ease her own discomfort, but perhaps she could ease H. Canning's. And suddenly she longed to be somewhere where there were no memories of Ryan, or of them being together; nobody who even knew Ryan existed. He was clinging to her like cobwebs, and she itched to brush them off.

Leah still lived in the flat, near Clapham

Common, that she had shared with Ryan. They had lived together for four years, moved in with each other after only two months of dating. She had never been as sure about anything ever before; and she wasn't normally an impulsive person. A love sceptic, she would have called herself, but along had come a man who could make her feel more alive just by being in the room. He didn't even have to touch her. She had quipped to her friends that she finally understood what pop songs were all about, but really it hadn't been a joke. She felt like her eyes had been opened—or perhaps her heart. Like she had been let in on a huge and wonderful secret. She was positively smug, for a long time; and afterwards her inner voices kept flinging cruel adages at her—about pride coming before a fall, and there being a fine line between love and hate.

She refused to move out of the flat, which she loved and had lived in for two years before she'd even met Ryan. She would go back to living in it by herself, she resolved. It was her place again, rather than theirs, that was all. But it wasn't true. It was saturated with him, with echoes of him being there, and memories of his touch. For weeks she could still smell him, and thought she was going mad until she realised that the bedroom curtain, near where he had stood every morning to spray on his deodorant, was giving off waves of the fragrance. She laundered the curtains at once, but not before she had crouched by the open washing machine door for twenty minutes, rocking on her heels, her face screwed into the dusty fabric.

*　　　*　　　*

After kissing Sam goodbye, Leah went back to the flat, packed a small suitcase, slung it onto the back seat of her car and joined the traffic queuing for the M4. It only took an hour to reach junction twelve, once she got rolling, and for some reason Leah was disappointed. Her big trip out of town, her mission, seemed belittled by how small England could be. Her satnav led her away from the main road, down a narrow, winding lane between high hedgerows still winter-brown and drab. It had been raining, and she bumped through potholes full of water, squeezing into the muddy bank and lurching to a standstill three times to let huge four-by-fours plough past. When her satnav announced that she had arrived, she was sitting at a junction looking out over a small triangular green, with pretty, crooked houses fronting the lanes on each side. There was a large horse chestnut tree in the middle, a postbox at one corner and a phone box at the other, and no immediate signs of life. Over the rooftops of the furthest houses, Leah saw a church spire rising against the mottled sky, and felt a flare of excitement. If the dead soldier had been friends with the residents of The Rectory, he had almost certainly attended a service at that very church. She parked the car, and set off towards it. The quiet was profound, and she almost walked on tiptoes, unwilling to break it. A soft, damp breeze wandered through the naked conker tree, tapping its knuckled branches together.

The churchyard was scattered with snowdrops and early daffodils, and little purple crocuses. The usual array of village dead lay beneath headstones—old ones weathered and furred with lichen nearest the church wall, and then forward in time across the field to some brand new ones, the cuts in the turf plainly visible, lettering still razor sharp in the marble. For some reason Leah found it uncomfortable to look at these. Like catching somebody's eye in a communal changing room, a tiny but definite invasion of privacy. The church itself was grey stone and flint, Victorian by the look of it. A battered iron cockerel stood on top of the modest spire, immobile in spite of the breeze. The door was firmly locked. Fliers advertising parish events on pastel-coloured paper curled and fluttered, held fast to the wood by rusty drawing pins. Leah twisted the flaking metal latch and gave it an extra hard shove, just to make sure, and then jumped when somebody spoke behind her.

'It's no good, love. It's locked except at the weekends these days,' a man told her, grey haired and with a heavy paunch poking out of an ancient donkey jacket. Leah caught her breath.

'Oh, OK. Thanks,' she said, brushing her hands on the seat of her jeans.

'Mrs Buchanan has the key, over at number four on the green; but I'm pretty sure she's out at her yoga at this time of day,' the man went on.

'Oh well, never mind. Thanks.' Leah smiled briefly and waited for the man to move on. He smiled back at her, and did not move. Leah had hoped to spend some more time snooping around the churchyard, perhaps even looking for some Canning headstones from the right era, but the man showed no signs of going about his business, whatever it might be. 'Could you please tell me how to get to The Rectory?' she asked, stifling her irritation.

'Happy to, happy to,' the man said. 'You want to go left out of here and keep walking about a minute until you get to Brant's Close. It's on the left. It's a new road, a cul-de-sac, with lots of houses on it. The Rectory is number two, not far after you turn off the lane. You can't miss it . . .' He followed her down the path as he explained all this, and for a moment Leah thought he would dog her steps all the way there, but at the church gate he halted.

'Thank you!' Leah called, striding confidently away. Oh, for the rude, unhelpful and unobtrusive people of London, she thought. The man crossed his hands on the gatepost, and watched her go.

Number two was a small brick house, a square box with a paved front driveway and a very neat little lawn. Early pansies nodded their purple and yellow faces from a row of identical pots beneath the kitchen window. A black slate plaque by the door proclaimed it to be The Rectory, and Leah rang the bell, suddenly unsure of herself.

'Yes?' A thin, middle-aged woman greeted her, smiling but with a hunted expression, as if she expected to come under attack at any moment. A lace doily of a woman, Leah thought at once, a little unkindly. Delicate and utterly useless looking.

'I'm sorry, I think I've got this quite wrong,' Leah said. The doily blinked rapidly, tucking her blue cardigan tighter under her arms. 'I was looking for The Rectory—the original rectory, as it would have been, about a hundred years ago?' she explained.

'Oh, The Old Rectory? Yes, you've rather come

to the wrong place, I'm afraid. It's out the other side of the village—only five minutes' walk. If you take the lane signposted to Thatcham, you'll find it on the right-hand side a little further along,' the woman told her, and began to close the door. Leah put her hand out quickly and stopped her.

'Sorry—you don't know by any chance when it went from being The Rectory to being The Old Rectory, do you? When it was sold off by the church, I mean?' she asked. The woman looked at Leah's hand on the door as though it wielded a weapon.

'I'm sorry, I really don't know. Possibly during the thirties. A lot of church property passed into private hands at that time.'

'OK, thanks. Thank you.' Leah released her and returned to the road.

*   *   *

When she reached The Old Rectory, Leah paused, stepping onto the sodden verge as a car splashed past. It was a lovely old building, Queen Anne, she guessed; square and symmetrical and halfway to rack and ruin. The red bricks stood proud, the mortar between them long since eroded away. The garden to the front was badly overgrown, although the remains of last year's geraniums, dead and bedraggled in stone troughs by the door, suggested that somebody still lived there, and made something of an effort. Leah couldn't see any cars parked anywhere on the driveway, or any lights on inside even though the day was gloomy and getting gloomier. She stood and watched it covertly for a few minutes, in case she saw movement within.

This, then, was the house where the letters she had pored over so avidly of late had been written. Her heart picked up a little at the thought. It felt like peeping through a tiny keyhole in a door, into the past. With some unspecified nerves, she went up the garden path and gave the dull brass knocker a good thump. She could hear the sound echo inside.

A youngish man opened the door, just a chink, and frowned out at her.

'What?' he said, abruptly. Leah got an impression of narrow grey eyes, short dark hair, several days' growth of stubble and a slightly bewildered expression.

'Oh, hello. Sorry to bother you—' she began, only to be cut off short.

'What do you want?' he snapped. Behind him, the house was in darkness. Leah tried not to peer past him too obviously. Suddenly, she longed to explore the place.

'My name's Leah Hickson, and I'm doing some research into—'

'Research? What do you mean?' the man interrupted again.

Leah felt her cheeks colour with irritation. 'Well, as I was about to explain, I'm looking for somebody who—'

'Are you a journalist?' the man demanded.

'Well, yes, I am,' Leah answered, taken aback.

'Oh, for fuck's sake!' the man exclaimed, rubbing his eyes viciously with his spare hand. Leah was too startled to respond. 'How did you find me? Who gave you this address? Can't you people take a hint—like bugger off? If I wanted to talk to any of you, do you think I'd have come all the way out here?'

'I . . . I can assure you that whatever you think, I—'

'Just don't bother. I've heard every possible sodding pretext from you lot over the last three months. Get off my doorstep. Is it just you, or can I expect a steady stream of you to start turning up?' he said, coldly.

'No, no—it's just me. I—'

'Good. Keep it that way. And get *lost*.' The man enunciated each word with furious clarity. He slammed the door in her face, and Leah stood still for twenty seconds or more, too stunned to move.

Eventually, her blood singing with indignation, and anger giving her a faint headache at her temples, Leah knocked again, as loudly as she could, and for a long time. But there was no response from the grey-eyed man, or anybody else who might be there, and no sounds from inside whatsoever. It began to rain steadily, and Leah was forced to retreat. She returned to her car, took out her notebook and wrote *Natives hostile* with an ironic flourish on the first blank page; then she sat and watched the rain for a little while, as it pattered and pooled and trickled down her windscreen. Ryan loved the rain. Even this reminded her of him, and she lived in a country famous for it. She thought of the dead soldier's wet hair, the way it had been slick against his skull. How much rain had fallen on his body, as he had lain undiscovered for a hundred years? She imagined it tickling skin that could no longer feel; soaking through clothes to flesh that could no longer shiver. Firmly, she banished the thoughts. She did not want the dead man turning up in her dreams.

She made her way back to the main road, then turned and followed the A4 into Thatcham. She parked up and wandered around for quarter of an hour, quickly establishing that she would not want to stay in any of the pubs in the small town. The main shopping street, called The Broadway, was occupied by bottom-end chain stores and tiny bank branches. People moved steadily through the growing downpour, their faces and eyes downturned, feet resignedly skirting the grubby puddles. It looked as downbeat and sad as only a small town at the messy end of winter can look. There was an old-fashioned bookshop, though, in which Leah spent a pleasant half-hour browsing and drying out. She bought two books on local history, and got a recommendation from the lady at the till for a good pub, The Swing Bridge, that did bed and breakfast, halfway back towards Cold Ash Holt and down a side lane next to the canal. Leah made her way there, and was shown to a room heavy with chintz and over-stuffed cushions. But it was warm, and had a wide, sweeping view of the rain-sodden water meadows lying to the east. In the distance, through a spindly row of poplar trees, Leah thought she could make out the spire of Cold Ash Holt church. She made herself a cup of tea from the tray, and sat, lost in thought, at the window.

* * *

The Swing Bridge had a largely local clientele who sat in groups at the bar and on benches along sticky wooden tables, and greeted each new arrival with nods and smiles and soft, drawled words.

Leah came down for her dinner at eight and was shown into the restaurant area, which was off to one side of the bar, colder, and painfully empty. She sat at a table laid for two, positioning herself so she could at least see through into the bar. The empty room behind her made the back of her neck prickle. She ordered fish and chips, and wished she'd brought a book with her for cover. She'd had vague ideas about joining a group of locals, and learning some local legends from them, but their conversations all seemed too personal, their groups so closed that she was suddenly too shy to interrupt. There were enough bones left in her fish to keep her occupied.

When she next looked up, she noticed with a start that she was no longer the only person sitting alone. Perched on a barstool, knees gaping uncomfortably to either side, was the man from The Old Rectory. Even though her view of him had been a shadowed glimpse, she was sure it was him. He hadn't bothered taking off his coat—a shapeless, faded green anorak—and he had a navy blue woollen hat pulled down low on his head. *Quite the casual local*, Leah thought; but when she looked down at his feet, his boots were of smooth brown leather, the laces tied tightly around sturdy brass studs. They were too clean, and too expensive. Leah's curiosity mounted. The man was clearly trying not to be noticed, trying not to be recognised. As it was, she saw more than one glance aimed in his direction, more than one muttered comment passed. The man stared resolutely at the drip tray in front of him, and drank a pint of bitter with dogged resolve.

Leah could not resist it. She got up quickly as

the man drained his glass and intercepted him as he turned for the door.

'Hello again,' she said, brightly. The man gave her a startled look, and then recognition drew down his brows. He tried to side-step her but she mirrored the move. 'We seemed to get off on the wrong foot before, and I'm sorry if I . . . disturbed you. I'm Leah Hickson, as I mentioned. And you are?' She held out her hand to him. He gave it a scornful look, and did not shake it.

'You know perfectly bloody well who I am. Now please get out of my way and leave me alone—is it too much to ask that I can go out for a drink on a Friday night without being followed . . .' the man said in a low tone, his voice tight.

'I assure you, I haven't the slightest idea who you are,' Leah interrupted him. 'And I didn't follow you—I'm staying here for a few days. I hear they do a good fry-up in the morning.'

'Oh, great. You just *happen* to be staying here. Is this going to be one of those "this is your chance to give your side of the story" offers? Because I've heard it all before!' the man snapped. There were knots at the corners of his jaw, and Leah suddenly realised that he looked exhausted. Grey bags sat heavy under his eyes, and tired lines tracked the contours around his mouth.

'Look . . . I hate to burst your bubble, but I really don't know who you are. You're clearly not as famous as you think. I am a journalist, but I'm working on a historical piece about a soldier of the Great War, and I came to Cold Ash Holt looking for information about him. He had links to The Rectory—which is why I knocked on your door. Whatever you've done—or not done—I'm afraid

115

I'm really not interested. Unless it helps me find out about my soldier, which I somehow doubt it will.' There was a long pause as the man considered this, his expression veering between relief, disbelief and anger.

'Are you sure you're not just . . .' he trailed off, twisting one hand in a gesture she couldn't decipher.

'I'm telling you the truth. I really am. And if you've got time, and can relax for a minute, I'd love to buy you another pint and ask you some questions about The Rectory.' The man stared at her for a moment longer then rubbed his eyes hard with the fingers of his left hand, just as he had at the door earlier on. A nervous tic, or a sign of fatigue perhaps.

'OK. Sure. If you're really who you say you are,' he relented.

'I am who I say I am,' Leah assured him, amused. 'Let's sit by the fire—I ate dinner in the other room and it was like a tomb in there.'

Quiet now, the belligerence running from him like water through a sieve, the man slumped into a chair near the fire, and Leah studied him covertly as she waited for the beer to be pulled, peering at his reflection in the mirror behind the bar. But she need not have worried about him noticing. He was staring into the air between his knees, picking absently at the edge of one thumbnail. With an agitated swipe he pulled the hat from his head, and she noticed that his hair badly needed washing, and quite possibly cutting as well. It lay flat to his skull, looking coarse and grubby. He was tall and lean, and the way his clothes hung from him it looked like he might have borrowed them from someone else, or perhaps lost a lot of weight recently. When she went over to the table he glanced up, pale-grey eyes alert again, on guard.

'One good thing about being out of London—you can get a pint without taking out a small mortgage,' Leah said as she sat down. The man paid no attention to the remark.

'So what do you want to talk about? That ridiculous thing about the fairies? That was shortly before the First World War, if I remember right,' he said, taking a long swig from his glass. Leah's pulse picked up a little.

'Sure, I'd like to hear more about that . . .' She left a convenient pause, but the man didn't fill it. 'I know you're sort of . . . incognito, but could I at least know your name?' she prompted him.

'Sorry, yes, of course. Sorry. It's been a . . . difficult couple of months. It's Mark. Mark Canning,' he said. Leah smiled, butterflies spinning in her stomach.

4

June 16th, 1911

Dearest Amelia,

I am writing to you of another new arrival to our quiet home: Mister Robin Durrant, the theosophist. I don't expect you to know what a theosophist is, so let me enlighten you—not that I claim to be an expert! I had to get an explanation from Albert, and half of that I did not understand. He describes theosophy as a quest for wisdom and spiritual enlightenment, and through the practice of it, theosophists hope to be able to release themselves from the ties of flesh, and commune with beings on higher spiritual planes. I had rather thought that this was what we strove to do with prayer, but apparently it is quite different.

Mr Durrant is a man that Albert heard speak a fortnight or so ago, in Newbury, on the subject of nature sprites and the like. Albert didn't talk about it a great deal at the time, but just a few days ago, he came in from his morning walk quite convinced that he had encountered such magical creatures— although apparently I ought not to call them this— out in the meadows around Cold Ash Holt.

I must say, the meadows are quite stunningly lovely at this time of year. They are simply glowing with life and wild flowers and fresh green growth. The grasses and reeds are growing so quickly, one can almost hear them at it if one stops and turns an ear! If nature can indeed put forth a spiritual body of some kind, then surely this would be the perfect environment for it to do so? I can't help but wonder, though. It seems such an extraordinary thing—as though he had come home and claimed to have seen a unicorn! But, of course, he must be telling the truth, and as his wife I must support him, and trust in his better judgement. He is a scholar, and a man of the cloth after all. I can make no such lofty claims.

And so this young man, Mr Durrant, is due to arrive later this morning, since Albert wrote to him about his observations; and will stay with us for a while—I admit I have not been able to get from Albert how long this might be. Mrs Bell is quite in a flap about lunch and dinner for three—it's a while

118

since she's had to cater for any more than just Albert and I. Which only goes to show, dearest, that a visit from you and my dear brother-in-law, not to mention sweet Ellie and John, is long overdue. Just name the date—your rooms are always ready for you. If he is to stay a while, this Mr Durrant, I do hope he is an amiable chap, and not too grand or clever and learned, else I fear I'll find nothing at all to say to him that he won't consider silly beyond belief!

Here is something that will surely make you laugh—but you mustn't, because I am quite serious. I have begun to worry that there may be something amiss with Albert. In terms of his physical conformation, that is—never with his heart or the essence of him, of course. I was coming back from the school just yesterday afternoon, and as we passed John Westcott's farm, I caught sight of his stallion being 'put' to a mare—I believe this is the term they use to describe this natural and necessary act. Westcott's daughters were out on the verge, cutting grass for their pigs, and they curtseyed to me most prettily, but I admit my attention was quite drawn by the spectacle going on behind them. Entirely improper of me, I am sure, and I should no doubt have averted my gaze, but such natural sights are common when one lives in as rural a place as this. I would not for one second compare my dear husband to a farmyard animal, but I can only assume that, on some terribly base level, the physical systems of most creatures are—at least very loosely—similar. But perhaps I am wrong in this as well? There. That will have to be all I say on the matter, since I am blushing and feeling horribly treacherous as I write this to you, and you are my own flesh and blood! If by some small mercy you understand what I mean by this *comparison, then your clarification, as ever, would be so welcome, my dear sister.*

I worry about Cat Morley as well. She remains so very thin, and looks so very tired all the time. It seems that her body is not responding to the wholesome life here, although what kind of body could resist such simple goodness, I can't imagine. Perhaps there is some deeper aspect to it that I have yet to discover, some perversion in her that runs deeper than I know. I have asked Sophie Bell to look in on her at night to see if she sleeps, but I understand that Sophie is a very deep sleeper herself, and finds it hard to rouse herself to check on the girl. What she might do in the long, dark hours of the night instead of resting, I can scarce imagine. It is an uneasy thought. And I also have it from Sophie that she barely eats, and upon occasion is in the act of eating and has to stop, gripped by some convulsion or sickness. I must get to the bottom of it. When I ask after her health she insists that she feels fine, and that the infection she had in her chest in London continues to improve. What does one do with a person who is sick, but will not admit to being so? I do my best to make her welcome, but it is not always as easy as it should be. She has the countenance of a hawk—a tiny, fierce bird of some kind; like a merlin, or a hobby.

Well, I had better finish this letter and make ready for Mr Durrant's arrival. I will of course write and tell you all about him in a few days' time, although forgive me if there is a delay—I am so fraught with the effort of getting everything organised in time for our Coronation Fête—one week today and still we have yet to find sufficient bunting. It's becoming quite a to-do. I dare say we shall get there in the end, but now is hardly the best time to have a house guest arriving. Poor Bertie—men have no clue about such things, do they?

Write soon, dear Amelia; and bend your thoughts, if you can bear it, to what I have written about the horse. What a dreadful thing to write!

Your loving sister,
Hester

1911

It is nowhere near lunch time when a smart knock at the door jolts Cat from her reverie. She has been distracted all morning, her gaze wandering far and away through the hall window which she's supposed to be polishing with balls of old newspaper. Thoughts of George Hobson tease her mind away from her work. She saw him again last night, drank enough beer with him to make her head spin and her insides glow. Now her head is spinning still, and her stomach feels weak, and a slow throb of pain has taken to beating behind her eyes. Fatigue makes her limbs heavy and her thoughts slow. Even this early in the day the air is warm, and a mist of sweat salts her top lip. When the door knocker forces her to move she turns, catching sight of herself in a heavy-framed mirror on the wall. A grey-white ghost of a girl, with dark hollows for eyes and a drab dress to set her off. That Holloway taint, still. Cat wears an expression of faint disgust as she opens the door.

'Yes? May I help you?' she asks the young man standing on the step. His face is every bit as fresh

121

as hers is not; he carries a leather holdall in one hand and a travelling case in the other, with his coat draped over it. In shirt sleeves and waistcoat, his jacket abandoned, Cat is reminded of The Gentleman's son, come down from university for a few days' break. That same luxurious disarray.

'Good morning. My name is Robin Durrant, and I believe I am expected.' The young man smiles. His teeth are very white and even; the smile curls his mouth slowly, like a cat stretching, and makes his eyes crinkle warmly.

'Do come in. I'll let Mrs Canning know that you're here,' Cat replies gracelessly. She takes the man's holdall from him, hangs his coat on the hall stand.

'Thank you. You're very kind.' Robin Durrant is still smiling. Cat turns away from his good humour abruptly, and goes along the hall to knock on the drawing room door.

'There's a Mr Robin Durrant here to see you, madam. He says he is expected,' she announces. Hester drops her pen suddenly, and looks up with a guilty blush on her cheeks. Cat wonders idly what hot gossip she was writing in the letter on the blotter.

'Oh, gracious! Not already? I've not had a chance to be ready, and Albert not even back yet . . .' Hester flusters.

'Nevertheless, he is here, and waiting in the hallway,' Cat says mildly.

'Right, well, yes—I shall come straight away, of course,' Hester says, but Robin Durrant appears behind Cat and clears his throat.

'I'm so sorry—I couldn't help but overhear—please do not disturb yourself, Mrs Canning. I am

122

early, which is frightfully rude of me, and I shall make myself scarce until the proper time. It's a warm day and perfect for a stroll. Please—don't get up,' he says cheerily. Hester gazes at him, quite at a loss, as he vanishes back into the hallway.

'Perhaps I ought to stop him, madam?' Cat suggests, after a pause.

'Yes, do! Do! He must not feel he ought to leave again . . .' Hester says, a little overwrought. Cat catches up with Robin by the front door.

'Excuse me, sir, but Mrs Canning insists that you mustn't go off again,' she says, flatly. 'She is quite ready to have you now.'

'Is that so?' Robin Durrant smiles again. His smile is ready and waiting, it seems; his face always half-primed to shape it. 'Then stay I shall. Who could resist such an invitation?' He gives Cat a knowing look that puts her at once on edge, and then returns to the drawing room.

* * *

'Was that him, at the door?' asks Mrs Bell, when Cat comes into the kitchen.

'It was. She'll be ringing for tea any second, once she's gathered her wits sufficiently to remember it,' Cat says, filling the kettle and setting it to boil.

'What is he—young, old, rich or poor?' the fat cook asks. From the table top, a fatty shoulder of lamb fills the room with the cloying smell of raw meat. Bluebottles circle it intently, waiting for a chance to land; but Sophie Bell is ready for them, dish towel in hand.

'Hardly poor, and very young. About the same age as the vicar's wife, I'd hazard.' Cat pours

123

herself a cup of water and drinks it in huge, messy gulps.

'Good grief, it's like listening to a cow at the trough,' Mrs Bell tuts. Cat shoots her a scathing look.

'Now you know how I feel, sitting down to dine opposite you every day,' she mutters.

'Any more of that lip and you're more than welcome to eat your supper out in the yard—or not at all, is what's more likely.'

'Indeed,' Cat sighs, unconcerned.

'You should call her "the mistress" or "Mrs Canning", not "the vicar's wife", so you should. Everything that comes out of your mouth sounds like disrespect towards somebody or other, and I really don't see that you're in any place to be giving it out,' says Mrs Bell.

'And why should I give respect to those that haven't earned it?'

'Because some people—most of the people in your life, I dare say—do deserve it, whether you think so or not. The mistress gives you a roof over your head, and a job of work to do when nobody else would give you one, not with your past . . .'

'I give myself a roof over my head by working every waking minute in this house! And as for my past . . . the governing classes make up rules to punish others by, just to have reason to punish them and keep them down, that's what I think. How can I not despise them when by accident of birth, by rules *they have written*, I am forced to answer to their every whim while they lounge about all day long, and can't help themselves with the simplest task? And I am supposed to be grateful to them for this, when in truth *they* should be grateful to *me*! Where would she be without me? To dress her and clean her clothes and feed her and make her bed? And without you to cook the food? They need us far more than we need them. If servants weren't all as ingrained with their rules as you, Sophie Bell, then we might forge some changes in this country.' Cat finishes her tirade, presses her hand to her throbbing head, pours another glass of water and drinks it just as hungrily. Sophie Bell blinks like a rabbit, her jaw hanging slack and bouncing amidst her chins.

'What on earth did they teach you up in London?' she asks in the end, quite stunned.

'What did they teach me?' Cat echoes. She considers this for a moment. 'They taught me that they will keep you down by any means, if their rules fail to curb you,' she says, more quietly.

Sophie Bell seems to wait, almost as if she would hear more, but when Cat does not elaborate she turns back to the shoulder of lamb and flicks at the flies with her towel, wearing a troubled frown.

'Nip out and cut us some rosemary for this lamb, Cat, there's a good girl,' she says, distractedly.

*　　　*　　　*

Hurriedly abandoning the letter to Amelia, which she has signed but not had a chance to put into its envelope, Hester smoothes the front of her dress, which is a touch creased, and pats at her hair. Without Albert to give her a lead on how she should treat this young man, and how much deference she should show, she feels quite at sea, and almost bashful about meeting him. She hears him approach and laces her hands neatly in front

125

of her.

'Mr Durrant, please do come in,' she answers his polite knock. 'I do apologise for any confusion, you were of course expected and are most welcome.' Hester smiles as her guest enters the room.

'Please don't apologise. My mother would quite berate me for arriving sooner than I was supposed to, and causing a disturbance. Delighted to meet you, Mrs Canning.' He shakes her hand warmly, pressing his thumb into her palm for just a moment. Outside the window, the gardener, Blighe, is trimming the privet hedge with shears that squeak when he opens them and squeal when he snaps them shut. This tortured sound punctuates the conversation.

'It's a pleasure to meet you, Mr Durrant. Albert spoke so highly of your recent lecture on theosophy,' Hester adds, hoping to have pronounced the word correctly. Robin Durrant smiles briefly in a way that makes her think she has not. She glances at him properly. He is of medium height and build, slim but quite broad at the shoulder. His hands, when they'd touched, had been every bit as soft and warm as her own. His face is heart-shaped, with marked cheekbones and gentle ridges over the brows, and there is the slight hint of a dimple in the chin. His hair is dark brown, rather long, and worn in a boyish, quite untidy style; all soft waves and stray locks. He has light brown eyes, a colour like clear toffee; and there is no trace of age upon him anywhere. Hester blinks, and realises to her dismay that she has been staring. She feels her cheeks redden slightly, and her throat is inexplicably dry.

'In fact, my lecture was less about theosophy as

a whole and more about the specific subject of nature spirits—my particular area of interest and expertise,' Robin Durrant continues.

Hester blinks again, and for a moment can't think what she ought to say. She is quite out of her depth. 'Yes, of course,' she manages at length. 'Won't you come and sit down? I'll call Cat for some tea.' She gestures to an armchair.

'Thank you. Very kind.' Mr Durrant smiles again, and Hester mirrors the expression. Indeed, it is hard not to smile at Robin Durrant.

'I suppose your husband is out and about at his pastoral duties?' Robin asks, accepting a cup of tea when Hester hands him one some minutes later.

'Yes, that's right. He always tries to be at church in the hours before luncheon. It seems to be when parishioners are most at leisure to call in if they have need of him. And if he's not there he's ranging all over the parish, visiting . . .'

'Tending to his flock, like a good shepherd ought,' Robin Durrant suggests, raising one eyebrow slightly.

'Yes, indeed.' Hester says. 'And you're from Reading, I understand?'

'I am. My mother and father still live there, in the house where I grew up, my brothers and I. Their work has moved them away from the area now, of course. Only I remain so close to the nest.'

'Oh, I am sure your mother is most pleased to have you nearby,' Hester says. 'I understand it's very hard, for a mother, when all her children finally fly away from her. Metaphorically speaking, of course. Tell me, what is it your brothers do, that takes them away from home?'

'Well,' Robin Durrant shifts in his chair, a

127

peculiar expression flitting across his face, 'my elder brother, William, is in the army. He's carving himself a most distinguished career as an officer, and has recently been promoted to colonel.'

'Goodness! He must be very brave! But how worrying for your family . . . has he been away at war?'

'He has indeed. In fact, it was an act of the very bravery you mention in Southern Africa that led to him being promoted recently, and indeed to him being decorated for valour.'

Hester's eyes widen appreciatively. 'He sounds like a true hero,' she says.

'That he is, and quite bullet proof, it would seem. He has been shot three times already, in his career—twice by arrows and once by a rifle shot, and yet he always seems to bounces back, quite unperturbed!' Robin smiles. 'It's become a family joke that he needs to keep his tail down more upon manoeuvres. It was the traditional poacher's injury he received, on two of the occasions.'

Hester nods slightly, not really understanding him. 'Shot by arrows! Good heavens, that the world is still populated with such savages!' she breathes. 'William must have the heart of a lion.'

'My younger brother, John, came down from Oxford with a first-class degree in medicine not three years ago. He is currently in Newcastle, where he has perfected a new surgical technique for the removal of . . . now, let me see. Is it the spleen? It quite escapes me now. Some organ or other, anyway,' he says, with a careless wave of his hand.

'My word, what an accomplished family you come from!' Hester exclaims, admiringly. 'And is your father a very distinguished man?'

'Oh, yes. He too was in the army for more than forty years, and was a Governor in India for many of them, until poor heath forced his return to more temperate climes. He is a great man, truly. He has never let any of his sons contemplate failure,' Robin Durrant says, his expression darkening slightly.

'Such a man might be hard to . . . live up to?' Hester ventures.

Robin takes a deep breath, and seems to consider this; then he shakes his head. 'Oh, no! He really is an old pussy cat. I only meant to say that he has always taught us to believe in ourselves, to expect the best from ourselves. Such an upbringing makes it easy for a child to excel,' he says.

Hester colours slightly, embarrassed to have misread him.

'Well, clearly you yourself are excelling at . . . theosophy.' She smiles. 'I know Albert was very impressed by the lecture you gave . . .'

'I fear that my chosen sphere is not one that my father readily understands. And it is not one in which, I think, a person can be said to excel— dealing as it does with the creation of a brotherhood of man, a coming together of equals, and the sacrifice of pride and personal gain,' Mr Durrant replies, quite solemnly.

'Indeed, yes, of course.' Hester nods. In the slight pause, the garden shears squeal and clack. 'Oh! I think I hear Bertie's bicycle!' she cries, with some relief.

*   *   *

Albert smiles widely as he shakes hands with Robin Durrant, his face alight with excitement in a way Hester can't recall seeing before. Certainly not on their wedding day, when he wore an expression of terrified concentration, as if in utter dread of doing or saying the wrong thing. She squeezes his hand fondly when he comes to stand beside her, glad to see him so animated.

'You'll want to see the site, of course. The hollow in the water meadow. I doubt whether we shall see any of the elementals themselves, of course, this late in the day and with the sun so high. It was early dawn when I first saw them, which was just as you mentioned in your lecture as being the best time by far,' Albert says.

'I should be very glad to see the place, indeed.' Robin Durrant nods. 'But I need not right this minute, if it will delay your lunch at all, Mrs Canning?'

'Oh, no, lunch will not be delayed. You don't mind, do you, Hetty? It needn't take very long,' Albert says, before Hester can reply. He does not take his eyes from Robin Durrant as he speaks, though he inclines his head towards his wife slightly, as if he knows he should.

'No, of course. You must do whatever you see fit, gentlemen,' Hester says. 'I will let Mrs Bell know that we'll sit down at two, instead of one. There's a lovely leg of lamb in the oven, I believe.'

'Perhaps . . . it's rather awkward of me, I know, but perhaps you might also give fair notice to your cook that I do not consume meat, of any kind.' Mr Durrant smiles, a touch diffidently.

'No meat?' Hester replies, before she can stop herself.

130

'Indeed, no meat. Theosophy teaches us that something of the animal nature of the beast that is eaten *physiologically* enters and is incorporated into the man upon his eating of its flesh, thereby coarsening him, weighing down mind and body and greatly retarding the development of the inner intuition, the inner powers,' the theosophist explains. All with a disarming smile.

Hester is dumbstruck for a moment. She glances at Albert, but he is shrugging on a lightweight coat, and patting the pockets to be sure he has a handkerchief.

'Well, then. Well. I shall of course let the kitchen know,' she murmurs, somewhat dreading Sophie Bell's reaction to the news. The men bustle from the house, and in the sudden quiet Hester is left to shut the door behind them. She stands at the hall window to watch them go up the path and into the lane. Albert talks avidly all the while, his hands moving in quick gesticulations; Robin Durrant walks steadily, and with his head held high. Hester takes a deep breath, and releases it in a short sigh. She finds herself wishing she might have been asked to go along with them. Albert does not look back from the gate, nor wave, as is his custom.

*   *   *

At the window in the drawing room Cat sees the men leave, and turns her face to the sun for a moment. She longs to chase the grey tone from her skin, to burn all trace of it away with the sun's glare. She has seen the farmer's wives, and their children, with their faces bronze and gold, and freckles like brown sugar scattered over their

131

noses. That is what she wants. When she is with George, she feels it ebb from her. The chill; the deathly, clinging taint. Memories of fear and pain. George and the sun, these two life-giving things, keeping her going by day and by night. She turns from the window and continues to dust, stroking the soft cloth slowly over the contours of a carved chair. She likes the satin feel of the wood beneath her hand. On the desk is the letter Hester was writing when Robin Durrant arrived. The letter that had her blushing over her pen. Cat walks idly to stand in front of it, and starts to read.

She reads that she might be checked upon in her room, to be sure that she sleeps. This makes her heart jump up into her throat, chokingly. Then it beats hard with rage. To be checked upon, kept watch over, kept captive. She is breathing hard, is too angry to enjoy Hester's concern over her health, or her worries about hidden perversions. When she reads the final paragraph an incredulous smile breaks over her face. She almost laughs aloud—not cruelly—but to read of the vicar and a rutting stallion in the same sentence . . . Then she hears a noise outside the door and hurriedly steps back from the desk. The duster had been clamped under her arm, and she can't quite get it to hand fast enough, can't quite seem to have been dusting, blamelessly, as Hester enters the room. The vicar's wife's expression is one of troubled distraction, but when she sees Cat she smiles, hesitantly. Cat smiles too, quick and curt, and hurries from the room.

She and Tess were discovered, of course. One of the footmen saw them, one Sunday afternoon, handing out leaflets outside the Liberal Party offices. Or rather, trying to hand them out. Men

132

brushed past them, rudely knocking their hands away, barrelling by as though they were invisible. One or two gave them dark looks, muttered 'For shame'. They had been wearing the best version of the uniform that they could manage—green, white and purple regalia, draped over their right shoulders, passing under their left arms. Ribbons in the colours tied around their bonnets. They could not afford the white golf coats they ought to have had, at seven shillings and sixpence; nor the short, daring green or purple skirts that brushed the leg just on the ankle bone. They were working class, as all could see, but they were still recognisably suffragettes.

They stuck together, working side by side, laughing at the men's rudeness, exchanging comments on their figures and dress, airs and graces. None of them took a leaflet, of course; but the girls called out their slogans nonetheless, and managed to give the literature to a few female passers-by. Then Cat saw Barnie coming along the street towards them, tucking a new packet of cigarettes into his pocket. She froze for a second, saw him recognise them, saw his expression change. He did not stop to speak to them, of course; would not be seen doing so in public. But as he made his way past he could barely contain a grin of stifled joy at his discovery. Barnie was excitable, and liked to make trouble, which he called 'joshing'. Both Tess and Cat had spurned his advances since he'd arrived at Broughton Street, so he dubbed them 'the sapphos', and his lust turned to spite.

News of what the parlourmaid and the second kitchen-maid were up to passed from Barnie to the housekeeper, then to the butler, then to The Gentleman. He called the pair of them to stand before him in his study. Tess shook from her curly hair to the worn-out soles of her shoes, but Cat squeezed her hand, and tipped her own chin up defiantly. She knew she could not easily be dismissed. Her mother had told her that, before she died.

'Well, now, Catherine and Teresa,' The Gentleman began. Upon hearing her name, Tess trembled even more; as if until that point she had been half hoping to go unnoticed. Cat met The Gentleman's eye and refused to look away, even though it took all of her nerve to do so. The study was an imposing, book-lined room; all dark mahogany on the walls and dark red carpets on the floor. Weak autumn light filtered in through the high windows, making the room reminiscent of a church. The quiet, dusty air was cool and still. The Gentleman was in his sixties, tall, broad and barrel-shaped. His jawline was described by grey whiskers, the bones themselves long since lost in a fold of flesh; but his eyes, though small, were jovial and kindly. Unless he had been drinking, or gambling of course. He was notoriously bad at both. 'I hear the pair of you have become rather hot politicos,' he said, smiling as if the idea amused him.

'I don't know what you mean, sir,' Cat demurred. Tess stared intently at the floor, as silent as the grave but for the snuffle of her anxious breathing.

'Come now, Catherine, don't play the ignorant serving wench with me—it just won't wash,' he reprimanded her. Cat blinked and let her iron gaze relax a little, seeing that they were not to be given a roasting.

'We were doing no harm. Our Sunday afternoons are our own. It's no crime to join a political union, or party; no crime to canvass on their behalf.'

'I understand that your Sunday afternoons are intended to be used for the visiting of relatives, or for getting on with some sewing or reading, or other such useful activity,' The Gentleman suggested mildly.

'Our Sunday afternoons are our own,' Cat replied, bullishly.

'Catherine! Why, you are every bit as stubborn as your mother.' He chuckled briefly.

'Thank you, sir,' Cat replied, with the ghost of a smile. The Gentleman took off his spectacles and laid them on the open ledger in front of him. He leant back in his chair, folded his arms and seemed to think for a while. The girls stood in place, like sentries.

'Well, you are quite right that there is no crime in what you do, handing out leaflets and such. I assume that you take no payment for this work? Good. But I can't pick up a newspaper these days without reading of some girl being arrested for some silliness or other in connection with these bluestocking rabble-rousers. They go too far. Unnatural creatures—quite unwomanly, what they get up to. But I am not the type to banish free thinking, not even amongst my servants. Carry on with it, then, if you must. But I will not hear of you out in the streets again, shouting slogans or harassing good citizens as they attend their own political meetings. No more of it, I say. I will not

135

have you bringing ill fame on this house with any more extreme behaviour. Do I make myself understood?'

'May we attend the meetings still?' Cat asked.

'You may retain your membership of the WSPU, and attend the meetings, yes. You may read their literature, if you must; but do not leave it lying around for the other servants to see. And I will not hear of you encouraging any of the other girls to join in this latest hobby.'

'May we wear a small token of the colours about our persons?'

'Whilst you are within the walls of this house, no, you may not,' The Gentleman replied, his eyes sparkling. He always had enjoyed a negotiation.

'Emma is allowed to wear a crucifix. Why may we not wear an emblem?'

'Emma is devout. Should you wish to wear a cross of Jesus, you also may. I hope you are not comparing our Lord God to Mrs Emmeline Pankhurst?' He smiled. Cat tried hard to keep her face straight, but could not prevent the corners of her mouth from twitching.

'Certainly not. For if God were a woman, we would certainly not have to fight so hard for basic social justices,' she said.

'If God were a woman! If God were a woman!' The Gentleman laughed. 'Catherine, you are a card, you really are. I should never have taught you to read. It's true that in women, a little knowledge is a dangerous thing!' he chortled. Cat stopped smiling, and resumed her steely stare. The Gentleman fell silent for a while. 'And with your mother's glare, to boot. Begone the pair of you, about your work.' He dismissed them with a wave of his hand. 'Let me hear no more about it.' Cat turned to go, rousing Tess with a tug on her hand. The girl seemed to have fallen into a trance. 'Wait, Catherine—here. Read these, if you please. Perhaps we shall turn you into a thoughtful socialist, rather than a scurrilous suffragette,' The Gentleman said, passing her a selection of pamphlets printed by The Fabian Society. Cat took them eagerly, and read the front of the uppermost: *Tract No. 144—Machinery: its Masters and its Servants.* The Gentleman knew her love of reading—it was he who had fostered it.

'Thank you, sir,' she said, genuinely pleased. He gave her a vague pat on the shoulder, and turned away.

Once they were back below stairs, Tess let out a massive sigh, as if she'd held her breath for the entire interview.

'Oh, sweet Lord, I thought we were out on the streets, so I did!' she cried.

'Don't be silly—I told you we wouldn't be, didn't I?' Cat said, taking her by the tops of her arms, giving her a little shake. Tess wiped tears of relief from her eyes, and smiled.

'I don't know how you have the nerve to speak to him the way you do, I really don't! I thought I would die of fright!'

'You don't know? Can't you guess?' Cat asked, solemnly.

'Guess what, Cat? What do you mean?' Tess asked, bewildered. Over her friend's shoulder, Cat saw Mrs Heddingly hovering in the dark doorway of her room. The housekeeper watched her with a censorious look on her face.

'Never mind. Come on, we'd better get back to

it,' she said. After this incident, they did not go canvassing again for a couple of weeks. And when they did start again, they made sure that they were well away from any of the shops Barnie visited for his fags or matches.

* * *

Hester finds Cat at the top of the cellar stairs, frozen, quite lost in reverie. Her stillness is unnerving, and for a moment Hester hesitates, unsure how to proceed. At last she clears her throat pointedly, and sees the girl jump.

'Ah, Cat. I wonder if you would be good enough to see me in the parlour?' she says, and retreats with the dark-haired girl following behind.

'Madam?' Cat says, coming to stand in front of her, hands hanging loose at her sides. Hester wishes she would clasp them either in front or behind her, but she does not know how to phrase such a request. It just seems so unnatural to leave them hanging in that way. As though she expects to have to use them in sudden violence.

'Cat.' Hester smiles. 'Now, I have had some mild complaints from Mrs Bell, that you do not always show her the proper respect— No, please, do let me finish,' she says, when Cat seems poised to speak. 'Obviously it has taken you a while to settle in here, and that's only to be expected after . . . what you have experienced. I quizzed Mrs Bell quite closely about your day-to-day work and she can find no fault in it. And I have to say, if Sophie Bell can find no fault in your work, then there can be no fault to find!'

'That woman hates me,' Cat says, flatly.

138

'Well! I'm sure she doesn't! If she is hard with you, well, then it's because she cares a great deal that things should be done in the correct way . . . Anyway. The vicar and I are quite happy with your work, and more than happy to have you continue here, but I must ask that you show Mrs Bell the respect due to one in her position—she is, after all, the housekeeper here; and she has been with me for several years now. It simply will not do to antagonise her,' Hester finishes. Cat gazes at her steadily, and says nothing, which Hester hopes is acquiescence. 'Well, that's settled then. Here, Cat—I made this for you. A little welcoming present to help you decorate your room.' She hands Cat the cross-stitch embroidery in its frame. Cat looks at it in silence for a moment, and when she raises her head again her eyes are bright with emotion.

'Thank you, madam,' she says, the words clipped, as if stifled. Hester smiles, seeing that Cat is near overcome.

'You're most welcome, child. Please do carry on,' she says, by way of a dismissal. Cat stalks from the room with her shoulders rigid.

*   *   *

In the kitchen, Cat throws the embroidery onto the table and stares at it, holding her bottom lip savagely between her teeth. The grocer's boy is bringing in boxes of goods, struggling to see through piled packages of flour and rice and gelatine.

'Can you believe this?' Cat demands of him, gesturing angrily at the frame.

'What, miss?' the boy asks. He is not more than twelve years old.

'This!' Cat picks it up and shakes it furiously at him. The boy steps closer, screws his eyes myopically at it, reads haltingly.

'Hum . . . hum . . .'

'Humility!' Cat snaps.

'Humility is a Servant's True Dig . . . nity,' the boy says, glancing up to see if he's got it right.

'Can you believe that?' Cat demands again. The boy shrugs, at a loss.

'Don't rightly know, miss,' he mumbles, and hurries away from her.

'What are you belly-aching about now?' asks Mrs Bell, waddling into the kitchen and slamming the kettle onto the stove.

'Nothing that concerns you, Mrs Bell,' Cat says, flatly.

'Everything in this house concerns me, my girl,' the housekeeper points out. She spots the embroidery on the table, picks it up and examines it. 'She's made this for you, has she?' Cat nods. 'So, what are you so steamed up about?'

'I . . . I do *not* agree with the sentiment.'

Mrs Bell eyes her shrewdly. 'No, well, I dare say you don't, being so full of hot air and your own opinions. Just you be grateful that you've the kind of mistress who wants to make pretty things for you, rather than beat you about with a stick. The first gentleman I worked for would come down and beat the kitchen-maids if he thought his tea was too cold, or too hot, or stewed too long; so you mark my words—you've landed on your feet here and you'll do well to remember it!' Her arms, folded over her bosom, look like ham hocks.

140

'Why should there be different rules for us, Sophie? Aren't we human beings, just like them upstairs?' Cat asks. She picks up the embroidered motto again, and examines it. Hester has stitched a small tabby cat into one corner, arching its spine amidst blue cornflowers. Cat runs her thumb over the neat little creature, and frowns.

'What are you *talking* about, girl? Of course there are different rules for them and us!'

'But why should there be?' Cat asks, keenly.

'Because it's always been that way, and it always will be that way! What can have happened to you that you've forgot your place in the world?' Mrs Bell blusters.

'I don't believe I have a place in the world,' Cat murmurs.

'Well, you have. It's here, in this kitchen helping me get the tea trays ready.' Mrs Bell bustles back to the stove.

*   *   *

Later on, Cat hangs Hester's embroidery on her bedroom wall, where once the crucifix had hung. Though she can't read the motto without her blood rising, she likes the little tabby cat, skulking in the cornflowers. Cat feels reckless this night. She hardly waits until the household has retired before slipping from her room, down the back stairs and out into the courtyard. Mrs Bell is not yet snoring. When she looks up at the house, bedroom lights are still lit. She could still be called upon, to make a hot drink or fetch a book from the library. The thought makes her heart beat faster. But she will not be kept in; she will not be checked

141

upon. Let the vicar's wife find her gone, she thinks, savagely. Let them cast her out. Better that than to be a prisoner. The night is still, and warm. From the meadows comes the occasional throaty call of a frog, the creak and whine of insect life. The scent on the air is of hot bricks and dry grass, the slight damp of dew falling.

Cat makes her way on soft feet to the far side of the house and to the little collection of outbuildings that flanks the courtyard. Here are the woodsheds and the gardener's den, the greenhouses and tool sheds. This latter is where the vicar stores his bicycle. Cat fumbles for it in the darkness, cursing when her questing hands make things shift and clatter; when her foot kicks a shovel, sending it toppling towards the concrete floor. She catches it at the last moment, with hands that shake. She has only ridden a bicycle once before—borrowed for a turn from the butcher's boy in London. She silently curses the soft squeaking of the wheels as she pushes it along the garden path and out of the gate. She does not see, behind her, the bloom of a cigarette in the darkness, nor Robin Durrant's gaze following her as he leans against the front wall of the house, blowing plumes of blue smoke up into the gentle sky.

Cat wheels the bicycle a long way down the lane before mounting it, in case she should fall; and fall she does, so startled to be moving forwards that she forgets to steer, and wobbles into the grass verge before clattering to the ground. She brushes grit from grazes on her hands and one knee, picks the thing up, gathers her skirt and swings her leg over it again. She will not fail at something the

142

vicar does so easily, with his too-short trousers and his milksop complexion. Gradually, she gathers speed, and finds that the faster she goes, the easier it is to stay upright, and to steer. With a few more near disasters she makes fine progress, wheeling the bicycle down the grassy path to the canal side. She does not need a light. The pale dusty towpath is straight and well visible, cutting through the deep green rushes and cow parsley, the thistles and dock and dandelions. Cat pedals as fast as she dares, the wind fingering through her cropped hair, making her eyes water and cooling her skin. She finds herself grinning in the darkness, thrilled and carefree. She would have cycled right past the barge boat where George sleeps each night, and sought him out in Thatcham, but there is a light on in the cabin, so she judders to a halt.

Suddenly still, Cat is dizzy, and stands for a while on the path, catching her breath, finding her feet. The water of the canal lies still and silent, and in the faint light of the stars she sees water birds drift noiselessly past. Reaching from the bank, Cat knocks softly on the side of the boat. Flaking paint comes off on her knuckles. There is a thump from within, the scrape of boots on wood. George opens the cabin door and holds up a lantern, which stabs at Cat's eyes, makes her clap her hands to her face.

'You'll blind me!' she calls. Talking makes her chest tighten, and she coughs violently, bending over at the sudden pain behind her ribs. This cough still waits inside her, then. It has not left her yet.

'Cat, is that you? Are you all right?' George peers into the darkness, shutting the lamp halfway to dim it.

'How many other girls call upon you in the night, George Hobson?' she asks tartly, when the fit subsides.

'Only you, Black Cat.' He smiles.

'Well then, it is me. Are you busy? Why aren't you in town?'

'I can't go to town every night, Cat Morley. I'd drink myself impoverished before long. Indeed, before very long at all,' he says, ruefully. 'Why are you puffing? Did you run?'

'I bicycled,' Cat says. 'I borrowed the vicar's bicycle, and got here in a fraction of the time it takes walking! So I can be back again in a fraction of the time, and can stay longer with you instead.'

'You *borrowed* his bicycle? That tends to mean you got permission . . .'

'Don't be daft. What he doesn't know can't harm him. What do you do in there of an evening, in such a small space?'

'Come aboard and I'll show you,' George offers. In the muted lamplight, his face is thrown into contours. The creases around his eyes that the sun has carved, the furrow above his brows, the strong line of his jaw. The bruises of his last fight have faded now, leaving only vague brownish smears, like grubby thumb prints. His shirt is open at the throat, the sleeves rolled up. So much skin he shows. So much of his living flesh; so much evidence of vitality. Cat drinks in the sight of him, feeling herself stronger with each second that passes. Something inside her unfurls when he smiles, like the new green leaves of a fragile plant. She takes his hand and steps onto the deck, but hesitates at the cabin door. The space within is confined indeed.

'I . . . I do not like small spaces,' she says.

'I shan't shut us in, if you don't want me to,' George says, not at all troubled by her admission. Cat goes down a couple of the narrow wooden stairs and then sits, wrapping her arms around her knees. Behind her head the night sky still spreads, huge and reassuring.

The cabin is low and narrow. Nothing in it really but a bed along one side, some shelves and a stove along the other. The bed is made up with rag rugs for a mattress, and worn blankets as covers. A tin kettle sits on the stove, but the embers within it have long gone cold. George watches her eyes flit briefly around his living space. He frowns slightly, seems suddenly uncertain.

'It's not much, I'll grant you. It must seem poor indeed, to one used to living in fine houses.'

'I work in the fine house,' Cat corrects him. 'But I live in a cramped attic room that swelters in this heat,' she says.

'It's hot indeed. I couldn't bear to light the stove, so can't even offer you tea, or cocoa.'

'You keep cocoa about the place, as a rule?' Cat asks, raising an eyebrow.

'Truthfully, no,' George admits. 'But I do keep ginger beer.'

'*Ginger* beer?'

'I've been fond of it since childhood.' George shrugs, bashfully. 'Would you like some, then?'

'All right then. I will. My throat's bone dry from coughing.'

'What is that cough? I hear it sometimes, when you talk. That there's a snag in your breathing, waiting to catch you.' He takes a brown bottle down from a shelf, pours the contents into two tin

145

mugs. Cat thinks before answering. She does not like to hear this—that others can detect the taint on her.

'I caught pneumonia, when I was in gaol,' she says, shortly. 'It lingers. The doctor said it would, though I admit I'd hoped it would go sooner.'

'It must have been a damp and dreary place, to give you an infection like that,' George says, carefully.

'It was. But that's not what gave me it. It was the handling I was given. The way we were . . . treated,' she says, sipping her ginger beer, eyes focused on the darkness at the bottom of the cup.

George puts out one thick, rough thumb, crooks it under her chin and lifts her gaze to meet his. 'I would have words with any person who gave you rough handling,' he says, solemnly. 'More than words, in fact. And you nothing but a slip of a thing. I've no time for those that box below their weight.'

'That's something I would dearly love to have seen. Pitting you against the villains in there that called themselves guardians.' Cat smiles. 'They could have done with a taste of their own medicine.'

'The job is one of cruelty and brutality, as I understand it. Small wonder that cruel brutes find their way into it. My father was gaoled once—and it was no bad thing for us kids, nor for my mother. He set about the rozzers that were trying to escort him home from the pub, drunk half dead as was his habit. They frogmarched him face down right past all his chums—that made his blood boil! I was glad they kept him in for we'd have felt the brunt of that indignity if he'd been allowed home.' He shakes his

146

head at the memory.

'What was his profession, your father?'

'His profession? That's not the word for it. He did labouring, farm work, odd jobs. Whatever he could get. If there was something needing doing that was too hard or too dirty for anybody else, they sent for my old man. He used to dock the puppies' tails, each time there was a new litter. He would bite them off.'

'He *bit* them off? That's horrible!'

'It's considered the proper way—the crushing of teeth closes the skin around the wound. But only a savage could do it thus, and so my father was called,' George explains. 'I remember hearing their poor little cries, all those pups. It made my blood run cold, but my father never flinched.'

'But I was no drunken brute. I only did what I was told to do, in gaol.'

'What the wardens told you to do? Always?'

'Well . . . perhaps not always,' she admits, dropping her face again. In truth she'd sought countless little ways to flout the rules, to pretend rebellion. It was her behaviour that brought Tess to the warders' attention, when she had been good and quiet enough to go unnoticed, until then. Cat swallows convulsively. 'Can we talk about other things?'

'We can talk about whatever you wish to talk about, Cat Morley,' George says, softly.

Cat looks around the cabin again, sips her ginger beer.

'Why don't you take rooms in town?'

'I used to, but then Charlie Wheeler, who owns and runs this barge and three others between Bedwyn and Twickenham, said I could stop on

147

board between jobs if I wanted, for no rent at all. It's good security, to have a man aboard, and this way I get to save my money up.'

'What are you saving it up for?' Cat asks.

George thinks a while before answering, then reaches to a pile of papers on the shelf, passes her a creased and much handled flyer.

'The canal trade is dying, Cat. Some stretches are so poorly kept up, you struggle to make headway for the growth of weeds and trees crowding in; and the locks leak so badly they scarce work. Few carriers still use it, now the railways are everywhere and so much faster. Charlie Wheeler is a traditional kind of man, and he keeps going with small loads and local trade, but soon enough even he will have to stop,' George says.

Cat examines the flyer. There's a grainy photograph reproduced on it, of a steamboat crowded with young girls in Sunday school uniform, all smiling at the camera man from beneath their straw boater hats.

'Scenic Pleasure Cruises?' she reads.

'Aye, that was what the man I met called it. He's up in Bath and Bradford, and once he was a carrier just like Charlie Wheeler. Now he makes a good living—a better living than he did—taking people for rides along the canal.'

'And you would leave to go and work for him?' Cat asks, her face falling. She knows, in an instant, that she could not stand life in Cold Ash Holt if it weren't for George.

'No! No, not at all—I would buy my own boat and do the same as he! It would have to be an old boat, for my purse to stretch, but I could repair and make good on it myself. I would moor it in

148

Hungerford, for there are no such pleasure boats there yet. The boat could be home and business in one, and I'd be free to make my own way, for once,' George says, his voice steady and resolute.

'That would be glorious. To be free!' Cat stares into the distance, caught up in the thought of it. She can hardly imagine what it might be like, to live as she pleased; but for a minute the idea scatters sparkles of excitement down her spine. Then she sighs. 'I doubt I shall ever be.'

'Anybody may be free. It's only a matter of finding a way.'

'And how long will it take you to save up your money, to buy your boat?'

'Not much longer. Four months, perhaps. Sooner if I can get more fights fixed up . . . and win them of course.'

'Of course you would win them! Nobody could beat you—I've seen you fight. You're like Hector, or Achilles.'

'Like who?' George frowns.

'Demi-gods of the ancient world.'

'Oh, indeed? And how on earth did you come to learn about them, then?'

'My father taught me to read at a young age. He lent me books that a working-class child would never have read, otherwise. I think it amused him,' Cat says, grimly.

'Why should it have?'

'He knew I would have no other station in life than the one I was dealt. Why did he bother to broaden my mind? To educate me? I've often wondered.'

'Perhaps he just wanted to give you a good start. Perhaps he thought you might rise above your station in life, with this knowledge he gave you?'

'He could have given me that start easily, and yet he made me a servant. It was a cruel gift; and an empty one.' She shakes her head.

'But a gift nonetheless, and perhaps well meant. My father gave me nothing but cuts and beatings.'

'Perhaps he gave you a gift without realising it— perhaps he taught you to fight, and now with the money you make from it, you will be your own man.' Cat puts out one hand, runs it the length of George's knotted arm, curls it behind his neck.

'Most girls would be put off to see me fight, to know what I do. It breaks the law, after all; and is hardly genteel,' George says softly, leaning towards her. She tips her head, and their foreheads touch.

'What need have I for gentility? It's nothing but a mask that allows men to be cruel and dishonest,' Cat murmurs. She kisses him and for one startled second he freezes, as if unsure; but then he puts his arms around her, lifts her effortlessly from the stair onto his lap and holds her tight. Cat lets herself be held against him, aware of the heat blooming between their skins, and the taste of his mouth, and the race of her heartbeat, so loud in her ears. She reaches an arm behind her to shut the cabin door as George pulls her backwards onto the narrow bed, and she does not care at all that the cabin is small, and the ceiling near. She does not even notice.

*　　　*　　　*

On Sunday, Hester stands beside Albert outside church after the service, politely greeting each parishioner. The sun is fiery bright in a clear blue

150

sky; the light so crisp it seems to outline every blade of grass in the churchyard, every sparkling fleck of mineral in the granite headstones. It glances brightly from Robin Durrant's tousled mop of hair, revealing gold and auburn strands Hester hadn't noticed before. A hand on her arm catches her attention.

'Is that your house guest?' Claire Higgins asks, in a low voice that the vicar won't hear. The sun isn't kind to Claire's face, showing up little hairs on her top lip, and a scattering of blackheads over her normally pretty nose. Hester suddenly worries how many of her own flaws are on such bold display.

'Yes. Mr Robin Durrant, the theosophist. He and Albert are engaged in a study of the spiritual side of our meadows,' Hester whispers back to her. Claire's gaze sweeps up from Robin's feet to his face. Her expression is one of languid appreciation, and it makes Hester slightly nervous.

'Is he married?' Claire asks, not taking her eyes from him; slowly, she strokes the silky end of the green ribbon holding her hat in place.

'No, dearest, but you are,' Hester points out. She raises her eyebrows censoriously at her friend, and they both laugh.

'Introduce me,' Claire hisses, as Robin saunters over to them.

'Ladies, may I accompany you back into the village?' He smiles at them, clasping his hands behind his back urbanely.

'Mr Durrant, may I introduce Mrs Claire Higgins, a good friend of mine?'

'Mrs Higgins, a pleasure,' Robin says, with a cheerful shake of her hand.

'I do hope you weren't put off by the curious

stares you were given during the service, Mr Durrant,' Claire says. 'I fear we receive few visitors of note here in Cold Ash Holt. And certainly none as exciting as a spiritualist.' The three of them turn away from the church and walk steadily along the gravel path towards the gate.

'Well, I fear I must disappoint you, Mrs Higgins, for I am neither very much of note, nor a spiritualist.'

'Oh? Is a theosophist very different from a spiritualist then?' Claire asks.

'Indeed we are, Mrs Higgins. A great deal different.'

'We held a seance with a local spiritualist just the other night, as a matter of fact. Only don't tell the vicar, or Hester will be in trouble!' Claire says, conspiratorially.

'Claire!' Hester protests, but Robin smiles so warmly at her that she relaxes again.

'Fear not, your secret is quite safe with me,' he says. Claire beams at him, and tightens her grip significantly on Hester's arm. 'But, perhaps I might urge caution in this area?' Robin continues. 'I fear that most *mediums*, as they term themselves, are quite fraudulent.'

'Oh, not Mrs Dunthorpe, surely?' Claire says. 'She is able to look beyond the physical world, and see into the world of spirit . . . We've both experienced it, haven't we, Hester? I am quite sure her powers are genuine.'

'And she talks to the dead, I presume?' Robin asks, seriously.

'Well . . . yes, indeed she does,' Hester replies, less certainly. 'Although I have never actually *seen* one of these spirits she talks to, or heard it . . .'

152

'I fear that you, like many good people, have been taken in by this woman.' Robin shakes his head. 'The spirits of the dead do not exist—not in the way such fairground mediums suggest.' He waves his hand dismissively. 'Upon the death of the body, the individual consciousness of man rejoins the universal soul, and waits in bliss for its eventual rebirth. The *personality* of the deceased is lost; so that ghosts, with any knowledge of their previous lives, simply *cannot* exist,' he explains.

'Oh dear! Is that really so? And she always seemed most genuine in her beliefs, her abilities . . .' Claire murmurs, quite crestfallen.

'I am quite sure she did, Mrs Higgins. Don't be ashamed to have been deceived in this way—thousands of others have before you! And I do not say she has no inner vision or ability at all, but that even if she has, she is untutored, and confused,' Robin says kindly.

'Well, perhaps we ought not to go again?' Claire looks at Hester with troubled eyes.

'Oh dear—I fear I have upset you, and spoiled your fun?' Robin stops walking and turns to Claire and Hester, pressing his hands together earnestly. 'Please, forgive me. I shan't move another step until you have, even if it means I miss my lunch!' He remains that way, all solemn and beseeching, until Claire giggles, and Hester feels a smile tug at the corners of her mouth. 'There, you have forgiven me. I can see it in your faces.' He grins broadly.

'Walk on, Mr Durrant. I would not have you miss your lunch,' Claire assures him.

'Well, at least that puts my mind to rest about one thing,' Hester says.

'Oh, what's that?' Robin asks.

'Well, at our last . . . sitting with Mrs Dunthorpe, she received a most dire warning from one of the spirit voices she heard. Or thought she heard, that is.'

'Oh—Hetty, that's right!' Claire says.

'Apparently, a source of great evil had come into one of our lives, and was going to bring dark times upon us. After some discussion, the conclusion reached was that the warning was for *me*,' says Hester, lightly, though she well remembers the cold shivers she'd felt, and the dark, watchful figure under the tree.

'For you, indeed? Well, fear not, dear lady,' Robin says. 'I am quite sure that Mrs Dunthorpe was hearing an echo of her own colourful imagination. I would wager my last shilling on it, in fact.'

'Mr Durrant!' Albert's voice comes from behind them. They pause, and turn to see the vicar trotting up behind them with a jerky, angular gait, his robe flapping around his knees. 'Mr Durrant, I wonder if you would be good enough to allow me to introduce you to somebody?' he asks, breathlessly.

'Yes, of course, Reverend. Ladies, if you will excuse me?' He gives them a graceful incline of his head. Albert nods briefly at his wife and her friend, and then guides the theosophist away with a hand hovering at his back.

'Well, he is quite delightful, isn't he?' Claire murmurs. 'Do you know what I think? I think your husband was a little jealous, seeing you walking and talking with that young man!' She nudges Hester lightly.

'Oh, no!' Hester laughs. 'I'm sure not. Do you really think so?' she ventures.

'Absolutely! Such a charming fellow . . . and so handsome. And I saw the way he smiled at you . . . perhaps the vicar has a good reason to be jealous?' she suggests, archly.

'Claire, *really*!' Hester admonishes her, but can't keep from smiling.

'And I'll tell you another thing—I'm jealous too. Of you, having such a wonderful house guest! Nobody interesting *ever* comes to stay with us at Park Farm. It's simply not fair,' Claire sighs, looping her arm through Hester's as they walk on again. Hester says nothing, a little ashamed by how pleasant it feels to be envied.

5

Cat hears the crunching of the dairy cart horse on the driveway, and goes out with the milk jugs to greet him. It's before seven in the morning, and the sky is as clear and colourless as glass. Barrett Anders, the dairy man, is thin and silent. His overalls stink of cattle, but his hands are scrubbed pink and clean. His mouth is lost beneath drooping moustaches, the same greasy grey as his hair.

'The usual please, Barrett,' Cat says, stifling a yawn. For the first hour after waking from her restless sleep she is chilled, shivery and stupid. She sets the heavy jugs on the ground as the dairy man measures out two pints of buttermilk, one of blue milk and one of cream; dipping into the churns with a long-handled tin measure. The horse, a sturdy cob with a massive rump, lifts its tail, farts loudly and expels a pile of manure onto the driveway. Cat rolls her eyes. 'It's me that'll have to pick that up, thank you very much,' she mutters. Barrett's mouth twists beneath the whiskers.

'Tha'll please the mistress, tha'll. Summat extra for 'er roses, free o' charge,' he drawls.

'Too kind of you, old nag,' Cat thanks the horse. After Barrett is back aboard the cart and rolling slowly away along the lane into the village, Cat lingers for a moment with the jug of cream in her hands. She likes the still and quiet, the cool dampness of the air. So sweet, it seems different stuff to the baked, heavy fug of the afternoon. Overhead, a phalanx of swifts goes screaming past, wings cranked back, bodies taut. Into the west, where the sky is a deeper colour. Cat stares after them, and longs to follow.

Just then she hears the door open behind her, and voices talking softly. She turns to see the vicar and the theosophist emerging from the house, all kitted out with their binoculars and bags. The vicar strides along smartly, tapping a polished walnut walking stick into the gravel as he goes, talking earnestly all the while. Mr Durrant wears a smart linen coat, one hand thrust casually into his pocket, the other carrying a boxy camera covered in soft brown pigskin and gilt decorations. As they pass her, Cat can make out the vicar's hushed words.

'. . . I do believe that the very reason I have always felt so deep a love for the countryside and the wild places of this earth, the very reason I have always been drawn to it and taken comfort from it, is that I have, all the while and unbeknownst to me,

156

been in the presence of these elemental beings; beings higher and closer to God than the whole of mankind,' he says. His face is quite rapt as he speaks, so much so that he doesn't even see his maid, standing in the dawn light with milk jugs at her feet.

'It may indeed be so, Albert. You must possess at least some small measure of inner sight to have seen the elementals in the first place, and that is where we all begin. Tell me, were you in any kind of a trance state when you saw them first?' the theosophist asks.

Cat frowns at them as they pass her by, at a distance of thirty feet. Her moment of peace is quite ruined. At the gate into the lane the theosophist looks back, unseen by the vicar, and gives her a smile too knowing, too familiar for her liking. She turns away, and picks up another jug before making for the kitchen.

They will be gone for at least an hour, Cat knows. The theosophist has fast adopted the vicar's habit of rising early, and joins him in his walks through the meadows before breakfast. No longer just walks, however. *Summonings*, she heard the theosophist call them, as she served him yet another cheese omelette the other evening. With curiosity, or something like it, gnawing at her, Cat goes upstairs on soft feet, and along the corridor to the guest bedroom that has become Mr Durrant's. She closes the door quietly behind her, in case Hester is awake and might hear, opens the curtains then stands with her hands on her hips, surveying the scene. The room is in disarray. Every morning she sets it straight, and every night she turns back the bed and shuts the curtains again; and yet in the short intervening space of time the theosophist manages to create more mess than a nursery full of toddlers. Clothes and shoes lie discarded on the chair and ottoman and floor; a plate covered in cheese rinds and grape stems is in the middle of the silk eiderdown, surrounded by greasy fingerprints; a high pile of books by the bed has toppled over; the sheets are a tangled mess, spilling off the bed. One pillow is entirely out of its case. 'For heaven's sake, was he pitching a fit?' Cat mutters, as she begins to pick up his clothes, shaking them out and hanging them neatly in the wardrobe. She makes the bed and matches up his shoes, putting one muddy pair by the door to take down and polish. She restacks the books, and as she does so an envelope falls out of the pile.

Cat picks it up, and the address catches her eye. *Mr R. Durrant, The Queen's Hotel, Newbury.* Was he living in a hotel then, before he came to the vicarage? Without hesitation, Cat opens the envelope and pulls out the letter, pinching it carefully in her fingertips. The paper is smooth and expensive, the ink profoundly black; the date is two weeks previously.

Dear Robin,

I fear you will not be pleased by the contents of this letter, but your mother and I, after much discussion, have agreed that what I propose is quite the best thing for you. You are of course dear to us, perhaps too dear to your mother—she does dote on you so, and would deny you nothing. I wonder sometimes quite how aware of this you are, and whether you tend to use her affection to your own

158

advantage. Perhaps it would be only natural for you to do so, perhaps we have been remiss in our raising of you. However, the time has come for you to stand by your own strength. This theosophy of yours will get you nowhere in the world, Robin. I do not suggest that you give it up; by all means continue with it as a hobby, if you wish. As a career, it is quite unsuitable. You must settle upon something with prospects, something by which you may build a name and a fortune for yourself. Look at your brothers—in medicine, and the military. They are carving fine niches for themselves. I do not suggest you should have taken up medicine—you haven't John's studious mind, after all. But I beg you again to consider the army. I—we—strongly believe that the discipline and order would help to settle you. And you would be following in my own footsteps, after all. But even if you insist that the army is not the path for you, I insist that you find some path—some worthwhile path. And so, though it pains me to write it, I do decline your latest request for funds. I cannot, with clear conscience, forward you any more money whilst I know it permits you to delay the pursuit of a proper occupation. I know you have it in you to do extremely well, just like your brothers, and I mean to assist you towards this end. I know you will not disappoint us, but will make us proud yet. Trusting that you are well.

With fond regards,
W. E. Durrant

Cat finishes the letter and folds it carefully back into the envelope. She slips it between two books and carefully stacks them so that nothing of the envelope is showing. She thinks about Robin Durrant's new linen coat, the expensive leather case of his camera. She tidies away his fine shoes, and she smiles.

*   *   *

After dark, Cat makes her way to meet George by the bridge at the edge of Thatcham town. Against the silhouettes of the wharf buildings he is one more shape, given away only by the movement of his arm, the orange flare of his cigarette. Up close she sees the pale shine of his teeth as he smiles, and as he lights a match for her his expression is at once possessive and shy. It makes something inside Cat reach out for him, pushes her inexorably towards him; he a magnet, and the very iron in her blood yearning for him.

'Into town, then?' she says, standing close to him; close enough to feel his warmth, to pick up the slight smell of sawdust and horses on his clothes. He reaches out and takes her hand.

'I would dearly love to see you by sunlight, one day,' he says. 'Always we're in darkness, like a romance between ghosts.'

'A romance? Is that what this is?' she says, archly. 'Well, by daylight I vanish in a cloud of mist.'

'I half believe it, Black Cat. I half do!' he says seriously.

'I could meet you on Sunday afternoon. Or will you be coming to the Coronation fête, in Cold Ash Holt? I could see you there,' she says; but George shakes his head.

'I go off with a shipment tomorrow morning. I'll

160

be several days away.'

'Oh,' Cat says, her heart sinking. 'Well, we'd better make the most of tonight then, I suppose.'

'That we had.' George smiles. 'Come on. I want to show you something.'

He leads her on, not towards town but away from the canal, into a tangle of deserted warehouses and ramshackle workshops that cluster around a small square, the depleted centre of the once lively canal trade.

'Where are we going?' Cat asks.

'We're here. Come on—up this ladder,' George says, pointing to a thin metal ladder bolted to the side of the biggest building.

'What's up there? Are we allowed to?'

'Since when has being allowed to ever bothered you, Cat?' he asks.

Cat shrugs ones shoulder, and starts to climb. 'You're quite right,' she says.

The ladder is long, the rungs too far apart for Cat, not having the reach of most men. When she finally reaches the top, and steps out onto a clay-tiled roof, she is breathing hard. She bends double, the air needling into her chest like a thousand glass splinters. She has time to draw in one more breath before the coughing starts, racking her body, robbing her of air. The pain is excruciating; is like knives. George can do nothing until it passes. He tries to hold her but the pressure on her ribs is unbearable and she bats him away feebly, with a hand that shakes. When it recedes, the coughing fit leaves her sitting on the roof, her knees pulled up and her face pressed into them. Her throat feels raw, but the iron bands around her chest loosen with each tentative breath.

161

'Are you better now?' George asks, anxiously. He takes her hand, rubs his thumb over her knuckles. Cat nods.

'It does knock me sideways, when it comes on like that,' she apologises. 'I don't think it's as bad as it sounds. The doctor said it's the body's way of being rid of whatever blocks it.' She looks up, sees worried lines on George's face lit softly by the stars, and feels a stab of guilt. Plenty of women left Holloway in worse shape than she did. Some may not have been able to leave at all—she has no way of knowing. She sees Tess with sudden, awful clarity—crumpled in the corner of her cell like a broken doll. 'Don't look so scared—at least it didn't start while I was on the ladder,' she says, her voice shaking slightly.

'I shouldn't have made you climb. I forgot . . . I'm sorry, Cat.'

'You don't need to be sorry, really. If a little more of the infection goes each time I cough like that, then you've helped me. So, what are we doing on a roof?'

'Look around. I love it up here. After a hot day, the tiles stay warm for hours, and you can just lie and bask, and watch the world. Look,' George says, and Cat obeys him.

They are as high as the tops of the chestnut trees; below them all around are deep shadows and the outlines of rooftops. To the east, the lights of Thatcham soak the air with a pale yellow glow; and further still the lights of Newbury are just visible on the horizon, glimmering faintly. Above their heads the sky is lilac and inky blue, pinpricked by cold white stars. Cat takes a deep, cautious breath, smells the hot tar of the roads, the parched wood

162

of the warehouses.

'It all looks so peaceful, doesn't it? You can see none of the arguing or the lying or the fighting from up here. None of the hardship. It all stays on the ground, like muck. It's almost like being far, far out at sea. Don't you think?' she murmurs.

'I've never been out to sea.' George puts his arm around her shoulders, his hand up into her hair.

'Neither have I. But I've read about it.'

'There's nobody around for miles. Apart from old Clement, who sleeps under the bridge,' George tells her softly.

'Then I am quite at your mercy.' Cat smiles. Their hushed voices are loud in the quiet night. There's a rustling beat of feathered wings in the tree next to them, as roosting birds are roused; the slightest touch of a breeze to cool their skin.

'No, Cat; I am quite at yours,' George replies. Their kisses are urgent, hurried. Cat pulls the shirt from George's body, runs her mouth the length of his torso, tasting salt. At first George is tentative and handles her gently, in spite of the need that lights his eyes, until Cat says:

'I'm no invalid, George Hobson.' He puts his hands through her cropped hair, pulls back her head to kiss her throat, and in one easy motion swings her up to sit astride him, tight to him; to make love with the quiet night air coaxing goose flesh along their arms.

*   *   *

The day of the fête to mark the coronation of King George V dawns without a cloud in the sky, and by mid-morning the ground shimmers with

163

heat. The beech tree leaves are curling, twisting slightly as they scorch to show their silvery undersides; and the brass band plays with streaming red faces, suffering in their smart uniforms. On the church field an array of tents and awnings have been set up, their sides rolled up and tied back in an effort to allow air to circulate. Brightly coloured cotton bunting is strung all around the village green and along the lane to the church; and Claire Higgins, who is in charge of the flower arrangements, darts anxiously from spray to spray, fretting as the blooms shrivel in the heat.

'Claire, dear, alas but I fear there's nothing you can do. Come and have a glass of lemonade before you fall down,' Hester calls to her.

'If I can just get the sweet peas into the shade of the tree, they might last another hour or so . . .' Claire says, shrilly, and won't be led away.

'At least carry your parasol!' Hester calls after her, and retreats into a white tent. The sun burns as soon as it touches. 'Cat! How is the tea coming along?' Hester smiles. Cat has been sweltering inside the tea tent all morning, keeping a small stove alight to boil kettle after kettle of water to fill the urn. The back of her dress is soaked and her hair is plastered to her head, but she may not take off her cap. On her neck is a mark where George kissed her too hard, and bruised the skin. Her hair is almost long enough now to cover it, and she tucks it hurriedly behind her ear to this end.

'It's ready, madam. But everybody wants lemonade. It's too hot for tea,' Cat says, flatly.

'Nonsense! I find tea most refreshing on a hot day. In fact I'll take a cup now, if I may.'

All day, Cat makes and serves tea to the people

164

of Cold Ash Holt. Hester and the other women arrange pastries and scones on pretty tiered cake stands, and give out bowls of strawberries and cream. Children with water ices lick them with desperate haste as they melt in seconds, dribbling down their arms to the elbow. Thus sugared, the children are pursued around the field by frenzied wasps. Robin Durrant proceeds from stall to stall with his hands clasped behind his back like a visiting dignitary, the vicar and a small knot of men and women following in his wake. Cat watches him, nonplussed, and wonders that he has made such an impression, in so short a time.

'So this is the Cannings' new maid. Catherine, isn't it?' Mrs Avery intones, on passing by the tea table with some companions. She raises her spectacles to the bridge of her bony nose, and peers down through them at Cat.

'I'm known as Cat, madam,' Cat replies, not liking Mrs Avery's manner.

'Well, I wasn't talking to *you*, girl. Pert, isn't she? Only recently down from London, and for reasons best left unmentioned, as I understand it,' Mrs Avery remarks to her friend. Irritation flares through Cat. She holds the teapot high in front of her, puts an empty smile on her face and affects a broad cockney accent.

'Tea, madam? A drop of the empire's finest?' she chirps.

'No, thank you,' Mrs Avery snaps, and saunters away with her nose wrinkled in distaste.

'Haughty old cow,' Cat mutters under her breath.

'Smile now, ladies! Look this way!' a man in a brown linen suit and bowler hat calls to them. He has a camera on a tripod, all set up pointing at the tea tent.

'Oh, it's the newspaper man!' Hester says. Cat walks to the front of the tent, still holding the silver-plated teapot with which she accosted Mrs Avery. She peers out from beneath the pungent canvas as the vicar's wife and the other gentlewomen of the village straighten their backs and tip their parasols prettily. The camera gives a loud clunk.

'And another one, if you please!' the photographer calls. 'Stay right as you are, big smiles now!' Cat stares into the lens of the camera, glowering in the bright light. She stares right down it, and seeks to corrupt the picture somehow. The ladies in front of her are a mass of white lace and frills, and gauzy muslin veils; they simper and smile for the photograph. It amuses Cat to know that she will be in the background, small and dark and bad tempered. She fights the urge to put out her tongue.

Her bad mood isn't only due to having the hottest, dullest job to do. There's also the fact that she won't have a moment free to enjoy the fête herself; and that when it's over and the clearing up and packing away done, she'll still have all her work at The Rectory to try to get done somehow. In *Votes for Women* that week, there had been glorious pictures of the Women's Coronation Procession, which had taken place in London the week before, on the seventeenth of June. Horse-drawn floats adorned with the colours, magnificent with swags and ribbons and garlands of flowers. Suffragettes from all over London wearing wonderful costumes; dressed as Liberty and

Justice, and as the four corners of the British Empire. Cat wishes she'd been there with them. Walking alongside the white ponies with a garland of red English roses, or carrying an eagle-topped staff. She wishes she'd been part of something so glorious and beautiful and above all *meaningful*. She gazes out of the tea tent as the village men begin a tug o' war, and the women gossip and fill their faces with cake. Then the man who has just taken her photograph ducks into the tent in front of her.

'Afternoon, miss. Is there some tea on the go?' he asks, unloading his camera onto a table and pulling out a handkerchief to mop his face.

'Plenty of it, and I'll give you the fresh, not the stewed, since you've got to spend the day working as well,' Cat says wearily.

'Hotter than Satan's toenails, isn't it?' the little man grins. He has a sharp face, boyish but beady, somehow feral; his cheeks and jaw sport a fur of auburn whiskers.

'That it is, and no cooler standing next to this tea urn, I'll tell you.'

'Will I still get the fresh brew if I tell you that I'm about done with work for the day?' he asks. Cat makes a show of pausing as she pours his cup, and the man grins again.

'Which paper will the pictures be in?' she asks.

'The *Thatcham Bulletin*. I'd hoped to pick up some gossip for the society pages while I was here, but everybody is being terribly polite and patriotic. In other words, dull.' He takes the cup of tea from her and slumps into a wooden chair with it.

'Haven't you met Cold Ash Holt's newest pet? The theosophist?' Cat asks.

167

'I met him briefly. He was quite keen to have his picture taken.'

'That sounds about right.'

'He and the vicar are working together on some academic paper or something. I couldn't really find out much about it. Sounded very dry, I have to say. You never could rely upon a vicar to give you a scandal.' He sips his tea, then looks up and catches Cat's thoughtful expression. 'Why do you ask, miss? Do you know something more?' She flicks her eyes at him, and considers.

'It wouldn't do for me to be found out, discussing their business. Let alone in the press,' she says, carefully.

'But, I don't know who you are—and I promise not to find out,' the man says, laying one hand earnestly on his heart.

'Well, then,' she says at last. 'Let me tell you a little bit more about Mr Robin Durrant.'

*　　　*　　　*

At the end of the week Cat collects the newspaper when it's delivered, and ducks through the narrow doorway to the cellar stairs. She perches on a step halfway down to the kitchen, and leafs through the pages until she finds the photographs of the fête. She smiles when she sees herself there, haunting the shade at the edge of the tent while Hester and the other ladies light up the foreground. In the bottom left-hand corner of the page is a poor, grainy photo of the vicar, Robin Durrant at his side, smiling smugly into the camera. Chin lifted, chest puffed out. Cat wonders what exactly has made the vicar burst out with pride like this. She

168

turns over to the society pages—thinly veiled gossip compiled anonymously by someone called Snitch. Cat skims her eyes over the text until the name she's looking for stands out.

Mr Robin Durrant graced the Cold Ash Holt fête with his presence, to the obvious delight of several ladies of the village. Mr Durrant, of Reading, claims to be able to see fairies, hobgoblins and other imaginary folk; and is here to hunt for the very same in our own water meadows, aided by Cold Ash Holt's worthy curate, the Rev. Albert Canning. The hunt has been going on for three weeks already, but alas, has so far proved fruitless. By what means Mr Durrant might capture a fairy, Snitch was not able to determine; nor what he would do with one if he caught it. It seems that Mr Durrant's father, the esteemed Wilberforce Edgar Durrant, one-time Governor of India, is less than enthusiastic about his son's unusual mission. Perhaps if young Mr Durrant is successful in his fairy hunt, he'll also find a pot of gold to raise his father's spirits?

'Cat! Where are you, girl? Come along down here and get these breakfast things taken up!' Mrs Bell's voice comes echoing up the stairs. Cat refolds the paper and trots into the kitchen on light feet. 'What's put that smile on your face then?' the housekeeper asks, suspiciously. Cat cocks an eyebrow, but says nothing. Mrs Bell grunts. 'Well, if it ain't proper, you better hope I don't find out, that's all,' she says. Cat takes up the breakfast

169

plates, lays the newspaper neatly on the sideboard, and waits.

*   *   *

Before lunch, she dusts the pictures all along the hallway and up the stairs. She uses a tightly twisted corner of her cloth to get into the curls and small gaps in the fancy moulded frames. Heavy oil paintings of Cannings gone before, ancestors of the vicar whose dignified likenesses have been trapped for ever on the canvas. *This is how the rich buy immortality*, Cat thinks as she studies each one, staring into their dead eyes. By discovering some new place, or inventing some new thing; by writing a book or a play. And for those not bright enough for that, not daring or talented enough, there was always a portrait, or these days a photograph. To make sure their names lived on, their faces didn't vanish into dust. *As I shall vanish*, she thinks. *One day*. The poor were too busy working, staying alive, to worry about preserving themselves after death. They vanished in their thousands every day, forever invisible to the generations of the future. *Nobody will ever know I existed*. Cat tries not to mind this, since it is all vanity; but it is not a comforting thought, after all.

Suddenly, Albert drifts across the corridor from the parlour to the library, and Cat gasps. The vicar is oddly absent from the house, not in body, but in spirit. He flits from room to room so quietly, so distractedly, that half the time Cat has no idea where he is. This is disconcerting, for a servant. A servant always knows, from the noises in a house, where the upstairs folk are to be found. A servant needs to know, so he or she can dodge around them, slip from place to place, clean and create order and never be seen. So he or she can catch the smallest break, to lean for a second against a warm hearth, or study their reflection in a gilt mirror, or peer from the window at the vast world outside, a world with which they have no business. Time and time again, Cat has risen from blacking a hearthstone, or turned from dusting a bookshelf, to find the vicar sitting in a chair behind her, reading or writing in his journal, quite oblivious to her. He is like a cat, found sleeping in odd places and almost stepped upon. She can't quite settle in the house when she knows he is in it.

Cat hears the door at the far end of the library squeak open and thump shut, and she pauses.

'Have you seen this?' Robin Durrant's voice is loud and abrupt as it breaks the silence. She hears the slap of the newspaper being thrown down hard.

'Robin!' The vicar's pleasure makes his voice ring. 'Our picture? Yes, I saw it. I think it's come out rather well, although—'

'I'm not talking about the *picture*, I'm talking about the gossip that's been printed about me by this . . . this *Snitch* character!' Robin snaps. His voice is rich with outrage; Cat can hear the angry sneer on his face. She bites her lip to stifle a sudden bubble of laughter, and takes a few tiny steps nearer to the library, peering through the crack between the double doors. Robin stands over Albert with his jaw working into tight, furious knots, while the vicar reads the short piece. *Touched a nerve, did it?* Cat thinks.

'Really, Robin, this Snitch person is the lowest kind of journalist, and everybody knows not to

171

heed a single thing he writes. Please don't let it trouble you . . .' Albert clears his throat diffidently, and speaks soothingly.

'*Imaginary folk*, he calls them. Imaginary! Does he take me for a complete fool? How dare he assume he knows more about such things than I do? How *dare* he?'

'Really, Robin, there's no need to take it so much to heart . . . nobody will pay it any mind,' Albert says, his voice now laden with growing anxiety.

'And that quip about finding a pot of gold for my father . . . what is that supposed to mean? Have they been to Reading, then, and pestered my father? Have they been asking the servants there what my father thinks about theosophy?' Robin demands. Cat holds her breath, waits in the agonising pause for him to put two and two together, and guess the source of the gossip. Her heart pounds in her ears.

The vicar murmurs something that Cat cannot hear, his voice meek and unhappy.

'They have no idea what they're talking about— these small-minded idiots, smirking at me through their moustaches . . . no idea whatsoever. And no idea who I am, or who I will become!'

'Robin, please . . . there really is no need to be so upset—'

'Oh, but there is! For years I've been surrounded by doubters and naysayers and people who like to ridicule what they cannot understand. I'm sick of it! I will *revel* in their contrition when my name is known around the world! When I am at the right hand of Madame Blavatsky herself! Then they will eat their words!'

172

'Indeed they will, Robin,' Albert says, uncertainly. Through the narrow gap Cat can see his stunned expression, the way he stands, face and body turned to the pacing theosophist like a flower turned to the sun. As Robin draws near he raises his hand, as if he would lay it on the other man's arm; but the theosophist turns away again, stalks angrily to the window. There is a long pause in which the vicar is frozen in shock and the theosophist squeezes his hands into angry fists. Cat daren't move in the silence. She can't trust her feet to go completely unheard.

'Our progress has been too slow. Far too slow,' Robin snaps at last. 'Almost a month I've been here, and we have seen *nothing*. I have felt their presence, yes . . . but they will not coalesce. That bungling photographic studio you sent me to returns blank, over-exposed frames, again and again. It will not do, Albert!'

'No, of course, I'm so sorry . . . Well, what must we do?' Albert asks, and Cat almost feels sorry for him, so complete is his supplication. 'How might we progress?'

'A theosophist must strive to live cleanly, ethically, and to benefit his fellow man with everything he does. Kindness, and generosity, and understanding.' Robin speaks as if to a child, biting off the words. 'Purity is of the essence. But above all, one must strive to bring the teachings of the Divine Truth to as *wide an audience as possible*. It is in this last respect that I must increase my own endeavours.'

'But how?' Albert presses. As they speak, Cat edges away along the corridor, so she can still hear them, but can dart away if need be.

'I mean to provide the world with incontrovertible proof that theosophy is the truth,' Robin says. 'A photograph. I will show mankind the reality of the elemental world; I will be the architect of an international acceptance of theosophy, and in doing so I will silence these fools who are so quick to ridicule!'

'I'll help you, of course. Whatever you need me to do. I am learning so much, all the time. I hope in the future to become wiser, more adept . . .' Albert says, eagerly.

'But you're holding me back!' Robin cuts him off. There's a startled pause, the sound of more pacing feet. 'Albert . . . I can only think that *you* are the reason I haven't been able to see the elementals yet. You are not adept, and your inner vibrations are discordant to them! Without the ability to tune yourself to their energetic frequency, you make yourself intolerable to them!'

'But . . . but . . . it was I who first saw the elementals, Robin . . . It was I who saw them first!'

'They *chose* to reveal themselves to you, it's true . . . And you are not without potential, I've told you. But there simply isn't time to wait while you reach a fine enough level of attunement. I must continue without you for now, my friend,' the theosophist says. There is a long, uneasy pause and when he speaks again, Robin's voice is low. 'Have you considered that perhaps they reached into your thoughts that morning and found *me* there— your memories of me from my lecture? Have you wondered whether, by revealing themselves to you, they were in fact calling out to *me*?' Robin demands, and much of the fury has burnt out of his voice, leaving something stony and cold in its

174

ashes. The vicar is silent for a long time.

'You no longer want my help?' he asks at last, and Cat frowns. His tone is like a child's, near heartbroken.

'No. Not on my summonings out in the meadows.'

'Perhaps, as with any wild thing, there is a trust to be built up before communion may take place . . .' Albert ventures.

'If I am to have a chance of capturing an elemental in a photograph, it will take all of my inner faculties, and I can't have you upsetting the balance . . . But continue with your studies, Albert. Ask me whatever you like, and I will teach you what I can,' Robin says, more gently now. 'You are only at the beginning of the long road to enlightenment, but you have taken your first steps—the first and most vital steps! Don't lose heart. Soon, when I have proof, you will be a part of the greatest revolution in civilised thought for a generation!'

'You're sure you will succeed, then? Where none have before?' Albert asks.

'I will succeed,' Robin replies, and his conviction is like steel in his voice. Suddenly uneasy, Cat slips from the corridor down to the kitchen, where she can be sure they will not follow.

*　　　*　　　*

Friday morning is hot as soon as the sun clears the horizon. Hester sits at her dressing table and starts to pin up her hair, feeling how damp it is close to her scalp. Albert is long gone from the room. She isn't even sure, looking at the smooth rise of his

175

pillow, that he came to bed at all. But she herself has been so restless in the night, and made such a knot of the sheets, it is hard to tell. She gazes at the pristine pillow, so bright where the sun lights it that it's almost painful to look at. Her thoughts turn to the theosophist's words, the many, many words he has spoken since his arrival; most of them to Albert. Words like drops of rain, falling from his lips. Albert seems to absorb them all like dry ground. She sees it on his face—that little frown of distraction, the way his eyes sink out of focus. Lately it seems that she doesn't see Albert unless she sees Robin Durrant as well. The theosophist is always right beside him. Or perhaps it is Albert who is always right beside Robin. Hester sighs.

As she pats cold cream into the corners of her eyes, she begins to compose a letter to Amelia in her head. *I wouldn't mind as much if I had some idea of how long he might intend to stay . . .* she drafted. *Bertie's stipend is as modest as ever it was. Modest enough to prohibit the telephone I would love to install. And yet we can apparently support this young man for as many months as it will take him to finish his project!* How she would love to hear her sister's voice. But even if they'd had the funds, Albert would probably still refuse her a telephone—his mistrust of modernity growing ever stronger. *I think if he could he would ban motor cars, dismantle all the trains and roll up the track! Thank heavens he can see the merits of electric lights, at least.* But now it sounds like she is criticising Albert as well as their house guest, and, suddenly feeling like a sulky wife and a graceless hostess, Hester discards the imagined letter. The bedroom is suddenly too quiet, too still. Hester feels desperate to talk to somebody.

Down in the parlour, she finds Albert sitting behind the morning paper, a dejected expression on his face. The theosophist, for once, is nowhere in sight. Hester stoops to kiss Albert's cheek.

'Good morning, my love. How are you?' she says.

'I am quite well, Hetty. Quite well,' Albert replies, distractedly. Hester's smile fades.

'I had no idea you were waiting for me. I'm so sorry to have taken such a long time to come down! I thought you would be out with Mr Durrant for some time yet,' she tells him.

'That's quite all right. It gave me a chance to read the papers before the day began and more important things presented themselves.'

'How is it that you didn't go out with Mr Durrant this morning?'

'Well, now. We are trying out a theory of his. Yes, a theory. But I've been reading some troubling things in the paper this morning,'

'Oh? Nothing too dire, I hope?'

'The police arrested seven men for gambling just the other evening. They have appeared today before the magistrates for it. Gambling—on a cock fight, of all things! Not two miles away in Thatcham—can you believe it? Of all the bloody and brutal ways in which a man can chance his luck, they choose to pit two poor dumb beasts against each other.'

'Oh, that is really too cruel! What a vile thing to do,' Hester exclaims.

'One of the men was Derek Hitchcock, from Mile End Farm. A Cold Ash Holt man, a member of my very own flock,' Albert reports, his voice

177

tinged with anxiety, face pinched with worry.

'Darling! You can't expect to be able to keep every last soul of the parish permanently on the straight path! Don't be so hard on yourself. Men will err—it's in their nature. You do an admirable job in bringing them closer to the word of God—'

'But this is just the smallest part of the impurity surrounding us, Hetty! It lies everywhere, in the hearts of all men, and women! Just the other day I called unexpectedly upon the Smith household, only to find the reason for their oldest girl's absence from church all too apparent—she is with child, Hetty! Heavy with child and only seventeen herself, and unwed.' Albert shakes his head, casting a look of desperation up at his wife. Hester sinks onto the arm of his chair and grips his hands tightly.

'Albert! Many a young girl has been led astray by the sweet whisperings of her beau . . . it's to be lamented, of course, and is a tragedy for her, but she may yet atone—she may yet return to God's favour, if she repents. And by far the majority of people here are good and kind and honest folk. Dear Albert, what's brought on this dismay?' Hester presses her hands tenderly to the sides of his face. Albert pulls away slightly, as if unwilling to meet her gaze, but Hester does not relinquish her hold.

'It was something Robin said to me, yesterday morning,' he confesses, wearily.

'What did he say?' Hester demands, more sharply than she intends. Albert glances at her, startled, and she smiles. 'What did he say, dearest?'

'He asked me not to go out to the meadow with

him in the mornings any more. He suggested that he might have more success with his photographs if I were not there with him. In case my untuned and impure vibrations are off-putting to the elementals.' Albert's voice is laced with unhappiness.

'Your impure vibrations? But this is nonsense! There is nobody purer of spirit than you, Albert . . .'

'He means more that I am untrained, theosophically speaking. I am not able to tune my inner self to . . . harmonise with them. It may be why we have not yet managed to capture them on film, and I have not managed to see them again. Because of my lack of initiation.'

'But . . . it was you who found them in the first place, Bertie! How can you be the reason that they stay away?' Hester asks.

'They granted me a glimpse of themselves, it's true. Perhaps I had indeed stumbled unaware into some trance-like state that I cannot recapture . . .' Albert speaks as if to himself. 'Perhaps that was it. Perhaps since seeing them my mind has been too unquiet, and I too caught up in the selfish desire to see them again, and to learn more. I must be a rough, clanging cymbal to them, so great has been my desire! Yes, I see it now—I have been foolish, and unworthy!'

'Albert, stop that at once! You have never been foolish in all the years I have known you—since we were children, Bertie! And never once unworthy. Only ever good and kind and generous. And if this theosophy is teaching you anything other than this, then it is plain wrong, and perhaps it would be better to learn no more!' Hester cries.

179

'Hetty!' Albert snaps, sharp with sudden anger. 'Don't say such things!' Hester recoils, stung.

'I do hope I'm not interrupting,' says Robin Durrant, appearing in the doorway as if he's been there all the while, one hand in his pocket, the other curled around his Frena camera. Hester jumps up from the arm of the chair and turns away, startled. Her skin prickles beneath her collar, and she feels breathless.

'Ah, Robin! No, of course not. Of course not,' Albert says, his cheeks colouring. In the uneasy silence, Hester takes a steadying breath.

'Good morning, Mr Durrant. I trust you slept well?' she says at last, her voice tight, higher than it should be. Robin Durrant smiles at her, in the languid way that he does, the curling shape moving slowly outwards from the centre to the far corners of his lips. For an instant his gaze seems to look right through her. She feels her face glowing hotly, and longs to look away, to put her hands over her eyes like a child. But that will not do. Her pulse beats hard in her temples, blood thronging to her cheeks in a blush she knows he can see. He holds her this way for a second longer, and then blinks, letting his eyes roam the room, quite at ease.

'I did, thank you. I always do here—the quiet of the countryside is such a tonic for body and mind. Don't you think?'

'Oh yes, quite so,' Hester manages. She clears her throat, knots her fingers together in front of her skirts. 'I've always found it very peaceful,' she adds, but Robin Durrant is looking at the vicar, and that same slow smile has quite a different effect. Albert seems to catch his breath, and a tentative smile of his own rises up to his eyes.

180

'Well?' he asks, and Robin Durrant smiles wider.

'Yes, Albert. *Yes*. I have seen them!' he says. Albert claps his hands together in speechless joy, holding the tips of his fingers to his mouth as if in prayer, his earlier anxiety evaporating. A sour worm of something fearful coils itself around in Hester's gut, but she cannot for the life of her either define it nor think what she should do about it.

6

In the sunshine late on Monday morning, Cat scrubs Hester's undergarments in a wooden butt of warm soapy water. She has come out into the courtyard to do this, where she can splash with impunity, and feel the sun on her face. These items are considered too fragile to be sent out to the laundress, and cleaning them is a painstaking process. Cat removes the stays from the corsets and washes them one by one; then she uses a soft scrubbing brush to gently sweep the satin fabric lengthways until all stains and marks and odours are gone. Each one must be rinsed under the pump, pulled and stretched back into shape along its whalebone pins, and laid flat to dry where the sun will help to restore its whiteness. She must check them every half an hour until they are dry, tweaking and coaxing and teasing them back into their proper shapes.

Hester's drawers are stained this week. Dark, bloody scuffs on the gussets and legs that turn brown in the water, and give off the smell of rusting iron. Cat wrinkles her nose as she scrubs, squeezes, rinses, repeats, her hands aching and puffy in the water. She is glad George can't see her in this labour.

'Haven't you finished that yet?' Mrs Bell remarks, leaning her head out of the scullery door. Cat angrily waves a stained garment at her.

'A twelve-year-old child could manage her courses better than the vicar's wife!' she exclaims.

'Hush your mouth!' Mrs Bell glances around, scandalised.

'I heartily wish the vicar would get his leg over and do his duty by her, so I would have fewer bloodstains to scrub for a term. Or don't men of the cloth do that?'

'It is hard to picture it, the two of them . . .' Mrs Bell chuckles, before remembering herself. 'Just you . . . show some respect,' she reminds Cat, hastily.

'I've never heard them at it, though. Have you?' Cat smiles, impishly.

'For shame! I've never listened out for it!' Mrs Bell replies, her eyes merry for once.

'One would have to listen closely, I suspect. More like the snufflings of a pair of bunny rabbits than the mighty roaring of a stag, I should think,' she says, and Mrs Bell laughs out loud, unable to stop herself.

'Cat, you are a devil!' she wheezes, and then coughs hastily and falls silent as Hester enters the courtyard from the far side gate, and walks towards them.

* * *

Hester has spent the morning teaching the smudged and bony children of the Bluecoat School, a small charitable school run for the poor families of the parish. The school house was once a chapel. A small and ancient stone building with a steeply pitched roof and low, narrow doorways, it huddles all alone, and rather forlornly, Hester always thinks, on the London Road at the edge of Thatcham. But on school days it lights up with the voices of twenty little girls, all chattering and laughing, their words skittering to and fro, rising up to bounce amidst the gnarled beams of the roof. When Hester arrives, the ragged girls quickly seat themselves at their desks, fall quiet and watch her with their big eyes shining like glass beads. Hester loves that moment. She stands with her hands clasped in front of her, feeling her heart bubble up in her chest.

She teaches the girls cookery and needlework, flower pressing, composition, deportment and grammar. Whatever she can think of that might benefit them, she tries to fit in some tuition upon it. And even though most of them are poor, and will end up married young and mothers themselves, ruining their bodies in the fields or going into service at one of the big estates nearby, Hester still likes to think that knowing a poem is never a wasted thing, and can bring comfort to the roughest of souls. She normally comes away from the lessons with a renewed energy for life, her mood elevated and spirits high. But not this time. Some vague sense of worry dogs her steps, as though she has mislaid something important. Her mind replays the recent weeks, retracing its steps, trying without success to find where exactly this crucial thing has been lost.

An unusual noise makes Hester look up, and she realises that Sophie Bell, standing over Cat at the wash tub, is laughing. Hester pauses, and realises that this is the first time she has ever heard her housekeeper laugh out loud. She smiles a little as she approaches the pair of them, but when they see her, the laughter stops abruptly. Cat continues to scrub and Sophie Bell looks away in such a guilty manner that Hester is left with the distinct impression that she has been the butt of the joke. To her dismay, unexpected tears fill her eyes, and she blinks hurriedly, smiling to conceal them.

'Good morning, ladies. I trust you're both well?' she says. Both Cat and Mrs Bell nod and murmur their assent. 'I called in on Mrs Trigg on my way back from school, Mrs Bell. She asked after you.'

'Oh, well. And how is she? Any better?' Sophie asks.

'Not a great deal, I fear. She's still keeping to her bed. I know she would dearly love to have more visitors,' Hester says.

Mrs Bell nods sharply, her chins rippling. 'I'll make sure I drop by to see her soon, madam,' she says. Hester glances down at the wash tub and sees the stains Cat is working on, the soap suds drying into a scummy ring around her elbows. Perhaps this is why they'd been laughing at her? Again, Hester feels her eyes stinging, and she looks away, ready to walk past them towards the front of the house.

Just then, there's a crash from inside the house; scraping sounds and a loud thump. All three women look quickly at one another. Hester edges past Sophie Bell, who needs more time to turn, and is the first one through the back door. Leading off the corridor, before it opens into the kitchen, is the door to the cold store. This is a small room built with three outside walls. It is dug a little deeper into the ground, with three steps leading down into it, and is stone floored, with shelves of solid slate slab that stay cooler for longer, even in hot weather. The only light comes from a tiny window, not six inches square, set high in the far wall opposite the door. There is no glass in the window, just wire mesh to keep out insects and vermin. It has the feel of a compact cave, which is the aim of its design. All meats and cheese, milk, cream and fruit—anything that will spoil in a warm room—finds a longer life on the cool slate shelves, or hanging from savage-looking hooks in the ceiling. Robin Durrant is leaning against the wall outside the cold store as Hester hurries towards it.

The source of the crash is immediately apparent. Smashed shards of a china basin sit in a puddle of white mess on the floor of the corridor.

'What has happened? That was the batter for the sausage puddings!' exclaims Mrs Bell, who has waddled along behind her mistress. Hester glances at Robin Durrant, who looks serious for once, and then into the little room, where Albert is filling his arms with foodstuffs.

'Albert? What on earth is going on?' she asks him.

'All of this stuff must be cleared out, Hetty. Robin has need of this room,' Albert says, quite cheerfully.

'But . . . this is the cold store, Mr Durrant. What possible use could it be to you?' Hester asks.

'Very considerable use, my dear Mrs Canning. I have decided to develop my own photographs, you see. My equipment was delivered to me this morning . . . The local laboratories have insufficient skill for work of such a precise nature as I am undertaking; and anyway they take far too long to return my prints to me,' Robin says. He stands up from the wall and links his hands behind his back, making no move to assist Albert in his labours. 'I do apologise about the batter, Mrs Bell.' The theosophist smiles at the simmering housekeeper.

'But . . . I don't understand,' Hester says. 'This is where we keep fresh food cold . . . what has it to do with your photographs?' she asks.

'Excuse me, dear,' Albert says, squeezing past them and towards the kitchen with arms laden with bacon and cheese.

'I need a dark room, Mrs Canning. A room where absolutely all light can be excluded, so that I may safely develop my prints. This room, with only a tiny window and such a good solid door, is perfect.'

'It's quite impossible, Reverend. In this weather! Nothing will last from one hour till the next, if I haven't a cold store for it! Perhaps we might do without it in winter, or even spring . . . but now? No, no—it will not do . . .' Mrs Bell protests.

'Nevertheless, Mrs Bell, this is the perfect—nay, the *only*—place that will do for it. Mr Durrant's needs are quite specific,' says the vicar, his voice steady and his expression adamant.

'And can he be specific about how I should manage without it?' the housekeeper snaps, much to Robin Durrant's apparent delight.

'That's enough, thank you, Mrs Bell,' Hester says, as soothingly as she can. With a black look on her face, the housekeeper disappears into the kitchen. Hester finds her pulse racing, and an odd rushing sound fills her ears. 'Albert,' she says, trying to get her husband's attention as he returns to the store and begins to pile up bowls of fruit and vegetables. '*Albert!*' She lowers her voice, aiming to speak only to him. 'There must be some other place we can install Mr Durrant's equipment! This is hardly appropriate—for one thing, it is below stairs, and Mrs Bell is quite right to resent the intrusion into her domain. And for another, in this hot weather it is madness to lose the use of this room for food! I do wish you had consulted with me about this beforehand . . . I could have pointed out earlier that this is really not the answer—'

'But it is, Hetty. Robin has searched all over the house, and this is the only place one might sensibly set up a dark room,' Albert insists.

'Well . . . what about one of the outbuildings? The old woodshed has no windows at all—surely we could arrange some worktops of some kind in there for him?'

'The old woodshed? It's full of dust and spiders, Hester! Don't be so ridiculous! How can Robin be expected to produce something as fragile and important as a photograph of an elemental when he is surrounded by crumbling plaster and sawdust? Really—you must desist with this obstruction!'

'But . . . but you shouldn't even *be* down here!' Hester whispers, unhappily. Two firsts in the space of five minutes, she thinks—Sophie Bell laughing, and Albert below stairs, within the female realm of the kitchen and utility areas.

'Excuse me,' Albert says again, passing her with the load of fruit and vegetables. Hester turns to watch him go, and catches the eye of the theosophist, still dallying in the corridor. She can't hold his gaze, and drops her eyes, filling with ill-defined outrage.

'I *am* sorry to be such a nuisance,' Robin says, not sounding sorry at all. Hester squeezes her teeth together and manages the briefest of smiles before walking past him after her husband. She cannot find it in her to accept his apology.

* * *

'I'm quite sure you will manage, Mrs Bell. You are a woman of great resource,' Albert says to the housekeeper, uncomfortably, as Hester catches up with him.

'Just the milk, then, Reverend? It can't hurt to let me keep the milk in there—it won't take up much room . . .'

'No, I'm afraid that's quite out of the question. The risk of contamination is too great. There. I apologise if you are inconvenienced, Mrs Bell, but the needs of our guest must take precedence in this instance. Our work is of the utmost importance. I would be grateful if you could bring out the rest of the food, and let us hear no more about it,' the vicar says, and walks away up the stairs.

'Madam, can't you talk to him? Everything will spoil!' Sophie appeals to Hester once Albert is out of earshot.

Oddly short of breath, Hester can only shake her head helplessly. 'I'm sorry, Sophie. Please just

'. . . do the best you can,' she says. She glances back along the corridor but Robin Durrant has gone out into the courtyard, leaving the cold store half empty and the spilt batter on the floor, attracting flies. Seconds later, Cat appears, drying her hands on her apron with a look of outrage on her face.

'The theosophist just sent me in to clear up his bloody mess, if you please,' she snaps, recoiling slightly when she sees that Hester is still in the room. 'Begging your pardon, madam,' she mutters.

'No, that's quite all right, Cat. If you wouldn't mind, please do see to it,' Hester says meekly, and flees the anger of the two women. At the top of the stairs she pauses, suddenly quite at a loss as to where to go or what to do next. It seems as though the house has changed somehow, as though somebody has been in during her absence and shifted all the furniture slightly, so that nothing is quite in its right place. *Our work is of the utmost importance.* Albert's words echo in her head. Is this where that important thing has been lost, then? Did it start the day Albert rushed indoors and told her he'd seen elemental beings? She'd hardly believed him serious, at the time. Feeling unsettled and almost afraid, Hester goes into the parlour and sits on the edge of a chair, quite alone.

*   *   *

Mrs Bell waits until Hester's footsteps have receded, then turns to Cat with her face pinched up in anger.

'What's all this?' Cat asks.

'Well, the young guest needs a *dark room*. To make photographs in, apparently, although what

189

pictures he can take in a room with no light, I haven't a clue. And my cold store is to be the place! No other room in the house will do for him—it has to be this one! And all the food will have to come out of it so as he can do his thing in it, whatever it might be. We'll have nothing by the end of the day but rancid butter and green curds!'

'All right—calm down. He'll be developing the pictures in the dark room, not taking them,' Cat says.

'Developing pictures? What do you mean?'

'The plates are very sensitive to light until they are developed—that is how an image comes to be imprinted upon them in the first place, of course. No other light must reach them until the right chemicals can be applied to set the image—even the faintest gleam would spoil it,' she explains.

'How in God's name do you know all this? No, don't tell me. You learned it in London,' Mrs Bell mutters.

'That I did. The Gentleman had photography as a particular hobby of his.'

'Of course he did. Well, perhaps with all the vast knowledge you gathered there you can think of a way to keep that milk from spoiling by lunch time?' she asks, acidly.

Cat thinks for a while. 'I might have the answer, you know,' she says, lightly. 'Does the vicar's wife have any mackintosh squares, for sitting herself on damp ground and the like?'

'I believe so, in one or other of the trunks. What on earth will you do with them?'

'Let's find them first, then I'll show you,' Cat says. She peers back along the corridor before she goes upstairs, and sees the outline of the theosophist, still standing out in the courtyard. She does not like to think that he will be down in the cellars from now on; that he might be around to overhear her speak, or watch her work. Without being able to say quite why, she would prefer to keep him at a greater distance—the safe privacy of the kitchens feels violated.

Cat finds what she is looking for in the chest of drawers in the hallway: two large squares of waterproof oilcloth. She fetches a ball of strong jute garden twine from the greenhouse, then she and the housekeeper pack all the meat and dairy foods into a hamper. With one of them at each handle, they go out into the back garden and make their way to the far corner of the lawn, where the ground is shaded by a stand of ancient apple trees that have mistletoe crouching on them here and there. Protected from the worst of the sun's onslaught, the grass here is longer and greener. It's a cool and calming corner.

'What are you thinking, girl?' Mrs Bell demands, when Cat puts her side of the hamper down with a bump. Cat points to a pile of crumbling stonework, topped with a rotting wooden lid.

'The old well,' she says, heaving the heavy lid to one side. Mould and cobwebs fur the underside of it; the dark entrance to the shaft breathes out a damp smell like fungus. Cat brushes the cobwebs aside, calmly flicking away a spider when it clambers along her wrist.

'*Ugh*, how can you bear to!' Mrs Bell shudders. Cat glances up at her.

'There are far worse things in life than spiders, Sophie Bell,' she says.

191

'That's Mrs Bell to you,' says Mrs Bell, but she speaks distractedly, as if from habit, and there is little feeling behind the words.

'So. We tie the stuff into bundles, good and tight, then we lower them a way down into the well, and tie them to the top somehow . . . to a cross bar—this'll do,' Cat explains, picking up a broken wooden slat from the grass and laying it across the round hole.

'I suppose it will be cool in there. Cooler than the kitchen, at least,' Mrs Bell concedes.

'Very much so.' Cat swings the lid of the hamper open, begins to unpack onto the lush grass.

'It won't do for the milk jugs. We'll have to stand them in basins of cold water back indoors.'

'And if it starts to turn by afternoon, we can scald whatever's left. It should at least keep until the morning if we do that,' Cat adds.

A soft breeze eases through the parchment leaves above them. Mrs Bell stands wide, catches her breath. She eyes the mouth of the well with dark mistrust, as if almost frightened by it.

'How did you even know this was here?' the housekeeper asks.

'Oh, you know. Just . . . getting my bearings,' Cat says.

'I'll bet. Snooping about is more like it.' Mrs Bell stands still and watches the well; she does not begin to unpack. Cat is drawing breath to demand help when Sophie Bell speaks again. 'I shan't be able to go too close to it, I think. No, I shan't. Not too close, and not to look into it.' She shudders a little, clamping her hands defensively into the enveloping flesh of her armpits.

'Why on earth not? What's to be scared of?

There's no way a woman of your girth could fall in there, after all,' Cat says, still unpacking. But when she looks up, she sees that the housekeeper's face is pale, almost yellowish white, like the butter she herself is holding. 'Are you all right?' she asks, more gently.

'I lost my Walter in a well. I tend to put it out of my mind, as a person might. Something like that. But now and then, you can't help but think of it,' says Sophie Bell, and her voice is different, much smaller than usual; deadened and defeated.

'Walter? I never heard you mention him before. Who's Walter?'

'My little boy, of course! Just five years old he was, when I lost him.' Sophie Bell presses her lips into a tight purse that puckers her chin.

'Down a well?' Cat asks quietly.

'The bigger boys dared him. Little buggers. They never meant no harm, I know, but at the time, of course, I wanted their hides. They dared him that he'd never climb down the rope far enough to touch the water. Silly boy, he went and did it—he wasn't to know any better. Nearly made it back up, they said, but then he slipped his grip on the rope and fell back again. Hit his head on the side and that was that.' In the quiet after Mrs Bell speaks, a robin comes to spy on them. Cat crumbles a tiny corner of the cheese and throws it into the grass for him.

'That's terrible, Sophie,' she says quietly, her throat gone tight with dismay. 'I'm so sorry to hear it.'

'Going on twenty years ago, but I still miss him. His birthday would have been next week. He'd not have been much older than you.'

193

'Were you married, then?'

'Of course I was bloody married! We don't all of us love scandal like you, Cat Morley. And you'll ask me next what became of my husband. Well, he up and died of a tumour. Not two years after Walter went down the well. No great loss to me nor mankind, but he gave me my Walter, so I had him to thank for that. He was a lovely bairn, he was— so kind, and so sunny.'

'I had no idea you'd suffered such loss,' Cat says, softly. She wishes she could put out her hand and take Sophie's, but the housekeeper's arms remain tightly folded. 'It must have been very hard for you, to go on with life after that. No wonder it soured your temper.'

'Hearing your pert remarks all day long does nothing to ease my sourness, young lady. You've a bad habit for speaking whatever comes straight into your head, do you know that?' Sophie remarks, and Cat smiles slightly.

'Yes, I've been told that before. But you could have married again, and had another child, couldn't you?' she asks. Mrs Bell shakes her head sadly.

'Only a lass who's never had a babe could think one so easily replaced. It takes the heart out of you, when they go. And besides, willing men were hardly queuing around the corner for the likes of me. It was probably too late to have another by then, anyway; even if I could have found somebody I liked.'

'Oh, I don't know. You could have cooked your way into somebody's good graces.' Cat smiles.

'You're just full of wise suggestions today, aren't you? Come on, let's get this done and get on with lunch. The mistress'll be wandering around with her belly rumbling before long. Not to mention this learned young man, whose work is so very bloody important.'

'Yes, who would have guessed how important? The vicar treats him like royalty,' Cat observes.

'Doesn't he just? Well, he must know something we don't, I suppose.'

'I'm not so sure about that,' Cat murmurs. Mrs Bell gives her a quizzical look, and Cat shrugs. 'The vicar should be careful. Apparently, Robin Durrant has no household of his own. It seems to me he's quite ready to take over this one instead.'

'In what way, take over?' The housekeeper frowns. Cat shrugs again.

'We'll see,' she says.

*   *   *

When the dinner plates are scrubbed, dried and put away, the dining table swept, and the napkins either refolded and pressed or put into the hamper to be laundered, Cat slips out through the back door, saunters into the courtyard and puts a cigarette between her lips. George is away on the barge for a few more days yet, taking a load of timber up the canal to Surrey. Square fence posts with sharpened points at one end, the newly hewn wood pale and moist. Cat saw the men loading them when she went into Thatcham to post letters for Hester. George's barge, and two others that had appeared to join it. The horses led from their ramshackle stables, snatching at the long green weeds as they were harnessed to the tow ropes, tossing their heads and flicking their tails at the crowding flies. The men wore thick canvas gloves, and had their trousers tied off with lengths of string just below the knee, to keep out the panicked rats that fled as the piles of timber were dismantled, reassembled on the barges. George, with his shirt plastered to his back, frowned in the sharp sunlight. She did not call out; felt wrong interrupting him at work. She likes the fact that she saw him, this time, but he did not see her. Like she owns a little bit more of his life than he meant to give. Now she wishes him back already. She could walk alone in the dark but there seems little point, with nowhere to go.

She fumbles in her pocket for a match but one blooms in the dark beside her, makes her jump. Robin Durrant leans from behind the orange flare, smiles a little as he proffers it to her. For some reason Cat can't define, her first instinct is to refuse it. But she accepts, takes a long pull on her cigarette and coughs a little.

'Thank you,' she says, guardedly.

'You're welcome, Cat,' he says, and his use of her name sounds too familiar. Cat measures him up in the weak light from the doorway. He moves away slightly, leans against the wall; his body curved into an elegant slouch, hips pushed forwards, head tipped back.

'What are you doing out here? You're not even smoking,' she points out. The yard has come to feel like her place; this after-dinner moment as her time.

'I was; I was. I finished it just before you came out. Sorry if I scared you,' he says, turning his head towards her. The contours of his face are softly lit. Clean, smooth brow, eyes lost in shadow. The long

196

sweep of his jaw. His face is beautiful, Cat realises. Quite perfectly beautiful, like a painting of a saint or a representation of love. But also opaque, unreadable. His affability looks like a mask.

'You didn't scare me.'

'No. I bet it would take something to scare you,' he says. Cat ignores him, takes another long drag. The tip of her cigarette glows fiercely. 'I hear you've been through it a bit. A bit of a firebrand, I hear,' he says, companionably enough.

'Who told you that? I thought the vicar's wife was sworn off gossip.'

'Oh, it wasn't dear Hester. But word gets around in small places like this. I should know—I heard myself called "the fairy man" just the other day, by a passing child no more than six years old. Explain to me how she knew to call me that, I beg of you.'

Cat smiles briefly. 'A little girl with dark brown curls and a turned-up nose, I'll wager?' she asks.

'Oh, indeed—you know the culprit?'

'Tilly. Daughter of Mrs Lynchcombe who takes in our laundry. I expect Sophie Bell has been filling her in on all your comings and goings, and the child is as sharp as a tack.'

Quite possibly. And yet, it is *you* I see, loitering behind doors when I am in discussion with the vicar or his wife. Listening hard, to all appearances,' he says, archly. Cat bridles, turns away from him and does not reply. Above her head, moths dive and flutter at the light in the corridor, bashing the soft dust from their velvet wings. 'Come now, Cat—you can't pretend to be shy. You're not the type.'

'What do you know of my type? What do you know of me at all?'

'I rest my case.' He smiles.

'You smile too much. People must guess that you're mocking them,' she says, blandly.

'A surprising few,' Robin concedes. 'You're unusual, for a servant, Cat Morley.'

'How should a servant be? I thought your Society made no distinction between class or race?'

'Indeed, it does not. But although such distinctions should not exist, perhaps they do nonetheless. Theosophy also teaches that if a person is made to toil or suffer in this life, it is to atone for wrong-doing in a previous life. The universal law and justice of karma.'

'Yes, I heard you speak of it the other night. I am a servant because I was a murderess in another lifetime, is that it?' Cat asks, drily.

'Perhaps,' Robin grins, pleased to have nettled her.

Cat thinks on this for a moment. 'Perhaps. Perhaps I was a starving pauper in a past life, but an exceptionally good one, and this is my reward. Perhaps you were a king, but a vile and corrupt one. And this is your punishment.' She gestures at him—his rumpled hair, his slightly creased clothes. Robin Durrant laughs softly. 'Karmic justice, you call it? It's no justice at all,' she says.

'Is the Christian way of thinking more just? That a deity should create a human soul and give it just one lifetime to exist, and in that lifetime he may bestow pain and suffering and misfortunes galore, and all of this is meted out for no reason at all? Or only to test that person? What a cruel God that would be!'

'But how may a soul, in a new body, learn from its past mistakes if it may not be allowed to remember them?' Cat asks.

'Well . . .' Robin Durrant falters. 'Well. By following the teachings of theosophy towards a greater understanding of their condition.'

'That is no answer. You say that to acquire knowledge they must first be in possession of that knowledge? How may a pauper living in the dust of darkest Africa even begin to guess at this grand scheme? There is no more justice in your theory of karma than there is in an arbitrary and unthinking universe.'

'Is that what you believe in? A great nothingness? You are an atheist?' Robin asks. Cat winces at the word, in case the vicar or his wife should hear it. She finishes her cigarette, grinds it into the bricks beneath her heel. The night is close and sticky. Sleep will be hard to find. In the distance, thunder rumbles ominously. The western horizon is an indigo smear, and all the usual night sounds are stifled, muted. Cat's body yearns for George, and his heavy, sure hands.

'I have been to the very edge of death. And I looked hard. And there was nothing there,' she says eventually, her voice clipped.

'You are very strange, for a servant,' Robin repeats.

'You eat no meat but you drink wine, and brandy, and you smoke tobacco. I should say you are strange, for a theosophist.'

'Ah, but the Society is not peopled with saints, Cat. Only with sinners who are trying to do better.' Cat rolls her eyes a little at this, standing up from the wall and folding her arms as she moves towards the door. 'Not bed, surely? Aren't you off out to see your sweetheart tonight?' Robin asks, quite pleasantly. At this Cat hesitates, shoots him a worried, angry glance. There is a hard edge to his smile now, a glint of knowing in his eye that makes her uneasy. Robin shrugs, too casually. 'Word gets about. But fear not. Your secret is safe with me.' His tone is nonchalant; makes a lie of the statement. Cat frowns, steps inside. 'Wait—won't you stay out and talk to me a bit longer?' he asks. That slow, lazy, gorgeous smile.

'Why on earth would I want to?' Cat snaps, and then remembers herself, checks her tongue a little. 'Goodnight, sir,' she amends, and leaves him in the darkness.

*   *   *

In the morning, Cat takes the small stack of letters from the postman and is arranging them on a silver-plated tray to take up to the breakfast table when her own name catches her eye. A small grey envelope, with her name and the address written on it in a round, childish hand that she does not recognise. The postmark is London. Cat's heart squeezes painfully. *Tess*, she thinks, slipping the letter into the pocket of her apron and hurriedly taking the tray up to the table. She dumps it rather abruptly in front of the vicar and retreats, not noticing Hester's polite smile of thanks, or the way Robin Durrant's eyes follow her. Ducking out into the courtyard she tears the letter open, squinting at the pale paper. The sky overhead is white with cloud so dense and uniform that is seems less like cloud and more as though the sky is too weary to be blue that day. But the letter is not from Tess.

200

Dear Cat,

I am writing to you because I no that Mrs Heddingly opened the letter what you rote to our Tess, who is not here any more. I did not think she should of opened it for she could of sent it on but she did not. We all saw Tesses name on the front of it and later on I stole a look at it in her room. This was not the proper thing to do neither but it was her that did the first wrong thing by opening it. I did not read it I swear it I only looked to see who it was from and I rote your new place out so I could rite this to you. Tess is in the workhouse now. Frosham House it is called and it is on Sidall Road near Soho. I hear it is not as bad a place as some but it is still not a good place and those what go there do come out thin and week if they come out at all. None of us could do nothing to help her having no money ourselves to give to her and her having no people of her own. I must also say that while Mrs Heddingly did wrong in not giving your letter on to her she did speak up for Tess after what happened but the Master would have none of it. Frosham House lets in visitors in the afternoon on the third Sunday of the month and no other day. Me and Ellen went to see Tess last month but she would not come out to talk to us. I hope you are in a better way Cat. It is not the same place here without you and Tess.

From Suzanne

The workhouse. Tess. Cat reads the letter again, heart sinking, feeling like lead in her chest. She shuts her eyes, and bunches her hand into a fist, the paper creasing and cutting into her. How could

201

he do it? The Gentleman, with all his bluff good humour and progressive ideas. He must have known that without Cat there Tess would have kept herself quiet and well behaved. He must have known that put out of her job with no reference, there were only two places that the orphaned girl would end up. Either earning money on her back, or in the poorhouse. The injustice of it burns in the back of Cat's throat like bile. At that moment, in spite of anything else, she hates him. Tess, just a baby still, given a choice like that. She would never have turned harlot. She was scared of men; still thought one day a handsome prince with gentle hands and a love of poetry would take a shine to her and marry her for her golden curls and her soft white body. And who knows—it might have happened one day. A tradesman or professional caller of some kind, rather than a prince; but still. Not now. Nothing for her now but endless toil and rat-eaten bread, and the stink of the old and infirm kept in damp rooms with nobody to help them. How she hates him!

*   *   *

Cat didn't realise, when she was released early from gaol, that it meant she wouldn't see Tess again. Cat was released ten days before her two months were up, with her chest consumed by infection, her skin drawn tight over her bones, her hair shorn away and her lips cracked, weeping blood whenever she spoke. The WSPU sent a welcoming committee to collect her and two other girls released that day, freed before their time because they were fading fast and the government did not want to create martyrs. They were taken in a cab to a meeting hall, where a reception breakfast was laid out for them, and speeches made in praise of their bravery. It was only these speeches that kept Cat from sobbing with relief, and with pain, the whole time. She kept a check on herself by saying nothing—keeping her ruined lips tight together other than to murmur thanks when her Holloway medal was pinned to her collar.

She could not touch the food they had prepared. The other girls did—one picking politely at the sandwiches and slices of pie and fruit, the other tearing into it, so quick and frantic that she made herself choke. The women urged Cat to eat, to start rebuilding her strength. They even brought out a mug of broth after she'd turned down everything else. Cat tried a sip but could not swallow it, and in the end she spat it back into the cup, as carefully as she could. In an extravagant gilt mirror hanging at one end of the room, she caught sight of herself. A pale, ragged spectre, with scabs around her mouth, bruises on her neck and wrists. Her clothes hung from her bony frame, her scalp was an ugly grey where it was visible around her hat. As they bustled around her, the women of the welcoming committee looked like round, glossy birds; plump partridges or doves with their billowing chests and bright, cheerful eyes. Cat stared at her reflection, and hardly knew herself.

Later, they took her back to Broughton Street, and then The Gentleman took her straight to see his own doctor. The first and only time she rode with him in his motor car. Dazed and exhausted as she was, still the novelty of riding in a self-propelled carriage was not lost on her. But it was only afterwards, when Tess was still serving her sentence and Cat was told a new position had been found for her in the countryside, that Cat realised she might not see her friend again, might have no chance to make amends. On the day she left London she was taken by bus to Paddington. Mrs Heddingly rode with her to be sure she caught the train, and tears streamed from Cat's eyes to drip unheeded from her chin.

*   *   *

'This Sunday? I am sorry, Cat, but it's quite out of the question,' says the vicar's wife, when Cat asks her. Hester Canning is sitting at the desk in the morning room arranging violets, yellow and indigo pansies and pink phlox into a suitable pattern in her pressing book. She works quickly since the heat of the day is making the petals wilt already. Several torn violets lie discarded to one side.

'But the place only lets in visitors the third Sunday of each month. That's this Sunday. If I can't go then I can't go for another month, madam . . .'

'But on such short notice, Cat, and with my sister arriving tomorrow with her family . . . you are very much needed here. I *am* sorry, but I cannot allow you to go. I promise you may next month. How about that? The third Sunday of August will be entirely yours, to make up for the afternoon you will lose this week. There's an early train which will get you to town in plenty of time to visit your friend.' Hester smiles brightly, as if the outing will be a fun one. She shuts the wooden cover of the pressing book and begins to tighten the screws, forcing the boards together with the hapless flowers caught between, flattened, stifled. Cat tries to breathe calmly but feels like her chest is pressed, as though Hester tightens screws upon her at the same time. How can she explain the way London workhouses are? The words will not form sentences, tangled in her desperate thoughts. By next month Tess might have faded and gone. Not dead, necessarily, but the light inside her extinguished, her innocence snuffed out, the spirit of her crushed like flower petals, and no pretty image of it preserved anywhere. Cat has seen people bought out of the workhouse. Empty shells, they seemed. Nothing behind their eyes but echoing space; shadows of loss and despair.

'Please,' she tries once more, her voice little more than a croak. 'It is of the utmost importance. Teresa is a very great friend of mine and it is only because of me that she finds herself put out of her job . . . *I* am to blame. I must visit her. I must take her some things to ease the hardship she is left facing . . .' she implores.

'Cat, please. Enough of this. I am sure the girl is being well looked after. The poorhouses are designed for such as her, after all—to give them shelter and food, and a way to earn these comforts. And she will still be there for you to visit next month, and every bit as pleased to see you then as she would be now, I am sure. It is only fair that I have more notice than this of you taking time off. Surely you can see that?' Hester smiles vaguely, quite unconcerned. Comforts? Cat stares at her, bewildered. Can the woman really think that there is comfort in such places? She stands in front of her, quite still, unable to move; not quite believing what she has heard. Hester continues about her hobby for a while, then looks up with an expression of mild discomfort. 'That will be all, Cat.'

*   *   *

For the rest of the stifling day, Cat works hard and fast, scrubbing angrily at the flagstones of the hallway until sweat marks a dark trail down her spine; pulling the sheets from the beds with enough force to tear them; chopping vegetables with sharp, agitated carelessness. She cuts her thumb this way but does not notice until Sophie Bell peers over her shoulder, curses in dismay at the sticky red smears all over the runner beans.

'What in heaven's name has got into you today?' the housekeeper asks.

'I want to leave!' is all Cat can answer, frustration making her voice tremble and holding her tongue half-paralysed.

'Well, by Christ, girl, there's the door!' Sophie Bell mutters. 'Hold still!' She binds Cat's thumb with a length of clean rag, ties it tightly with string. Almost at once, the blood blooms out through the fabric, unfurling like a rose. 'You cut yourself deep. Foolish girl,' Mrs Bell observes, and the words sound profound to Cat—a judgement on more things than Sophie Bell can know.

In the early evening, the rain finally comes. Thick blankets of cloud had lain warm and damp over the house all afternoon, growing steadily darker and heavier. At half past five the first drops fall, warm as bathwater, soft as melted butter. Cat serves the dinner, disgusted by the luxury, the excess; the way the theosophist turns down the meat, his expression blasé, sanctimonious. How many others in the world have need of that meat, Cat wonders? When now it will go back to the kitchen and spoil, and be thrown away and wasted because the cold store is full of this thoughtless young man's toys. She snatches up their plates with her lips pursed and her face in a frown. And afterwards, when all her work is done, she slips out into the pounding rain and is soaked to the skin in an instant. She takes the vicar's bicycle from the shed and wheels it clanking along the side of the house, the rain hiding any sounds she might make. By the gate she pauses, swings her leg over the saddle and tips back her head, lets the rain wash away the day and all it brought. Her anger is like a scent on her skin, a clinging stink that she can't get rid of. The rain almost hurts on her face, it falls so fast. Lightning makes her see red—the inside of her eyelids, glowing. She can feel the thunder in her chest like another heartbeat, irregular and uncomfortable, making her blood run faster. If lightning were to strike her, she thinks, she would not mind. She would not feel it. A hand on her arm makes her gasp.

'Off out again? In this inclement weather?' Robin Durrant asks, his voice raised against the onslaught of the rain.

'What are you doing out here?' Cat demands, bewildered by his sudden appearance. He holds his jacket above his head but it is soaked, water dripping through it, running down his arms, drenching his shirt.

'Well, I went to your room but you weren't there. I guessed you must be leaving for one of your assignations. He must be a very fine lover, to tempt you out in this storm.' Robin smiles.

'That he is!' Cat snaps back at him, but Robin only smiles wider. Splinters of a new worry work their way into her mind. He went to her room? Who knew if he could move softly, if he was careful. 'Now let me go.'

'In a second, in a second. I have a job for you. Meet me at the stile along the lane at first light on Sunday.' Robin runs his tongue along his bottom lip, licking the rainwater there.

'I will not!'

'You will. Or I will have to let slip to the Cannings about these evening jaunts of yours. The vicar is very much concerned with the purity and moral probity of his flock. I dare say he would have something to say about it within his own household.' This he says in a light tone, conversational, even slightly bored. Cat glares at him, tries to see if he would indeed betray her this way, and to guess why he might. 'First light on Sunday,' he says again, and grins at her like an excited child, without malice; as if he is not threatening her, not controlling her. Cat snatches her arm away, strains against the pedals to be away from him. She can hardly see in the rain and the dark, she can hardly breathe through the rage in her heart. George is not there for her, but still she pedals as fast as she can, the bicycle careening wildly through puddles, along the little stony lanes. Just to be away from The Rectory; just for the illusion of liberty.

Hester hears the sound of the pony and trap on the driveway and her stomach gives a childish little lurch of joy, mixed with something almost like relief. She hurries to the front door and waves as her sister, her niece and her nephew climb down from the cart, and Mr Barker undoes the straps around their luggage and begins to pile it on the ground.

'Oh, careful with that one, please! It's rather fragile,' Amelia cries. Mr Barker clamps his jaw into his moustaches and nods in a surly manner.

'Darling Amelia! It's so wonderful to see you! Come here, children, let me look at you,' Hester calls. She holds the two children at arm's length: eleven-year-old John, who has sandy hair and a rather pinched-looking face, and is all skin and bone; and eight-year-old Ellie, who is plump and cheerful, with pale grey eyes and a tucked-in chin like a china doll. Her little blue and white sailor dress is tight across a round tummy, and creased from the journey. *Just as I would have looked at that age*, Hester thinks, with a tug of affection that is almost painful. 'Goodness me, how you've grown! I can scarcely tell it's you! You're enormous!' she exclaims. Ellie smiles but John rolls his eyes a little and looks down, scuffing his feet in embarrassment.

'John! Don't make that face! Give your aunt a kiss,' Amelia instructs him sharply.

'Oh, there, there.' Hester crouches down and smiles at them. 'I've never liked forced kisses, only freely given ones. What do you say, John?' Hester's nephew leans forwards and kisses her cheek quickly, and Ellie puts out her arms for a hug, which Hester gladly gives her. 'Run around the garden and stretch your legs, children. Off you go! Come and have some lemonade when you get too hot!' she calls after them, as they gratefully trot away and are lost amidst the high flower borders and sun-beleaguered shrubs.

'Oh, thank goodness!' Amelia sighs, putting down her vanity case and hugging her sister. 'John has been vile all the way here! It's not his fault— he's so disappointed that their father hasn't come with us . . .'

'Yes, where is Archie? Didn't he mean to come?'

'He did, until the very last minute. I'm so sorry, Hetty! Typical of him—he had a prior engagement at his club that he hadn't told me about, and had forgotten about himself. But I am here, and so are the children, and we shall have a wonderful time without him, I'm sure.' Amelia smiles. She is five years older than Hester, and has a grace and elegance that her younger sister has always envied. Feline cheekbones and a delicate jaw, and the most perfectly blue, almond-shaped eyes. As a débutante, her beauty was the talk of the season, but now there are slight hollows in her cheeks and under her eyes, and her skin has lost the first vibrant glow of her youth.

'Amy, you look a little tired. Are you quite well?' Hester asks, solicitously. Amelia's smile shrinks a little, and to Hester's shock tears appear in her eyes, sparkling in the sun. 'Amy! What is it? Whatever's the matter?' she demands, grasping her sister's long-fingered hands.

'Let's not talk out here,' Amelia says, lowering her voice as Cat appears in the hallway behind them. 'Are we in our usual rooms?'

'Ah, well . . . Mr Durrant has taken the room that the children would normally have, I fear . . . I thought it impolite to uproot him, since he has been with us so many weeks and got so well bedded in . . .'

'Yes, so you mentioned,' Amelia replies, wryly.

'But Cat has made up the west end bedroom for them—I'm sure they'll be comfortable in there.'

'But there must be somebody to help the girl take our luggage up, surely?' says Amelia, eyeing Cat's thin arms and shoulders as she hefts one of the trunks, her whole body arching backwards to take the weight of it.

'I'm quite able to manage, thank you, madam,' Cat grinds out tersely, scarce able to breathe.

'Here—let me take that from you,' Robin Durrant says, appearing in the doorway. He takes the case from Cat, lifting it easily out of her hands and carrying it into the hallway.

'Oh! Mr Durrant . . . how kind of you. May I introduce you to my sister, Mrs Amelia Entwhistle? Amy, this is our resident theosophist, Mr Robin Durrant,' Hester says, trying to keep her tone from betraying her. She isn't sure what it is she is trying to hide, but lately there is something. There is definitely something. Robin gives Amelia's hand a gentle shake.

'Very pleased to meet you, Mrs Entwhistle,' he says, smiling his widest, most disarming smile; and Amelia can't help but return the expression.

'Likewise, I'm sure,' she says.

'Well, I'm off to the station, and thence into

Reading. I have a few things I must attend to . . . but I do hope to meet you properly at dinner, Mrs Entwhistle. Is there anything you'd like me to fetch for you while I'm in town, Mrs Canning?' He turns his smiling eyes on Hester, who finds it hard to meet his gaze.

'No, thank you, Mr Durrant.' Her voice is clipped in spite of herself.

'Then I'll bid you fine ladies a good day.' He makes them an ironic little bow and saunters away towards the gate. When he passes out of sight, Amelia turns to her sister and gives her an appraising look.

'We have much to talk about,' she says, as they walk into the house. Inside the hall, Cat bends down again, and sets her back to the heavy case for the second time.

*　　　*　　　*

The two sisters settle themselves in the shade of a cherry tree on the terrace to the rear of the house, where the slightest of breezes stirs the torpid air. They sit on iron filigree chairs, which are so hot that they glow through their skirts onto the backs of their legs. Amelia wafts air gently over her face with a beautiful silk fan, her gaze instinctively following her children as they weave and skip around the garden, playing with an almost grim determination, their eyes screwed up, brows furrowed.

'I have never known such heat as this summer!' she exclaims at last. 'On my way here just now, we passed a group of children playing in the street, and do you know what they were doing? They were collecting bubbles of melted tar from the road on twigs of straw, and using it as glue to stick the pieces onto the side of a barn, to make letters and pictures! Melted tar, at not ten in the morning!'

'It is extraordinary. I find it most draining, don't you?' Hester agrees.

'Truly. You didn't mention in your letters that Mr Durrant was quite so very . . .'

'Very what?'

'So very young and handsome,' Amelia says, watching her sister closely.

'I must have said he was young? As for handsome . . . I hadn't really noticed, to be perfectly honest. Is he?' Hester replies, evasively. She feels suddenly self-conscious, as if caught out in a lie.

'You know he is—don't play the innocent with me. You have eyes, haven't you? Or do you only have eyes for Albert?'

'Perhaps that's it . . . Anyway, he's our guest. Of course I don't think of him that way. And besides . . .' She trails off awkwardly, not quite sure what she had been about to say.

'Yes?'

'No, nothing. But tell me, Amy, please—what's troubling you?' Hester asks, keen to change the subject. Cat comes over to the table with a tray of iced tea and lemonade, freshly cut oranges and slices of Madeira cake. Cloudy droplets of sweat scatter her brow. Amelia waits until the servant has gone back indoors before she sighs.

'You must never speak of it to a soul, not even to Albert. Do you promise? Well . . . the trouble that you have with Albert, dearest . . . the trouble that you write to me about? I fear I have just the

213

opposite trouble with Archie.' She touches her fan to her lips as if reluctant to let the words out.

'I . . . don't quite understand you, Amy,' Hester whispers, as the children run close by, faces flushed and hair damped down with sweat.

'I found him . . . making . . . making a fool of himself the other day. With the upstairs maid, Danielle.'

'*No!* Oh, my darling . . . that is *dreadful*! Are you *sure*?'

'Very sure indeed, I fear. Oh, I've got rid of the girl, of course. This all happened just this week, and truth be told it's why he's not come away with us on this visit. And it has happened before, though I never told you, Hetty. I was so ashamed . . . But he promised, he *promised* me it would never happen again. Now he says that he has drives he must satisfy, and that he cannot help himself,' she says, with an angry little catch in her voice. 'Do you think that can be true? Do you think a man may be made a slave to his desires?' Hester thinks carefully before answering. She takes her sister's hand, but their skin is hot and soon grows clammy where it touches.

'I think . . . I think any person *can* be a slave to their desire, if they allow themselves to be. Surely the measure of any person alive is in their behaviour—in what they *choose* to do, in spite of what other options are available to them?'

'You're right,' Amelia says, bleakly. 'There is no excusing what he has done. It is despicable.'

'Now, Amelia, you of all people know that I can't be counted as any kind of authority on the wants and desires of men,' Hester says, smiling a little. 'Archie has committed a great sin, both

214

against you and against God. But perhaps . . . forgiveness is the Christian thing to do? Once the guilty party has repented, of course . . .'

'But that's just it, Hetty! This time . . . this time he didn't even seem repentant. He seemed . . . angry with me, if anything—for interrupting him at his sport! Oh, it was dreadful! Intolerable!' She sinks her face into her fingertips and begins to cry quietly.

'Darling Amy, please don't cry! The children must not see . . . Please, dearest, take heart. Archie loves you, and the children. I *know* he does, and you know it too. Perhaps men are indeed governed by stronger forces than we women . . . I can scarce credit a good man such as Archie behaving in such a manner if this weren't the case. Can any of us see into the heart of another? Truly? Please don't cry.' Gradually, Amelia lifts her face and blots her eyes on her handkerchief.

'Well, I have told him the contents of my heart. He is killing my love for him with his infidelity. Perhaps only one more incident, I told him, would be enough to wipe it away completely,' she sniffs. Hester is too shocked to say anything to this. 'And what of your marriage, Hetty? Do you fare any better of late?' Amelia asks. Hester looks down, at her fingers nestled in the cotton folds of her dress. Such plump, smooth fingers; the nails buffed and clean. For some reason, she can hardly stand the sight of them, feels such a spasm of dislike for herself that she curls them into fists and squeezes until her nails bite into the heels of her hands.

'I married for love, Amelia. As you know . . . as our parents lamented, albeit in their soft way. And I thought that, though I chose a humble man of

215

limited means, I would have love, and be loved, and raise children surrounded by love . . .' She looks across the scorched lawn to where John is teasing his sister, holding a ribbon he'd pulled from her hair above her head and snatching it away when she makes a grab for it. The little girl jumps and reaches quite amiably, always smiling, never losing her patience, and again Hester feels a violent pull of sympathy for her, of fellow feeling for their shared path in life.

'And . . . are you not loved?'

'Oh, I am loved. As a sister, as a friend. Not as I love him, I feel. Not as a wife. Not as a . . . lover.' She takes a deep breath and sighs slowly, feeling the weight of her own words settling ever more heavily on her spirits. 'And now he has a new friend, a new confidant, and I fear I am slipping further from his thoughts every day.'

'Surely not, Hetty? Albert has always been so devoted to you,' Amelia says.

'Perhaps he was, once. But now, everything has changed. Even his parish is suffering the effects of his diversion by Mr Durrant.'

'How do you mean?'

'Well . . . For example, the other day, Pamela Urquhart called in to see if the vicar was unwell, since he hadn't been to visit them for two weeks or more. Let me explain—Mrs Urquhart's father is very old and infirm, and has been awaiting death for some time now. He suffers a great deal, poor man, and finds his faith tested daily, and he hasn't been able to come to church for many months. Albert made a habit of calling on him to offer comfort and prayer, at least two times a week, but his visits, since the theosophist arrived, have ceased. I just don't know what to make of it, Amy. It's so unlike Albert to neglect his duties, but this new interest seems to be taking precedence over all other concerns.'

'This new interest—do you mean in theosophy, or in Mr Durrant?' Amy asks, pointedly.

'Theosophy . . . or rather, both, I suppose,' Hester says, looking up at her sister and trying to read her expression.

'This is a troubling evolution, indeed. I wonder . . . I wonder quite what it is about the man that draws Albert so?'

'You think it's the man, then, and not the ideas he's brought with him?'

'Well, don't you, dearest? After all, I expect Albert has known about fairies and theosophy for quite some time. How is it that only when Mr Durrant appears does it become all-consuming?'

'Amy—I don't understand,' Hester says, desperately.

'Perhaps I am wrong. I must meet the young man again, and get to know him a little better,' Amelia replies, leaning back in her chair and letting her gaze fall into the distance. Her tears, already dried by the sun, have left faint pink streaks in her face powder.

'Well, of course you shall,' Hester says, still trying to make out her sister's meaning.

*   *   *

In the kitchen, Cat slides the empty tray onto the table top and crosses to the sink. She thrusts her hands into the basin of water where the milk jugs are standing, supposedly keeping cold, but the water is blood temperature. She splashes some onto her wrists and wipes her wet hands over the back of her neck nonetheless, hoping to feel it cool her.

'This milk will have gone by the evening,' she warns Mrs Bell, who sits wedged into her chair, the newspaper spread open on the table in front of her.

'It'll turn all the quicker if you keep dipping your hot hands into the basin,' the housekeeper observes.

'I can't help it. As soon as I move in this heat, I swelter. And *somebody* about this place had better keep moving,' she mutters, but with little feeling. Sophie Bell's face is puce, her cheeks mottled with cracked red blood vessels; and when she moves about too much her top lip turns white, and her eyes slip out of focus. Cat does not want the woman to faint. Lord knows, nobody would be able to pick her up, and they'd be forced to step over her carcass all day until the temperature dropped and she roused herself.

'Over there,' Mrs Bell sighs. 'I kept some of the iced tea back for us. And pour me a glass while you're at it.' Cat whisks the linen cloth from a jug on the sideboard, scattering a handful of parched flies that had been waiting in vain to drink. The chunks of ice in it, collected that morning in a block from Thatcham, have melted clean away, but the drink is still cool and tangy with fresh mint and lemons. Cat gulps hers down like a child, shutting her eyes at the chill shiver it gives her. 'At least with the men out all day there'll be a bit less work,' Sophie Bell says. 'Where's the fairy man gone off to, did you hear?'

218

'Reading, he said,' Cat says, wiping her mouth on the hem of her apron. 'Some "things I must to attend to" was all he said.'

'Huh. Well, I bumped into Dolores Mickel in the week, whose sister works at a big house in Reading, and she says the family her sister works for knows the Durrant family of old. Mr Robin wasn't always a theosophist, she told me,' says Sophie Bell, her eyes glinting slyly as they always do when she gossips.

'No?' Cat asks. She finds herself keen to know more about the man. *Know thy enemy*—the words jump into her head. *My enemy?*

'No indeed. He was off at his studies for a long time, and then for a while once he was back, there was a different story from his parents each time they came to dinner. First he was a poet; then he was writing for the papers. Then he was going into the clergy—a Methodist minister, if you please. He went to Greece and was there for quite some months, though nobody seemed to know what he did there. Then when he came back he ran for parliament, just like that! The Liberal Party, but he didn't get hisself elected. Next thing you know, he's a theosopher, or whatever he is now, and insisting that it was his true course all along.' Mrs Bell dismisses the man with a small flap of her hand that sets the meat of her arm swinging.

'Theoso*phist*. Well. Sounds like he doesn't know who he is or what to believe in, doesn't it?' Cat smiles, unkindly. 'Interesting.'

Mrs Bell glances up at her, her eyes narrowing suspiciously. 'Now, don't you go bandying it about—least of all to him. I've heard you talking to him, out in the courtyard. Don't be getting careless

219

with yourself, will you, Cat?'

'No, Sophie Bell. There's no danger of that.'

*   *   *

In the afternoon, when she has an hour to rest, Cat keeps to her room, and holds her breath when she thinks she hears a footstep out in the corridor. But it's only the house, groaning in the heat as its beams and boards expand. Outside her open window the sky is simmering blue. She can hear the vicar's wife and her sister, talking in low voices that spiral, on and on; the children complaining breathlessly to one another, their voices drawing near and then receding, like a small flock of birds on the wing. She cannot wipe from her mind that Robin Durrant came to her room in the night; that he knows about her sleepless life. It's like a nagging itch, or a buzzing insect that she can't shake off. And that he means to use the knowledge against her somehow. If it's for him to take out his lust, she thinks grimly, he is in for a disappointment. She will claw his eyes out before she lets him touch her. But she will meet him, as he told her to. If for no other reason than that, beneath her anger, she is curious. Dwelling on such thoughts, precious time slips away. Cat shakes her head, grips the pencil tighter and writes. Another letter to Tess, this time addressed to Frosham House. Guilt makes her stomach churn, washes through her like acid, makes it hard to think. *I can't bear to think of you there. I will find some scheme to get you out, I swear it*, she writes. But what scheme? What can she do? She bites her lower lip hard between her teeth, writes *I swear it*

220

again, so that she will have to think of something. *Please be strong, Tessy. Hold on until I can think of a way.*

* * *

Tess grew weary of the suffragette cause as time passed, even as Cat grew more and more committed to it. Tess had only been interested in it as a way to get out of the house where they spent so much of their lives, as a way to escape; never really for the politics themselves. She joked, giggling in hushed tones, that she wouldn't know who to vote for even if she were enfranchised. It was an exciting diversion from work, which stopped being exciting after several weeks of handing out leaflets and selling ribbons, hawking copies of *Votes for Women* and shouting slogans and being scowled at by respectable men and women.

'I don't see why they should disapprove of us so,' Tess said one day, hurt by the cold treatment they got from rich women. 'It's them that'll benefit, after all.' She stuck out her lower lip like a child, tucked her hair behind her ears and straightened her cuffs self-consciously; twitching just like she did when Mrs Heddingly or anybody senior came to inspect her work.

'Because the rich will ever disapprove of the poor doing anything but catering to them,' Cat told her, keenly. 'Cheer up. Another half an hour and I'll buy you a cup of hot chocolate,' she said, giving Tess's shoulders a squeeze. Soon it became clear that these little treats were the only thing keeping Tess active in the WSPU, and Cat knew she

221

oughtn't to pressure her friend into going with her. But truth be told she wanted the company, wanted to share the adventure. Tess had introduced her to the movement, and it wouldn't have felt right going out on a Sunday without her, or sneaking to evening meetings when they were able to, listening to the great and good ladies of the society speak about rights and laws and votes and justice. She would not have felt half so brave or daring without Tess there, always less sure, always needing to be encouraged. Cat pauses in her letter writing, shuts her eyes tight with anguish. She had used her friend. Used Tess to show her a reflection of herself that she liked seeing; to afford herself some scrap of power over another person for the first time in her life.

Two months after they had paid their shilling each and joined the society, Cat let the secretary of their local branch know that they would be willing to take on more active duties. She said it quietly, as if they might be overheard, but the lady in the office looked up sharply.

'Window breaking? Invasion of political meetings?' she said, abruptly. Taken aback, Cat nodded, and her heart thumped loudly in her ears. The older woman smiled briskly, looking up over the top of half-moon spectacles with piercing dark eyes. 'Excellent, comrade. Good girl. I shall keep you in mind.' Cat smiled a tight little smile, nodded, and went back out into the main room of the office, with its piles of leaflets, its walls laden with banners and slogans, and framed photographs of suffragette martyrs. There was a glorious portrait of Saint Joan of Arc, patron saint of the WSPU, gazing down fiercely from behind a row of volunteers as they folded leaflets into envelopes. The room was stuffy with the smell of paper and typewriter ink, the air thick and warm with a constant buzz of busy voices and footsteps and machinery. It was the hub of a war campaign, where battles were planned and losses accounted. Cat loved it. Industry that had nothing to do with cleaning or cosseting, with making life easy for those too idle to do it themselves. Tess was not there when Cat volunteered them both for militant action. Tess was waiting outside, watching the hurdy-gurdy man with his little monkey in a tiny top hat and red waistcoat, and laughing quite delightedly at its tricks.

*   *   *

Robin Durrant arrives back from Reading in time to stride through to the dinner table, face glowing, hair tousled and untidy.

'Forgive me. I do hope you haven't been waiting for me?' he snaps, looking briefly at Albert, Hester and Amelia in turn; and for once his eyes are too quick, his smile a little strained. There is agitation in his whole expression, Hester notes.

'Not at all, Robin. Not at all. I trust you were able to find what you needed in town?' Albert asks. The vicar is as neat and tidy as ever, his soft hair set back, his whiskers neatly combed and trimmed. Hester glances at him, since they had indeed been waiting for Robin, and the hour is gone nine; but Albert's face is open and unconcerned.

'Indeed I did. And I called in on my parents while I was there, as it's been some weeks since I last saw them. My younger brother is visiting, so I

223

was able to see all three at once,' he says, sitting almost before the ladies have settled, dropping his napkin into his lap with a flick of the wrist, and reaching for his glass before realising that Cat has yet to fill it. Albert notices the gesture, and gets up himself to fetch the wine from the sideboard. Hester can feel Amelia's questioning gaze across the table, as the theosophist's glass is filled before hers, the female guest's.

'And how were your family? In good health, I trust?' Hester asks.

'Oh yes, very well. *Very* well, thank you . . .' Robin says, with odd emphasis.

'This is your brother the doctor, is it not?'

'Surgeon, actually—and there is a difference, quite an *important* one, as he would no doubt be quick to tell you,' Robin says, acidly. The room, even though the windows were left open all afternoon, is close and warm. Robin runs a finger around the inside of his collar; a film of sweat is making his face shine.

'It *is* too warm in here, isn't it?' Albert says. 'When the maid comes up I shall have her open the windows again.' But moments after Cat does as she is bidden, the first moths and other insects begin to invade the room, cannoning headlong towards the lights and making Amelia emit little screams of horror. Cat closes the windows again, and gazes with an expression of mild amusement at the array of winged life circling the room. 'That will be all!' Albert snaps at Cat, whose face hardens as she turns to go. Hester happens to look at Robin, and is sure she sees the merest of winks narrow his right eye as he watches Cat go; but when she looks at Cat the girl's face is averted, her

224

shoulders set.

'I recently asked my class at the Bluecoat School what they thought fairies looked like, and what they thought they did. All of them had an opinion, and they drew me some lovely pictures,' Hester says in the strained pause that follows. Robin nods, a frown still ghosting the skin of his brow.

'Pretty little girls with butterfly wings, I would guess?' he suggests, curtly.

'Yes, variations along those lines, certainly,' Hester agrees.

'I think a great many children are in fact clairvoyant, until the onset of puberty causes the mind to close off, and earthly distractions to mar the inner vision,' Robin says. 'That's why they're all so familiar with the elementals—and why stories of fairies abound in children's fables. I should very much like to come along and talk to the children in your class about what they've seen, Mrs Canning.'

'Oh, well, of course you might have, Mr Durrant, but I'm afraid the school is closed now, for the rest of the summer. I shan't be teaching again until after the harvest.'

'Oh. Pity.' Robin shrugs.

'But why should these nature spirits take on human form? Why should they assume the forms of girls at all, albeit with wings and other non-human attributes? If they are the guardians of the plants and trees—the souls of these plants, as Hester put it earlier—then surely they should look like the plants?' Amelia asks, in a tone of open scepticism. Hester feels her heart beat faster, and a prickle of unease makes her shift in her seat. She sends a silent plea to her sister for peace. Robin smiles tightly into his soup for a moment before answering.

'Why, because the elementals are able to reach into our thoughts, of course—into our very minds, and take on the forms that they find there; forms in which they can present themselves to us and be understood. Forms that they find beautiful, and which we do too.'

'They can read our minds?' Albert asks, sounding slightly appalled by the idea.

'Certainly—perhaps not in a lucid or coherent way, but to draw upon images and feelings, certainly. To pick up emotions and the vibrations of a person's inner energy, most definitely,' Robin says, gazing so intently at Amelia that she is forced to look away.

'But their behaviour is purely . . . functional, is it not?' Albert asks, as if keen to clarify things to the women.

'Indeed. They act solely within the bounds of their purpose, that is, to distribute energy to their charges. They are carrying out abstract orders from their superiors, the *devas*—a race akin to a lower order of angels.'

'A lower order of angels? Indeed?' Amelia asks, not hiding the doubt in her voice. 'And what do *they* look like?'

'I have never seen one myself. It would take a higher degree of initiation than I currently possess, though one day I hope to progress to such a level. Those who have seen them describe their enormous size, and the tremendous power of them. They have been much associated with ley lines, and the earth's own massive energy flows. I believe that it is the *devas* who lie at the core of our folkloric traditions of dragons and giants.'

226

'*Dragons?* Indeed?' Amelia casts an amused glace at her sister.

'I can assure you there is nobody more knowledgeable about these beings than Mr Durrant, Mrs Entwhistle.' Albert speaks up, defensively. Thoughts chase visibly across his face and cast troubled shadows over his eyes. Hester wishes she could reach out and take his hand, but it would not do at the table.

'Oh, I'm sure of that,' Amelia says, with an ironic tilt of her brows. Robin smiles, a narrow, thoughtful smile, as though at a private joke. Hester searches desperately for a way to lead the conversation in a different direction, but Robin speaks again before she can.

'There is plenty of evidence, in spite of the basic nature of these elementals, that they are leading lives of greater freedom and joy than all of mankind. The purpose of theosophy is to redress this imbalance; to allow mankind, in the full knowledge of his position and condition, to live more freely, less caught up with the mundane and the material,' he says, putting down his spoon and lacing his hands before him on the table. 'Geoffrey Hodson, a very great clairvoyant, has witnessed undines—water elementals—in Lancashire, sporting in the waterfalls of a fast-flowing stream. The creatures, some twelve inches in height, were hovering in the rainbows cast by the spray, absorbing the vital energy from the sun and water until it grew too great for them to contain. He saw the effort and concentration with which they gathered and held the stored energy until they were fit to burst. Then they released it in a powerful moment of climactic euphoria, their

227

colours flaring to great vibrancy, their eyes shining with expressions of extreme joy and rapture, after which they fell into a dreamy state of relaxed bliss.' Hester stares at her soup, at her spoon frozen above it in her hand. She doesn't dare look up at anybody at the table. A scorching blush floods her cheeks.

'And what are we to make of this event?' Amelia asks, frostily.

'That perhaps by the constraint of our own . . . natural rhythms . . . with social rules and conventions, we remove ourselves yet further from the elemental plane, and the divine processes of nature,' Robin says, his voice entirely innocent of any impropriety. 'The ecstasy of the undines visibly nourished the water and the plants surrounding the stream. They absorbed this gathered life force upon its release.'

'Are you suggesting that . . . humans might achieve something similar to this?' Amelia asks, though Hester inwardly implores her to desist. Robin glances from Amelia, to Albert, to Hester, who feels his gaze upon her and can't help but look up.

'I'm suggesting . . . it couldn't hurt to try,' he says. In the silence, the moths and flies buzz and bump against the glass chandelier, making the little drops twist, sending small sparks of light to bounce from the walls. Albert clears his throat.

'Another slice of bread, Mrs Entwhistle?' he says softly.

*   *   *

Cat does not sleep on Saturday night. She thinks of

the moths in the dining room, which will be sleepy and dazed or dead by the morning, clinging to the folds of the curtains and the corners of the casements. For some reason it bothers her, that they've been lured in and imprisoned on the whim of the vicar. The sister is very beautiful, with the same blue eyes as The Gentleman. Cat was taken aback when they first swept over her, first locked onto her own eyes. She expected to be scolded, or instructed. She expected to be recognised, but the blue eyes carried on, brushing lightly, carelessly over her features in the way the rich always look at servants; and she was pointlessly affronted. Long after midnight there is a loud bump from the floor below. Cat winces, her pulse speeding up. It could be one of the children, out of bed; it could be Robin Durrant, sneaking about for whatever reason. Beautiful, careless, treacherous Robin Durrant. *What does he want?* She had wanted to sleep a little. George is due back the following day, by noon. In the evening she will see him, and she had not wanted to look haggard; to look grey or flat. But sleep will not come. She is waiting, listening too intently.

Death comes to stalk her room, to offer cold company. Cat slides into an exhausted trance, and returns to her mother's deathbed: gloomy and dark behind drawn curtains, the iron smell of blood in every corner and the lurking reek of death behind that, not improved or hidden by the flowers she bought and set about the bed, or the herbs she threw on the fire. Her mother's pillow was encrusted with crimson. Each time she coughed, more bright red sputum came up. She turned her head weakly to the side, let it soak into the cotton

229

sham. They had given up trying to blot it with handkerchiefs. They did not own enough of them. She could no longer lift her head to spit into a bowl, and Cat could not lift her to do so, not every time. So many times. Consumption, the doctors pronounced, months before, with no hope or promise or hint of comfort in their voices. And it did consume her—she was a wraith by the end, sunken in on herself, robbed of speech, of strength. Her eyes dulled to grey, like her hair and her skin. One more shadow in the room. So unlike herself, so lifeless already that Cat only knew she had died because the scraping of her lungs quietened, and then stopped. There was no change in her appearance. Cat stood and watched her for a while, and was not sure what to do. That ragged wet rattle of air, as regular as her own heartbeat, had been her company for so long that the silence unnerved her. She stood, and she trembled, and she listened until the silence hurt her head. She had been twelve years old at the time.

*   *   *

At the first lightening of the sky, Cat is up, shaking off the impression insomnia gives of years having passed, of ages of man dawning and dying whilst the night has ticked slowly by. There are kinks in her spine, knots in her muscles from working all day and then lying too long in one position. When she stretches, joints pop. She arches her back like a dancer, feels the sinews burning back to life. Cat washes her face, the trickle of water into the basin as loud as thunder cracks; combs the raven feathers of her hair; dresses in silence and slips down the back stairs on the softest feet. The house is silent now, no movement of person or structure, of trapped moth or sleepless child. The air is as still and smooth as a silk blanket, softly grey. Cat lifts the latch on the back door as carefully as she can, skirts the edge of the garden until she can escape through the side gate, into the lane. The sky glows palely, a non-colour somewhere between grey and yellow and blue; the sun is not yet near the eastern horizon. With her stomach hot and empty, Cat thinks back, tries to remember when she last ate. She picks a handful of wild strawberries from the hedge, and bites each one deliberately, liking the sharp burst of juice between her teeth.

Robin Durrant has beaten her to the stile that crosses into the meadows. Cat pauses when she sees him, surprised. She had half thought he would not come, half thought nobody but she existed at this hour. But of course this is an illusion, brought on by loneliness. From the far side of the village a cow bellows, its plaintive cry echoing through the still air from where milking has already begun. Robin Durrant looks up when he hears her coming, his face indistinct in the near dark. Cat pauses, keeping her distance, and she sees the pale flash of his teeth.

'You can come closer, I won't bite you,' he says, softly.

'I have scant idea what you will or won't do. And I'll stay right here until you tell me what this is about,' Cat replies.

'Come on. Let's get away from the road a bit. I don't want anybody seeing you.'

'What does that mean? Where are we going?'

'Into the meadows. I've found the perfect spot.' He holds up his hand to help her over the stile, but Cat does not move. She sets her jaw, stares hard at him. Robin shakes his head, lowers his hand. 'Look, I swear to you that I have no intention of laying a finger on you. I give you my word.' Cat considers this a moment longer and then relents, vaulting over the stile and still ignoring his proffered hand.

'What use is the word of a charlatan?' she mutters, walking to one side where she can keep her eye upon him. He has a broad leather bag over one shoulder and his Frena camera in the other hand; he swings it nonchalantly as they go.

'A charlatan, am I? That's a strong word, Cat Morley, and not a fair one at that. What makes you call me it?'

'I know what I see. Who but a charlatan would charm the vicar, befuddle his wife, and blackmail the maid all in the same day? You're like a snake that dazzles with its beauty and grace, before it strikes,' Cat tells him.

'A snake, now, am I?' He laughs quietly.

'I know what I see,' Cat says again.

They make their way through the tall, tussocky grass, soaking their shoes with the fresh dew and kicking up insects which bumble away groggily. The dawn chorus grows louder as each second passes, flooding out across the grassland like a rising tide. In spite of everything, Cat feels herself grow calm. Impossible not to be calm, when the world seems so still, so at peace.

'I love this time of day,' Robin Durrant says, taking a deep breath and letting it out slowly. At once, Cat is on edge again.

232

'Where are we going?' she demands. It is cool, more so than she had expected. Goose pimples stand out on her skin, and she folds her arms tightly.

'It's not much further. There's a wonderful old willow tree by a kink in the river . . .'

'Yes, I know it. What of it?'

'You know it? How do you know it?'

'Can't a person go for a walk, and use their eyes? Even a servant?' Cat asks, tightly.

'Why do you fight your status so? The Cannings are an easy pair. Why aren't you happy with your lot?' Robin seems genuinely curious. Cat glares at him suspiciously.

'I hear you were a poet, for a while. A minister, a politician?' she says. Robin looks at her, frowning, and Cat smiles. 'As you told me, Mr Durrant, word gets about in a small place like this.'

'Well, what of it?'

'Would you have been content if you had been told, when you were still a child: you shan't be a poet, or a minister, or a politician. You shall be a clerk in a bank. Would you have been content, never to have been allowed to try other things? Never allowed to find out what you wanted to do, what you wanted to be?'

'A clerk in a bank? Why—'

'For the sake of argument!' Cat snaps.

'But you are working class, Cat. Such things are immutable . . .'

'Oh?' She pounces. 'And what makes them so? What makes me working class?'

'Your . . . lack of breeding and education . . . your birth, Cat. Surely you can see that?'

'Ah, there we have it. My birth. Something in my

233

blood. A servant is born, as Mrs Bell says. You agree?' she asks. Robin looks at her, puzzled, and thinks before nodding.

'I suppose so, yes.'

Cat smiles bleakly. 'Well, there is your answer, then,' she says.

They reach the willow tree after walking for ten minutes, with the village entirely out of sight behind them apart from the church spire, pointing up grey and fragile into the marbled sky. The land falls gently into a bowl, sloping down to the edge of the river, where the old tree hangs its branches, motionless; its supple twigs trail forlornly in the water, carving furrows in the glassy surface.

'We must be quite quick now,' Robin says, dropping to one knee in the wet turf and opening the leather satchel. 'I don't want the sun to come up. And it wouldn't do for the vicar to get impatient and come looking for us.' Over the river, a haze of pale mist hangs in the air, to shoulder height, shimmering and shifting as the sun's light grows brighter in the eastern sky.

'What is this, for God's sake? What game are you playing?'

'No game, Cat Morley. I simply want to take your picture,' he replies, now pulling paper-wrapped items from the bag.

'My picture? With the camera? What on earth for?'

'Yes, with the camera. I haven't time to draw your portrait myself. And besides, a drawing would not give the same . . . proof. But the camera . . . the camera cannot lie.' He glances up at her and smiles, then stands and hands her the packages.

'What is this?'

'Open them.'

Cat does as she is told. One package contains a garment of the finest white gauze, swathes of it like clouds of fleece. Cat fingers the fabric, confused; puts it over her shoulder to open the second parcel. She nearly drops it in shock. Human hair, masses of it. Long, slippery, white-blond tresses, coiled like satin ropes in her hands.

'Is this real hair? I don't understand.'

'Put them on—the dress and the wig,' Robin Durrant says, impatience creeping into his voice. He is readying the camera, unscrewing the lens cover. 'But take your dress off first. I don't want it to show through.' Cat thinks for a minute, then tips back her head and laughs. 'Quiet!' Robin hisses.

'It's a *costume*? You mean to dress me up, take my picture and tell the world I'm an elemental?' She laughs again, incredulously. Robin's face flushes angrily.

'Just do it. Put them on!' he snaps.

'You are a fraud! A phoney! You no more believe in fairies than I do!' Cat scoffs.

'I am *no phoney*!' Robin Durrant shouts, lurching to his feet and towering over Cat, anger swelling his chest and darkening his face. His declaration bounds off into the mist, and is swallowed up at once. Cat gazes up at him, unafraid.

'At last, I can see inside you,' she says, quietly.

Robin takes a deep breath. 'I am not a fraud. The elementals are real. My belief is real—in truth it is *knowledge*, not belief. Intuition, not faith. They are real. It is all real.'

'Then why must you pose a maid in a wig to catch a photo of one?'

235

'I . . . I don't know. Why I have failed. Why they will not be captured with the camera, as other beings not of the flesh have done in the past . . .'

'You truly believe in them? In fairies?' Cat eyes him intently. Robin nods. Cat studies him closely, then shakes her head. 'Astounding.'

'They will be the making of me. This . . . this *revelation* will be the making of me. It *must* be so,' he declares.

'I have never met somebody who really believed their own lies before.'

'It's not lies. And what of the vicar? You say his God is a lie, and yet he believes it.'

'That's true,' Cat concedes. 'Very well then, you are every bit as deceived as the vicar, if that makes you happy.'

'Cat, Cat.' Robin smiles. 'I am not deceived. The world, blindly going about its petty business, unaware of the grand order of things . . . it is the world who is deceived. And this picture I will take of you may well be a falsehood, of a kind, but the most pressing demand of theosophy is that its followers strive to bring it to a wider audience. Strive to convince and enlighten people who would otherwise go through their lives unaware of the great truths our adepts have learned. And I have learned that people cleave to their ignorance as if it comforts them. They will not see reason unless they are made to. I will make them see reason. I will give them no recourse to back away,' he says, with quiet zeal.

'You have lost your mind,' Cat tells him, blandly.

'No,' he says. 'I have found it. Put them on. Or I will tell them what you do, and where you go; and that will be the end to it,' he snaps, the words short and hard. 'Do it—quickly. I could ruin you, if I chose to. And don't think for a moment that I would hesitate.'

Cat falls still, her eyes hardening. 'What grace there is, in this theosophy with which you hope to enlighten me.' Her voice is bitter. Turning her back on the theosophist, she strips off her work dress and puts the gauze gown on over her shift. It is long and loose, but so light that when she moves it clings closely to her body. She leans forward as she has seen ladies in London do, and positions the wig over her own hairline. Upside down she sees a damsel fly, not an inch from her nose, clinging to the underside of a pale iris leaf—electric blue body, glittering rainbow wings vibrating, warming up for flight. *So many hidden things, such hidden beauty*, she thinks. *Such lovely things truly do exist, and yet they are never enough for us. We must always search beyond.* The wig is heavy, and threatens to pull itself off with its own weight. Only the bobby pins Cat happened to be wearing keep it in place. She straightens it, then turns to Robin Durrant. He stares.

'Well?' she demands. The long tresses hang around her face. She can feel the unfamiliar weight of them bumping against her back. Not long ago, her hair was long—although perhaps not as long as this. How quickly she has got used to it being gone, when at the time it was shorn she felt as though she had been stripped naked in a public place.

'You look quite lovely, Cat,' Robin says, softly. 'Yes. You will do very well indeed.'

'Then let's get this charade over with,' she replies. Robin watches her for a moment, and then chuckles.

'It won't work if you just stand there scowling with your arms folded, my dear girl.'

'I am not your dear girl. And how should I stand, then?'

'Do not stand at all. Dance. Over there—down by the water's edge where the mist is thickest. And take off your shoes.'

'*Dance?*'

'Dance,' Robin says, quite firmly.

Cat walks away from him, the grass cold and wet on the bare soles of her feet. The soft fabric of the dress brushes the skin of her legs lightly, makes her shiver. She has never danced. Not properly. Occasionally, The Gentleman had musical evenings, not big enough to be called balls, but with a quartet of musicians to play waltzes and quicksteps for twenty or thirty glamorous pairs; and the staff would sneak to the bottom of the stairs, or even to the doorway of the grand salon, to listen, to grab each other and make a parody of the steps that set them all to laughing. This is her sole experience of dance, and this will not do now, she knows. An elemental would not waltz with an invisible partner. She thinks of the way she felt the first time she managed to ride the vicar's bicycle all the way to George's barge. The push of the wind in her face, the way her blood ran faster through her veins; the thrill of speed and movement. She thinks of Tess, in the workhouse; of The Gentleman who did not save her. Cat draws in a shaky breath, anger making her burn.

She throws out her arms and leaps, as high as she can; arching her body and tipping back her head. She lands heavily, coarse grass stems jabbing into her feet. She pauses, takes a deep breath and

238

then runs forward, gaining more momentum and leaping again. And even though she feels ridiculous at first, feels as though the world is laughing at her, capering like an idiot, she soon forgets this. Her heart beats hard and she breathes fast, running and jumping like this, lifting up her front knee, pointing her toe behind her, holding her arms out wide or pulled back or high above her head. She kicks and storms and spins, and there is freedom in this, in the abandonment of propriety; the burn of her muscles and the rush of air into her nose and mouth. She pounds them all beneath her feet—Robin Durrant, The Gentleman, Mrs Heddingly, Hester Canning. She dances until she is out of breath, and leans against the old tree to rest, Robin Durrant and his camera all but forgotten; and then she dances some more, the same exhilaration in movement coming back to her—the possibility of life and freedom. When she falls still at last, the damsel fly circles her curiously, wings humming, flashing blue as the first rays of the sun creep into the sky. She catches her breath, and realises that she is not coughing. Does not need to cough. She smiles, until in the corner of her eye Robin Durrant stands up, slowly screwing the lens cap back onto his camera.

With a sinking feeling, Cat lets her arms fall to her sides, and the damsel fly darts away, vanishing into the widening day. She tugs the wig from her head, runs her fingers through the sweaty hair at her brow and walks towards him.

'That was simply wonderful. You looked . . . amazing. Beautiful, Cat,' Robin tells her; his voice quite different, almost deferential. Cat looks away, holding out the wig for him to take.

239

'There's no beauty in a lie,' she says, coldly. 'Can I go now?'

'Yes,' he says, meekly. 'Yes, we should get back before you're missed.'

'You have important work to do,' Cat says sarcastically, nodding at the camera.

'You must never speak of this to anyone, Cat. Not even to the man who can tempt you out in a thunderstorm. We must keep each other's secrets from now on,' he says, his tone peculiarly companionable. Cat glances at him in disgust, and walks a few steps ahead, to keep her back to him. An odd, desperate feeling gathers in her gut. She feels suddenly powerless, vulnerable. She feels that she will never quite be free of what they have just done.

8

2011

Leah drove all the way into Newbury to find a comfortable café with free wi-fi. The sky was low and sullen for the third consecutive day, and she frowned at the road as she crawled along, stopping at incessant traffic lights, hearing grey water crackling beneath her wheels. Finding a café from a chain she recognised, she collected a large hot chocolate from the counter, tucked herself into the corner of a sofa and turned on her laptop. The tips of her fingers were pink and numbed with cold. Blustery rain hurled itself at the window panes, smearing them with crystals of sleet, and the floor shone with watery footprints. The place stank of wet coats, wet hair; a pile of wet umbrellas by the door. She scanned through her inbox, finding little of interest until she got to the previous day's emails. There was a message from Ryan. Leah's heart gave an exaggerated thump. She took a deep breath, hating this reaction that any contact from him caused in her, and opened it.

What no goodbye? Most unlike you—you were always so fond of them. Thanks for taking on the little project I found you, I appreciate it. And so does our dead chum here. He's been rather sidelined since you left—bumped back into the cold store. We've had a fresh batch in from the building site of a new housing estate—I tell you, corpses are ten a penny round here. Oh well, keeps the likes of me in pin money. Let me know how you get on. I'm coming over in a couple of weeks for Dad's sixtieth. Perhaps we can meet up then to discuss what you've found? I did enjoy meeting up with you again over here. Really. Even if you did let me pay for dinner, and then didn't stay for breakfast.
Keep in touch.
Ryan

Leah read it twice, and then flicked the cursor angrily to the delete button, where her finger hovered, shaking ever so slightly. After a hung few seconds she sighed, moved the cursor away. She logged out instead, and ran a search of *Cold Ash Holt Fairy Photographs*. Various paranormal and

241

new-age sites came up in a list and, halfway down the screen, the village's community website. She opened this page, and steered away from church announcements and adverts for local workmen by clicking on the *History* tab. Two paragraphs sketched the life of the village from its meagre Domesday listing to the decline of the canal trade and the Second World War. There were black and white photographs of the church, and of long-dead farm workers leaning on their pitchforks in front of half-built hayricks. Leah stared into their eyes with the fascination she always found in old pictures of anonymous people. Eyes shrouded by shadow and blur—just pinpricks of white, or the steel grey of an iris. People who could not have known, when their likenesses were captured, that eighty years later she would be sitting in a café, getting to know their faces. Their lives, their thoughts, lost for ever. At the bottom of the page was a separate section of text, which read:

Perhaps the most unusual episode in Cold Ash Holt's history was the publication, in 1911, of a set of photographs, taken by a leading spiritualist of the time, which claimed to show fairies living in the water meadows on the edge of the village. Robin Durrant enjoyed a brief period of fame when the pictures were first published, and were widely accepted as genuine both by his fellow spiritualists and by the general press. They were later discredited, despite the unswerving support of Cold Ash Holt's vicar at that time, Albert Canning. Are there fairies in our fields? You decide!

Below were two grainy black and white photographs. The first showed a wide, level meadow, carpeted with high summer grasses and thistles, with tall trees out of focus in the background. In the middle of the picture stood a single tree, a weeping willow by the looks of it; its trunk gnarled and twisted with age, leaves pale as silver. A change in ground levels suggested that it was standing on a river bank, although the water was invisible through the grass. To the right of the tree was a small figure, slightly blurred. It was female, and appeared to have been caught in the act of leaping or dancing. Midway through a giant, exuberant stride, arms and head flung back in abandon, hair so pale it seemed white, streaming out behind it, long and wild, almost half the length of the figure's overall height. Its face was indistinct, the features not quite captured. Just the juts of a delicate nose and chin; pale, pale skin, and its eyes seemingly closed. It was hard to get a true impression of the figure's size, since the willow tree might have been fifteen feet high or thirty, the grasses a foot tall or three. It was an oddly unsettling picture. The sky was a flat white, the same colour as the figure's shapeless, diaphanous dress. The fabric clung to a thin body, flat like a child's, yet there was something adult in the angular arms and legs; the proportional size of the head to the body. The whole picture had an other-worldly, washed-out glow. As though the light had been peculiar that day, or the air unusually hazy. It was an eerie picture, and Leah stared at it until her eyes ached. The figure seemed more ghost than fairy to her.

243

In the second picture the figure was even harder to make out. The willow tree dominated the shot, much closer this time, and in its shadow the figure was a pallid smudge, body pressed tight against the trunk, arms reaching up towards its branches, head turned to the side and downwards, so again the face was lost, this time in shadow and behind tresses of its own hair, hanging like long cobwebs down past its waist. Wishing she had a printer, Leah studied the pictures for a long time, her nose creeping closer to the screen. If you wanted to believe in them, you could, she decided. They were odd, and ambiguous enough; the figure androgynous and indistinct, and yet still giving the impression of great beauty and delicacy. She knew from Mark Canning that the man who'd taken the pictures, Robin Durrant, had been staying at The Rectory at the time, as a guest of the vicar and his wife, Mark's great-grandparents. In Mark, without even really trying, she had found a direct descendant of the woman who had written letters to the dead soldier; but having access to her DNA would not help with the identification of the soldier. Those were not letters written to a family member, Leah knew instinctively. Had they been written to this Robin Durrant?

Outside, the sun came out, blisteringly bright, making her screen hard to see. Blinking in the sudden glare, Leah turned her body away from the window. She skipped through a few of the paranormal websites, where the pictures and story took second place to the better known Cottingley Fairies, famously championed by Sir Arthur Conan Doyle. On one site she found a short biography of Robin Durrant, describing him as a theosophist

244

rather than a spiritualist. Leah jotted the unfamiliar word down in her notebook. She leaned back and looked out of the window, at people marching by, squinting. The street outside was rendered black and white by the sudden harsh light; people and buildings were silhouettes, hard outlines. The same sun in a different season would soften everything, and coax out all the many colours. Now it was as sharp and unforgiving as a knife. Leah looked at her watch. Mark Canning had invited her to have a look around The Old Rectory at midday—in an hour's time. He had told her, in The Swing Bridge pub, that the fairy photographs had always been a source of mild embarrassment to his parents and grandparents, who were deeply logical people and had no time for such things. That an otherwise unimpeachable ancestor, the vicar Albert Canning, had been taken in by such blatant trickery was considered quite baffling, and tragic.

Leah thought about Mark, picturing him as she had last seen him—in the darkness outside the pub as they had said a stilted goodnight. A tiny muscle in the grey skin under his eye had been caught in a spasmodic twitch, a little hiccough visible even by the wan light of the single bulb above the door. A sure sign of exhaustion, and Leah had put her fingers to her own eye socket, pressing them into the skin in sympathetic agitation. Mark had not seemed to notice the odd gesture. She hadn't asked him anything more about himself, except in the broadest terms—to establish his relationship to Hester Canning. She had been itching to ask more, but he was so extravagantly cagey about it that she didn't want to frighten him off. His violent reaction

245

to the idea that she was a journalist and might have an interest in him had of course only served to make her more interested. With only a tiny niggle of guilt, she turned back to her computer and googled him. News articles from recent archives appeared. Not huge headlines, but the kind of story that rumbled on for weeks, getting two or three columns on page eight or nine. She skimmed through a few of the articles, her lip clamped between her teeth in fascination, eyes widening. Vaguely, she now remembered hearing a short piece on the news about the case, but it had been early in the morning when she had been staring listlessly at the TV over her breakfast, and not really listening. Small wonder he did not want to talk to a journalist. The press had given him a rough ride over the previous six months.

*   *   *

At noon she walked up the overgrown path to The Old Rectory again. Drops of rainwater on the knocker wet the palm of her hand, made her shiver and tuck her chin into her scarf. In the ruined vegetation of the garden, small splashes of colour were beginning to show. Occasional purple grape hyacinths, and pale yellow narcissi; the minty green spikes of tulip shoots, nosing their way between swathes of rotting brown foliage. Leah was reminded of *The Secret Garden*, one of her favourite books as a child. And in spite of the drifts of dead leaves that lay all around, half a foot deep in places, by summer, even if nobody paid it any attention, the garden would be a rich jungle. Plants need much less help to grow than gardeners might like to think, Leah thought. She looked to one side of the door. The wooden frame of the nearest sash window was rotten to the core. The paint was a pattern of chipped scales, the putty securing the glass all but gone; a waxy-looking orange fungus frilled the sodden wood here and there. She jumped slightly at the sound of bolts being drawn back from the door.

Mark opened it with a heave that made it shudder.

'Bloody thing always did stick in wet weather. Come in out of the rain,' he said. He'd had a shave since she last saw him, and washed his hair. He still looked worn out, but calmer than before.

'Thanks. I was just admiring the garden,' she said, smiling away any implied criticism.

Mark rolled his eyes. 'I know. The whole place has gone to seed, not just the garden. Dad really let it get away from him. I should have helped him more but . . . you know how it is. Life gets in the way. It's been empty for half a year now. Since Dad . . .' He hesitated.

'Oh, I'm so sorry—you lost him?' Leah asked, gently.

'In a way, yes. Come through.' Leah stepped into the hallway, which was wide but gloomy. She looked up. There was no light bulb in the single socket that dangled overhead. Spiders had built a cone of dusty webs around the wire. The air was incredibly still, as if one occupant was not enough for the place, could not hope to fill it. It smelled of damp plaster and cold, gritty floors; and the chill of winter seemed to linger even more than it had outside in the rain. 'I won't offer to take your coat—you'll need it,' Mark said wryly, as if reading

247

her mind.

'Old houses can get so chilly.' She grimaced sympathetically.

'Especially this one. The boiler's packed up. The kitchen's the only warm place in the house—I've managed to get the Rayburn going. Coffee?'

'Yes, please.'

They went along a corridor towards the back of the house, where the kitchen light was casting a warm glow out into the shadows. Leah peered through doorways and into corners, her curiosity irresistible. It didn't look as though the decor had been updated for twenty or even thirty years. In a sitting room, the sofas and armchairs bore deep impressions in their cushions, moulded and flattened by years of being sat upon. There was a thick layer of dust on the mish-mash of furniture, most of which was dark oak, a wood which Leah had always found oppressive. Dog-eared motoring and fishing magazines in a rack in the hallway were a decade out of date. The shades of reading lamps were faded, bleached by the sun of many summers gone by; and beneath her feet were rugs so threadbare and worn that the original patterns and colours were lost, and only the criss-cross of warp and weft remained. Glancing over his shoulder, Mark caught her quick appraisal of the place.

'Don't be too horrified. He's an old-fashioned bloke, my dad. Saw no reason to change something if it still functioned. And in the months before he moved out he was in no state to redecorate.'

'I'm not horrified,' Leah replied hurriedly. 'I'm just so curious about this place. I've read the letters your great-grandma wrote here so many times over—'

'Did you bring them with you? I'd like to read them,' he said, pulling out a stool for her at the kitchen island.

'Of course.' Leah rummaged in her bag.

'No rush. Coffee first.' He filled a battered metal kettle, plonked it on the hot plate. A coal scuttle sat next to the stove, pitch black dust twinkling on its lip. The acrid, sooty smell of it filled the room, and a fine layer of smuts speckled the sticky vinyl counter top. A long, sagging green sofa was set against the opposite wall, with a messy stack of blankets at one end, and a small television sat amidst empty cups on a low coffee table next to it. The kitchen units were as dated as the rest of the decor—a fake white marble top, with fake beechwood door fronts. Mark jimmied a drawer open, gritting his teeth in irritation. He gave up after a while, snaked his hand in up to the wrist and withdrew it with a teaspoon pinched precariously between his fingertips. 'You can see why I thought this would be a good place to hide out. It's the house that time forgot,' he said, grimly. Leah wondered whether to say anything about the newspaper articles she'd read. She stole a glance at his careworn face, and thought better of it. There was such tension behind his grey eyes; she knew she needed to tread very carefully. But it was all over, supposedly—the court case, at least. He'd been acquitted, and yet he acted as though he was still waiting for a judgement of some kind.

'It must have been a gorgeous house in its day. I mean, it still is, obviously, it's just . . .' she floundered.

'Don't worry. I know it's in a state—no offence taken. The rectory was often the grandest house in

249

small villages like this, not including the manor, of course. Back in the days when the vicar was the most important person after the land owner.'

'How is it the house stayed in your family when it stopped being the actual rectory?'

'I'm not sure. My great-grandparents must have bought it from the church at some point, I suppose.' He shrugged.

'Do you have any childhood memories of her? Of Hester Canning?'

'No, none at all. Sorry. She died before I was born. I remember my grandfather, Thomas, though—Hester's son; although he died when I was still just a boy.'

'So this house passed to your parents? Did you grow up here?'

'No, no. It passed to my uncle and aunt. My cousins lived here as children. I visited sometimes—a few Christmas holidays. The house only came to Dad when my uncle died ten years or so back.'

'Not to your cousins?'

'One died in a car accident when he was twenty-two; the other fell out with the family and moved to Australia. Not heard a word from her in fifteen years.' He put two mugs of coffee on the work top, and caught her expression. 'I know, I know. My family isn't exactly blessed with luck or harmony.' He smiled ruefully. 'Witness my own current situation,' he added, almost to himself. 'What about you? Domestic harmony or *Jeremy Kyle Show*?' he asked. Leah smiled.

'Domestic harmony, for the most part. We're very conventional. Home counties, golden retrievers, that kind of thing. My mum is in the WI;

Dad plays lawn bowls. You get the picture.'

'Sounds nice. Wholesome. Do you see a lot of them?'

'Yes. I suppose so. They never want to come up to London though—too loud for them. I always have to go home to see them.'

'What made you move to London?'

'What makes anybody? Work, friends, culture. Isn't that why you moved there?' she asked, without thinking. He stiffened, his face darkening.

'I thought you didn't know who I was or anything about me?' he demanded. Leah held up a placating hand.

'I googled you this morning. Sorry. You were so mysterious the first time we met . . .' She tried to smile but Mark's expression was thunderous.

'For good reason,' he said.

'I know. I mean . . . I understand. I'm not going to ask you about it,' she replied. He stared morosely into his coffee cup for a while, dark brows beetling, hooding his eyes.

'Thank you.'

'Here are the letters. Have a read,' Leah said, quickly passing them over.

Mark scanned the pages. 'Well,' he said, as he let the sheets of paper fall back onto the counter. 'I can see why you're interested in them. Very dramatic, aren't they? She was in a right knot about something. Living in "fear and suspicion", and "everything so strange and dark . . ."'

'I know. Nothing rings any bells, does it? Reading through them? No family gossip or legends or anything she could be referring to? Or any idea who she might have been writing to?'

'Come on, Leah—this was nearly sixty years

251

before I was born! I never even met the woman. The only family scandal I know about was the fairy thing. Not much of a scandal even—a guy manages to convince a handful of people of the existence of fairies. And then they all change their minds again,' he said, in brief summary.

'I wish she'd dated the letters. Or we had the envelopes with a dated postmark on, or something. If this theosophist guy was around a lot that year, there's a chance she could have been writing to him, I suppose. He could be the dead soldier—Robin Durrant. I need to find out more about him. Like what is a theosophist, anyway?'

'Never heard of it. Some odd branch of religion or spiritualism, clearly. A lot of people believed in a lot of strange things back then. Like God, for example.' He smiled.

'You shouldn't joke about that—you'd be amazed how sensitive people can be about it.'

'Oh, I know. Bit of a double standard, I've always thought. Anyone can come to my door and tell me the error of my ways according to their particular deity, but if I stand up and say that there is no God, people get very huffy.'

'Sounds as though you're speaking from experience?'

'My sister-in-law. Just one of the many facets of this whole bloody mess.'

'I thought you didn't want to talk about it?'

'I don't,' he said, with a quick, agitated shrug. He glanced away, out of the kitchen window, and Leah took a good look at his face. Long, straight nose, thick hair peppered with grey. He had a gaunt look, slightly starving; his spine curved into a weary slouch, shoulders fixed high and back, the bones sharp and angular beneath his faded jumper. His eyes slipped out of focus all too easily, gliding past her into the middle distance as if helplessly chasing thoughts that ran away with him. Suddenly, Leah saw how fragile he was—that he was stretched far too thin by life. She recognised the exhaustion dogging his every move—remembered it well from the long days of crisis after she'd left Ryan. It was there on the tip of her tongue: *I know how you feel.* Mark took a long breath and sighed sharply through his nose. 'Are you hungry? Do you want some lunch?' he asked.

'Sure. Thanks.'

With Mark's permission, Leah took herself on a tour of the house while he cracked eggs into a bowl and cut up mushrooms for an omelette. She climbed the wide staircase with a sense of growing excitement, a childish effervescence that made her smile to herself, made her breathe a little faster. Desiccated floorboards squealed beneath her feet, for if the ground floor was tainted with damp, upstairs the air was as dry as old bones; so dry it prickled the back of her throat, made the threat of a sneeze linger maddeningly at the top of her nose. She looked into the master bedroom, which had been Mark's father's room until relatively recently. Curtains with big sprays of fat roses, once red, now a rusty brown like dried blood. A wardrobe, dressing table and chest of drawers, all too small for the wide room. The bed had a massive mahogany headboard, and was covered in piles of dusty feather duvets and eiderdowns, pillows gone the orangey-yellow of beeswax with the sweat and grease of generations of sleeping heads. The smell of it was at once familiar, repugnant, and

253

comforting somehow. Like a favourite garment, unwashed and worn long enough to echo exactly the shape and smell of the body. A clock radio flashed 00:00 in red LED digits, giving a faint electric buzz each time the numbers lit up. There was a Teasmaid at least thirty years old; a dusty trouser press; a collection of wire coat hangers bundled on a hook behind the door. Leah stared into every corner of this sad, neglected room, finding it at once depressing and exciting. She was spying, but on a world so quiet, so out of date that it bore no resemblance to life as she knew it.

Through a doorway in one wall was the en suite bathroom: a trail of blue-grey limescale in the bath, channelling a steady drip of water from tap to plughole; a splayed and dishevelled toothbrush in a chipped yellow mug that said *Rise 'n' Shine!* in bold letters on the side; a razor furred with dried soap and traces of stubble. The carpet was dark with mildew around the sink and toilet pedestals; the lace curtains had moss growing along the hem, where the window did not shut properly and a small puddle of rain had found its way onto the sill. Leah pushed the window open slightly and peered out, over the back garden where the grass was knee-high, choppy and beige after the winter frosts. To the far left she could just see the high wall of a courtyard, and a selection of haphazard outbuildings, one of which had a gaping hole in its roof. Two fat wood pigeons huddled up to one another on the ridge tiles, their feathers fluffed against the rain.

Leah continued her tour, drifting from room to room on soft feet as if she might disturb somebody; but none of the other rooms seemed to have been occupied in years. They were full of random items of furniture and junk—one bedroom contained three commode chairs and a shop window mannequin—and crumpled cardboard boxes of books and magazines and blankets and toys and kitchen oddments. The attic bedrooms appeared to have been used as storage space for decades. Boxes and trunks stood in lopsided piles in all three of them. Leah picked her way to one of the dormer windows and peered out at the view. On the window sill, a dusty old fruit box held a stack of pictures in frames, most of which had lost their glass. Leah brushed some mummified flies aside, and flicked through them. Bleached watercolours; a small print of Charles I; another of kittens playing with wool; an embroidery sampler, the motto so faded she could hardly read it, with a small striped cat arching its back amidst flowers in one corner; a sepia picture of the house, with the caption *Cold Ash Holt Rectory, 1928* typed neatly along the bottom. Leah drew this photo out, and took it down to show Mark.

The downstairs was better furnished, and better equipped, but it all had an air of long neglect that made Leah slightly sad—gave her a feeling of nostalgia, as though she herself missed the people who had once lived here as much as the house itself appeared to. A door that seemed to go down into the cellars was locked, and Leah left off rattling the handle with a tug of regret. She went back to the kitchen, where Mark had turned on a tinny radio and the lunch-time news was filling the room. His back was to her, at the stove, gently frying the omelette with a meditative air. Leah slid onto her stool, and he looked around as her knee knocked the counter.

'I don't suppose you know the property features writer? I suppose the place should go on the market. For a while I'd hoped Dad might come back to it, but he's not going to. The sooner we all accept that, the better,' he said absently, as if she'd never left the room.

'The property features writer? Like I said, I don't work for a paper. I'm freelance,' Leah reminded him carefully. His moods seemed to chase across him like clouds on a windy day, and they consumed him. Even now, with his back to her, tension seemed to radiate from him. Leah shuffled Hester Canning's letters and put the old photo of the house to one side, at a loss for something to say.

'What's wrong with your father? Is he ill?' she asked, before she could stop herself. Mark glanced at her again, as if trying to read her face, to judge her worth. A heartbeat later his eyes softened, and his face fell into the tired lines she was becoming familiar with.

'He's in a care home. For the elderly.' Leah studied him, trying to guess his age and therefore how old his father might be. Mark caught her scrutiny and smiled a tiny, bitter smile. 'He's seventy years old, in case you're wondering. But he has early-onset dementia.'

'Oh. I'm . . . really sorry to hear that.'

'It's wretched. It's a wretched, awful thing to happen to a good, kind man; and it's completely unfair. Which is how life is, I suppose. The last time I went to see him, he didn't recognise me at all,' Mark said, in a monotone, as he came over to the island with the frying pan and served the omelette onto two plates.

'Thank you,' Leah murmured.

'Don't mention it.' He sat down opposite her and started to shovel the eggs into his mouth as if she wasn't even there, his gaze far away again, jaw working mechanically. Leah picked up her fork and began to eat slowly. He'd scorched the bottom of the omelette, and the mushrooms hadn't cooked through, sitting hard and dry inside the folds of egg. She picked at it politely, trying to keep a smile from her lips as she watched Mark chew and chew at his raw mushrooms, his attention finally returning to the room, and to her. 'This is bloody awful,' he said at last, and Leah smiled ruefully, nodding her head. 'Come on, let's go to the pub.'

*   *   *

After a better lunch of sandwiches and beer, they walked out into the water meadows. The rain had cleared and left the sky china blue, with fat white clouds bowling above their heads as they made their way along a footpath that ran beside a lake, away from the canal. The ground squelched beneath their boots, the turf seeming to bounce as if floating on liquid.

'These lakes probably weren't here when Hester wrote the letters, and the fairy pictures were taken,' Mark told her, marching along with his hands thrust into his pockets.

'How come?'

'They're flooded gravel pits, for the most part. There are still some gravel works around here, even today. It was big business at one point.' He sniffed—the cold breeze was making both their noses run, and had brought a flush of colour to his cheeks, a shine to his eyes that made him look more alive.

'I suppose it would have been more open, too—less footpaths and fields and more common land and water meadow?' she asked. Mark shrugged.

'Yes, I'd have thought so. Here's a bit of the river. It weaves in and out of the canal all the way along here—between Newbury and Reading. Sometimes the river and the canal are the same thing, sometimes they're separate. And all the way along there are these little streams and tributaries and lakes.'

'I suppose the chances of the tree in the picture still being there are . . .'

'Slim to nil, I'd say. It looks like an old tree in the photos, and if it was old a hundred years ago . . . well, even if it wasn't chopped down to make way for something, it would have come down of its own accord,' Mark said. He stopped to consult the photos again. In the study at his father's house, they had found an original copy of a pamphlet written by his great-grandfather, Albert Canning, about the pictures and the circumstances of their production. In it were the two pictures Leah had seen online, and a couple more besides, in which the thin figure was less distinct. 'Well, there are rows of tall trees like that here and there all along the canal and the river braids.' He glanced up at her and shrugged one shoulder. 'We'll never know if we're looking at the exact ones, but those over there are as like them as any, and there's a hollow in front of this bit of the river, just like in the picture. It's as good a guess as any,' he said, handing Leah the pamphlet and gazing around at the landscape.

Leah studied the picture hard again and then looked up. Mark was right—the landscape was as similar to the picture as any they had seen that morning. The sun seemed preternaturally bright after so many wet days, and she shielded her eyes with the pamphlet. The stream by their feet was quick and clear, cutting through the cropped turf with keen efficiency as it hurried by. On its bottom were brown and orange pebbles, chips of grey and white flint and knots of green weed that streamed with the current. The short grass was peppered with pellets of sheep and rabbit shit, and the hedgerow beyond was pocked with burrows and rodent diggings. Suddenly it was spring, as though all it took was the sun to shine for Leah to see it. Dandelions with fat yellow manes; the little white daisies of childhood; tiny purple blooms with hairy leaves that she did not recognise. She crouched and picked up a stick from the ground, throwing it into the stream and watching it whisk away. On the other bank, a startled pheasant bolted away from them, legs pedalling comically. Leah smiled and took a deep breath. The breeze was damp and cool, and tasted of earthy minerals, soft rainwater; but the sun on the top of her head had warmth—a wonderful glow of heat she hadn't felt since the September before. She tried to imagine the eerie light of the photograph, settled over the bright scene in front of her. Had the photographer used a filter of some kind? It didn't appear to be misty, exactly, but there was some kind of unfamiliar, pallid glow, softening all the outlines just slightly, just enough to allow doubt to creep in. Doubt, or belief. Leah took another deep breath, all the way to the bottom of her lungs.

'God! It's nice to see a blue sky, isn't it?' she exclaimed, standing up again and wiping her hands on the seat of her jeans. She turned to Mark and found him watching her with an odd, wide-eyed intensity. 'What's wrong?'

'Nothing,' he replied. He shook his head and the look was gone, the old troubled scowl back in its place. 'I used to come here and play with my cousins as a kid. In summer we used to swim—not right here, a bit further along where there's a big bend in the river and the water is slower. It was freezing.' He shuddered at the thought. 'Bone-achingly cold, every time. But I had to go in, of course. Couldn't be the one left out.' Leah put her hands in her back pockets and turned in a circle, surveying their surroundings. 'What do you want to do now?' Mark asked. He sounded genuinely interested, and slightly resigned; as if entirely at her disposal. She looked across at him, squinting in the sunshine, and realised that he didn't have anything else to do. Small wonder, then, that he was such a prisoner to his moods and memories.

'I don't know,' she confessed. After all, she admitted to herself, the fairy pictures might have nothing at all to do with what Hester Canning had been writing about. 'Let's walk on a bit—make the most of the fact that it's not pouring down. Then I wouldn't mind having a better look through the books in the study, if you don't mind? There might be something in there about theosophy, or this Robin Durrant guy.'

'Sure.' Mark nodded. 'The footpath carries on to the corner of the field there.' He turned towards it, the hems of his jeans dark and sodden with water from the long grass. He stopped when he got to the muddy path, watched her clambering towards him, waiting for her to reach his side before leading her on, like a taciturn tour guide.

*   *   *

Later, Leah returned to the study at The Old Rectory and began to search the shelves. She found old books on theosophy, their spines chipped and faded, papery shreds hanging from the covers; another slim volume about fairy photography; and precious little else that related to the incident at all. Vast rows of *Reader's Digest* condensed works; a huge set of encyclopaedias; novels by the ton, most of them dated historical romances, the heroines on the covers invariably clad in a low-cut bodice, bosoms heaving. Leah rummaged and leafed and felt as though she was achieving something, although she suspected that she probably wasn't. She resisted the urge to go through the drawers of Mark's father's desk, a vast leather-topped affair that crouched like some sleeping beast in the shadow of the mezzanine gallery; but the papers left on top, when she nudged them lightly with her fingertips, were bank statements and utility bills; torn-off calendar pages from two years before; and lists of crossed-out items, scribbled so comprehensively that all the words were lost.

Mark brought her a mug of tea as the sun began to set. He flicked on the lights as he came in, making her flinch. She hadn't noticed the gathering gloom, pooling like water in the corners of the room.

'Thanks,' she said, as he put the mug carefully on a stack of old newspapers beside the tub chair she was sitting in. The leather was worn through on the arms, and she had been running her fingers over the exposed stuffing as she read, picking absently at its gritty innards. A scattering of crumbs lay across her knees and on the floor at her feet. 'God! Sorry! I didn't even know I was doing it!' she exclaimed, brushing hastily at the evidence. Mark smiled briefly.

'Don't worry about it, really.' He looked around the study, from the dusty swags of the curtains to the cluttered shelves. 'Sometimes it takes an outsider to make you see what's staring you in the face,' he said, half to himself. 'The whole place is crumbling like that bloody chair. It all needs to go. The lot.'

'But . . . this house has been in your family for generations . . .' Leah said, gently. 'Aren't some things worth keeping?'

'I don't think I could ever be happy here. And I'm the only one left. Well—my nieces and nephew, my sister-in-law. But I don't think she'd come here. I don't think she'd bring them. At least, not while I'm alive,' he said, darkly. Uncomfortably, Leah flicked the last of the stuffing from her jeans.

'But your father's still alive, isn't he? And it's his house. *Could* you do anything, even if you decided to?'

'Yes. I have power of attorney.'

'Oh,' Leah said. She sipped at her tea, unfolded her legs from beneath her. She had been sitting too long that way, and pins and needles blazed down into her calves and feet like wildfire, like a million

262

biting ants. Unable to stop herself, she drummed her feet on the floor like a child to get the blood moving.

Mark glanced up, gave her a bemused look. 'Stand up and jump up and down,' he instructed. 'It's the only way.' With a grimace, Leah obeyed him. Hopping with her two feet together, up and down the stringy carpet of the study in her socks, with the floorboards wobbling underneath her feet and the dim light bulbs buzzing overhead. When she stopped she was grinning at her own idiocy, and Mark was smiling stiffly, as if his face was unused to the shape. 'Better?' he asked, and she nodded. 'What do you want to do now?' he asked, for the second time that day. Leah stopped smiling, and looked him carefully in the eye.

'Can I meet your father?'

*   *   *

The care home was a crisp, modern, brown-brick building, clad in Virginia creeper and surrounded by neatly kept gardens; windows shining clean, cars parked in neat rows. It was two days since Leah had asked Mark's permission to visit. He parked his car—a mud-spattered Renault—on the pristine tarmac drive, and a look of grim anxiety covered his face, making Leah nervous. He turned off the engine and they sat in silence for a moment, listening to the hot metal tick.

'So, did you find out anything more? About theosophy and this Durrell person?' Mark asked, at length, as if they had come out in the car for a chat, and no other reason.

'Durrant. No. I think he was a bit of a flash in

the pan—there's no information about him in any of the books or pamphlets after 1911, the year he took those pictures at Cold Ash Holt. I couldn't find anything online either. I suppose if he was discredited, he might just have slunk off back into obscurity. It's like he just disappeared, after that summer,' she said. 'Perhaps off to the war, but that wasn't for another three years; and it also seems an unlikely thing for a theosophist to do. From what I've read, he'd almost certainly have been a conscientious objector. All life was sacred to them. But perhaps he stopped being a theosophist after that year. However—you can ask me *anything* about theosophy. I'm a pocket expert now. Eastern philosophy meets Western spiritualism, the many levels of the spirit world, the many orders of spiritual being, and spiritual awareness. Reincarnation. Asceticism. Karma. Clairvoyance. Inner vision . . . Ask me *anything*.' She smiled, counting them off on her fingers. Mark's hands still gripped the steering wheel, and he looked sideways at her, his face pinched and heavy.

'Are you ready to go in?' he asked. Leah's smile faded.

'Are you?' she said. Mark nodded, unclipped his seatbelt.

'Just . . . don't expect too much, OK?' he warned her.

They were greeted at the reception desk by a smiling young nurse with soft red hair, who took their names and gave them visitors' badges to clip to their clothes. Inside, the building was bright and overheated, and Leah pulled at the funnel neck of her jumper, which was suddenly too tight and stifling against her skin.

'You picked a good time. We're definitely having a *good* day, today,' the nurse chirped, passing them a register to sign. Leah wondered if she was referring to the day in general, or Mark's father in particular.

'Good. That's good,' Mark said. When he didn't move, the nurse gestured along the corridor to the left of the desk.

'Room eleven, you remember?' she said. 'You can make a hot drink in the common room, if you like.'

'Thanks,' Leah said, and turned towards the corridor. A heartbeat later, Mark followed her, never quite catching her up, so that Leah walked two steps ahead, counting up the room numbers with mounting unease. The smell of the place was strong and pervasive. The slightly greasy, fusty smell of people and worn clothes, some harsh artificial air freshener, and underneath it all the nauseating tang of ammonia and bleach. Leah took shallow, cautious breaths, just like when Ryan had shown her the body of the dead soldier.

Geoffrey Canning was sitting in an armchair by the window in a small room that overlooked the front gardens and the driveway along which Leah and Mark had recently driven. The carpet was green, synthetic, and very hard. The furniture looked brand new—pale beech veneers, flimsy looking, the chairs padded with more hard fabric. The window was shaded by vertical blinds, turned to their most open position. Geoffrey himself was a strong-looking man. Even sitting down, Leah could tell from the length of his back and legs that he was tall. There was none of the stoop of old age about him. He looked fit, and strong; as though he might

265

get up to greet them with a hearty handshake, hearing Mark's diffident knock at the door. He did not. He kept his face turned to the window, his hair smooth to the side of his head, thick and silvery.

'Dad?' Mark said, hovering uneasily just inside the door. Leah crowded behind him, trying to smile. Geoff looked over at them briefly, his face registering nothing. Mark gritted his teeth and Leah saw stress knotting every joint in his body. She gave him a soft bump with her arm, which made him glance at her, and then cross the room to his father.

'Dad? How are you? It's me, Mark.' He bent forwards in front of Geoff's chair and patted one of the broad, wrinkled hands that gripped the arms. Geoff made a slight harrumphing sound.

'There you are! Where did you get to? You were gone for over an hour,' Mark's father said, quite calmly.

'Uh—sorry, Dad. I had to . . . pop out for a bit.'

'Well, well. Not to worry. I told them you wouldn't be long,' Geoff said, with a slight smile. 'Pull up a chair, son, don't stand about. Your mother'll be along in a minute with the tea.' Leah saw this remark visibly strike Mark. She gripped his arm briefly in support, then fetched two hard plastic chairs, like school chairs, from the other side of the bed. The soles of her shoes were scuffing static from the carpet, and when she touched the chairs tiny sparks flew, stinging her fingers.

'Thanks,' Mark murmured to her. Geoff had gone back to staring out of the window, nodding his head slightly as if agreeing with some general point that had been made. Again Mark had to touch his father's hand to get his attention. 'Dad? This is Leah Hickson, a friend of mine,' he introduced her. Leah smiled, murmured 'hello', but Geoff did not look at her. It seemed so odd, and uncomfortable, to be rebuffed in this way, even though she knew he was not to blame. He had the same grey eyes that had passed to his son, and they drifted from one side of the gardens to the other, without blinking, as if searching for something. The same raw cheekbones as Mark, the same lean look and straight nose. Mark had a smaller frame than his father, was shorter and not as broad, but the resemblance was still strong.

'You look just like him!' she said quietly to Mark, who nodded sadly.

'No, indeed! I take after my mother's side. Everybody has always said so. These are *Giddons* hands!' Geoff told her, speaking so suddenly that they both jumped. He put his hands up, fingers spread, in front of Leah's face and held them there long enough for the muscles in his arms to protest, and a slight tremor to stumble along them from shoulder to fingertip.

'That's right, Dad,' Mark said, gently guiding the old man's hands back into his lap. Geoff looked crestfallen and bewildered, as if he couldn't remember why he'd raised them in the first place.

'I don't know why you keep calling me that,' he muttered, plaintively. Mark cast a bleak look at Leah.

'Shall I make us some tea?' she asked brightly, getting up when nobody answered her and slipping from the room. In the common room at the end of the corridor, she filled three mugs with hot water from a steaming urn, dropped three tea bags into them and put them on a plastic tray with a small steel jug of milk.

'Are you from the club?' an old lady asked her, appearing behind her so quietly that Leah jumped. She was tiny, bird-like, and so papery thin that it hardly seemed plausible that she should be standing unaided. Wisps of white hair stood out around her wrinkled scalp, as fine as a dandelion clock. *A blonde, at one point*, Leah guessed.

'No, I'm not.' Leah smiled, awkwardly. The woman's face fell, as if this was a terrible disappointment.

'Well, when are they coming? I was told Tuesday, that's what I was told. It'll be too late, if they don't come soon . . .' she quavered, anxiously.

'I'm sorry . . . um . . . I don't know when they're coming,' Leah told her. 'I'm sure it'll be soon.' The old woman said nothing more, but still stood, looking up at her with such great expectation that Leah gathered up the tea tray clumsily and walked away, feeling a terrible, ill-defined guilt. The place was like a doorway, a crossing-over point into a myriad other worlds, she thought. A place where time and meaning shifted from person to person, and the worlds in which they lived, real, past or imagined, converged.

Back in room eleven, Leah dunked the tea bags, squeezed each one and lifted them out. As she busied herself with the task, Mark asked his father a few more questions, about his health, and how he was being treated. He got few replies, and most of them non-sequiturs.

'I've been to see your lovely house, Mr Canning. The Old Rectory,' Leah said, as she put two mugs of tea in front of the men. 'I love old buildings. It

268

must be wonderful to live somewhere with so much history.'

'My grandparents bought it from the church, you know. After the war. He was a man of the cloth, you see,' Geoff told her, as clearly and lucidly as if they had been chatting about it all morning.

'That's right. The Reverend Albert Canning,' Leah encouraged him, but Geoff harrumphed again, fumbled with the handle of his mug as if his finger wouldn't fit through, though this was not the case.

'Make sure the children aren't playing near the well, won't you?' he said, raising a warning finger towards her.

'Yes, I will,' Leah said, carefully. Geoff nodded, satisfied. 'Do you remember your grandparents, Mr Canning? I was hoping to ask you a bit about them, actually. About your grandmother in particular—Hester Canning? I've found some letters that she wrote . . .'

'I'm not deaf, you know.' Geoffrey sounded mildly offended. Leah checked herself. She had been speaking loudly, hoping to get through.

'Sorry,' she apologised, glancing at Mark. He shrugged; smiled a quick, wintry smile. Leah waited for a while, but Geoffrey had gone back to his sweeping survey of the garden.

'Never play near the well. The ghost of a boy lived in it, you know. A little dead boy,' the old man muttered, his voice growing thin and brittle.

'Which boy, Mr Canning?' Leah asked, trying to join up his disjointed remarks.

'Who are you, miss?' Geoffrey asked her, looking at her again with that sudden,

269

disconcerting speed.

'I . . . I'm Leah . . .' she started to say, but Geoffrey turned to his son, gave his knee a conspiratorial nudge with one hand.

'Blondes have more fun, eh?' he said, with a mischievous smile.

'So I hear,' Mark agreed, raising one eyebrow at Leah. She took a deep breath, uncertain of how to proceed. Geoffrey's thoughts seemed to jump about and twitch like nervous sparrows, taking flight, scattering in a heartbeat.

Outside it had clouded over—puffy, mottled, grey and white clouds, fat with unshed rain. The light in the room went ashen, leaching the colour from their faces and from the bright, functional furniture. Mark burst to his feet, quickly switching on the overhead lights as if he couldn't bear it.

'Mr Canning? Can you tell me anything about your grandparents? Anything at all?'

'You're wasting your time,' Mark told her flatly, as he came back to his chair. He crossed his legs, picked at the seam of his jeans with one thumbnail.

'Or anything about a family scandal? Something that happened, before you were born?' she pressed.

'Leah . . .' Mark protested, wearily.

Geoffrey Canning turned to look at her, a pleasant, uncomprehending smile on his face, eyes slightly worried, as if he knew he had forgotten something important. Leah smiled reassuringly, and squeezed his hand.

'John Profumo. That was the scandal of the day, my word! Yes. Lovely girl—what a cracker she was!' he told them. 'And the other one—the blonde.' Geoffrey nodded sagely. Mark shook his head incredulously.

'Of all the things he would remember! He always did have a crush on Christine Keeler.'

'I guess the chances of him remembering any family gossip he'd heard are pretty slim,' Leah said, somewhat deflated.

'The memories are there, it's just . . .' Mark twisted his hand in the air between them. 'Getting to them. They're all knotted up. The pathways between memories and thoughts don't work the way they should any more. It's all disconnected . . .'

'He may not even know anything about the fairy photos. It wasn't much of a scandal, after all. It was probably forgotten about a couple of years afterwards . . .' Leah sighed.

'Fairy photographs? That wasn't the thing, Mandy! No indeed. There were *big* secrets, things we weren't allowed to talk about. Whenever I asked I was told "fairy photographs", but that wasn't it. I *heard* them talking. That wasn't the big scandal in our house, oh no,' Geoff told her, shaking his head adamantly. Leah's heart beat faster, she gripped his hand tighter and he smiled delightedly.

'What was the big secret, Mr Canning?' she asked, intently. Geoffrey leant towards her, relishing the drama.

'*Murder!*' he whispered loudly, eyes as wide as a child's. 'Bloody *murder!*'

A shiver slipped between Leah's shoulder blades. There was something in the way Geoffrey Canning's eyes lit up, something in the way he whispered it, as though mimicking exactly how he'd first heard it. She was suddenly sure it was a real memory; that it had happened, and that this crime was what had haunted Hester Canning

271

so. *Murder!*

9

1911

'These are . . . simply marvellous. Marvellous. Truly, the most *wonderful* pictures,' Albert breathes, leaning forwards over the table top and putting his face close to the photos, as if unwilling to defile them with his touch. Robin Durrant smiles, his face alight, jubilant with triumph. He seems unable to speak, and instead puts out one hand to grip the vicar's shoulder. Albert reaches up with his own hand and covers the theosophist's, grasping the other man's fingers tightly. For some reason, the ardour in that touch distracts Hester from the pictures, and she moves closer to her husband, putting her own hand gently upon his other shoulder. There they stand, Hester and Robin, either side of the vicar as he sits at his desk with the pictures Robin had taken that very morning arrayed before them, still reeking slightly of the developing chemicals. After a pause, Robin gently removes his hand from Albert's, but the vicar does not reach up to take Hester's hand instead. She fights the urge to pinch him, to lean her weight, make herself felt.

Instead she reaches forward and picks up one of the prints. 'Careful, Hetty,' Albert cautions her. 'They are easily damaged by fingerprints and the like.'

'I shan't damage them, dear,' Hester tells him. She examines the photo as closely as she can focus her eyes. The odd, androgynous form, swathed in diaphanous white and with copious hair flying out behind it. In most of the shots it is just a blur, features impossible to make out, form lost in the swirls of fabric. But in two or three, a human-like figure is clear to see, leaping with its thin limbs cast out wide. 'And is this like the ones you saw, Bertie? The ones you described to me?'

'Yes,' Albert says, although he does not sound entirely sure. 'Though, this one seems to be better formed, and rather taller . . .'

'That is only to be expected,' Robin says, swiftly. 'I expect, from your descriptions, Albert, that what you saw were some slightly lesser beings than this—perhaps elementals allied to some wild flower or meadow herb. I have seen just such beings myself in the meadows here, and they are indeed smaller and of a less sophisticated form. This, I believe to be the guardian of the old willow tree.'

'A dryad?' asks Albert.

'As it would have been called, in ancient times, yes. Like the tree it nourishes, this elemental being is a larger and more sophisticated entity. I did endeavour to engage it in a dialogue, but it was wary of me, and perhaps wisely so, though I did my utmost to emanate waves of love and welcome towards it.'

'Perhaps that was rude,' Hester says, before she can catch herself. Robin glances at her. 'Well, I mean . . . if it has lived with this tree in the meadow for many long years, perhaps you, as the visitor, ought not to have bade it welcome to its own

273

home,' she explains. Robin smiles slightly.

'Really, Hetty. Don't be so obtuse. Robin means only to speak in general of his emotional vibrations. There is no social etiquette to be observed here,' Albert says.

'Well,' Hester says, taken aback. 'I'm sure I didn't meant to imply—'

'No, it's quite all right, Mrs Canning. I understand what you meant. One must of course tread carefully with something as pure and reactive as these beings,' Robin says, benignly.

'Look—look at this one. The face is almost discernible. And lovely—quite, quite lovely . . .' Albert holds a particular photo up to the theosophist, who takes it and studies it closely, his eyes lost in thought.

'Lovely indeed,' he murmurs.

'Robin—we must publish these at once! The whole world must see them! I shall call the papers myself—is there a particular one you should like to have the pictures first? Can copies be made?'

'Of course, of course. We shall do just as you say, Albert,' Robin soothes the trembling vicar.

'Well, gentlemen, I shall leave you to your . . . great work. Amy must have got the children dressed by now, and we have promised them a trip into Thatcham to buy sweets,' Hester says brightly, but if she hopes to cause a stir with her departure, she is disappointed.

*   *   *

'I'm not sure what to make of it,' Hester confesses to her sister, as they walk slowly along The Broadway in Thatcham, parasols on their shoulders with the sun beating down on them, almost like a physical weight. Ellie and John lag behind them, squabbling over a bag of liquorice twists. The town is quiet and stifled. From the smithy, the clank of hammer on metal is slow and irregular, as if, however used to the heat he might be, even Jack Morton's arm is too heavy that day. Those people of Thatcham that are about walk slowly, their faces screwed up against the onslaught. Fat flies buzz around their heads with aggravating tenacity.

'Come on, children. Let's go down to the river and see the ducks,' Amelia calls over her shoulder, her voice brittle with impatience. 'These photographs of his, you mean? I'm not surprised you don't. I shall have to see them myself before I pass comment, of course, but . . .' She shrugs.

'But? You suspect them to be . . . not genuine?'

'How can they be? I'm sorry, Hetty, but it's just too much. *Fairies*. Really! And you say he was quite alone when he took the pictures, and when he developed them?'

'Oh, yes. Albert doesn't go with him into the meadows any more, and nobody is allowed into the cold store. His dark room, that is.' Hester steps carefully over the butcher's brindle-haired dog, fagged out flat on its side in the middle of the pavement. It twitches an eyelid as her skirt tickles it.

'Well, there you are then! He's had ample opportunity to doctor the images . . . I can't see how he will hope to convince anyone if he has produced them in such secrecy,' Amelia declares.

'Well, they do seem . . . that is, it does look like a real . . . person—figure, that is. It's just that . . . it's

275

so blurred it's hard to tell if it is a fairy or just a . . . woman,' Hester says, hesitantly. 'But it can't be a person. Who could it be? Nobody would partake willingly in such a deception. Nobody from the village has hair so long and fair, nor would be out in the meadows before sunrise. No. There is some other explanation . . . Perhaps it *is* real,' she concedes. 'Albert certainly believes it.'

'Yes. It's clear that Albert is rather . . . caught up in it all.'

'Oh, yes. He is quite convinced by whatever Robin says,' Hester agrees, not trying to keep her unhappiness from sounding.

'Remarkable, how quickly they have become so close.'

'Indeed. So very close. Sometimes . . . sometimes I catch Mr Durrant watching me with a most peculiar expression on his face, and I wonder . . .'

'What, Hetty?'

'I wonder if he knows things about me that I would rather he did not.'

'You mean, that Albert may have been indiscreet? About your . . . marital affairs?'

'Perhaps, as I confide in you, Albert has . . . confided in Robin,' she says, hesitantly. Amelia takes a short breath and considers this for a moment.

'That speech he gave last night, about the undines in their ecstasy . . . do you suppose he was referring to . . . ?' she suggests.

'You would know better than I if that was what he was referring to,' Hester says, miserably.

'I thought he merely meant to cause a stir! Rascal of a man!' Amelia's voice is low and

276

scandalised. 'Well, that only confirms to me something I suspected from the very start, dear sister.'

'What did you suspect?'

'That Mr Durrant is not what he seems to be. Be careful, my dear. Do not let him get the better of you, and . . . try to distance yourself from this whole fairy business.'

'How can I distance myself when my husband is so very involved?' Hester asks. Amelia is silent, and appears deep in thought for some minutes.

'It is a difficult situation, I do see. I think the best thing will be to speak of it little beyond the walls of The Rectory; to try to encourage scepticism in Albert, if it is at all possible; and to hope that the whole affair blows over quickly. A madness of this hot weather, and nothing more,' she says at last.

'Scepticism? Albert is busy writing a pamphlet about it all! They mean to go to the press, and publish the pictures . . . Surely that must mean that Robin is genuine? That he does not mean to dissemble? Surely he would not risk exposing himself in this way otherwise?'

'But what has he to lose, Hetty? He is an unknown, who seeks to be known . . . whereas Albert has a reputation, an important role of long standing in the church and in society . . . He lends respectability to the project, but if there were to be a scandal . . .' Amelia says seriously.

'Then Albert would suffer more damage from it than Mr Durrant?'

'Indeed he would, dearest.'

'But . . . what can I *do*?' Hester cries, fear making her tearful. Amelia takes both of her hands

277

and squeezes them.

'Don't look so frightened! It will more than likely come to nothing at all! And perhaps it could be a good thing for them to publish the pictures— if they cause a stir, Mr Durrant may well take himself off on a tour with them, or some such. It may hasten his departure from The Rectory.'

'Oh, do you think so?' Hester says, hopefully.

'You must hope so; and wait to see,' says Amelia, and though she smiles at her sister, her eyes are grave.

*   *   *

At the river, Thatcham's children are sporting in the greenish water, leaping from the bridge with whoops of delight, paddling haphazardly from bank to bank, where the grass is being trampled muddy. Ellie and John watch them with envy and rage, knowing better than to even ask their mother if they can join in. They stare, and chew their liquorice glumly, running blackened tongues over greyish lips. The air is cooler by the river, where tall horse chestnut trees shade it and the water soothes it. The two sisters walk very slowly and find a bench to sit upon. No ducks to feed, not with the racket the children are making.

'I do wish you didn't have to go back to town tomorrow, Amy,' Hester says softly.

'So do I, darling. But . . . we must. I have much to talk to my husband about.'

'What will you tell him?'

'Just what I told you. That if he continues, I will love him no more. Perhaps that will not bother him.' She shrugs sadly. 'Perhaps it will. But what else can I do?'

'What can any woman do?' Hester agrees. She thinks of Cat, and smiles. 'My maid, Cat, would tell us off for such defeatism. She went to jail to earn us the vote, after all.'

'Was that what it was all about? How ridiculous. They do more damage than good, those foolish vandals.'

'Indeed,' Hester murmurs. 'And have you any more words of advice for me? Regarding my . . . marriage bed?' she asks, and though she tries to make her tone light, the words come out with a quaver that sounds fragile, at breaking point. Amelia squeezes her hands again.

'Only this. If you are lying close to him, smiling and asking to be taken into his arms, then your part is done, dearest. Anything that is lacking is lacking in Albert, not in you. So I cannot help you, because you are not the problem,' she says.

'Yes. That is what I have come to fear.'

*   *   *

'So, I suppose this will take Mr Durrant to pastures new,' Hester says to Albert, lying on the cool sheet with the blankets cast off, in the sudden darkness of the bedroom after the lamps have been extinguished. The window is still open, to freshen the air, and the distant sound of a dog barking echoes in from the village. She turns onto her side, facing Albert, as she always does in bed, and can trace the shape of his face in the pale glow of the starry night sky. His eyes are open and shine softly. He does not reply for quite some time, and when he does his voice is tight with anguish.

279

'I truly hope not. Perhaps, for a while at least. He means to go up to London with them, to the headquarters of the Society. But afterwards . . . I pray he will return to us. To the elementals of our meadows.'

'You wish him to return?' she asks, already knowing the answer.

'Yes, of course. He is teaching me so much . . . I feel that my mind has been opened, in these weeks since he came to me. The world is quite a different place.'

'Yes, he has been full of . . . instruction,' she says.

'I don't know what I would do if he didn't come back again. I don't know . . . how I would continue,' Albert whispers, in a distracted way, as though to himself.

'Come now, Bertie—you will always have me, even if house guests come and go,' she says robustly, putting out her hand to stroke his arm reassuringly. 'Won't you?'

'Yes, of course, Hetty,' Albert says, not sounding in the least bit comforted.

'He can't stay with us for ever, after all. For one thing, we couldn't afford to keep him,' she says, pointedly.

'But can't you see, Hetty? He's *right*. Everything he's told us, since he arrived—and I saw you take some of it with a pinch of salt—no, don't deny it. I know you too well, dear Hetty—all of it was *true*. And now he has the means to prove it to the world . . . do you understand *how important* this is, Hester? How important what has occurred here this summer is?'

'Yes,' Hester whispers, and feels close to tears

280

because she does not feel it in her heart. She cannot feel the truth of it, nor share her husband's conviction. The pictures show her a pretty figure, a thin figure, a barefooted dancer in a water meadow. Try as she might, she cannot see a fairy. And she does not want Robin Durrant back. She wants Albert back—wants him to belong to her again, if not in body then in spirit. She watches him for as long as she can, but while her own eyes grow heavy and her eyelids droop, his stay wide open, gleaming with the light of the heavens in them.

*   *   *

For the first time since she mastered the bicycle, Cat walks the distance to Thatcham. After days without George, she is so eager to see him that it feels almost like fear, makes the tips of her fingers shake and her thoughts buzz inside her skull like trapped insects. It is a mauve and indigo night, the landscape quite visible and full of noisy life— scrabbling movement in the bulrushes, the whirr and clatter of cricket wings, the harsh cries of startled river birds. Fatigue makes her head feel light. She has not slept for a day and a night and a day; has eaten little; has thought of Tess and George and Robin Durrant so much and so intensely that they have blurred in her mind's eye, spiralling queasily into one another. Her dance in the water meadow could have happened a week ago, or a year, or ten years. Time is behaving oddly. Mrs Bell caught her earlier, up to her elbows in the scrub bucket, clutching a chemise when the water had long since gone cold. When she took her hands out the skin was puffy and

281

wrinkled. Her steps along the towpath are a clock ticking, a metronome. One follows the other, left then right, and by this means alone, she finds her way.

His boat is moored in its usual place, and the cabin light is on. Cat stops beside it, feels puzzled and delighted and relieved. She walks the gangplank, slowly, carefully, unsure of her own body, her balance. All of the power she felt as she danced has gone now. When George hears her and climbs out of the cabin, she falls into him.

'Cat! What's happened? Are you well?' He has caught even more sun, the skin of his face dark brown but for little pale lines around his eyes, where during the day he squints.

'No, no, I'm not ill. Just tired. I have not slept,' she says, smiling drunkenly up at him. He searches her face for a moment; runs his hands the length of her as if to check all is in place; brushes back the short wisps of her hair; plants a kiss on her mouth.

'Sit down, Black Cat. You look done in, girl.' He smiles. 'Look—I bought some beer while I was away. Will you have some?'

'Ginger beer?'

'Yes, though I bought plain ale as well if you'd rather.'

'No, I like the ginger,' she says.

'What happened while I was away?'

'Need anything have happened?'

'I can see it in your eyes, Cat. Is it bad news?' George takes two cups from hooks, pours their drinks.

'It's all bad news. I am bad news,' she says, and he waits for an explanation. 'My good friend Tess, who was arrested and gaoled with me—on account of me, if truth be told—has found herself in the workhouse, with nowhere else to go. She's only a child! Not yet eighteen, even. And I would have gone to see her today, since today is the only visiting day, but the vicar's wife would not allow it. And it is all my fault! And The Gentleman . . . he could have kept her out of it. He could have let her have her old job back . . . he knows she was no trouble, not really. Not like me. Or sent her here, that's what he should have done! Sent her here in my stead. I deserved the poorhouse, perhaps, but she did not. She did not.' The words tumble over one another, and before she knows it, tears are sliding down her cheeks and she can't keep her throat from closing.

'Hush now, stop that! It won't help her to tear yourself up over it,' George says softly, holding her face in his hard hands, catching the tears with his thumbs.

'I must help her, though . . . I must. Perhaps I spoke the truth just now . . . perhaps that's it!' she cries, her eyes widening.

'Cat, love, you're not making sense . . .'

'She should come here, and take this job. I hate it . . . I can't stand it. It's all lies and . . . and captivity! But Tess doesn't fight things like I do. She would be a good maid to them, and grateful as people would say she should be. They must hire her!'

'And where will you go, if they do? They'll not keep you both on, I'll warrant,' George asks, frowning slightly and catching Cat's hands as she gesticulates wildly.

'I'll leave. I don't care. I'll just go . . . I don't care where,' she says, then falls still as she considers her words. 'I can't stay there for ever. I can't be like Sophie Bell. I will turn mad,' she murmurs.

'I have an answer to this, perhaps,' George says quietly. He lets go of her hands, crosses to the far side of the cabin where his kitbag is stowed beneath the narrow bed. He pulls it out, rummages inside for something. 'I had meant to ask you another way, and perhaps not this evening. But still.'

'I could find some other job, perhaps. Not as a servant. I could learn to type . . . Or I could work in a factory somewhere . . .'

'That's just another kind of servitude. Cat, listen to me.' He kneels in front of her, so that their eyes are level. 'I have the answer, I'm telling you.' Cat frowns, struggles to focus her eyes on him, her thoughts on him. There's a flash of silver in the palm of his hand. 'This ring was my grandmother's. I called in on my folk, while I was away. They've kept it in case I ever had need of it, which now I do.'

'You mean to sell it? The money . . . would not be enough to support . . .' Cat shakes her head, gazing at the thin white band.

'No, I don't mean to sell it, you dunce. I mean to wed you with it!' George exclaims. Cat stares at him. 'I mean to wed you with it, Cat. I love you, truly. I would have you with me always. And you can leave your post, if that's what you wish. We can take rooms in Hungerford, until I can save enough for the boat . . . Find other work if it pleases you, or I'll keep you, as a man should . . .' In the face of Cat's silence, George's words stumble to a halt. He looks hard into her eyes, which are inscrutable. 'Have you no answer for me, then?' he says, anxiously. Cat puts her hands through his hair, runs them the length of his thick arms. She kisses his neck, his eyes, all over his face, and puts her arms around him. He is more real and alive than anything else she knows, and though she is asleep within seconds, she wonders, at the last, how she will explain her refusal.

*   *   *

Cat wakes, by chance alone, as the sky is turning pale silver. For a while she lies still and wonders why her back aches, and why her feet are cold, and where she is. For a while, she revels in the glorious sensation of having rested. Her stomach rumbles hotly. Then she lifts her head and sees George. No room for two people side by side on the narrow bed. He has lain all night on his back, with Cat on his stomach as though he were a mattress. He snores softly, shifts his spine when she moves, and a spike of fierce love for him startles her. Panic soon replaces it. Dawn is on its way, and she has passed the whole night fast asleep in his arms. In less than an hour she must be washed and dressed and ready to open the house and make breakfast and start the day, yet she is miles away, and has slept in her clothes which are creased and stale. And she hasn't even got the vicar's bicycle with her to speed the return journey. She slides to her feet as softly as she can, but George opens his eyes.

'Where are you going?'

'It's morning!' she snaps, anxiety making her curt. 'I can't believe I slept so long . . . I have to get back! They'll notice . . . and I look like a vagrant!'

'Don't fret so . . . the sun's not yet up, you've

time.' George sits up, twists his shoulders to free up the muscles. 'Tell you what, for a slip of a thing you aren't half heavy after a while.' He smiles.

'I can't believe you let me sleep on like that.'

'You needed it. I was going to wake you when it got late, but you looked so peaceful. So I shut my eyes for five minutes, and must have drifted off as well.'

Cat rakes her fingers through her hair and brushes roughly, pointlessly, at her skirt and blouse. Pulling on her shoes, she turns to climb the steps. George catches her hand.

'Wait! Wait a second, Cat. You never did answer me. My proposal.'

'There's no time now, George,' Cat says, trying to pull away and be gone.

'Yes or no—both very short words, and quick to say,' he counters, and his tone is guarded now. 'I would be good to you, Cat Morley,' he adds when she hesitates, won't meet his eye.

'I know it. I know you would. But I can't marry you, George.'

'Why not?' he asks, his face falling. Cat hugs her arms tight around herself, suddenly cold and queasy. 'Why not? Do you love another?' he presses, sounding both angry and afraid.

'No!'

'Am I not good enough for you?'

'You would be good enough for any woman, George, and that's the truth,' she says, sadly.

'Then why won't you marry me?'

'Because you would own me! I won't be owned, George! By you or anybody . . . bad enough that I am slave to the vicar and his wife. I would not swap that one kind of slavery for another.'

'I'm talking of marriage, not slavery . . .'

'But it's the same thing! If you'd only heard some of the accounts I have, from women in London—how marriage has served them, how they have been treated. If I wed you it would be your right to beat me! To take my money, my children, everything I own, though God knows I own precious little . . . It would be your right to take your pleasure with me, whether I wanted it or not! To shut me indoors and never let me see the light of day . . . It would be your right to . . .' She runs out of breath, and coughs; finds her hands shaking in fear at her own words.

'I would do none of those things! Is that what you think of me?' he asks, stricken.

'No! I don't think you would do any of them, George; I speak only of the *state* of marriage, and why I will not enter into it. With you or any man!' she cries. 'I *will not* be owned!'

From outside the boat, in the wake of her words, comes silence. George turns away from her, sits back down on the bed and does not look at her. Cat swallows, her throat parched and painful. She hesitates a moment, then climbs out of the cabin and makes her way back towards Cold Ash Holt.

The Rev. Albert Canning—from his journal

TUESDAY, JULY 18TH, 1911

Today Robin has gone up to London. He sent a telegraph ahead to propose a meeting with the upper echelons of The Society, and although he had not had a response before he left, I am sure they will be most thrilled to see the evidence he has procured here, and to think and plan in which way best to use it, to further the teaching and enlightenment of the people. It is like walking in God's very shadow, to know such things are so close at hand. It is a constant distraction, and a glorious one. I can think of little else. I yearn to be in the meadows at dawn, with Robin at my side; to be suffused with the overwhelming sense of rightness which overcomes me at such times. Yes, I yearn for it. Afterwards, the human race, in the full light of day, seems a paltry and unworthy thing indeed. I find my parishioners almost disgust me, with their sicknesses and their impiety and their material obsessions and their lasciviousness. Bringing them to the truth would be a task indeed, and I confess, to my shame, that some selfish part of me would rather not try, and would rather keep this exquisite discovery between myself and Robin. But this is not the way of theosophy, and I must work to oppress such thoughts.

I have not been able to sleep of late. I lie awake until the birds begin to sing, captivated by thoughts of the wonders of the earth, and how close I am coming to communing with them. For knowledge is the first step to enlightenment, and from enlightenment the path to a clearer inner vision and higher consciousness unfurls. I think that I cannot sleep because my inner sight is awakening. When I do sleep, in the first hour or so after dawn, I am beset by dreams, most troubling dreams. My own human doubts and fears return to mock me, and to test my resolve. Robin Durrant's face comes to me often in such dreams, as though he has reached out, and wishes to guide me. Even when I wake, his face remains. He is in all my thoughts, and I feel his benign influence in my every action. The days will be long indeed, and empty while he is away. I wish he had asked me to go with him, so that I could remain at his side and help him in this time of great change.

I cannot sufficiently explain the aura of blissful harmony and knowledge that emanates from the theosophist. He is an exemplary man. This is how a person should be! His patience and learning, and how in all things he is both passionate and rational. He is the actual embodiment of an unsullied human spirit. How else to explain the feelings of completeness, peace and joy when I am in his company? Hester does not understand. When she speaks of him she is petulant, and is at times foolish. I should not reprimand her for it, since she does not know the truth, and can have little understanding of such esoteric ideas. Women were ever less pious than men, ever less studious, ever less able to commit to serious thought. Wisdom is not in their make-up, and they are not to be blamed for it. Though theosophy teaches that, within The Society, no such discriminations are made between the sexes, I do not claim to agree with every one of its tenets.

While Robin is away I will go myself into the meadows, and I will recapture the quietness of spirit that first allowed me to see the elementals. I will do this. I must not fail. For if I cannot do this I am no better than the gamblers in the pub, the fornicators in the dark corners of the streets. I will fight their assaults on decency, and I will fight my own impurities, the materialistic urges that have made it impossible for me to see again what I first saw. For as Charles Leadbeater himself says, for the elementals to be near an average man is like to be assaulted by a hurricane—a hurricane that has first blown over a cesspool. I will not be an average man any longer. If I can achieve this, Robin will truly have something to come back to. A proper companion, a proper acolyte to his teachings. For he must surely come back.

1911

For a while after she wakes, Hester can't quite place what is different. Downstairs, she hears Cat opening the shutters quietly, the gentle clonk of wood against wood as they concertina away into the panelling. The air is still, and close, and too warm. Her skin itches slightly, hot and clammy wherever the sheets touch her, and her thoughts feel drowsy and slow. Then she realises—she is not alone. For the first time in as long as she can remember, she has woken up before Albert, and he remains in bed beside her, asleep on his back with his jaw fallen slack and the tiniest of frowns puckering his brow. The soft sound of his breathing fills what would normally have been silence. It has been six days since Robin Durrant went up to London, and there has been no word from him; and while Albert seems agitated and impatient at this, Hester is pleased, and feels happier than she has in weeks. She rolls over gently so that she can lie facing him. With the curtains still closed the light coming through the thick fabric is a rich, shady ochre. Albert has kicked the covers off in the night, and lies with his legs and arms jumbled wide, carelessly. Hester smiles fondly at him as he murmurs something unintelligible, and shifts his head a little.

To sleep in, Albert wears a long, loose shirt of unbleached linen over a matching pair of trousers. These are rumpled now, from a restless night, and lie bunched and creased in a way that would be most uncomfortable had he been awake. Hester puts out her arm and rests it gently on his stomach, and then recoils in surprise. There is a hardness at his crotch, beneath the pale linen, that she has never felt before. Albert murmurs again, more softly now. Hester stares at her husband's body, but try as she might she can't think what form of thing it might be that would feel that way—odd and almost unnatural, as if wholly disconnected from the rest of his relaxed, supine form. With her pulse quickening, Hester, ever so gently, fumbles at the buttons that fasten Albert's trousers. The fabric is rough and she has to use both hands, though she does so with her lip gripped in her teeth in consternation, in case he should feel it and wake. He does not. And there it is. A curve of hardened flesh, arching up to rest against the soft down of his stomach, the skin satin smooth over an array of ridges and vessels; a deep, flushed, pinkish-brown colour, and a musky smell unlike any she has ever noticed him having before.

For a second, Hester is stunned, then revolted and afraid. She thinks that perhaps this deformity is the reason her husband has never wanted to hold her, or lie truly close to her at night. She lies rigid, propped on one elbow, transfixed and bombarded with questions and anxieties. But the more she thinks about it, the more some of the things Amelia has written to her drop into place, and she begins to understand that this . . . state is what is needed for their bodies to enmesh with one another. And now she is witnessing it, finally, for the first time. Cautiously, with one eye on Albert's sleeping face, she touches it, letting her fingertips brush lightly against his skin. It feels feverishly hot, satin smooth, and strange. Albert whimpers quietly and arches his spine a little, twisting as if in nightmare. Hester considers waking him, but in the end is too fascinated by this new exploration of his anatomy. She curls her hand around it and squeezes ever so slightly, testing its rigidity, trying to discern what makes it so. Albert sighs, squirming slightly beneath her caress. The thing in her hand seems to grow yet harder, and she fancies for an instant that she can feel the beat of his heart within it. Running her hand along to its tip, which feels like the finest chamois, Hester smiles, surprised and pleased to finally learn something new about her husband. If he had been shy about this organ of his, then surely now she has seen it, he will not be? A warm tingling begins between her thighs, and spreads to the pit of her stomach, and on impulse she leans over and kisses his mouth.

Albert wakes with a sharp inhalation of breath and a look of extreme bewilderment in his eyes, as if he expected to see somebody entirely different. The look persists even as he moves his head away from her slightly, and draws breath to speak. With her hand still circling his shaft, Hester feels, very precisely, the moment that its hardness begins to soften, and its size to diminish. Albert leaps away from her, scrambling from the bed and fumbling with the buttons of his trousers.

'*Hester!* What are you *doing?*' he cries, his voice breathless and tight, either with fear or with outrage.

'Nothing, my love—it's perfectly all right, really . . . I was so delighted to wake up beside you for once . . . I merely wanted to touch you, and I saw . . .' She gestures at his lower body, her smile falling from her lips as she sees the thunderous expression spreading over his face.

'Silence!' he snaps, finishing with his fly and pulling on his dressing gown with desperate haste. He knots the cord around his middle with such ferocity that he will struggle to undo it again. 'You must *never* touch me like that when I am sleeping! Or ever!'

'But, Bertie, I only—'

'No. We will not discuss this! We will forget it—'

'I don't want to forget it! Albert, this is nothing to be ashamed or . . . embarrassed about, my darling. It's perfectly natural,' she says, still hoping against a nagging uncertainty that this is so. 'And I am your *wife* . . . we are married. There should be no secrets between us, nothing that the one does not understand about the other . . .' She trails into silence. Albert goes to the window and throws the curtains wide, as if inviting the world in, unwilling to be alone with his own wife. His arms hang limply at his sides, fingers flexing occasionally.

'It was most improper and . . . indecent of you, to touch me like that!' he says, his voice charged with some emotion she cannot define.

'Bertie, please—'

'We will not speak of it,' he says.

'But I *want* to speak of it! We must start to talk about these things, Albert, or remain forever in the dark!' she cries in desperation.

'What do you mean, in the dark? It's you who

will bring darkness upon this house, with such indecency!'

'*Indecency?* Is it indecent for a wife to touch her husband—the man to whom God has joined her? Is it indecent to want to live as man and wife, rather than as . . . brother and sister? You are a man of the cloth, Albert. I know it, and I respect it. But you are not a monk! What is the point of marriage if not to allow us to . . . lie together, and touch one another, and to make a *family*, Albert?' Her voice shakes with emotion.

Albert stands and stares at her for some time, his jaw working, knotting at the corners. 'You don't understand . . . how could you?' he says at last, his voice hard and low.

'No, I don't. I don't understand this, and increasingly I don't understand you, Bertie, or what I have done to make you treat me in this way . . . Please, explain it to me!'

'I . . . I have always been kind to you, haven't I? And a good husband?'

'Yes, but—'

'Then please, Hetty, don't *pester* me like this all the time! Is this . . . physicality all you want from me? Are you so desperate for it that you're willing to steal it from me, against my knowledge while I sleep? Like the worst kind of wanton strumpet?'

'How can you accuse me like that? How can you use the word wanton when I, your wife of over a year, am still a *maid*?' she gasps at him, struggling to speak as sobs take a stranglehold on her.

Albert's face is pale, and shining with sweat. He looks unwell. 'I . . . I'm sorry,' he says at last, quietly. His eyes are wide and unfocused. He swallows, and looks down at Hester as she weeps as though she is a wild and unknowable animal. At length, he turns and walks slowly away towards his dressing room, and Hester flings out her hand, clutches the fabric of his robe.

'Albert, wait! Please, don't go . . . stay and talk to me!' she begs.

'Now, now, Hetty,' Albert murmurs vaguely. 'I must get ready.' He goes into his dressing room and shuts the door, his expression both fraught and distant.

Kneeling on the bed, Hester puts her hand over her mouth and catches the musky smell of him clinging to her skin. She is still sobbing, and though she tries to stop she can't. She shivers in the warm room, and sits until these symptoms ease. In their place come confusion, and doubt, and desolation; and with them the new, unwelcome realisation that it had been when he'd opened his eyes and seen *her* that Albert's state of arousal had waned. Hester moves to the edge of the bed, and sits with her feet dangling over it. She ought to get up, and get dressed for breakfast, but it all seems so pointless. Entirely as pointless as she feels herself to be.

*   *   *

Cat hears the jeering before she sees the unfortunate butt of the abuse. She has walked to Thatcham, and posted letters and a parcel for Hester, and now has to pick up fresh meat from the butcher. This she has to do more regularly than ever, since the weather continues to seethe and stew, and they can't keep it from spoiling at The Rectory. After more than a day hanging in the well it comes up silvery green, and slick with a wet shine that greases the fingers, smells sharp and vinegary, and turns the stomach. As Cat walked past George's boat, just now, her heart lurched and her throat went dry. But the cabin door was firmly shut, with no sound from within or signs of its occupant. She walked on past with a slight fluttering in her stomach—butterfly wings of panic, threatening to grow stronger. She wonders what they mean. At the far end of The Broadway, where a wide open area between the flanking rows of shops forms something of an unmade square, a plump woman is standing on a rickety wooden platform. Her bonnet is no match for the powerful sun, and her face is flushed and shining. It's the colours that draw Cat's eye, make her catch her breath: a banner of white, green and purple hanging in swags behind the woman; a sash to match, draped over her; ribbons in the colours hanging limp in the still air. *Arise! Go Forth and Conquer!* the banner reads, painted by hand in purple letters that stand bold from the white sheet. A smaller placard propped beside her reads *Newbury WSPU—Bicycle Corps*. Licking her dry lips, and with a strange longing inside—almost like when her mother died, though not as strong—Cat makes her way over to the crowd.

It's mostly men making all the noise, though some women join in too; laughing, passing remarks to one another, firing scandalised looks through their eyelashes. Those folk at the front of the crowd who might have wanted to hear the speech have little chance to. The strain of making herself heard above the din is forcing the plump woman to fight for breath.

'As Mrs Pankhurst herself explained . . . as Mrs Pankhurst herself explained, the vote is first of all a symbol! Firstly, a symbol; secondly a safeguard; and thirdly, it is an instrument! Sisters! Comrades! Your lives will never improve until the government of this country is made accountable to you all!' she shouts, to a fresh round of whistles and abuse. The speaker, short in stature with curly brown hair and a wide, gentle face, casts a glance over the hostile crowd with a helpless look in her eyes. 'The vote is the instrument by which we may redress the imbalances in education, and law, and employment, all three of which remain to this day weighted so very heavily in favour of the male sex!' she says, the words all but lost in the din. 'They say that men and women occupy two different spheres of existence—the home for women, and work and government for men—and that these spheres have been ordained by God, and should remain separate. They say that the political world is too dirty and raucous a one for women. Well, if the home may benefit from a woman's gentle nurturing and purity, then surely public life could not help but be benefited by the same? If it is so dirty and raucous, then let us cleanse and civilise it!' she cries gamely.

'Be quiet!' Cat says, the words seeming to arrive directly upon her tongue, without first passing through her brain.

'Yeah, stop your mouth up!' a man next to her says, looking down at her and grinning his approval.

'No . . . *you*, all of you! Let her speak! Haven't you the least common decency?' Cat shouts.

'Oh, Christ, here's another one,' the man

297

mutters to a friend, stepping away from Cat and eyeing her coldly.

'Let her speak!' she shouts again, louder now. A few more people turn to look at her. The speaker struggles bravely on, but Cat can no longer hear her. There is a buzzing in her ears that has nothing to do with the jostling crowd or the rising tide of their voices. The stink of sweat and sweltering skin is everywhere. The air tastes used, soiled; commingled breath, hot vapours and sour mood. The man beside her and his friend begin to sing, linking their arms and tipping back their heads in music hall parody.

'Put me upon an island where the girls are few; put me among the most ferocious lions at the zoo; put me in a prison and I'll never, never fret; but for pity's sake don't put me near a bleedin' suffragette!' they carol, and fall about laughing at their own cleverness. At the mention of prison, Cat feels a black fury building in her chest, bitter as bile.

'Shut up! Shut your mouths, you worthless whoresons!' she spits at them.

'Here, you want to watch that tongue of yours, slut. It'll get you in trouble,' the first man tells her bleakly, through tight lips. He holds his finger, thick and dirty, right up to her face, and she slaps it away. Just then, a scream from the stage causes a momentary hush to fall. The speaker is looking down in horror at her white skirts, now streaked with red juices. Someone in the crowd has pelted her with a handful of rotting tomatoes, and they cling to the fine muslin; blackened seeds and flecks of skin and pulp.

'Good shot!' a man shouts, to much laughter.

'Really, I . . .' The speaker falters. 'I have every right to come here and speak to you, and speak I shall!' she rallies, but her voice lacks the courage of her words.

Cat pushes her way through the wall of people, and as she climbs onto the platform more missiles are launched. Eggs land with soggy little crunches, and one hits Cat on her arm as she straightens up, turns to the crowd. Breathing hard, she glances at the stranger, whose face is pinched and startled. The woman's eyes dart nervously from Cat to the crowd. Cat grabs her hand and turns full face to the crowd's contempt.

'*Shame* on you! Shame on all of you! We're *not* afraid of you! You can't just shout abuse and expect us to go away! We're not children!' she shouts. She ducks to one side as more festering fruit is thrown, and an empty beer bottle, sticky and brown. 'That's your answer, is it, when a woman speaks up for herself? Attack her! Wound her! No doubt you treat your wives and daughters the same way, since that's the only way men can continue to impose their illegitimate domination of women!' Her voice grows louder, hoarse with fury. The speaker hangs from her hand, astonished.

'Our wives have better sense than to stand about in public shouting about things they know nothing of!' one man calls up at her.

'And how can they know anything about it? About politics, or education, or their rights, when they spend all their time in the home, addling their brains with housework and the raising of children?' she demands.

'And who else should do those things, then?

299

Their menfolk?' This to general laughter.

'I say—' The speaker tries to interject, but Cat squeezes her hand tighter.

'Why the bloody hell not?' she shouts. But this is the final straw, and more objects and insults are thrown, and Cat cannot hear her own words for the cacophony of abuse and name hurling, though she knows she is shouting because her throat aches with it, and the speaker is pulling to free her hand, which Cat will not relinquish; and somewhere behind it all she hears police whistles blowing, and then a dead rat hits her legs, stinking, its eyes filmy and its tongue a dry curl between snarling teeth, brown fur matted with filth on which flies resettle, almost at once. It smells sweet and rank and putrid, so strong that for a moment Cat falters, clamps her teeth together to keep the stench out.

'Oh, good Lord.' The speaker quails, the blood draining from her face. She sits down heavily, her eyes sliding out of focus, legs splayed inelegantly. A smattering of laughter comes from the crowd, and Cat grinds her teeth in fury. Kicking the rat to one side she bends down, picks up what she can of the eggs and vegetables and hurls them back at the crowd, shouting furious curses at them all the while. She aims the beer bottle at the head of a man whose eyes are streaming with mirth, forcing him to duck hurriedly. It shatters into pieces on the street behind him, and he flinches as a fragment hits his cheek, makes a tiny cut there.

'Let that wipe the smile from your face, you son of a bitch!' Cat yells at him. She keeps it up as long as she can, trading insults and missiles with the raucous crowd until heavy hands clamp around her limbs and she is carried off, twisting like a snake.

*   *   *

Cat's upper arms are tender, and she touches them tentatively. Rolling up her sleeves, she finds bruises shaped like finger marks, dotting her skin like tokens of some plague. The lock-up at the police house is cool, the walls constructed of thick stone and coated in cream-coloured paint that bulges and cracks into craters in places; but Cat can't appreciate the respite. She can't even worry that she has jeopardised her position, has jeopardised everything, by losing her temper that way. All she can do is sit on the hard wooden chair and stare up at the tiny window with its dirty pane of glass behind strong metal mesh, and take her thoughts away, far away so that she does not panic. She must be anywhere, anywhere else but locked in a cell. The bitterness of bile burns in the back of her throat, and cold sweat trickles between her breasts to her stomach, seeping into the waistband of her skirt. If she were to pay attention, if she were to acknowledge her incarceration, she might lose her mind; burn out like a match in an instant of pure fear and be nothing but cinders, charred remains of herself. Frowning in concentration, she makes sure she is anywhere else but there . . .

She is in the house where she grew up, as they carry her mother downstairs and out to the waiting hearse. She had waited at first, and not told anybody that her mother had died. She didn't know what she would do next; she didn't want to start life again without her. Her mother had said somebody would come for her, when the time came. Cat had twisted and tried to turn away, but

301

her mother had insisted, her eyes fever-bright, the whites gone grey, pupils huge in the shadowy room.

'No, you must listen. This is important. When the time comes, somebody will come and collect you. You're to go with her, and do as you're told. Do you understand? It's all arranged. It's the best I can do for you. You will be looked after there. The Gentleman of the house . . .' She paused, her voice little more than a whisper, and fought to keep a storm of coughing at bay. Cat willed her to succeed. She could not bear the agony these fits caused her mother. 'It is a good place. The Gentleman of the house . . .' she tried again, but this time succumbed to the fit, and was too exhausted afterwards to speak any more. So Cat, when she died, waited. She waited, and she wondered, but did not care, what would happen next. And when a neighbour had called round the next morning, and found her alone, and when they had taken her mother out, a strange woman did appear in the doorway. Buttoned tightly into a black coat, her face motionless beneath steel-grey hair, looking as though it had never worn a smile in a lifetime.

'You're to come with me now, young lady. Do you understand?' she asked. Mute, Cat nodded. 'This is what your mother, God rest her soul, has arranged for you. Go now and pack up your things. Others will see to the rest. Go on, now,' the woman said. Cat did not want to. She wanted to go with her mother, even with her shut away in a box, even with her body so very empty and silent and wrong. She did not want to go with this hatchet-faced woman with her thin, censorious lips or her spidery

302

hands. Mrs Heddingly. But her mother had told her to, so she went . . .

When the door is opened some time later—she has little idea how much time—Cat does not break off her reverie. Only when the police constable shakes her shoulder, tentatively, as if she might explode, does she blink. She twists her head, hears him speak.

'Come on, I haven't got all day. Or do you want to stay in here, is that it?' Behind him the door is open, and Cat is up in an instant, bolting through it without a word. She runs headlong into George.

'Cat! Steady, girl! You're all right, are you? Not hurt?' he asks, holding her easily with one solid arm, though she would have run right by him, out into the sunlight.

'George! They locked me in!' she gasps.

'Hush, hush, I know they did. But you're out now. Slow down, Cat. Look around you,' he says, softly. Cat does as she is told, taking a deep breath. She is in the front room of the police station, and behind George the door is wide open, the street dazzlingly bright.

'You're letting me go?' she asks the constable who roused her just now.

'This time. But just you stay out of trouble, you hear? I've heard rumours about you, Miss Morley. We've no need for any more of your public exhibitions, understand?'

'But . . . they wouldn't let her speak. She had a right to speak! And . . . they threw things—a dead rat, for God's sake! At two defenceless women!' she cries. 'Are you going to lock up the man who threw that, are you?'

'If I knew who it was that threw it, aye, I would.

303

And you hardly strike me as the defenceless type, I must say. Luckily, Mrs Hever has spoken up for you, and told us you were only trying to protect her from the crowd's . . . hostility. And George Hobson here has . . . vouched for you. So you can go.' He scratches absently at his moustache with one hand. Sweat glazes his face and is staining the stiff collar of his shirt. 'This heat,' he mutters. 'It's turning people frenzied, I do believe. Go on and begone with you, and I don't want to see your face again. Things might not go so smoothly if I do.' He dismisses them. George marches Cat from the room before she can speak again.

They walk in silence for a minute or two. The Broadway is all but deserted now; the sun dipping in the west, growing fat and glowing, honey-coloured. At the south end of the street a scattering of debris is all that remains of the trash that was hurled at the WSPU speaker. Cat can smell her own sweat, sharp and rank. She stinks of the fear that gripped her inside the cell, rather than from the heat. George walks with his eyes down and his shoulders tense. Cat peers up at him, tries to read him.

'You vouched for me? What does that mean? What did you say?' she asks him, hesitantly.

George shrugs, puts one hand in his pocket and then takes it out. 'I said you were my woman,' he says, gruffly. 'I said I would keep you out of trouble.'

At this, Cat can't help but smile. 'Oh, really?' She knocks him playfully with her elbow. 'I'd like to see you try.'

But George does not smile back at her. His eyes are troubled. 'Please, Cat. I can't afford to bail you another time,' he says, then pulls himself up short, and clamps his lips tight together.

'You can't *afford* to? What do you mean?'

'Nothing. Forget I said it.'

'George—did you have to pay that man, to let me go?' she whispers. George aims a kick at a pebble in the road, sends it bumping into the verge.

'Perhaps he would have let you go anyway. Later today or tomorrow. Or perhaps not.'

'How much?'

'Never mind it.'

'How much, George? Tell me,' she demands.

'I won't. Enough,' is all he says. Cat stops walking and hangs her head in shame, tears blurring the image of her feet in their dusty shoes.

'But . . . your boat, George! You shouldn't have done it!' she says, the words sticking in her throat.

'I had to, Cat. You were locked up! I knew . . . I knew how you would be feeling. I didn't know if you could manage it . . . and I couldn't bear the thought of it.'

'But you shouldn't have! I can't repay it! We can't get it back!'

'I'll make it back. It'll just take more time,' he says, grimly. 'Perhaps I'll sell that ring, as you suggested. If you'll not wear it. A small sum, indeed, but a start, I suppose.'

'George . . .' she whispers, turning to face him. She puts her arms around his middle, not caring who might see; lays her face against his chest and feels the mass of him through his shirt, the deep, steady beat of his heart. 'I'll not be your wife, but I *am* your woman. Just as you said. If you still want me.' The words muffled and sad.

George grips her shoulders, gives her a little shake. 'Of course I still want you! I'll always want you! I've never known anyone like you. But we *must* wed, Cat! I want you as my wife. And it's sinful not to—'

'Sinful? I don't believe in it.'

'Well, I do. And so does God. Marry me, Cat!' he says, taking her face in his hands, not letting her look away. But he can read the refusal in her eyes, and she sees it, so she does not need to answer him. She is adamant.

'I will find the money to give back to you, George—no, I will!' she insists, when he shakes his head. 'I will find it. And I am yours, whether you would have me or not,' she adds; and finds, to her shock, that it's the possibility he might say no that causes panic to flutter inside her.

* * *

Hester hears Mrs Bell's voice, loud and sharp, coming up the cellar steps, so she knows that Cat has made it back to The Rectory at long last. It has been five hours since she was sent for meat, and to the post. Steeling herself, Hester goes down the steps and into earshot of the tirade.

'. . . and after all of it, you come back with no beef! What am I supposed to make for dinner, with no beef? Answer me that, little miss good-for-nothing!'

'I said I was sorry . . . I got held up! I couldn't help it, and then the butcher had shut up shop—'

'Sorry isn't going to feed the five of us, now, is it? You're a useless slattern, Cat Morley, and I'll tell you another thing—'

'Mrs Bell, that's quite enough,' Hester says, as calmly as she can. The housekeeper visibly bites her tongue, her nostrils flaring, and settles into her chins with a sulphurous expression. Faced with her glittering eyes, Hester feels herself flinch. Cat, in contrast, looks pale and exhausted, her clothes dusty and creased, her hair out of its pins, matted. 'Cat, would you come with me, please?' Hester says, and turns to go back upstairs. She thinks for a moment that the girl is not following her, but when she turns to look there she is, treading so softly that she makes no sound. More like a wraith than a person.

Hester leads the way into the drawing room and then turns to stand with her hands clasped in front of her. She has been rehearsing the wording of a reprimand for the past three hours of the blazing afternoon, never having had to give one before—not a proper one. But now it comes to it, it hardly seems appropriate. Cat sways slightly on her feet, her face slack, utterly expressionless. Hester notices blood around several of her fingernails, where they have been torn off too close to the quick, and a purple-grey bruise spreading along one collarbone where it juts through the open collar of her blouse. Two buttons are missing from the blouse.

'Heavens, child! What happened to you?' she exclaims, filling with concern rather than ire. 'Were you set upon?'

Cat blinks, and takes a long, deep breath. Hester fancies she sees thoughts flickering fast behind those dark eyes, as if the girl is phrasing her response quite carefully.

'In a way, madam. I am most sorry to be so late

307

back, and not to have got the meat for dinner tonight—'

'Never mind the meat. Mrs Bell will think of something, I'm sure. Just tell me what kept you?'

'There was a woman in town . . . she was giving a speech. Mrs Hever, she was called. Only the crowd was most discourteous, and wouldn't let her have her say. They called her all sorts of names, and they threw rotting food at her, and . . . and a dead animal, madam, which made her faint. I stood up for her.'

'You stood up for her? How do you mean?'

'I . . . stood next to her, and I . . . told them to let her speak. But they would not. The police came, and I was made to wait in the police house until . . . Mrs Hever had come to speak up for me. Then they said I could go. But I could not have got away sooner, madam, or I would have,' Cat says, and sounds sincere enough. For the first time since her arrival, Hester sees some definite, unambiguous expression on her face—anxiety. The girl is deeply troubled by something.

'I see. And, tell me, what was it the woman was speaking about in the first place? Or trying to?'

'It was . . . she was . . . from the Newbury WSPU. Come to talk about the vote,' Cat answers, reluctantly.

'I see. Cat,' Hester sighs, 'it will not do. That is all behind you, and there it must stay. No, no—I dare say you were indeed acting honourably towards this Mrs Hever, and it sounds as though the good people of Thatcham were behaving far from honourably in return. But though my husband and I were quite willing to hire a maid with a troubled past, I am not sure we would be

308

able to keep one with a troubled present. Do you understand? Here, you are our maid of all work, and as such you *cannot* also be a suffragette. Cat? I must stress this. Put it out of your mind. It will not do . . .'

'I cannot change the way I think, madam,' Cat replies, her voice low but strung tight with emotion. 'Though I may not take part in the campaign, I must be allowed to think as I see fit!'

'Well! Your thoughts are your own, indeed; though I might find them unnatural . . .'

'It's not unnatural for women to want control of their own lives, their own destinies, madam . . . it is not unnatural for them to want to better things for themselves, and their daughters after them . . .'

'They may by all means want those things. But these militant tactics . . . this unwomanly behaviour only goes to show that the gentler sex is not fitted for government, nor politics. Women would do better to make sound marriages, and encourage their menfolk to fight to improve the country for everybody. We are angels of the hearth, Cat; not warriors of the battlefield. God ordained it thus, and thus it should ever be. I am quite sure that by improving her husband, by soothing him and imparting a feminine softness to some of his masculine fire, a woman would make far greater gains than she might by . . . smashing windows and behaving like a common thug . . .' Hester takes a deep breath, and glances at Cat to find the girl's face registering something like pity, or perhaps contempt. Either way, she wipes it quickly, and reverts to her customary glassy stare. 'Anyway. Go and get yourself cleaned up. I can see you're very worn out. I would say to rest this evening, but

309

Mr Durrant is due back in time for dinner so I fear we will need your help. Take half an hour now to wash and rest, and let us hear no more about this. Or again in the future. It's fortunate that my husband has been addressing his pastoral duties all afternoon, and was not around to learn about any of this.'

'Robin's—Mr Durrant is coming back again, this evening?' Cat asks. Hester glances at her sharply, and though the neutral look is there, something else that she cannot read is written in the maid's eyes.

'He is,' she replies, and cannot keep her own discomfort quiet. It makes her voice higher than normal and pinches the words uncomfortably, makes the phrase slightly shorter than she means it to sound.

'You must be so pleased,' Cat says, and an expression passes swiftly over her face, just for a fraction of a second—a twitch of the brows, and one corner of her mouth—that loads her statement with irony.

Hester's cheeks colour slightly, and she is not sure how to answer. 'Indeed,' she says.

*   *   *

With Cat gone from the room, Hester crosses to the window. At least, she thinks, she has dealt with the little crisis calmly and sensibly, and all can now return to harmony. Keeping the house running smoothly, and keeping the servants cheerful and discreet about their work is very much a part of being a wife. It does not do to allow your husband to witness housework half done, laundry half dry, or the servants bickering or being reprimanded. She is glad Albert stayed away, so she could deal with the matter efficiently, away from the tin-tack gaze of Sophie Bell. She looks out at the parched garden, where her crimson roses are dropping petals like waxy tears onto the lawn.

It is no good. She can't convince herself, even with this piece of wisdom, that she is glad Albert has been out all afternoon. Since she woke him with her unwelcome caress . . . since she set eyes upon that one part of his anatomy that until then had been such a mystery, he has been more out of the house than in it, and his early mornings have begun again. So early that she woke that morning to find it still dark outside but her husband already up and gone. She has no idea where he has gone, or why, since he no longer talks to her about his day. She watches a blackbird dash a snail to death on the flagstones of the path. The sharp *crack crack crack* of its last moments feel like fine fractures shooting through her thoughts, splintering them until none make any sense. Something has gone very, very wrong, and is driving a wedge between Albert and herself, but she can't tell exactly what it is, nor see a way to make things right.

*　　　*　　　*

Cat deliberately doesn't look at Robin Durrant as she serves them their dinner. The vicar is all animation. He has burnt the skin across his nose and cheeks, giving him a look of constant excitement. He asks question after question about who the theosophist has spoken to, and what they

311

have said, and what is to be done next about the grand design to bring truth to the masses, and whether Robin would review the pamphlet he has been working on regarding their discoveries. Robin's answers seem somewhat subdued in comparison to the vicar's urgent questions, and it is only with great force of will that Cat can keep herself from studying him, from trying to find the truth of things in his face when she knows it's not to be found in his words. She knows where to meet him, and later, when she goes out to the courtyard, she sees him waiting in the far corner, smoking, pacing; his shoulders hunched.

'Well? How well did they swallow your lie?' Cat asks him, smiling mirthlessly. Robin shoots her a censorious look, flicks open his packet of cigarettes and offers her one. She takes it, holds it between her lips as he lights it, cupping his hand to shelter the match from a lively breeze that comes curling through the courtyard, blessedly cool.

'You make it sound awful,' he says, distractedly. He shifts from foot to foot, as if at any second he might be called upon to run, or fight.

'Isn't it?'

'No! All I have manufactured is a representation of the truth. A *tangible* proof, for those that struggle to accept the more intangible ones ...'

'Manufactured. Everything that needs saying about this sorry matter is in that one word. And you know it,' Cat says, blandly. She takes a long pull on the cigarette, exhales blue smoke into the streaming air. Robin smiles, and then laughs shortly.

'Do you know, it's almost a relief to hear you speak of it? Such decisive dismissal, when all I've

312

heard for days has been prevarication and dithering and uncertainty,' he says.

'They didn't go for it?'

'Some did, but not altogether; some wanted to, but weren't quite able; some didn't, but thought it was possible . . .' He shakes his head. 'It did not go quite as I had hoped, no. I think more is required.'

'More?' Cat asks, instantly on her guard.

'I might need you again, Cat. Some members of The Society hinted that . . . perhaps the image of the elemental had been painted onto the film before development. Though I am no artist, as I tried to explain. Maybe they think I have an accomplice. They might send somebody to witness the production of another set of pictures, if I succeed in meeting and photographing the elemental again . . .' he says, letting the implication of this linger.

'That could be interesting. It might be hard to explain me away, in my wig and chiffon gown.'

'No, no. Nobody can be present for the actual capturing of the image, obviously. But I can argue that case easily. A stranger would upset the equilibrium, and cause the spirit to remain hidden. Their expert could then come with me into the dark room . . . yes. I may have need of you again, Cat.'

'Why do you fight so hard for this?'

'What do you mean?'

'Men. Why do you fight so hard to carve your names into history? To . . . leave some mark of yourselves for after you've gone?'

'Is that what you think I'm doing?'

'Isn't it? You tried poetry, you tried politics . . . now you will try theosophy, and you will perjure

313

yourself to succeed at it. Why not just live, and let it be? You will die and be forgotten, just like the rest of us,' she says, shrugging one shoulder and regarding him through lowered eyelashes. Robin blinks, seems taken aback by her words.

'I don't want to be forgotten. I . . .' He raises his hands, at a loss. 'Is that the difference between men and women then? Is that why men excel, while women just exist? Why it's the names of men that last for ever in history?'

'Nothing lasts for ever. Haven't you read *Ozymandias*?'

'Keats?' he asks, and Cat shakes her head.

'Shelley. But the joke's on you. On men. Women *are* immortal. We leave traces of ourselves in our children, and our children's children; while men are out trying to be the first to claim a mountain.'

'Oh? And aren't there traces of the fathers in these children as well?'

'Yes, if the man troubles himself to imprint upon them. If he's not too busy trying to claim a mountain. Or discover fairies. Perhaps you might consider this as a better way to immortality than posing a housemaid in a costume, and lying to the world?'

'Settle down and take a wife and spawn a few brats? I think not. But I will be immortal, Cat. I will make my name, and a name that will always be remembered. Even when the world turns and my brothers' heroics seems commonplace, this will be remembered.'

'You would do all this for sibling rivalry?' Cat asks incredulously. 'How sad.'

'Who are you to pass judgement on me, Cat Morley? Perhaps nobody will ever remember who

314

you were, but with me you have the chance to be part of something truly world-changing,' Robin says, still pacing restlessly, a few steps one way and then the other.

'Well.' Cat takes another long pull on her cigarette, thinks for a moment. She tips back her head to exhale, watching clouds pour overhead, caught by the wind. It's not yet wholly dark, and faint slivers of the palest blue show here and there through plumes of indigo. 'I might have something to say about that,' she says.

Robin stops pacing and watches her closely, his expression hardening. 'What do you mean?'

'It seems to me that I am acting as your model. That I am the only person who can act as your model.'

'And?'

'And I believe it is customary for models—be they working for artists or photographers—to receive remuneration,' she says, meeting his gaze and not wavering.

'And pay you I do, with my silence; with my collaboration in your wanton behaviour,' he says, his smile twisting to one side, and cold.

'Well, I believe that . . . my silence is every bit as important as yours, now. Even more important, perhaps. I have the option to leave here, you see. I have a proposal of marriage. There is little you can do to punish me, should I choose to speak out about your photographs; and yet I think it would cost you dear if I did.'

'A proposal of marriage? But where is your ring?' Robin snaps, his face thunderous.

'Being fetched down from his mother's place,' she lies quickly.

315

'Tsk tsk, a badly prepared proposal indeed,' Robin says. He turns away from her on his heel, thrusts his hands into his pockets and throws back his head. He stays this way for some moments as Cat waits, heart bumping painfully against her ribs, bending all her will to an outward show of resolute calm.

Finally, Robin Durrant turns back to her, so suddenly that she jumps. Snaps his head around like a bird of prey.

'Very well. I can see you have me backed against the wall on this occasion. What is the going rate for a photographer's model, do you think?' he asks, his voice flat with anger.

'For a model who must hold her tongue for ever more . . . twenty pounds.'

'*Twenty p*— You've lost your mind!' Robin exclaims, his voice falling sharply from a shout to a furious whisper. 'If I had that kind of money to throw at serving girls I wouldn't be back here lodging with the bloody Cannings, I can tell you!'

'The rest of my life is a long time to keep silent. I am the very linchpin of this career you wish to build, I am the key to your lasting fame—'

'You're a brazen villain, Cat, to threaten me like this—'

'You threatened me first, remember? More fool you if you thought I would take it lying down.'

'Ten pounds, and not a shilling more. I mean it, Cat. Don't push me,' he says, standing so close that she must tip back her head to look at him. She can almost hear his heart beating, loud with outrage.

'Up front. Soon. Before we take any more pictures.'

'Half now. You'll have it when I've been to the

bank tomorrow. Half when we take the next set of pictures.'

'When will that be?'

'I can't say. They will dither some more and take their time to find the right kind of expert to send down to me, I'm sure, once I have suggested the plan. Two weeks, perhaps three.'

'Agreed.' Cat smiles. 'I look forward to receiving my back pay, for services already rendered.' She turns to go but Robin's hand strikes out, fast as a snake, and grips her arm to prevent her.

'If you run off with your fancy man before I have taken more pictures then I warn you, Cat Morley, I will find you and make you pay for it,' he says, so calmly and assuredly that Cat goes cold. She holds her breath to hide a shiver, and refuses to flinch even though his fingernails are gouging into her skin. After a silent struggle she pulls her arm free, and glares at him.

'Be careful, theosophist. Karma might catch *you* up if you did. And my betrothed has twice your weight and reach.' She fights to keep her voice even when she wants to shriek at him. Her legs feel weak and unreliable. As she turns to go inside, she sees Hester at the window on the stairs overlooking the courtyard. She has seen them talking, stands watching with her face close to the glass to cut out the reflection of the bright lights behind her. Talking is no crime, nor smoking; and yet Cat shivers again, and pretends not to see her, turning her face to her feet as she walks quickly through the door. Again the breeze comes, and lifts the black lengths of her hair, running curious fingers over her scalp, examining, questioning, making her conspicuous.

317

*   *   *

The next night, Cat knows where to find George. He has a bet to make, though he has a shipment to take west, early the next day—gravel to be moved to Bedwyn for the building of new houses. A few fine spots of rain are falling, hitting her face as she pedals hard, the bicycle clattering along the towpath, skidding here and there on loose stones. Cat squints into the darkness. With the heavy cloud, with no moon or stars, she can hardly see the way. She is upon the bridge before she knows it, the sudden hunched black shape of it looming in front of her, and behind it the weak glow of Thatcham's street lights. Braking hard, Cat slides to a halt. She dismounts, carefully stashes the bicycle in the bushes at the foot of the bridge, where nobody would see it without first stepping on it; and runs steadily the rest of the way to The Ploughman.

The doorman and the publican know her now, and instead of barring her way they nod, mutter a good evening. A few people inside turn to look at her, to gawk at the girl with the shorn-off hair, who wears no corsets and is rumoured to have slit the throat of her lover, her employer, her father; to have set fire to a church in London; to have robbed a shop, a bank, the mail train; to have done things so awful that the vicar's wife is too scared to mention them. Cat's blouse is damp, and sticking to the skin of her back. Catching her breath, she goes straight through to the back room, into the familiar, claustrophobic stink and roaring din, where bodies cram and press all around and her nostrils fill at once with the pervasive reek of liquor and humankind. It is familiar now, almost dear to her; so far removed from the quiet sounds and cooking smells of The Rectory, from the soapy aroma of clean laundry, the gentle souring of milk in the kitchen, the hot fusty smell of the hallway rugs where the long ticking clock marks the passing of life with the slow swing of its pendulum.

It's no boxing match tonight, but a fight of another kind. Behind the curses and shouts of the audience, shrill shrieks and cackles can be heard, ugly and enraged. Cat crouches slightly, her face at the height of the men's hips, and through their jostling bodies she can see the cocks, their feathers fluffed, combs bright red and droplets of blood flying from the spurs on their legs. Bright eyes, flat with hate; their beaks open and panting. They thrust and parry and crane their necks, dancing and stabbing at one another. Across the ring, Cat sees George watching the fight, his face serious. She makes her way around to him, touches his arm to greet him.

'Why do they fight?' she asks, curiously.

'Why do dogs bark? It's what they do. Two males cannot abide to be near each other.' George shrugs. 'Come here to me.' He puts his arms around her waist, tightens them. 'You choose, then.'

'Choose?'

'Say which bird will win and I'll bet a penny on it,' George says. 'I can't decide on a winner.' The heat in the room has put a mottling of dark flecks on the shirt over his chest. Cat puts her hand on the fabric, feels the damp heat of his skin. George leans into her touch, a look of wanting in his eyes.

319

Smiling sharply at him, Cat turns back to the ring. She watches the birds fight for a moment, their bronze and gold feathers shaking, flying; black claws at the ends of grey, scaly legs. Cat has never seen two animals so set upon each other's destruction. There is none of George's measured grace in the way they fight. Only the urge to maim and kill.

'That one,' she says in the end, pointing to the slightly smaller bird, whose wings are greenish-black.

'Are you sure? It looks to be coming off worst.'

'But look how furious it is about that,' Cat points out. George calls out to a fat man who has stripped himself of his shirt, and stands upon a chair sweating and wobbling in his stained vest. The coin is passed, the bet acknowledged with a scrap of blue paper. 'Watch him now,' Cat says, her eyes fixed on the cut and bleeding birds.

For a while, the smaller bird continues to do badly, falling back from the repeated charges of its opponent, screeching in outrage when spurs rake its body, when its face is pecked and cut. But it never loses the mad look in its eye, and it never backs down or gives up. 'He's a fighter. He'll not let himself lose, even if he dies for it,' Cat murmurs, her words lost and unheard in the din. With a final surge of strength, the smaller bird launches itself into the air, comes down with its talons aimed at the other's face. One spur takes out an eye, the other shears a chunk of flesh from the unlucky bird's face, which bleeds into its remaining eye, blinding it. The wounded bird squats in defeat, shakes its head helplessly. It is soon finished off, pecked to death by the smaller bird, which then stands, wings loose, tongue poking out in exhaustion.

Cat stands mesmerised. She had not known that violence could still shock her. Mistaking her sudden silence, George looks troubled.

'He's better off out of it, that dead bird. With only one eye he'd have been no use. Turner would have wrung his neck, had he lived,' he says. 'Perhaps he would not have wanted to survive it, knowing he'd lost to a smaller bird,' he adds.

Cat shakes her head. 'All creatures want to live,' she says. Frowning, George collects their winnings from the fat man, and gives half to Cat.

'I shouldn't have half—it was your penny.'

'But you chose the winner. I would have picked the stronger bird for sure, and lost out.'

'Keep the money. What would I buy with it? I can't buy myself out of my bonds. Keep it and put it towards your boat—towards what I owe you,' she insists, pressing the coins back into George's broad hand. He gives her a puzzled look. 'And here,' she says. 'Here's more as well.' She smiles, pulling her purse from her pocket and holding it out to him.

'What's this?'

'I have more money for you—though I don't know what you paid that policeman. I have some now, and I will have more later; and it's best you don't ask where I got it from.'

'What money? How much, and where did you get it from?' George asks, leading her out of the crowd towards the edge of the room, where the din is less.

'Money for your boat. I have five pounds now, and the same again before a month is up, most likely . . .' She weighs the purse in her hand.

321

George closes his own around it, pushes it hastily into the folds of her skirt.

'*How much?* And you brought the whole of it here to be picked from your pocket!'

'Nobody has stolen it, see. It's all there, and all for you.'

'This is far more than I paid for you. I will not take it.' He sets his jaw stubbornly.

'But you will take it. And whatever you did not pay to free me, you can keep and put towards the boat. Our boat. Our future, and our freedom,' she says, seriously. George looks hard at her, thinks for a while.

'Then . . . you will marry me?'

Cat looks away, fingers the strings of the purse for a while. 'No, George. I stick by what I said. But I will come away with you, if you'll let me. Will it be enough? When I have the other five pounds—will that be enough to take rooms, to buy the pleasure boat and begin again with it?' she asks, eagerly.

'It will be enough. More than enough. But—'

'No, don't say but! Say I can come with you! Say I can leave off this life that I hate, and that you will give me a different one.'

'As my *wife*, Cat, you would have all of that and more,' he pleads. Pressing the purse into his hand, Cat draws breath to answer but is cut off.

Shrill whistles pierce the air, and the door from the front room is pulled open with the squeal and crunch of splintering wood. Policemen rush in, blowing their whistles and holding lanterns aloft to light the winners collecting their pay, and the losers tearing up their tickets. They fan out to catch as many as they can, scurrying like beetles in their dark uniforms and helmets. In an instant, every man tries to be far from the bloodied birds, tries to be rid of his ticket if it is worthless, or to be gone with it if it will later be redeemed. There is a surge of bodies towards the back doors, which are hastily thrown open, and the crowd knocks Cat off her feet, carrying her away like a piece of driftwood.

'Oi!' George bellows, wading after her.

'Stop there! Everybody, stop there!' one of the policemen shouts. With her ribs crushed and bruised, Cat fights to regain her feet. The air is suddenly sweet and clear, and she realises she's been carried clean out through the doors. Eyes searching, she can see no sign of George amidst the struggling bodies. More whistles are blowing, and the sound of running feet in heavy police boots echoes towards her.

The police have pushed from the front of the building, and cast a net at the back to catch the fleeing gamblers. Cat fights her way to the edge of the mêlée, dodging officers left and right. Suddenly she is barrelled from behind, by a man fleeing with his hat pulled so far over his eyes to avoid recognition that he doesn't even see her, and cannons her to the ground. The wind is knocked from her lungs, and she stays down for a second, fighting to breathe. Then a voice rises high above the police whistles and the grunts of captured men, loud and incongruous. Cat looks up and sees Albert Canning, approaching through the darkness with a fire in his eyes that seems to light his way. He steps into the pool of light spilling from the pub and there is so little thought, yet so much conviction, suffusing his expression that Cat is chilled by it. In spite of her contempt, and the many weeks she has lived with the vicar, scarcely noticing him, she is suddenly afraid. He wears a smile quite sickly and deranged.

'Repent! Examine you all the error of your ways! The gravity of your sins! Cast aside these foolish and perilous ways, for they are the path to your downfall, to your destruction, and to the destruction of all that is clean and pure and good in the world!' the vicar shouts, his voice high and excited, face lit with a zeal so bright that it outshines the electric back room lights. Cat's heart plunges into her gut, which twists in protest. She coughs, fighting for air, flinching as booted feet thunder past her, near her head and hands and legs. He must not see her. She tries to get up but too soon, and a wave of dizziness forces her back onto the dusty ground. The vicar is walking forwards slowly, one childlike step at a time. He holds aloft a gilt cross fully twelve inches high, which gleams like his eyes. Brandishing it, he inches slowly towards a pair of officers who are wrestling a man to the ground, a man who fights tooth and nail not to be taken down.

'Leave off me, you filth! I only came down here for a pint!' the man cries, raggedly.

'Then what's this betting slip in your pocket, Keith Berringer, and how come you've two weeks' wages in your purse?' one of the officers asks. 'Been saving up for a rainy day, have you?' he says, and his colleague laughs as rain begins to fall steadily, turning the dust to mud.

'Repent, my son! Cast off your corrupted ways like an old skin! Be born anew in the love and fear of God!' the vicar implores, standing as close to

324

the struggling man as is prudent.

'Christ! You needn't have brought the bloody church along with you! Haven't I enough to deal with?' Keith Berringer complains bitterly.

'Well, that weren't our idea,' one of the officers mutters in distaste, as Albert stands before them, beaming, breathing hard. Still coughing, Cat gets to her knees. She knows it would be better to turn her face away in case his gaze shifts, but she can't take her eyes from the vicar. If he were to look down, if he were to look to his right, he would see her. Her heartbeat bangs in her temples. She is on all fours like an animal, her fingers sinking into the gritty earth as the rain wets it, her clothes filthy with it. She clenches her teeth but can't keep another fit of coughing at bay. The spasms in her chest are agonising, and she lets her head droop down, close to the ground. For a second the noises all around recede—the whistles and shouts and stamping feet, the slamming doors and the vicar's thrumming voice and the laughter of the police— all are lost behind a wall of muffled thumping that storms her ears. Shadows crowd her vision, sparkling with bright motes of light. *Do not faint!* she commands herself. She can't be arrested, can't be seen. Can't be found lying helpless in the mud.

Gradually, air returns to her lungs, and she breathes more easily, and her head clears and sound comes back into vibrant clarity. She gets to her feet, and glances to her right. The vicar is looking for a new target. The police have made off with Keith Berringer, who seems keener to go with them than stay and be preached to.

'The path to righteousness is one of purity and chastity, one of cleanliness and honesty . . .' the

325

vicar announces to fleeing figures left and right, waving the cross at them as though he can cure them with one glimpse of it. *Run, now*, Cat tells herself. But it is too late. She has risen into his eye line, and he turns upon her, pounces. 'You! Young woman! You have no place here! Women are created mild, the meek vessels of subservience to Godly rule . . .' His voice tails off to silence. Their eyes meet. For a second, she thinks he will not recognise her. Many are the men who would not know their own servants outside their uniforms, outside the house, least of all in the dark and muddied. But he frowns, struggles to place her, and in the second before she flees, Cat sees that he does. His eyes widen with shock.

10

Hester wakes briefly in the night and stretches out her hand to find Albert's side of the bed empty. Thinking it must be near morning, she sleeps again, with a shroud of ill-defined hopelessness weighing her down. She feels listless, as if there is little point in her waking up at all. But when the morning comes, and brash sunshine lances between the curtains to wake her again, she sees that Albert's pillow is smooth and plump, and the sheet on his side of the bed is still pulled taut. He had been sitting up with Robin Durrant, deep in discussion, when she came up to bed the night before. Now it seems that wherever he's slept, it has not been in his own bed. Hester dresses herself as neatly as she can without calling for Cat to help her. She feels strangely uneasy, after seeing Cat and Robin Durrant talking in the courtyard. He had seemed agitated, pacing up and down. The way he'd stood so close to her, the way he'd gesticulated, all seemed far too familiar. As though they knew each other well, as though they had a relationship of some kind that she knew nothing about. Amelia had called Robin beautiful; perhaps Cat found him so as well.

She pins up her hair, smoothes her cheeks with a little powder and goes downstairs in her morning dress, only to find Albert sitting in the parlour, hands on his knees, staring straight ahead. The hems of his trousers are caked with dust and grime, his shoes encrusted with it. Of Robin Durrant, there is no sign.

'Albert! Are you all right? Where have you been?' she asks, standing close to him, taking one of his limp hands in hers. He looks up at her slowly, like an old, old man, and blinks once or twice before seeming to recognise her.

'Hetty! I was waiting for you. Forgive me. I was too troubled to come up to bed. I thought it best not to disturb you until now . . .' he murmurs.

'Disturb me? Why? What on earth is going on?' Hester holds his hand tightly. She does not like the way his gaze seems to come from a great distance, the way his voice is soggy with fatigue and bewilderment.

'I fear there is a pariah in our very midst . . . a spot of rot and blight to blemish the purity of our home,' Albert says, grimacing as though his own words taste ill.

'A spot of rot? Albert, please, you're not making

327

sense!'

'The servant girl. The dark-haired one. We must be rid of her at once,' he says, more decisively.

'Cat? Why must we? What has happened to her?' Hester asks anxiously. *A spot of rot.* She thinks of what Amelia had caught her husband doing, and of the familiarity she had witnessed between Cat and Robin. Her throat goes dry. 'Is it Mr Durrant?'

'What? What do you mean? This has nothing to do with Robin! Is he back? Is he back from the meadows?' Albert half rises from his chair only to slump back again, wearily.

'I don't know . . . Albert, where did you sleep?'

'No, no. I couldn't sleep. I can't sleep. There is too much to think about . . . The girl must be gone from here . . . as soon as possible. No wonder! No wonder I have not managed it! Tainted! With debauchery . . . it taints everything it touches . . .' Albert throws up his hands abruptly, face falling into despair.

'Debauchery? What debauchery?' Hester struggles to keep up, crouching beside him and trying to read his face. It is closed to her, thoughts she cannot read churning behind his glassy gaze. Without warning, tears spring into her eyes, hot and stinging. 'Bertie, *please*. Explain this to me,' she begs. Albert looks down at her and smiles; a small, sad-looking smile.

'Of course you don't understand. You, who are everything a wife should be,' he says. Hester smiles too, glad at least that the argument following her unwanted caress seems forgotten. 'I went with the police last night, to a notorious gambling den in Thatcham. I went to try to convince the men to

328

change their ways, to give up such ungodly pastimes . . . I tried to explain the damage that they do to themselves, to all of us . . . to the whole of mankind!'

'But . . . what has this got to do with Cat?'

'With Cat? Who is Cat?

'The *maid*, Bertie. You said the maid would have to be let go . . .'

'Yes! By all means, she must go! She was there, Hetty—she was there, fleeing like one of the rats as the police stormed in and turned out the nest of them . . . I saw her! I knew her at once!'

'You must be mistaken, Bertie . . . why in heaven's name would Cat be in Thatcham, and gambling, for pity's sake? It couldn't have been her—she was upstairs and in bed, I'm sure of it!'

'No, no, you are not sure. *I saw her*, Hester. A liar and a gambler and no doubt a lascivious doxy besides . . .'

'But you *must* be mistaken,' Hester insists.

'I want her gone. She will be the ruin of us all.'

'No, Albert! On this you must listen to me— please. You're mistaken. She's a good girl! She works hard—'

'It has come to a fine state of affairs that my own wife should doubt my word,' Albert says, coldly. 'Call her up, and ask her. Ask her, then, and let's see how deep the roots of her dishonesty go!'

*   *   *

Hester finds Cat making up the master bed with fresh linens, the dirty ones twisted into a bundle by the door. Hester steps over it, suddenly finding her feet like lead, and her tongue made of wood. She

329

smiles weakly when Cat looks up, and notices the dark shadows under the girl's eyes and that, however well brushed they have been, her shoes still look dirty, muddy.

'Sorry, madam. I won't be a moment, but I can finish this later if you'd rather?' Cat says quietly.

'No, no, Cat. It's quite all right. There was . . . actually something else I wanted to talk to you about,' Hester says reluctantly. Cat throws her arms wide and a clean sheet billows out, falling slowly and with expert aim into just the right position. She twitches it a couple of times, and then stands up, turning to face Hester with a look of such calm resignation that Hester knows the answer before she has asked the question. 'It's true then? You were out in Thatcham last night? And gambling? My husband says he saw you there . . .' She trails off, surprised by the way her nerves jangle, and to find that she has been hoping it has all been a mistake. Praying it, even.

'He saw me there, it's true. But I was not gambling, madam,' Cat says, looking straight at Hester without flinching; that black, disconcerting stare of hers.

'Oh, Cat! How could you? How . . . how on earth did you *get* there?'

'I borrowed the vicar's bicycle. I've done it many times before,' Cat announces, tipping up her chin defiantly, as if daring Hester to rebuke her. Hester stares at her, dumbfounded, for a long moment, until Cat speaks again. 'I suppose I shall be let go?' she asks, and though her defiance remains, there is a slight tremor in her voice.

'I don't know . . . I don't know. If the vicar finds out you took his bicycle . . . You have done it many

330

times?' Hester breathes. 'But, to do what? When do you sleep?'

'I do not sleep easy, madam. Since I was gaoled I . . . I do not sleep easy. And you never said I could not go out of the house when the day was over. It was never said that I shouldn't! All I wanted was to have some taste of life beyond these four walls. Is that a crime?'

'No, no, it's not a crime, Cat! But it is not seemly! Those places in Thatcham, and at that hour of the night, unaccompanied . . . it is no place for a young woman on her own! Anything could have happened to you! People might have thought the *very* worst of you! It's just not the done thing, Cat! I never said so explicitly because I never thought it needed saying! And you know I have the right of it!' Hester cries, her voice rising higher and higher, beyond her control.

'I was not always unaccompanied,' Cat mutters.

'Oh, and who went with you? Not Sophie Bell, I know that for sure . . .' Hester falters, as Cat's meaning becomes clear. 'You mean . . . you have a sweetheart?' she asks. Cat says nothing, but a flicker of emotion kindles in her eyes. 'I see,' Hester says, quietly. Was that what she had witnessed, in the courtyard? A lover's tiff? She looks out of the window, at the far green blur of distant trees. Birds are singing, as they always do. The air is bright and dry, but suddenly the house feels far away, removed. Or perhaps it is she, Hester, who is far away. Disconnected from all the things she thinks she knows. 'But,' she gropes weakly for some redeeming feature in it all, 'but you were not there to gamble? Last night?'

'No, madam. I was not there to gamble.' Silence

331

falls in the room, and the dust sent up by the billowing sheets slowly settles, one twinkling mote at a time, onto the polished surfaces of the furniture. Hester weaves her fingers together in front of her and studies them for a time, and she can just about hear Cat breathing, fast and shallow, like some cornered creature, ready to fight. 'Shall I pack my things then?' Cat says at last. Hester shakes her head.

'I must . . . speak with my husband about it. I believe you are good at heart, Cat; I do believe it. If you are to stay, I must have it from you that you will stop these visits to town. Perhaps you might walk out with your . . . gentleman friend on a Sunday afternoon, when you have free time. But you must not go to the public houses in town any more, and you must not sneak out in the night. Can I give my husband your word on this?' Hester asks, her voice shaking. The hardness in Cat's eyes softens a little, and her mouth thins, pressing into a single line of unhappiness; but her answer, when it comes, is resolute.

'No, madam. I cannot swear to it.'

*   *   *

Hester pauses at the top of the stairs before going back down to Albert. She puts out a hand to grasp the banister, and sees that it is shaking. Her whole body is shaking. Suddenly it seems that the world is a place where nothing is as simple as it had once seemed; a place where she has little understanding, of anything. And she knows that she ought to be outraged by these admissions of Cat's, but somehow she is not. She is shocked, and she is worried, and she is . . . not *envious*, surely? Could that be what is causing the lump in her throat, what is making her long to fly into Albert's arms? But she is not outraged. She is afraid. Swallowing, she begins her descent, and realises that she had paused for a specific reason. She needed time to think of an argument, to think of a way to persuade Albert to let Cat stay on. Because, suddenly, the thought of her going, of one more familiar thing transforming, of one more failure, is more than she can bear.

But nothing she says has any impact on her husband. She promises him, in spite of what Cat said, that the girl will never go out at night again. She lies, and says she has Cat's word. She does not mention the bicycle at all, nor Cat's sweetheart; she swears that Cat had not been gambling, that night or any other, and that she had merely wanted to exercise a little freedom from the constraints of her position, and to explore her new surroundings; something to be expected in one so young, and one who has seen so much trouble in her short lifetime. She even argues that they would not be able to afford to replace her, since a less troublesome girl will command a higher salary. But the vicar is every bit as adamant as Cat. He hardly seems to listen, sitting with an impassive expression on his face, his arms and hands limp in his lap as she speaks, on and on, presenting the same argument in three different ways. When she finishes, and grasps his hand in supplication, he merely pats her hands, absently.

'You are a good and charitable soul, Hester. But she must go. At once. She is a *spot of blight* upon this house, at a time when it is utterly crucial that there be *no stain* here. No pollution. Do you see? Do you see, Hester? *Everything* depends on this!' he says, with such a strange light in his eyes that Hester feels a wave of desperation crash through her.

'Albert, please. Please do listen to me. There is no stain on our house! This theosophy has skewed your thoughts, my darling . . . Haven't I always run a good household? Shouldn't I know best about what servants to keep, and how such things should be done? I must insist that this matter be left in my hands!'

'Hester, your eyes are blind. You do not have the proper understanding,' Albert says, resolutely.

'I have not been . . . altered, you mean. I am not controlled by the teachings of Robin Durrant!' she says, her voice a strained whisper.

At this Albert merely smiles. 'And for that very reason, Hetty, you must do as I say.'

'Albert, *please*,' she implores. Albert pats her hand again, as though she is an unthinking pet of some kind, whose bewilderment is lamentable but to be expected, then rises and goes to his study, shutting the door behind him. Her words are quite lost upon him. In the deceptive calm of the house the clock ticks like a dusty heartbeat, and Cat's light footsteps, as she makes the bed that Hester will lie in, cause the floorboards to creak.

*   *   *

Hester is still perching on the edge of a chair in the parlour when Robin Durrant returns. She turns at the sound of his lively footsteps, sees him make his way to the door with a purposeful stride, let himself in like a resident, not a guest; and then hears him putting down his camera to hang up his coat and hat, all unconcerned. His buoyant walk makes locks of his hair bounce against his forehead, like a boy's, and he hums, ever so softly, just under his breath. A tuneless staccato which might have been formless words, bubbling irrepressibly from within him.

'Albert!' he calls, as he strides along the hallway. *In he crashes*, Hester thinks, *like a tidal wave, like a blowing wind*. His head and shoulders appear around the doorway, grass-stained fingers leaving smears on the cream paint of the panelling. 'Hester! You're very quiet in here.' He smiles warmly.

'Should a person not sit quietly in their own home?' she replies, unable to meet his eye. Robin pauses, seems to think, to slow down.

'Is everything all right? Are you upset?' He comes into the room and stands with his hands clasped behind his back, arranging himself more formally all of a sudden.

'I'm not upset,' she says, but to her chagrin her voice breaks as she says it. Wanting to hide it from Robin Durrant only seems to make the weeping harder to hold.

'Hester! You poor creature . . . tell me what the matter is,' Robin commands. He puts out his hands and moves towards her, as if to offer an embrace, but Hester rises hastily from her chair.

'Don't touch me!' she cries. 'It's your doing!' Her pulse races, makes her fingers shake; but the words are out now, and she cannot take them back.

'Then you must immediately tell me how I have troubled you, so that I can apologise and be sure

335

never to do so again,' Robin replies carefully. His words are smooth and unhurried. As seamless as the rest of him.

'My husband . . . saw our maid Cat at a tavern last night. It seems she has been keeping late-night trysts with a sweetheart, and now he says she is to go and he will not hear another word on the matter. Such notions of purity he has now, you see.' She shoots the theosophist an angry glance. 'Such notions that he has half lost his . . . sense of proportion, and will brook no argument.' As Hester speaks she looks up, just briefly, and is shocked by Robin's expression. It veers here and there between shock and anger and consternation for some seconds before he manages to wrestle it back into his control. Hester catches her breath. 'Did you know something of this before, Mr Durrant?'

'I . . . no, of course not,' he says, but without conviction. Hester stares at him, her eyes widening. 'That is, I had seen her, once or twice. Going off in the evening. Just for walks, I assumed.'

'I see. And you did not think to mention this to Albert or myself?'

'My apologies, Mrs Canning. I had thought no harm could come of it,' Robin replies smoothly, and all expression in face and voice is gone, masked behind a careful neutrality.

'Well, harm has come of it, Mr Durrant. I wonder if that was all you knew about it. I wonder if you might not have some inkling as to the identity of her gentleman friend?' Hester says quietly, her voice shaking with nerves. Robin Durrant watches her, a new expression forming on his face. One of slight surprise and amusement. One of new understanding. Hester looks away, down at her hands. His eyes are too familiar, suddenly; they seem to laugh at her.

'Hester, how has your opinion of me changed so much of late that you no longer trust me to speak the truth?' he asks; a touch of soft menace in the words.

Hester fidgets, twisting her handkerchief tightly one way, then the other. 'I have seen the two of you . . . speaking together. In the evenings,' she stammers.

'What of it? You don't mean that *I* am her mystery man, surely? A few polite words exchanged between guest and maid, over a cigarette, and you have construed an affair from this?'

'That's not what I saw. It was not . . . polite,' Hester whispers. Robin Durrant crosses the room towards her with a slow, deliberate step, and she fights the urge to back away.

'You must have been mistaken, I assure you. There is nothing whatsoever between me and your maid,' he says, standing so close to her that she can feel the warmth of his body, the moist touch of his breath as he speaks. She turns her face away, heart racing in her chest, and endures the silence for a long moment, until she thinks she might scream. 'Still, if you'd like me to speak to your husband on behalf of the girl, I would be happy to do so. Perhaps I can persuade him to let her stay on, if that is what you wish?' Robin murmurs, so close now that she can hear his every breath as it rushes gently in, between his parted lips, over teeth and tongue. Her eyes well again, tears splashing messily onto her cheeks. Without hesitation, the theosophist puts out his fingers and brushes them away. Hester is rooted to the spot, too shocked to move.

'I don't understand what power you have over my husband,' she says, her voice so constricted she hardly knows it.

'Don't you? No, I suppose you wouldn't. Unbesmirched as you are. *Virgo intacta*, a lily whiter than white; so kind and clean and innocent,' he says, his mouth twisting to one side in cruel amusement. Hester's jaw falls open in shock.

'How do you . . . ?' she whispers, inadvertently.

'Albert told me. One day whilst extolling his own purity to me. He could hardly boast of his own virginity, and not by default proclaim you to be in the same state, could he?' Robin says, with a lupine grin.

Hester shuts her eyes, her face burning. In the darkness behind her eyelids the room seems to spin, and her thoughts to match it.

'I think you should leave this house. Leave and not return!' she says.

'Hester, Hester. You and I need not trouble one another,' Robin says calmly. 'We *must not* trouble one another,' he adds, making the statement a command, a warning. The hand that gathered her tears lingers, moving softly over the skin of her cheek, along her jaw and from chin to neck, neck to collarbone, until the air freezes in her lungs and she can neither protest nor move nor turn away. 'Dear Hetty. I'll speak to Albert. I'll convince him. You can keep your maid—a gift from me to you, to make up for whatever I have done to turn you against me,' he says, his eyes alight and savage. His

338

hand stays a second longer on her skin, his fingers warm, wet from her own salty tears. They seem to burn her, and his light touch is like a yoke of iron, fixing her to the spot. Then he is gone, across the hallway to knock softly on the study door. Released, Hester heaves in great gulps of dizzying air and flees the room with blind, faltering steps.

*   *   *

Mrs Bell opens each hamper of laundry as it comes back from Mrs Lynchcombe, lifts out each item and checks it off the list, her eyes screwed up with the effort of reading her own cramped handwriting.

'That should be six pillow slips—did I count six?' she mutters; this and similar comments. Cat has seen this process many times, and knows she may as well ignore the remarks. Mrs Bell, despite a close and apparently friendly acquaintance with the laundress, seems convinced that the woman will one day conspire to rob the household of a napkin or a nightdress, and cannot be satisfied without checking the hampers herself each time. She blows out her cheeks, wipes her sweaty brow, puts her hands on the vast slabs of her hips and studies a lace-collared blouse, pressed and neatly folded in front of her. Is this the one that was sent away? Or has it been switched with one of lower quality?

'Your own suspicions must tire you out,' Cat observes.

'What's that? Don't mumble behind my back, if you please,' Mrs Bell grumbles.

'I said you should be commended, for such

thoroughness.' She smiles briefly. Mrs Bell laughs a short bark of a laugh.

'Ha! You never said that in a month of Sundays!' She goes back to her examination of the hampers. Cat shrugs. She is breaking up the salt, which comes from the grocer in a large, hard block. She uses a round pick with a smooth wooden handle, so smooth that the effort of keeping her grip on it cramps her hand. The muscles in her forearm burn. She stabs repeatedly at the block, at just the right angle that small, usable chunks are broken off; not big pieces that must be broken again, not small gritty pieces that she will struggle to collect from the worktop. The right-sized pieces are packed into earthenware jars and sealed until they are needed. They will be ground by hand, as the need arises, to fill the silver cruet. There is some satisfaction in the repeated stabbing, the controlled violence of the job. Precise work is needed; blows of the correct weight and speed, over and over again. Cat's mind clears as she does it; some of the odd, cold rage that has filled her all morning starts to dissipate. An odd rage indeed, hard and numbing. She hardly knows who it is directed at. The vicar, for seeing her? The theosophist, for sending him out on crusade? Hester, for forbidding her to go out again? George, for insisting that she wed him? Or just because her secret has been found out. Because she has no secret any more: the one thing that belonged to her alone, now taken. She stabs, she breaks the block, her muscles burn, and she grows calmer. Cat kicks off her shoes, lets the cool of the flagstones press into her aching feet.

'I may be gone from here, soon. Tonight, even,'

she says at length, her tone betraying no dismay at the prospect.

'What are you talking about?' Sophie Bell asks, finishing her inspection and slumping into a chair. With a sweep of her arm, she pushes away a pile of peas to be podded, so that she can spread her bosom, her mottled arms, across the table top.

'I think I am dismissed. The vicar's wife is speaking to him on my behalf, but I doubt she'll convince him,' says Cat. The housekeeper gapes.

'But . . . what for, for Christ's sake? What 'ave you done, you minx?'

'I . . . go out in the night. I don't sleep. I go out into Thatcham, and places. And now he has found me out in this. So I am dismissed.' She shrugs, as if the future were not suddenly an amorphous thing, shapeless and menacing and empty. No reference for a dismissed servant. No further positions for her, with this last chance spent.

'Cat Morley . . . Cat Morley . . .' Mrs Bell says her name as if it is a very curse to be uttered in disbelief, in extremis. Her sliver eyes are wider than ever before. 'How could you be so stupid? And you so bright?' she asks, and this is so far from what Cat expected, so far from the scorn and the derision, that at first she can't think how to reply.

'I . . . I love a man,' she says at last, pausing with the pick buried deep in the salt, stuck fast there. She jabbed it too hard, drove it too deep. Mrs Bell shakes her head.

'A man! What good is a man? You had everything here!' Cat wrestles mutely with the pick. Flies circle the stuffy room, and Mrs Bell seems, for once, to be robbed of words.

'What everything? Truly? What have I here but

341

every day the same, like I am not a person at all but a machine? And to be told that this is my lot, and I should be happy for it while others have it that they can lie around and . . . and . . . press flowers all the livelong day!' she cries, her voice shaking treacherously.

'What everything? A bed! In a clean, warm house . . . three meals a day and an income—employers that don't beat you, but tolerate your lip when it gets away from you! That's what everything!' Mrs Bell says. 'Is that not enough for you, when countless thousands would wish to be so fortunate?'

'No,' Cat tells her solemnly. 'It is not enough. I can't abide it. I can't.' She waits, and watches; but the housekeeper merely stares ahead, then down at her chapped and ruined hands, and does not speak. Cat takes a slow breath. 'If I am gone by tonight, I wanted to say I'm sorry about your boy. About you losing him. And I'm sorry you lost your husband too. I'm sorry if I . . . scorned you, for being a good servant. You are everything you should be. I am the one with no place in any of it, as you've been telling me from the start,' she says, in a measured tone.

'Don't give me contrition, girl. It don't suit you,' Sophie Bell replies, but the whip-crack tone of her voice has gone slack, has lost all its sting, and wanders instead like her gaze around the room; unravelling like a loose thread from a hem.

*　　　*　　　*

Robin emerges just a quarter of an hour later. Hester is in her room, but she hears the study door

342

open and then close with a soft, resolute thump. There had been voices, low and muffled, the entire time the theosophist was in with her husband. Mostly Robin's, as far as she could tell, with a few loaded pauses; a few hesitant, barely audible words in Albert's voice. Even through the floor she could sense his uncertainty. And yet she knows, as she hears the theosophist's footsteps go first into the parlour, and then along the hall to the bottom of the stairs, that he will have got his way. For whatever is Robin's way is now Albert's way as well. She sits at her dressing table with her powder puff in her fingertips, poised by her cheek. She had been about to repair the damage her tears had done, but had caught her own eye in the mirror, and halted. Her eyes are puffy, and below them her cheeks seem more sunken and drawn than ever before. Her hair is flat and lifeless, and in the bleak light from the window it has no lustre at all. She is a dull creature indeed, she thinks. No wonder Albert should prefer his fairies, his beautiful theosophist. The powder puff trembles a little, sending a scatter of fine, pale dust down onto the mahogany table top.

Robin's footsteps on the stairs make her heart jolt. His walk is so instantly recognisable—he makes no effort to be subtle, to tread quietly. He bangs about like a thoughtless child . . . but no. Hester can no longer think of him as childlike—however unruly his hair, however quick his grin. He knocks respectfully at the door, and she does not answer.

'Hester? Mrs Canning?' he calls. She hears the mocking way in which he interchanges these two forms of address, as if it is up to him to choose

343

which one to use, appropriate or no. 'Hetty? I have good news,' he says; and though her pulse beats hard inside her head, she still does not reply. In the mirror she sees her lips pinch tightly together, a grim line that makes her even less lovely. There is a long pause, and then he chuckles. 'I shan't huff, or puff, or blow your house down . . . but I have it from Albert that Cat can stay on. There—doesn't that cheer you up? He has some . . . conditions to this, which she's not going to like, but I did my best. At least she's not to be cast out into the world without means. Hester? Aren't you going to thank me?' he asks. *No!* she cries silently, suddenly sure that whatever the reason he has done this thing, it is in his own interests. 'Very well. Perhaps you are resting. Perhaps you are sulking. Either way, I shall see you at dinner, Mrs Canning; and thanks to me there will be a maid to serve it to us.'

His footsteps drift idly away, back down the stairs, and Hester breathes again, and tries to be relieved that Cat is not to go. But even this makes her uneasy, because it is his doing and he proclaims it to be on her behalf. Her head is aching, a tight band of pain around her skull. Slowly, she rises, and lies down on the bed. She had meant to think, to plan, but her mind is both full and empty, and she can make no sense of her thoughts, nor find anything in her experience or education to inform her how to act in this alien situation. And neither can she sleep. So she merely lies, in dread of the dinner hour.

*   *   *

Before dinner, and at a crucial point in its

preparation, Mrs Bell is summoned under protest to go upstairs and be addressed by the vicar and his wife.

'Watch those pies, Cat—another five minutes to brown the crusts is all they want,' she says as she waddles from the room. Cat stares steadily at the doorway once the fat housekeeper has gone through it, and tries to guess what it might mean. The whole house is loaded with tension, paused in anticipation like a clock wound too tight. Perhaps it is only the heat, but perhaps not. Cat watches the pies, and finishes scrubbing the carrots in a bucket of water, and fetches the cream for dessert from the well; and on her return to the kitchen Mrs Bell is back, and will not look her in the eye, and snaps:

'Never you mind!' when Cat asks what the summons was about. A while later, she speaks again. 'You're to put their food on the dresser when you take it up. Don't take it to the table— they'll serve themselves. The vicar . . . the vicar don't want you too close to him,' she says heavily, her voice laden with disapproval as she passes on this injunction.

'What does he think—that I'll infect him with something?' Cat asks, incredulously.

'How should I know what the man thinks? Just mind what he says and be thankful you're still here!' says Mrs Bell.

So Cat serves dinner with a feeling of angry suspicion to make her hands clumsy. She glares at them as she puts each dish on the dresser, but only Robin Durrant will look at her, and he smiles and thanks her with ostentatious ease. Hester's eyes are fixed with a kind of desperation at the precise centre of the white tablecloth, and the vicar gazes around him with a serenity that seems wholly out of place, wholly disconnected from the room. Afterwards, when all is cleared away and she has been out for a cigarette, keeping close to the eaves of the house as a few bloated raindrops begin to fall, Cat returns to the kitchen to find Mrs Bell standing with her hands in the pockets of her apron and a look on her face that Cat has never seen before. She pulls up short. Something in that look tells her to run, but she ignores it.

'What is it?' she asks, warily. Mrs Bell is breathing hard, her nostrils flaring whitely. She almost looks afraid.

'I'm to accompany you to your room. To make sure you go into it,' she says at last, the words clipped.

'Ah, so you're to be my warden now? They have pitted us against each other.' Cat smiles resignedly.

'I may not like it, but that is what I am instructed to do. To see to it you go to bed at the end of the day, and not out to any *dens of iniquity* . . .'

'The vicar's words?'

'The very same.'

'And I suppose nobody will take my word on this any more?'

'I think you've done that to yourself, Cat,' Mrs Bell replies; and Cat smiles again, just fleetingly.

'Very well then. Let us go up.'

Walking ahead of the housekeeper on angry feet, Cat is up both flights of stairs and outside her room, arms folded defiantly, by the time Mrs Bells puffs her way laboriously along behind her.

'Well then, here I am. All ready to be tucked in,' Cat says.

'I'm to see you inside your room, and ready for

bed.' Cat steps over the threshold, walks to the bed and sits upon it.

'Will this do? Or must I strip off and get beneath the sheet?'

'I don't like it much, Cat. But you've brung it on yourself,' Mrs Bell replies. She reaches out, takes the door handle and begins to close the door.

'Wait! I never close it all the way . . . I can't stand it. Leave it ajar, if you please,' Cat says. Mrs Bell hesitates, her face falling even more, a troubled frown making deep folds between her brows. Her spare hand fiddles with something in her pocket, and then she reaches for the door handle again, and her other hand emerges from her apron, and Cat sees a glint of metal in it, a warning flash of reflected light that she has no time to react to.

'I'm sorry about it, girl,' Mrs Bell mutters; and then the door is shut and there is a telltale click in the lock.

Cat is on her feet in an instant, and flies to the door.

'No, no, *no!*' she shouts, twisting and heaving at the handle, which creaks in protest but does not yield. Behind it, Mrs Bell's weighty footsteps recede as hastily as they may along the corridor. With sudden violence Cat doubles up, her stomach lurches, and a thin string of bitter mucus drips from her mouth to the floor. When the spasm passes she finds the walls pressing in around her, her heart squeezing as if it will burst, and black shadows of panic swelling up inside her head. The floor seems to lurch beneath her feet, rolling like deep water. She throws her arms out for balance, such a buzzing in her ears that she can't even hear her own voice as she shouts for Sophie to come back. She hurls herself at the door, scrabbling at the wood, heedless of the splinters that drive themselves beneath her fingernails. She pounds her fists against it, feels the shock of each blow rattle her bones. But the door does not yield.

*   *   *

Hester, on the floor below, lies sleepless and alone in her bed. Albert retired to his study after dinner, and shows no sign of emerging. So Hester lies and listens to Cat's shouts, her sobbing and swearing and the way she begs, until she can hardly bear it a second longer. The girl calls for Sophie for a long time, then she pauses, and Hester pictures her catching her breath.

'Mrs Canning! Mrs Canning! Please let me out! I can't be locked in! I can't!' Cat's ragged voice comes clearly through the ceiling. Hester goes cold. She holds her breath, prays she will hear no more. *'Please . . . I won't run off! I won't! Please, let me out!'* On and on it goes. Hester shuts her eyes and puts the pillow over her head, but she can't block out the girl's distress completely. She has no choice but to hear it, and finds in it, as the night progresses, an echo of feelings deep inside her own heart.

2011

Leah stormed back to her car, climbed in and slammed the door. In the sudden quiet she caught

348

her breath, and the wind whipped a scattering of damp yellow tree blossoms onto the windscreen. Her scarf was too tight around her neck, her gloves were making her clumsy. The car was stuffy, the air stale, and Leah felt a huge irritation boiling up inside her. She groped in her bag for her mobile, and dialled Mark's number.

'Yes?' he answered with a bark; his default setting of suspicion and barely contained hostility.

'It's me,' she replied, just as shortly.

'Oh, hello . . . how did you get on?'

'I'm at the library now—well, I'm in the car park. Apparently you have to book an appointment to use the microfiche machines, and the local papers from 1911 aren't online yet, and the machines are booked up all day. The earliest I could get one was tomorrow. How ridiculous is that?'

'Steady on, Leah—it's not long to wait. You're not in London any more,' Mark said, sounding amused.

'I know. It's just really frustrating to get held up like this . . . perhaps I should go back up to London for the day, and look in the national press?'

'What's the rush? The guy's not going to get any less dead. Or any deader, for that matter. Are you always this impatient?' he asked, slightly too quickly.

'Yes! Probably. With a story, anyway.' She took a deep breath and let it go. 'How did you get on with the schools?'

'Stroke of luck there, actually. I rang most of the schools in the area and was getting nowhere— several of them weren't even founded until the fifties and sixties—but then the headmaster of the last one, a primary school, by some miracle wasn't too busy to talk to me, and happened to be a local history buff. I told him what Hester said in the letters, and he thought it pretty unlikely that a vicar's wife would have worked full-time as a teacher—it just wasn't really the done thing once a woman was married. He says it's more likely she was volunteering a little time each week—perhaps for Sunday school classes, or cookery—and he suggested we check out The Bluecoat School.'

'The Bluecoat School? Where's that?'

'It's in Thatcham. It's not a school any more, but it's still known by that name. I'm standing right outside the building now, as it happens,' Mark said.

'You're there? Without me? Where exactly?' Leah demanded, starting the car.

'Relax—it's not going anywhere. Come along the A4 into Thatcham and you'll see me.'

As Leah drove the sun began to break through widening cracks in the clouds—dazzling shards of light that hurt her eyes. She waited impatiently at traffic lights, fingers drumming on the wheel, and was almost out the other side of Thatcham before she saw Mark, hunched into his raincoat. He pulled one hand from a pocket and waved to her, and she swerved into the kerb, the car behind giving her a loud blast of its horn. She waved vaguely in apology as it sped past, and wound down the window.

'I almost drove right by you! This is the main road—are you sure this is the right place?'

'Yes, I'm sure. It's probably best if you pull off here—there's parking just a little way up that street,' Mark said as a lorry squeezed past, narrowly missing her rear bumper.

'OK, hang on a second.' She pulled back out into the traffic, got more angry gestures and honks, and followed Mark's instructions. As she walked back to where he was waiting, she studied the building that had been The Bluecoat School. Now she came to look at it closely, it stuck out like a sore thumb. It was clearly ancient. A tiny, ancient building with ochre plastered walls and a steeply pitched roof, its shape echoed by the porch over the main door. The stone mullion windows were boarded up, the glass blank; a door in the side wall was barely five feet high, and there were several vacant niches around the walls.

'But—this must be a chapel, surely?' Leah asked, as she came to stand next to Mark.

'Correct. A very old one—almost certainly the oldest building in Thatcham, possibly one of the oldest in Berkshire. Originally the chapel of St Thomas, it was used as an auxiliary school building for years, and then as an antiques shop. Now the council own it, have fixed it up and are wondering what to do with it,' he said. Leah glanced at him and smiled.

'You seem to know a lot about it.'

'That headmaster pointed me to the website,' Mark admitted.

'And he thought this was where she would have taught?'

'He said it was the most likely candidate. It was used as a kind of overflow classroom for the local charitable school, which would have been the most likely to need volunteers like the vicar's wife to fill in teaching gaps.'

'But . . . what about the main school buildings?

Couldn't she just as easily have taught there?'

'Yes. But this place has one crucial advantage.'

'Which is?'

'It's still standing. The rest of the old school buildings were pulled down to make way for new housing between the wars.'

'Bugger.'

'Quite. But at least there's a chance that this is the place she was talking about—where she hid whatever incriminating evidence it was she'd found.' He shrugged.

'I suppose so. Can we go inside?'

'It's locked,' Mark said, with a shake of his head. 'The caretaker should be here any minute—he's agreed to show us around. I told him we're researching a book on ancient chapels, so make sure you act like a scholar.'

'What did you tell him that for? You could have just told the truth.'

'I thought this would sound better. And I didn't want to say we might want to pull up the floorboards and look underneath them. Besides . . . it's more fun this way,' Mark grinned.

'You really have been living quietly lately, haven't you?' Leah said, wryly. Mark shrugged amiably. 'Pulling up the floor might be a tricky one. We'll have to think of a way to see if there are any loose boards . . . perhaps I could ask for a tour of the outside and leave you inside to check it out, or something?' she suggested.

'Excellent! It's like we're going undercover,' Mark said.

'I think you might be getting a bit carried away.'

'Possibly. This is probably him now—the caretaker. Don't forget, you're a scholar and an

352

expert on ancient chapels.'

'Got it.'

As she spoke, a thin man in a dark blue cagoule appeared, walking briskly around the corner, slumped into a kind of apologetic cringe. He came towards them with his hand extended in front of him like a white flag on a pole. The caretaker's name was Kevin Knoll; younger than Leah had expected, and blinking like a mole in the spring sunshine. His light brown eyes watered behind thick pebble glasses. His mouth was small, his nose pointed. His whole face and body appeared gripped by some terrible anxiety, but he smiled readily enough as they introduced themselves.

'Well, I'm sure you're itching to get inside. It's such a joy to meet people who still care about these places,' he said, glancing rapidly to and fro between them. 'Chapels like this are so quintessentially English, to me. They represent so much of our history.'

'Oh, I . . . couldn't agree more,' Leah said, as she followed Kevin to the front door of the building and waited impatiently as he fumbled with the keys. 'So, I imagine you know a great deal about the history of this building? Its uses over the years?' she asked. The key clunked in the lock, and the door swung open.

'In we go. Yes, I suppose I know as much as anybody. Not that I'm an architectural historian like yourselves, of course,' he said, in modest qualification. Leah shot Mark a quick look, and he winked.

'Our, uh, research tells us that the building was used as part of a school, about a hundred years ago—is that right?'

'Yes, that's right. The local charity school for the children of the poor. Once that closed another local school used it—for their home economics classes, I think it was.'

'I don't suppose you have any information about what was taught here? And by whom, back in the days of the charity school?'

'No, I'm afraid not,' Kevin said, and did look a little afraid not to have the answer. 'I'm awfully sorry. I don't know where you'd even look to find that out. I doubt that records survive, if there ever were records . . . I admit, I rather thought you'd be more interested in the *fabric* of the building itself?'

'Oh, we are. It's just always nice to get a bit of colour into the history,' Mark said, clearing his throat. 'It makes a book so much more accessible to readers.'

They walked into the centre of the single room inside the chapel. Pale daylight was streaming through a Gothic arched window in the east-facing wall, reflecting brightly from the whitewashed walls. The incandescence was surprising. Leah had been expecting darkness and gloom, age-old shadows. The windows facing the road were blocked off, as was the tiny side door, but still it felt open, alive. The breeze had followed them in and circled the floor, sending a few bundles of dust to scud around their feet.

'I've always liked to imagine that window in its prime, full of beautiful stained glass . . .' said Kevin, looking at them expectantly.

'Oh, yes—it almost certainly would have had . . . a truly magnificent piece of artwork in place; before the Reformation,' Mark agreed hastily. There were empty stone niches here and there

354

inside, but little else to see. No plaques, no tombs. 'And . . . er . . . I understand the building is being used as community space now? And there are plans to extend it?' he floundered on. But Leah wasn't listening. She was staring at the floor in abject disappointment. She walked to the far end of the room and turned to face the empty space, bathing herself in white light. Was this where Hester Canning had stood? *I know what lies beneath my feet* . . . Leah looked down again. *So there it stays, beneath the floor*. But this was not the floor Hester Canning had walked. Not the floor she could possibly have hidden anything beneath. Leah took a deep breath, filling with frustration. The floor was made of fresh oak boards. Entirely even, flat and secure; entirely modern.

'When was the floor replaced?' she asked, interrupting Kevin as he told Mark about the plans for the building.

'Oh . . . fairly recently. Just last year. It was one of the first things we had to do in order to make the space usable, you see; grade one listing or not. The old boards were quite lovely, but entirely eaten away by wet rot and woodworm. They were loose and uneven. They just crumbled around the nails as they were lifted, I understand. We couldn't even reuse them for anything. They were ruined,' Kevin told her. Mark was looking down now, following the line of one board with his toe, and frowning.

'Did they find anything underneath them?' Leah asked. Kevin gave her a puzzled look. 'It's just, you know—with buildings this old you can often make . . . archaeological discoveries, just by doing something as simple as lifting the floor. Sometimes

355

the original craftsmen have left something behind, something that can give an insight into the time of construction . . . that kind of thing . . .'

'Yes, I see—or superstitious offerings, perhaps?' Kevin said. 'Children's shoes are quite common, aren't they?'

'Probably. So, did you find anything?'

'I'm afraid not. That is, not that I heard about. I wasn't here every day, of course, while they were doing it, but I'm sure the builders would have mentioned it if they'd found anything . . .' Kevin looked at her crestfallen expression and smiled nervously. 'I *am* sorry to disappoint you . . .'

'Oh, no . . . it's just, these incidental finds are a particular passion of mine,' Leah said, woodenly.

'Would you like to take some pictures? For your book?' Kevin asked.

'Great, thank you,' said Mark.

*   *   *

A short while later they stepped back out into the cold daylight; Kevin Knoll locked the chapel and took his leave. Leah and Mark walked slowly back to where they had parked their cars. Leah had the tantalising feeling she was beginning to get somewhere, was beginning to track down the story behind the soldier's letters, and the thought of losing momentum again was almost unbearable. While she had the ball rolling, she had a purpose. When it stopped all the vagueness, the limbo state of her life became obvious again. A heavy feeling of pointlessness; the needle of her inner compass swaying drunkenly to and fro. If Hester Canning had got locked into just such a state—if her life

356

had got stuck on one particular thorn of a problem, never to be worked free, then perhaps it was fate that, in working it free, Leah could unlock her own life at the same time. And she wanted to be able to hand a complete report to Ryan when she saw him next. She wanted to succeed, and give him a name.

As if reading her mind, Mark spoke. 'Shame. I thought we were really starting to get somewhere then. So, have you got a deadline for this investigation?'

'Not exactly . . . the sooner the better. I . . . my contact at the Commonwealth War Graves Commission is here in the UK in about ten days' time. I said I'd meet him and hand over whatever I'd found out.' Leah kept her eyes to the front as she said this, and was trying so hard not to give herself away that she felt self-conscious, as if her every inner thought was written large across her face. To her dismay, she felt heat in her cheeks, and sensed Mark's gaze, thoughtfully taking all of this in.

'Your contact?' he echoed, and left the question hanging between them. Leah sniffed. The breeze and bright light were making her eyes water and her nose run. She thought about changing the subject, and about saying nothing. Neither seemed appropriate, somehow.

'My ex. He got in touch a few weeks back, for the first time in ages. He's been working over in Belgium, near Ypres, and they found the body— the soldier's body. When he found Hester's letters, he called me in to investigate.'

'Your ex? An ex, or *the* ex?'

'Oh, quite definitely *the* ex. My friends are furious with me for going over there. But it's the story I'm interested in. Truly. I've been so blocked since . . . well, for a while. Having something to work on again is . . . just what I needed,' Leah said, quite truthfully.

They stood in silence for a while, by the parked cars. Mark was frowning, thinking.

'It's meant to be the same process as grieving, you know. Breaking up with a long-term partner. You supposedly go through all the same phases—shock, denial, anger, depression, acceptance . . .'

'Really? I'm not so sure. When somebody dies, they can't butt back into your life half a year later and kick you off that neat trajectory, after all.' She shook her head.

'True, true. Better not to see them again, I suppose, until you've been through it all, and come out the other side,' he said carefully.

'Now you sound like Sam. My best friend,' Leah said. She stared along the busy Bath Road for a few seconds, squinting at the cars pushing impatiently by. 'But that's just life, I suppose.' She shrugged. 'The best-laid plans, and all that.'

'Sorry. It's none of my business.' Mark looked away and pulled his car keys out of his jacket.

'It's OK,' Leah said. She changed the subject. 'Mark, about what your dad said—do you really think there was a murder at The Rectory?'

He raised his eyebrows, the sun making his grey eyes pale, as glossy and hard as polished granite. 'If there was, I never heard anything about it.'

'But he did say it was some big family secret.'

'He also thought you were Mandy Rice-Davies.'

'Yes, but what if there was? That would be bad enough for Hester to write those letters about, wouldn't it? She keeps mentioning guilt and a

358

crime and her silence making her complicit, doesn't she? And finding something in the library?'

'It would be bad enough, for sure. But it's equally possible that Dad was remembering an episode of Inspector Morse . . .'

'I don't think so. He seemed . . . really convinced. Excited, just like a child would be if they overheard the grown-ups talking about something like that.'

'Well, who do you think was murdered?'

'I've no idea. But I mean to find out.'

'Shall we walk somewhere for a while? I feel like some fresh air,' he said.

They made their way south along The Broadway, over the railway crossing at the station, and down onto the towpath beside the canal. The cloudy green water slid silently by, flat and smooth. The path was busy with cyclists and joggers, dog walkers and young mothers. They walked eastwards by unspoken consensus, back towards Cold Ash Holt. The sun blanched the water-coloured sky and soaked the landscape with a sudden warmth that made the air muggy with moisture. Leah stripped off her jumper and tied it around her waist, only for Mark to pull it free again, throw it over his shoulder.

'You'll ruin it that way. The sleeves will stretch,' he said, absently.

'Sorry,' Leah said, bemused. A few narrowboats were moored near town, but they soon left them behind to walk between high banks of vegetation. Trees to the north of the water, fields of spindly brown stalks, as high as their shoulders, to the south. Yellow catkins gyrated in the breeze, and each and every twig ended in a shiny bud; waxy, ready to split. The horse chestnut blossoms were almost out—tall candelabras of fresh green stems, the white flowers still furled, waiting. A breeze scudded westward along the water's surface, so that it felt as though they were moving faster than in reality.

About a mile out of town they turned south across one of the fields near the village, where the stream had been marshalled into neat, manmade cuts between the gravel pit lakes. They watched the water birds, squinting as the sunlight shone from the water's surface. There was nobody else in sight now, and no noise.

'It's strange to think how much this has all changed since your great-grandmother was here. None of these lakes. The A4 still just the London Road, with hardly anything on it that wasn't pulled by a horse,' Leah said. She felt so close to the woman, when she read her letters. Could almost hear her voice. Then she looked around and found herself a hundred years, a whole world, away. 'And The Bluecoat School, full of children, full of life. It looked kind of sad today, didn't it? Sitting there with all that traffic thundering past it.'

'Well, that's what the council is trying to change. There's a charitable trust now as well, raising money to extend it and use it as community space,' said Mark distractedly, snatching up a long stem of grass and picking last year's dry seeds from it, a thumbnail full at a time. High above their heads two buzzards circled, their faint cries carried down on the wind for a split second, and then blown away.

'Are there any pictures of Hester? Or Albert? Back at the house?' Leah asked suddenly.

'I don't think so. Sorry. I think I remember some from when I was a child, but . . . I haven't seen them for years. It's possible Dad got rid of them. When the dementia started he did some odd things. We could look, if you like?' he offered. Leah nodded. She was putting her piece together already, though there were more blanks to fill in than filled. A long article, with pictures, and extracts from the letters. Laying it all bare, making it all clear. And without thinking about it explicitly, Leah felt she would be doing this for Hester Canning; a favour for a long-dead stranger.

'How did it start? His dementia?' she asked gently.

Mark took a slow, deep breath. 'So gradually. Around about the time I went up to university, I suppose. That's the last time I remember him just how he used to be. And Mum was still alive—they were so chuffed. Nobody ever thought I'd make it through A-levels.' He smiled, wryly.

'Why, were you a tearaway at school?'

'No, I was as meek as anything. But I'm dyslexic, and the school I was at didn't believe in dyslexia.'

'Oh, I see. Forward thinking of them.'

'Quite. But numbers—numbers I can deal with. So I did maths, and then went into investments . . . it all worked out better than anyone had predicted, and they were *so* happy for me. By the time I graduated, Dad was starting to forget words. He'd get halfway through a sentence and get stuck, trying to find the next word. Not difficult words either. "Car", or "then", or "February". Random little words that just sneaked away from him. We all laughed about it for the first couple of years,' he said, bleakly. Leah had no idea what to say.

'At least,' she began, hesitantly, 'at least the care home seems nice. You hear such horror stories . . . at least you've found him a clean, friendly place where they look after him,' she ventured.

'Sometimes I think it'd be better if he'd died,' Mark said, bleakly.

'Don't say that.' Leah frowned. 'You don't know what he's thinking—it's quite possible that a lot of the time he's quite content.'

'Do you really think so?' he asked, with an edge of desperation in his voice. They stopped walking, and turned to face one another.

'Yes, I do. Wrong to call it a blessing, of course, but at least with dementia the person suffering from it is unaware of it. At least, most of the time,' she said gently.

'Very wrong to call it a blessing,' Mark said sadly. 'I just . . . whenever I go and see Dad I get into a spiral of . . . rotten thoughts. Why him? Why so young? What did he ever do to deserve this?'

'I don't think it works that way. Not unless you believe in karma. Which I don't,' Leah added, firmly. Mark nodded slowly, his face so stricken that Leah's heart ached in sudden sympathy, and she touched his hand briefly, running her thumb across his knuckles. 'Come on. Let's go and look for photos,' she said.

They walked back to their cars in Thatcham and drove to The Old Rectory, made coffee and started to search the house for family photographs. Leah thought of the boxes in the attic rooms, but after a fruitless hour she had searched barely a fraction of them, and her nose and eyes were streaming. She gave up and went downstairs, her jeans smeared with dust, her fingers grimy. In the library, they shamelessly rifled through the many drawers of the vast desk, but to no avail.

'Here's something,' Mark said, climbing down the rickety ladder that ran along a rail around the room, giving access to the highest shelves.

'What have you found?'

'Nothing that exciting—it's Thomas, my grandfather. When he was still a young man.' Mark passed her the dusty photo in a crumbling leather frame, and Leah took it eagerly.

'So this is Hester's son. The one she talks about in the letters,' she said, wiping the dust from the glass and studying the image closely. A solid, oblong face with mid-brown hair, combed back from his forehead; deep brown eyes and the trace of a smile. His skin was completely smooth and unlined. 'Quite handsome,' she remarked. 'Do you think he took after Hester?'

'Your guess is as good as mine, I'm afraid. I honestly can't remember what the photos of my great-grandparents looked like,' Mark said with a shrug.

'Still, at least this is something. Can I make a scan of it at some point? It'd be great to include it in my article, especially since she mentions him in both letters.'

'Of course you can.'

As the sky began to darken outside, they stopped searching and, by unspoken agreement, settled into opposite armchairs to read. Leah went through the vicar's pamphlet for the second time. The prose was flowery, and the praise glowing, to say the least. The vicar's excited rapture over these elementals, as he called them, shone from every page, as did his admiration for Robin Durrant, the 'eminent and learned theosophist' who had unveiled them to the world. He wrote as if a host of shining angels had descended upon him, rather than a handful of sketchy photographs of a girl in a white dress. She peered closely at the supposed elemental again, trying to pick features out of the grainy smear of her face. The more she studied them, the more she thought she could see, in the dancing picture, a thin, dark line along the edge of the figure's forehead.

'It's a wig!' she announced, glancing up at Mark to show him what she'd spotted. He was fast asleep, his head tipped sideways onto the wing of the armchair, mouth clamped shut, brows drawn down severely. Leah watched him for a while, noticing the grey in the stubble along his jaw and at his temples; the gaunt shadows under his cheekbones; a slight cleft in his chin. His bony knees were drawn up, and his arms wrapped around them like a child playing hide and seek. From behind the chair, you wouldn't have known he was in it. There were holes in the toes of his socks. His breathing was slow and deep, as regular as Leah's own heartbeat. There was something deeply calming, deeply pleasing, in watching him sleep. Leah smiled to herself, and scribbled a note for him, leaving it on the arm of his chair. *I'll be back for dinner—not omelettes, thanks.* She got up quietly and let herself out.

*   *   *

The evening was crisp and clear, the sky turning the palest turquoise after sunset, with a tiny high moon like a silver fingernail. In spite of the chill, the scent on the air was soft and damp. A green smell, slowly rising from the grey and brown smells of winter. Leah went to The Old Rectory on foot, having checked the route across fields from the towpath on a map. Her boots were soaked with dew, and her torch beam wobbled in front of her along the ground. From a distance, the lights inside the house made it clearly visible, standing alone on the lane at the edge of the village. She paused, slightly breathless after the brisk walk. Did Hester Canning ever see this view? Or Robin Durrant? Possibly not. It probably wasn't normal to wander the fields after dark if you were an Edwardian vicar's wife, or guest. But nevertheless Leah stood for a while and gazed, and with little effort could imagine herself back in time. Opening the door to find the house warm and alive; clean, bright. A piano playing, perhaps, and voices from behind the parlour door; ghosts of laughter echoing up the kitchen stairs. But she stopped herself. This was not how Hester Canning last knew the house, after all. She wrote of its shadows and secrets. She wrote as if it were her prison, as if she were afraid of it; of something within it. Leah shivered slightly and walked the last stretch quickly, watching her feet in the darkness.

Mark opened the door with the usual brute force, smiling as a wave of cooking smells rushed out around him.

'I really must put a bulb in this light fitting,' he said, by way of greeting.

'Something smells good. Doesn't smell like burnt omelette,' said Leah.

'I'll let you in on a secret—I'm actually a bloody good cook. I was just . . . not really trying before.'

'I had my suspicions.' Leah smiled.

'Well, I admit I was a bit surprised that you invited yourself for dinner, after the last debacle.'

'Sorry. That probably was quite rude. But I did bring wine.' She handed him the bottle as they went through to the kitchen. With the hotplates open and a fan heater whizzing in the corner, the room was warm and almost cosy. Mark had lit some candles and set them around the room.

'As much for heat as for atmosphere,' he said, with a slightly awkward smile. 'Just as well—you look frozen.'

'I walked here,' Leah explained, stripping off several layers of clothing.

'Really? Why?'

'I just fancied it. And it really is a lot shorter as the crow flies. And I wanted to be able to have some of the wine,' she said. Mark took it, and peered at the label. 'Oh, no—you don't know about wine, do you? It's only plonk.' She winced.

'I do know a bit about wine. And this is not a bad plonk at all. There's a corkscrew in the top drawer, if you can get it open, that is.' He went back to the stove as Leah opened the wine. His hair was still damp from washing, and his face looked a little less drawn, a little less hard.

'So how was your nap?' she asked.

'Not bad. Too long. I woke up with a horrendous crick in my neck, and my legs completely numb. You should have woken me.'

'No way. You looked much too cute, tucked up in that chair. Like a dormouse.'

'Great. I feel so manly,' Mark said ruefully, and Leah smiled. 'How do you like your steak?'

They soon finished the bottle of wine Leah had
brought, and Mark disappeared into the cupboard
under the stairs to fetch more. They ate and talked
until late about their lives before, and about
Hester Canning and the fairy photographs, and
Mark's family history. Leah took her cue from him,
not mentioning his brother or his father until he
did; and not mentioning Ryan at all. And she
might have been imagining it, but she thought she
could feel Ryan in the room, feel them stepping
carefully around the subject of him, and of what
had happened between them. As if Mark's
curiosity was a thing she could see or touch,
spreading out to probe the room. His gaze was so
keen that she felt it penetrate her thoughts if she
held it too long, felt that she gave secrets away
without saying a word.

'That was delicious. All memory of the omelette
has been wiped from my mind.'

'I'm very glad,' Mark said, refilling her glass.
Leah took a sip and felt the alcohol warming her,
making her languid.

'So what *will* you do next? Once you've . . .
finished here?' Leah asked, to break a silence
between them that was becoming loaded.

'Once I've finished skulking, and licking my
wounds, you mean?' He lifted one eyebrow.

'Skulking was your word, not mine.'

'I really . . . don't know. Job hunting, I guess.
Once it's all died down.'

'It kind of has, you know. I know it hasn't for
you, but I honestly had no idea who you were,
when you first told me your name. Other than

367

being excited that I'd found a Canning, that is.'

'Yes, but I get the impression you've been out of it yourself, lately. Out of the loop, I mean. No offence,' Mark said, holding up one long hand in apology. Leah glanced at him, annoyed for a second that she should be so transparent again.

'How could you possibly know that?'

'Takes one to know one.' He shrugged. 'But perhaps you're right. I'm sure my flash in the pan is over with. It just . . . doesn't feel like it. But I'm going to sell the house. That I have decided.'

'Oh,' Leah said, with a pull of sadness inside, though she couldn't think what possible right she had to feel anything about it.

'Will you tell me about it? Your war wound—what it is that makes your face drop like a stone sometimes?' he asked softly, intently.

'Does it?' she said airily, looking away across the room.

'You know it does. Come on, Leah.' He tilted his head to catch her eye.

Leah sighed, shrugged. 'There's really nothing to tell. Split up with boyfriend last year. Slight broken heart. Not quite ditched the emotional baggage, blah blah blah . . .'

'Did he sleep with someone else?'

'I really don't want to talk about it,' she said, more sharply than she'd meant to. For some reason, discussing Ryan with Mark was intolerable. It made her want to jump up from the table and run, to hide her head in her hands. But what did she have to be ashamed of? Why should she be the one who felt like curling up in shadows somewhere, where nobody could ever see her or touch her again? *Because I didn't guess. Because*

I'm a bloody, bloody idiot, she answered her own question. *Because I still love him*.

'There, see? Not easy, is it. People are supposed to be able to talk their way through anything these days,' Mark murmured, watching her closely.

Leah looked at him, frowning, and considered her answer carefully. 'I talked about it to all and sundry right after it happened. And yes, he did sleep with somebody else, but it was far, far worse than that simple phrase makes it sound. A while back I couldn't stop talking about it, as if I could . . . argue my way out of the situation I was in. But now . . . now I think there's not much more to say about it. And when I do say something it . . . infuriates me,' she said, struggling to explain. Mark said nothing. Their hands, on the table between them, rested two inches apart; fingers curled. 'What about you? Have you . . . talked through what happened to your brother?' As soon as she spoke, Leah regretted it. At the mention of his brother, Mark recoiled as if she'd slapped him. 'I'm sorry,' she said quickly. 'I shouldn't have said that. It's . . . a completely different thing, I know.'

'How do you know?' he said; sadly, not unkindly. 'How can anybody know about something like that? I had no idea, until I lived through it.'

'You're right. I don't know,' Leah said in contrition. She gulped her wine uncomfortably.

'I haven't talked about it to anyone. Who could I talk to? Dad?'

'A friend?'

'They disappeared, a lot of them. It was . . . too huge,' he said, pouring more wine. 'It made them uncomfortable.' In the pause after he spoke, the

369

candles bobbed in the many draughts creeping into the kitchen, dancing merrily to a private tune.

'You can . . . tell me. If you want,' Leah said.

'But you know already, don't you?' Mark said, abruptly.

'I know what the papers wrote. I don't know the truth. I don't know what it was like.'

'And do you want to know?'

'If you want to tell me,' she said. Mark looked away, at the black window glass and his own dim reflection in it. Leah saw the muscle begin to twitch beneath his eye, and his jaw clench spasmodically. A physical reaction to even the thought of speaking about it. She put out her hand instinctively, and squeezed his arm. Beneath the layers of his clothes, the flesh was hard and unyielding. Skin over sinew and bone, and tension in every fibre of it.

'You don't have to,' she said.

'I know. But I can't feel any worse, and maybe I might feel better . . . I don't know how much you've read in the papers, so I'll just tell it from the start. My older brother James was my hero when we were kids. He was just the archetypal best big brother. He helped me build my model aeroplanes, taught me how to bowl a cricket ball, how to actually hit something with my air gun. How to chat up girls—very badly, I must say. I suppose the age gap between us was big enough that we didn't compete for things. We didn't fight much. He was five years older than me. Anyway. I loved him very much. We stayed close even once we'd grown up and left home. I loved his wife Karen, too, when they got married fifteen years ago. He'd always been a bit of a cad with women, I suppose. He

370

didn't mean to . . . he just seemed to attract them, and had a hard time resisting them. He had a long string of girlfriends and sometimes they overlapped more than they ought to have; but Karen was different. She sussed him out straight away, and let him know she wasn't going to put up with any of his nonsense. She's Catholic, so they got married before anything else, and I can honestly say he'd never been happier. His job was going great—he was a lawyer, making good money. They were muttering about making him partner. The kids came along, everything was fine. Domestic bliss. I went there every Christmas— Mum and Dad too. He loved it—lording it up, showering us with hospitality.

'Then he got ill. He started to lose his balance— worse some days than others. He was moody and distracted—which was a sure sign something was wrong. James was always cheerful. Why wouldn't he be? He led a charmed life.' Mark paused, turning his glass around in front of him. Slowly, slowly; anticlockwise. The foot of it vibrated against the table top, sending shivers down Leah's spine. 'He had unexplained pains, stiff joints. He couldn't grip things any more. He got clumsy, kept tripping over. He choked a lot on his food, and . . . sometimes when he wasn't even eating. Just watching TV . . . choked on his own saliva. Then his speech started to slur. So eventually he went to the doctor's. Put it off as long as he could, like a typical man. A man who'd never taken a sick day from work in his life. They sent him for a raft of tests and I was expecting him to come out and say it was an inner ear infection, or something up with his circulation. A nasty, lingering virus at worst. It

371

was motor neurone disease. The diagnosis floored him—floored us all. Amyotrophic lateral sclerosis, to be exact. Life expectancy three to five years. James was in a wheelchair within nine months of the diagnosis. This for a guy who won the tennis club tournament four years running, and had three kids under the age of twelve.' Mark looked up at Leah. She had stopped fiddling with her own wine glass and was listening in mute agony. There was nothing she could say, nothing she could do. She felt like a prisoner at the table, trapped in the inevitability of his story.

'And he knew . . . he *knew* how he was going to end up. Incontinent. Unable to speak, to feed himself, to do anything. Slowly dying. He was wasting away right in front of our eyes . . . every time I saw him . . .' Mark shook his head, swallowed convulsively. 'I knew what he was going to ask us to do. He called Karen and me into the room one afternoon; sent the kids outside. And told us, the two people who loved him most in the world, that he wanted to die. Karen went crazy. She called him a coward, and worse—that he didn't want to fight it, that he was giving up. Accused him of abandoning her and the kids. God, she said some terrible things! I thought she was just . . . wild with grief. I thought she'd come around. Because I was willing from the start. I didn't want to lose him—I'd have done anything to keep him. But there *was* no keeping him—he knew it and I knew it. And I'd have done anything to stop him suffering. I thought Karen would accept it eventually, but . . . she didn't. She was adamant. Suicide was not acceptable to her, and of course neither was murder. That's what she called me, when I tried to persuade her. A murderer.

'Another six months of this went by, and even though we didn't talk about it much it was there. Every time I went to visit. Every time I saw Karen, she had this look in her eye—this awful, angry, admonishing look. Daring me to mention it. Warning me not to. And every time I was alone with James, he begged me to help him. He couldn't even get himself in and out of his chair by then. They had carers coming to the house four times a day. His worst nightmare was coming true.' Mark paused again, put his hand over his mouth for a second, as if to stop the words from coming out. 'I wrote letters for him saying it was what he wanted and that I was only doing what he'd begged me to do. He signed them as best he could. One morning he gave the kids an extra thorough goodbye before they went to school. Then while Karen was taking them there, I gave him sleeping pills. As many as he could swallow. I bought them on the internet . . . God knows what was in them. But they worked. He . . . died. He died.'

'Mark, I'm so sorry . . .'

'You haven't heard the best part yet. Karen reacted . . . as was to be expected, I suppose. And more so. She tore up the letters when I showed them to her. My own stupid fault—I should have made copies. She destroyed them and went straight to the police to report his murder. I just don't know . . . I don't know why she *did* that! I still don't understand . . . that she could be so deeply in denial, and not know in her heart that this was what James wanted. That it was the best and kindest thing anybody could have done for him. Then his will was read and he'd left all that money

373

to me—money to keep Dad in the home for a bit longer, without having to sell the house. Once the press got hold of that they tore me to pieces.'

'But the trial was over in no time . . . everybody could see you'd acted from compassion. The judge even said it should never have gone to court . . .'

'Tell that to Karen and the kids. And to the journalists with their bloody "Cain and Abel" headlines. She's told the kids terrible things, Leah. I don't know if I'll ever get to see them again. If they'll ever forgive me.'

'But . . . did they know he was dying? Did they know that?'

'I'm not sure. I never spoke to them about it . . . Karen told me she was handling it. So I don't know. I don't know.'

'But . . . once they're older, once they can find out for themselves how ill he was . . . I'm sure they'll want to see you,' she tried.

'Well. I suppose only time will tell. So now it's just me and Dad. He's the only family I've got left. That's willing to speak to me, anyway. Some of the time.'

'That's terrible. Mark, I . . . I really don't know what to say,' Leah said, helplessly.

'There's nothing *to* say. But now you know; and I wish I could say I feel better, telling you about it. But I really don't.' He took a deep breath, released a long, shuddering sigh.

'It's far too soon for you to be thinking you ought to feel better,' she told him carefully. 'You lost your brother, and all the shit afterwards meant you didn't have a chance to mourn him.'

'Well, I've got time now, haven't I? Work fired me, of course. So much for innocent until proven

374

guilty. They said my work had been falling below par for some time and it had nothing to do with the impending trial. Which is bollocks.'

'We could take them to a tribunal,' Leah said. *We*. How unexpectedly that word had slipped from her tongue. Her stomach gave a tiny jolt, but Mark didn't seem to notice.

'What's the point? I don't want any of it back. Any of that old life. How can you go back to things, anyway? When everything is torn apart? You just have to start all over. Might as well be in a new place. A new job,' Mark said, finally sipping his wine.

'You do have to start all over,' Leah agreed. The lines on his face had faded away, smoothed out of relief by the candles' glow. She took his hands across the table top, meaning only to hold them briefly, to give strength through the touch of human skin. But Mark gripped her fingers tightly, and didn't let go. Leah met his gaze, as the pain she felt for him changed, became something like fear.

'Stay tonight,' he said. Leah opened her mouth but no words came out, and her heart lurched into her throat to choke her. The silence stretched and Mark let go of her hands. 'There're plenty of bedrooms, after all,' he said, awkwardly.

Leah took a steadying breath. 'I can walk back to the pub. It really isn't far,' she said.

Mark's mouth twitched into the slightest of smiles. 'Of course,' he said.

*   *   *

In the morning, Leah rose early and drank a coffee

standing at the window of her room at The Swing Bridge, where the glass panes were misted by a night of her own damp exhalations, and the day outside was tentatively bright. Her head was heavy and tender after the wine of the night before, and she couldn't marshal a clear thought about Mark or what he had said to her. Downstairs there were sounds of movement from the kitchen, metal pans and cutlery rattling. The smell of bacon wafted up the stairs and under her door, and her stomach rumbled; but she didn't have time for breakfast.

Leah was at the library for when the doors opened at half past nine. She was shown the microfiche collection, and how to use the machines, and was soon scrolling through the local papers from a century ago with her heart speeding in anticipation. Following a hunch, she started with the year that Robin Durrant's discredited photographs were taken, and taking the hints from Hester's letters, she started with the summer months. Not even halfway into August 1911, she caught her breath, clapping her hand over her mouth inadvertently. There it all was, just like that; the story stretching out for a few weeks, into the autumn of that year. She read, and read again, and tried to scribble a few key facts into her notebook, but her handwriting had gone wild and erratic, barely legible. Smiling, she gave up and pulled out her phone, ignoring the glare and tutting of the person using the machine next to her as she dialled Mark's number.

'Leah? Found something?' he answered, and in his clipped tone she read something of the same ambiguity she herself had felt that morning. Storing this fact away for now, she took a deep breath.

'I've found *everything*, Mark. It's all here! And pictures . . . wonderful photos of Hester and Albert, and of the theosophist . . . Everything!'

'You mean, something did happen? When?'

'*That summer*—the summer Hester was talking about. The summer of 1911,' Leah said, her voice tight with excitement. 'And I think . . . I think I know why our soldier kept those two particular letters of Hester's . . .'

'Leah—tell me what happened! Was it a murder?'

'Oh yes, there was a murder. A dreadful and violent one.'

'Well, who was it? Who was killed? And by whom?' Mark pressed.

11

August 4th, 1911

Dearest Amelia,

How I wish you were still here, to help and give me strength. This house is no longer a comfortable place. I don't quite know where to start. Albert. Albert is not himself. He is strange and distant and so caught up in his desire to see the wretched elementals again that he has no space left in heart nor mind for me, or the parish, or his duties or anything. He eats little, and will no longer touch meat of any kind, and I have not seen him sleep in days. He has taken to lingering outside the inns and public houses of the district, preaching to passers-by about their many sins. Amy! I am quite distraught about it all! And I can trace only one possible cause of these unsettling changes— Mr Robin Durrant. Who is still lodging with us, after all these many weeks, though he contributes nothing to the running of the household. When I mentioned this to Bertie he seemed almost to find it funny. To find me funny. He describes Mr Durrant as 'our esteemed guest', and believe me—he could not possibly hold the man in higher esteem. Whatever Mr Durrant suggests, Albert agrees to. It is that simple. It's as though my dear husband has quite lost his own mind!

Cat, our maid, is also beside herself. Albert saw her in one of the pubs in Thatcham, and declared that she must be dismissed for this misdemeanour. I protested, and spoke up for her, as I have come to like and value her; but it was only when Robin Durrant spoke up that she was allowed to stay. Albert insists that she be kept locked in her room at night, which she has been; but I understand that since her incarceration in London, confinement is something she really cannot abide, and she is most terribly upset every time the door closes. I think it's a cruel and unnecessary thing to do, but Albert insists, and this time Robin chooses not to argue with him. Perhaps it amuses him to hear her in distress. Oh! I know I am writing terrible things about him, but suddenly I find that I do not trust him, and that I do not like him, and that I do not want him here!

Cat has a sweetheart, in town. That was why she was wont to go out in the evenings—to meet up with him. I thought when she first hinted at it that it was Robin Durrant with whom she was keeping trysts. I have seen them together, outside in the courtyard.

378

Talking in a most familiar way. But he insists that he knows nothing about it, and actually I can't think that Cat would be interested in him. Perhaps this is why I feel so much sympathy towards her, for if she loves this man as I love Bertie, then keeping her away against her will is even more inhumane of us. I suggested that she write him a note to explain her staying away for the time being, but she tells me that he cannot read. Poor, simple soul he must be. I have made sure Albert hears nothing about any of this. In his present mood I think he would march them straight to church and wed them, even if the most tenderness they had shared were a kiss, or a clasping of hands. It breaks my heart a little to think I am party to their being kept apart. For that is how I feel too—cut off from Albert, separated. I miss him, Amy!

I shan't commit the details to paper, but a week or so ago, on the last occasion that Albert came up to our bed at night, something occurred which demonstrated to me just how the thing that is supposed to happen between us, as man and wife, should go. I understand, you will doubtless be relieved to hear, after all this time. But no sooner had I made this discovery than I found myself even further from my husband than I have ever been. He recoiled from me, Amelia. From the very touch of my hands. There. What possible direction can I go in from here? Because I know, though I can't explain exactly how, that if there is to be any improvement between Albert and me from here on out, then it cannot happen while Robin Durrant remains in our lives, and under our roof. When he is here, it's as though Albert is not. Or perhaps, I am not. Am I making sense?

Well. Perhaps you have read about our elementals in the paper? I understand that a couple of the national papers are printing the story now, after the storm of correspondence that followed the publication of the pictures in our local paper. It seems a great many people share your reaction to the photographs, Amy. Mr Durrant has yet to receive official support from the Theosophical Society, which annoys him greatly. He is petitioning them to send somebody to witness another picture being developed, to prove that the images are real. How do I know all this? By listening at doors, dear sister. Yes, in my own home! Albert's pamphlet fares less well. He has yet to find a book shop to take on a stock of it, and has run an advertisement in the paper instead. He sends out two or three a day by mail order, for three pence apiece.

I wish you were here, with all my heart; and am also glad that you are not—for I would not wish the atmosphere of this house upon another living soul right now, let alone one as dear as you. But how about you? And your own troubles with Archie? I do so hope you have managed to come back to some state of accord, and that your house is a happier one than mine. I wish I had some advice to give you, but I am fearfully ignorant. I can't think what advice you will have for me, mine being such an unusual and unwelcome set of circumstances. But if you do have any, please dearest sister, write it soon and send it to me. I am not sure what to do, what not to do, or how much longer I can stand it all.

With all my love,
Hester

1911

When the key turns in the lock, there comes such a roaring in Cat's ears that she fears her head might explode. It doesn't matter that Mrs Bell's face is heavy with anxiety and displeasure as she does it. It does not matter that through the window the moon still rises, and sets the glass ablaze with silver light. It does not matter that come morning she will be let out again. None of it matters but that she is a prisoner again, and powerless, and hasn't the freedom to come or go as she may. She is like The Gentleman's canary, which tipped its head at him and would not sing. Silence was its last weapon, the last thing of its own that it had control over. Cat's voice is her last thing. In fear, in rage, she shouts at the door, shouts her throat raw; shouts to be louder than the thumping inside her head. She will not rest, and neither will the household. She hammers her fists against the wood; stamps her feet; curses and swears and sobs. She thinks she is loud, too loud for anybody to ignore. But when at last she slumps, exhausted, to the floor, she can hear Sophie Bell's snores, sawing gently from two doors down the hall.

So she sits, when she's too tired to fight any more. Sits with her back to the door and the rough wooden floorboards snagging the skin on the backs of her legs. Her throat is burning, her skull wrapped around with tight bands of tension and pain. She tries to think of George, of the way she feels when she is with him. The life he seems to breathe; the soul of her, drawn patiently from the hard kernel inside by his smile and the touch and the taste of him. She tries to think of her mother—her mother as she was, before the consumption; or Tess on the first afternoon they sneaked out to a public meeting, with her delight painting her face like a rainbow. But the thoughts won't stay to comfort her. George slips away into silhouette, into shadow, as if distant in her memory. She is left with his outline only, as if he sat with the sun always behind him, and her eyes could not cope with the light. Sickness and death take her mother; gaol, and now the workhouse, take Tess. Cat is back in her cell, with chill, clammy walls and the stink of piss and shit from the pail in the corner; with lice scurrying over her scalp, driving her wild with itching. They were in the bedding. In the ticking of the mattress, the seams and stitching of the meagre blankets. She did not think to check—had never before been anywhere where lice lay in wait like that; waxy grey speckles to swarm the unwary. The stone walls were damp; thick mildew crawled up them, shading the mortar black.

The working-class girls had none of the soft treatment of their middle- and upper-class comrades. No privileges, no luxuries. They were not allowed to write letters, or wear their own clothes. They were allowed out of the cell block for one hour a day, to shuffle around a cramped cobbled yard. Cat and Tess walked together, huddled close, their fingers meshed. Cat tried to make Tess laugh by sharing gossip and making up wild stories about the wardresses, and the other prisoners, and the vast feasts of cake they would eat upon their release. One wardress was the most feared by all the women. She was built like a snake,

382

thin and wiry. All sinew and bone; no hint of a curve to soften her hips or bust. Her face was hard. She had dark hair which she pinned back severely; cold blue eyes; a cruel, lipless mouth turned up at the corners in an expression that had nothing to do with good humour; and a sharp, pointed nose. Cat dubbed her The Crow for this reason, and made up mocking rhymes about her in the long hours she was alone, to sing to Tess as they walked around the yard. Tess didn't laugh, but she managed to smile. Her eyes were always full of tears, swollen and pink.

The wardresses slapped them for insubordination—a charge that encompassed walking too slowly, or too fast, coughing too much, or swearing, blaspheming, whistling, singing, talking back. By the second morning of her three-month sentence, Cat, who had never been struck in her life before, had a split lip, and a wobbly tooth behind it. Word passed around quickly that they had to go on strike against this treatment. This was what they did—suffragettes. They ought to have been classed as political prisoners, not common criminals. They ought to have been in better accommodation, with better food and treatment, and the privileges due to them. They were told all this by the WSPU before they were sentenced. Cat knew it as she passed through the massive stone gates of Holloway, crenellated like a fairy-tale castle, but with no happy endings inside. They had to demand these things, and they had to refuse to eat until they got them or were allowed to go free. Cat didn't mind the closed-in space. Not at first. It did not bother her, the first night that the door was locked. She hadn't known then what it meant. She

383

had not tested the boundaries of her new world, and found out how close they were, how much they could hurt.

* * *

The first day without food was a blessing. The bread was always hard and stale, the soup little more than the water in which the wardresses had cooked their vegetables. Thin and bad-smelling. Cat was used to the good food of Broughton Street, and before that the home cooking of her mother. She could hardly touch this stuff without retching. Her stomach soon felt hot, and knotted itself in protest, but she was more than able to ignore it. The food she did not eat was left to go foul. The wardresses slapped her for her rebellion; The Crow twisted her arm up behind her back and yanked her around her cell by her hair. She bore it all, because they couldn't force her to eat. They couldn't win. Five days this went on, and by the sixth she couldn't get up from the mattress. The cells all around her were quiet too, since all the suffragettes were housed together, and she lay still and listened to that silence. It was a companionable silence, and spoke of their shared weakness—the listlessness of their bodies, the strength and determination of their minds. The silence didn't last beyond the end of the sixth day. New sounds came to fill it.

The squeal of trolley wheels. Multiple footsteps, moving with purpose. The rattle of keys, of metal equipment of some kind. Cat raised her head from her rancid mattress at the unfamiliar noises. She thought about getting up, and pressing her face sideways to the tiny grille in the door, to see if she could see what was coming. Needles of unease pricked at her skin, and she couldn't say why. Then more sounds started, and she knew her instincts were right. Shrieks, scuffles. The thump of furniture, knocked against the wall, the clank of metal again, the wardresses swearing, and male voices too. Two of them, muttering in low tones, as though through gritted teeth. The shrieks became screams, rose higher in panic, and then were stifled, choked off; replaced by coughing, retching. Hideous animal sounds like none Cat had ever heard a person make before. And when the source of the noises exited that cell, they left silence behind within it. A terrible, stunned, weighty silence. As the trolley wheels came towards her door, Cat's heart pounded hard enough to break through her ribs.

She was next. Three wardresses, their hair in disarray, scratches on their arms and cheeks. Their faces grim as death. The Crow was one of them. The two men she had heard were wearing white coats like doctors, splattered and smeared with some substance. Beige smears, with flecks of red. The five of them brought with them a stink of sweat and fear. Slowly, Cat sat up. Her head spun wildly, a shock of dizziness that made it hard to think, hard to act. 'Now, you give us any trouble and you'll only make it harder on yourself. You hear?' The Crow told her. The woman who, several days ago, had smiled as she split Cat's lip with a sharp, back-handed slap. 'Get away from me,' Cat said. She tried to stand, but her legs felt boneless. She grasped the mattress for support, tried to push herself up once more. 'It's for your own good, young lady,' one of the men said. 'Let's keep her on the bed, then,' a wardress said. Cat shouted out, shouted: '*No!*' But they were on her in an instant, two of the women holding her down by her arms, one of the men coming to hold her head. She bucked her body as hard as she could—which was not very hard—tried to twist out of their grasp. Her joints popped, skin bruised where they held her. The second man filled a tin cup from the trolley and passed it to The Crow. She put her knee on Cat's chest, and the man lifted her head up, and the cup was pushed into her mouth. She smelt the sickly, milky smell of gruel and clamped her teeth together as hard as she could, wouldn't yield. The wardress pushed the cup ever harder, scraping it along Cat's teeth until the metal rim cut her gums, and she felt blood wetting her lips. But she did not yield. A tiny bit of gruel found its way into her mouth, and as soon as the woman was off her chest she spat it violently at her. Bright red swirls in the milky mess. 'Christ! You're a bloody idiot,' The Crow told her.

Cat panted, gasped for breath. She strained every muscle, cursed them with every foul word she had ever heard coming from the mouth of a street hawker. The man at her head glanced at the man by the trolley. They nodded to one another. Her head was let go momentarily, but then The Crow took over, gripping her skull hard, pressing her thumbs cruelly into the pressure points at Cat's temples. She screamed. When she opened her eyes, the men were upon her: one held a thin rubber tube, the other attached a funnel to the far end of it. Cat didn't understand. She squeezed her teeth together again, thought that in this way she would beat them. But the tube was pushed into her nose. Into one nostril, uncomfortable at first, alien, and then excruciating. Like a knife stabbing behind her eye. She screamed, her mouth wide open at last, surrendering, but they stuck to their course. The tube was pushed in ever deeper. She felt it at the back of her throat and she gagged, her mouth filling with acid. She couldn't breathe, her eyes bulged with panic as she choked, coughed, gasped little snatches of precious air. 'That's it. Ready,' the man manoeuvring the tube announced curtly. His colleague poured the gruel into the funnel. For five minutes, which felt like a lifetime to Cat, he poured, watched the stuff trickle down the tube, poured again. When the tube came out at last it left a sticky wet dribble of milky slime in her throat, which trickled into her lungs. Her nose bled profusely as the tube slithered out, and her mouth tasted of blood and bile. They left her on her side, filthy and coughing. Deep, ragged coughs to clear the muck from her lungs. The pain in her head and chest was astonishing. She coughed for hours. She coughed for weeks and weeks. 'Same again at teatime then, petal?' The Crow said, sweetly. 'That's enough,' one of the men snapped sternly. 'There's an anti-emetic in the mixture, but check on her in half an hour. If she has vomited at all, let me know and we will repeat the procedure.' Cat lay in misery, in outrage and pain; every bit as violated as if she'd been raped. *Same again at teatime.*

* * *

'Cat?' There's a gentle knock at the door, rousing

387

her from the waking nightmares that beset her. 'Cat, are you awake?' It's Hester's voice, soft and quiet. Cat blinks, looks around her, finds it is still dark. She has no idea what the hour might be.

'Yes, madam,' she says, and then clears her throat. It feels raw and rough, as though the men with their tube really have been back to see her.

'May I come in?' Hester asks, and Cat has no idea how to answer her. Then there's a rattling, a joyful little grating sound, and the door is open. Cat's legs have gone to sleep. She struggles to her knees, turns her body, grips the edge of the door and feels the push of air through the gap. Light blooms behind her closed eyelids. She can't tell if it's Hester Canning's little candle lamp, or relief, joy, liberation. 'Oh, Cat! Your poor hands!' Hester says, setting the candle on the dresser and helping Cat to stand. The skin across her knuckles is tattered and bloody.

'Please. Please don't lock me in again,' Cat says. She's not sure how many nights it has been, since the first time. Perhaps only two or three; perhaps more.

Hester's eyes are full of pity. 'Nobody even knows I've got this key. It opens every door in the house,' she says, holding it loosely in her palm. 'Come—come and sit on the bed. I'll wash your hands for you. Oh, you have so many splinters!'

'I can do it, madam. There's no need,' Cat says, flatly. She won't let Hester make amends for this. Won't let her forgive herself. There's an awkward silence. Hester wraps her dressing gown more tightly around her, tucks the ends of the belt away neatly, nervously.

'Was it so very awful? In gaol, I mean?' Hester

asks. Cat stares at her, wonders how to explain.

'It was,' is all she says in the end, the words little more than a croak.

'Cat, I have always wondered . . . what was your crime? Why did they imprison you?' Hester asks. As if here, in the dark, here in her servant's room, she is no longer in her real world. She can ask things she would never normally ask, because the rules are not the same. Cat smiles a bleak little smile.

'Everybody wants to know,' she says. 'Two months I was locked away, and my friend Tess and others with me. And for what? Obstruction.'

'Obstruction?'

'That was the charge. We had intent to cause a breach of the peace as well, they said. I had half a brick in my pocket, but that was for later. I hadn't thrown anything at the time of my arrest, but they found it in my pocket, and they knew what it was for. And I would have done it.' She tips her chin up defiantly. 'Through the window of the milliner's shop on West Street, that was my intention. It had the most lovely, huge plate-glass window; all the fine feathery hats inside on fake ladies' heads. Hats the likes of Tess and I would never have cause to wear. I wanted to smash it. I would have done it!'

'Hush, Cat! We mustn't be heard,' Hester whispers. 'But you didn't throw it?'

'I didn't get the chance. Six o'clock, that was meant to be when we would all split up, go to our various target areas and wait. When Big Ben struck the half hour, we would attack. But first, in the afternoon, we went to a Liberal Party meeting. We had placards to hold, and we were to shout slogans as loudly as we could, so that everybody who'd gone to hear the speakers inside would hear us too, since we weren't allowed in to ask our questions, or make our demands. There were twelve of us, all the active duty girls from our branch of the WSPU. And Tess. Tess, my friend. She didn't want to be on active duty, but I made her. I *made* her.' Cat pauses, takes a long, shuddering breath and shuts her eyes. It's unbearable to think of it. 'We had strict instructions. There's no law against doing what we were doing, as long as you stay in the street. If you step onto the pavement, they can call it obstruction, and cart you away. Standing in the street to shout a slogan is no crime. Standing on an empty pavement not a yard away to shout a slogan *is* a crime. How fair and reasonable the law is! So the policemen who turned up, they began to herd us. I didn't realise at first what was happening. The officers linked arms and moved towards us, just ever so slowly. A half a step at a time for twenty minutes or more. Until we had no choice but to fall under their feet, climb onto each other's shoulders or step up onto the pavement. So we did the latter, and we were arrested. Each last one of us.'

'You were gaoled for months for *that*?' Hester says, incredulously.

'See now what a violent miscreant you have in your employ?' Cat asks, bitterly.

Hester stares at her with wide eyes, robbed of words. In the end, she looks away, gets up and goes to the window, though there is nothing to see outside it but a solid black sky.

'I scarce know what is right or fair any more, Cat. But that you should be gaoled for that small crime is not right. Not right at all,' she says, unhappily.

'We were beaten in gaol, madam. Beaten and . . . handed out worse treatment than I know how to describe to you! And now . . . and now I am a prisoner again! Do you see? Can you understand— I can't bear it!'

'Yes, I see! Quiet, Cat! Here—take this.' She holds out the skeleton key to Cat, who stares at it incredulously. 'Take it. You can unlock the door once Mrs Bell has locked it and gone. She takes the key from the lock when she goes, I have checked.' Cat snatches the key, holds it tightly in her fist as if Hester might try to take it back again. A cold, iron lifeline, a talisman even more powerful than her Holloway medal. 'But you must swear, Cat, you must promise me you will not go out of your room at night. Please—swear it! If you do, if Albert finds out that I have given you this key . . . Please, swear to me,' Hester begs, crouching down in front of Cat and forcing her to meet her eyes.

'I swear it.' The words drag themselves from Cat, reluctantly. 'But, I must get word to . . . to George. To my man. We were arguing, before. He might think I keep away because, because I don't want him any more.' To Cat's bewilderment, Hester's eyes fill up with tears; her lips tremble slightly and she presses them together.

'Do you love him?' Hester asks. So alien, it seems to Cat, to speak so freely with the vicar's wife. But the night is dark and the room is a cell, and Hester Canning has offered her reprieve.

'With body and soul, madam. With all of me,' she answers; and Hester drops her head, a tear falling with a minute splash onto her clasped hands. For a long time Hester is quiet, breathing

391

shallowly, and seems to fight for control of herself. Then she looks up again.

'I will send you on some errand, tomorrow afternoon. Some errand in Thatcham. You may seek him then. But promise me—not in the night time. Not when your freedom might be noticed.'

'I promise you,' Cat says, and is surprised to find that she means it.

'Well then. Hide the key, and keep it carefully! Turn the lock again in the morning before Mrs Bell comes to let you out. It wasn't right to lock you in, Cat. I never thought it was right. But lately I seem to be mistress of this house no longer. There are two masters instead,' Hester says forlornly, getting to her feet and picking up her candle once more. In the warmth of its glow, with her hair tumbling over her shoulders, eyes wide and glistening, the vicar's wife is quite lovely.

'Only one master, as I see it,' Cat says darkly. 'Can't you be rid of him?' Since they are speaking openly, Cat will have her say.

Hester blinks, startled. 'I have tried to suggest that it's time he went home . . .'

'As far as I can tell, and as Mrs Bell's gossip informs me, the man has no other home. And not much money to his name, either. His father keeps him on a very tight stipend. He is expected to make his own fortune,' Cat says carefully. She watches Hester Canning, sees her digest this unwelcome information.

'No home? He doesn't even keep rooms somewhere?'

'No, madam. It will be hard to shift him, I think, while the vicar makes him so very welcome.'

Hester nods her head, resignedly. 'You

understand a great deal, Cat Morley.'

'Nobody knows a household and its occupants like its servants, madam. It's inevitable.'

'And what else do you know about Mr Durrant?'

'Only this: do not trust him. He is a liar. If you can find some way to move him on, then do it,' Cat says, gravely.

Hester stares at her, alarmed, then nods once and turns to go. 'In the morning,' she says, from the threshold of the room, 'it must be as though none of this has passed between us.' Her face betrays some discomfort.

'Of course,' Cat says, quite unperturbed. With Hester gone and the door open, she lies down on the bed and sleeps for the first time since it was locked.

*   *   *

The following day is one of simmering heat. In the kitchen, Cat and Mrs Bell make jam from the overflowing baskets of raspberries and loganberries that the gardener, Blighe, keeps bringing to the kitchen. The fat housekeeper is at the stove, stirring and stirring, making sure all the sugar in the vast copper pan has dissolved. Cat scalds the glass jars, boiling kettle after kettle of water to sterilise them before filling. Both work with sweat running down their faces and backs, between their breasts, into the folds of their clothes. Their cheeks are as red as the bubbling fruit pulp, their eyes flat with a kind of dull, resigned anger; ill-defined, aimed half at the heat of the day, half at the blameless raspberries. The room is sweet and heady with the scented steam. It clings to their hair and their faces and hands. Cat burns herself for a third time, hisses at the pain and plunges her hand into the bucket of cold water where the milk is kept. Mrs Bell hasn't the energy left to reprimand her, or urge more care.

Once the jam has been left to sit for a quarter hour so the fruit will settle evenly, there are more burns as it's poured. Splashes, piping hot flecks find bare wrists; dribbling overflows must be wiped away, the hot jars braced with wincing fingertips.

'Dear God, if only that was the end of it! In a week the blackcurrants will start coming in,' Mrs Bell sighs, putting her hand to her mouth and sucking where a blister is forming.

'I've got to get out of here,' Cat says, leaning her elbows on the sticky table top and bending forwards to stretch her back. 'It's suffocating me.'

'It's hotter than hell, I'll grant you,' Mrs Bell agrees. All day Cat has looked to the doorway, looked to the stairs, looked to Hester as she put the lunch dishes on the sideboard; waiting to have her errand, her means of escaping to find George. All day it has not come, and the wait has chafed her more as each minute ticked past. She takes the tea tray up at four, with a bowl of the fresh jam and a plate of scones. Her legs feel like lead as she climbs the stairs; her movements are wooden. No amount of water she drinks seems to quench her thirst. In the drawing room, the vicar and his wife sit with Robin Durrant, listening as he reads from a letter. Hester Canning's face is flat and shiny, her hair a frizzy mess around her forehead. She seems lost in thought, and does not notice Cat, however hard Cat tries to catch the woman's eye. The vicar can't seem to keep his eyes still. They flit from

Robin's face to his hands to the letter he holds, and when Cat draws near he shuts his eyes and turns his head away, shuddering slightly, as though the smell of her offends him.

Gritting her teeth in fury, Cat puts the tray down with exaggerated care, and transfers the tea things to the table as slowly as she may without it appearing deliberate.

'*It is a source of tremendous satisfaction to us both that you have at l— that you have begun to make such a name for yourself as an authority in your chosen field. You are to be congratulated in the advances you have made of late. I look forward to our next meeting, and to a further discussion of both the nature and implications of your discoveries, since the newspapers' reporting of it, which we follow most keenly, has been somewhat stingy with the facts of it all, and over-exuberant with either excitement or derision. I am sure that your continued diligence and endeavour in the field will only bring you greater prospects and wider renown. Yours etc . . .*' Robin Durrant lets the letter drop into his lap and smiles widely at the Cannings. 'There! What a wonderful letter to receive from one's father!' he exclaims. 'I know for a fact that the old man can't for the life of him grasp the esoteric theories of theosophy, and yet he offers me his support and, I think, begins to respect the fact that in this field at least, my understanding outstrips his. And that of my brothers,' the theosophist says, his voice vibrant with excitement, smiling with achievement. When neither of the Cannings replies to him, it clearly annoys him. He prods them as one would a listless pet, Cat thinks, requiring it to play. 'What say you, Albert? Hester? Don't you think it wonderful that a man as staid and traditional in his beliefs as my father can be persuaded to open his mind to this new reality?'

'Oh, yes. Robin. You are to be congratulated, indeed,' Albert obliges him, still keeping his face averted from Cat, and swallowing convulsively after he speaks. Beneath the sunburn that bridges his nose and cheeks, his face is an ashen grey. He looks unwell. *No more than he deserves*, Cat fumes inwardly. Hester seems about to speak, but clears her throat instead, and fumbles with the handle of her fan until the theosophist's gaze returns to her husband.

'Will that be all, madam?' Cat asks pointedly, catching Hester's eye and filling her face with significance.

'Oh, yes, thank you, Cat,' Hester replies, distantly. Cat glances at Robin, glares balefully at the flawless, self-satisfied smile on his face, and then leaves the room.

*   *   *

'Damn and blast the woman!' Cat swears, as she returns to the kitchen and pours herself a cup of water.

'What now?' asks Mrs Bell. She is writing out labels for the jam, crouched as close to the pen as she may, her face screwed up with the effort of concentration. Her writing is as small and cramped as she is large and flowing.

'Let your pen move as freely as your thoughts,' Cat says, peering over her shoulder. 'Let the ink flow like a slow river.' Mrs Bell shoots her a black look, and Cat retreats. 'That's how I was drilled, when I was learning to write.' She shrugs.

'Well, I'm not learning. I'm plenty good enough at it,' Sophie Bell grumbles.

'Sophie . . . I have to go out,' Cat says suddenly.

'You what?' She does not look up from her labelling.

'I have to go out. Please—only for an hour. I just have to get some fresh air, and be out of this house for a little while. I'll be back in time to clear up the tea things, I promise . . .'

'Oh, promises, promises. You'll be off to see George Hobson, I know, and not back until you've made your bed with him,' the housekeeper says. Now she looks up, to find Cat's jaw gone slack with surprise, and her mouth robbed of words to protest. Sophie Bell smiles, not unkindly. 'You of all people ought to know there's little goes on around this parish that I don't know about, Cat Morley. You've been seen with him enough times, by enough people.'

'And I suppose you condemn me for it?'

Mrs Bell frowns a little, turns back to her pen but does not write. 'There's scant enough fun to be had in a servant's life. I'm not so old and *sour*, as you called me, to begrudge a youngster getting out and about a bit. George Hobson's an honest enough sort, rough as he is,' she mutters.

'Sophie Bell . . . of all the people I would not have placed on my side in all this . . .' Cat shakes her head in wonderment.

'Shows what you know, don't it?'

'So, then—please. I need to go and see him, just for a while. I just need to ask him something, that's all. And I can't send a note because he can't read. Please. If I'm missed, tell them I came over all faint and went to lie down for half an hour . . . I'll come straight back again, I promise.'

'I don't know . . . it's one thing for you to put your own job at stake, quite another thing to start doing it to mine, isn't it?'

'Lie, then. Tell them I slipped out without a word, and you were none the wiser. When I get back . . . when I get back I shall tell you a secret,' Cat says, teasingly. Mrs Bell looks up, studies her for a moment and then chuckles.

'Whatever it is, I'll bet you I know it already. Go on, then—and be quick!'

*   *   *

The sun is like hot metal in the sky, fierce and heavy. Cat goes via the front gate, not caring if she is seen. She walks quickly, breaks into a jog from time to time. In her pocket is the stub of a pencil and a scrap of paper—an old laundry receipt. Though she can't write George a note, if he is not aboard his boat, Cat will leave some mark, leave some symbol to show she came to look for him. She thinks of the very thing, and smiles. A black cat. That's what she'll draw. But, twenty minutes later, as she comes upon his boat and her throat is so dry that it feels torn, she sees him on the deck. Lying on his back, knees bent, bare feet flat, arms crossed over his face to shield them from the glare of the sun.

'George!' Cat calls, and can't keep from smiling, a wide and compulsive smile. 'Listen!' She stands by the boat and takes a deep breath—huge, all the way to the bottom of her lungs. They are dry. No catch, no bubble; no fluid to make her cough.

George squints at her, confused for a moment, and then he smiles.

'You've got it licked at last, then,' he says. Cat nods, wipes one hand over her slick brow. Her hair is wet through at the back of her neck.

'The last of that muck they poured into me, finally gone. Can I come on board?'

'You can.' George nods, getting up to take her hands as she wobbles along the gangplank. Standing close to him, so close she can scarce focus her eyes, Cat takes another deep breath. The smell of him, so familiar and enticing. Like the warm wood of the boat; like the dank canal water; like the fresh, pungent foliage all around them. All have sunk their perfume into his skin, mixed and made it wonderful. So wonderful she shuts her eyes, sways on her feet, surrenders herself to the hold of it. 'You stayed away a good few days. I'd wondered if you would come again after the fright of having the police close in like that,' George says. His voice is even, the words without emphasis. But when she looks up, his face is pulled apart with emotion, with uncertainty and relief, with love and fear and wounded pride.

'I didn't mean to. They've been locking me in, George! I couldn't get word to you . . . the vicar saw me at The Ploughman. He's quite lost his mind! He wanted me sent packing, but somebody spoke up for me. But I've been locked in my room, each night when work's done!'

'They lock you in? That's not right . . . they've no right to!'

'I know it. The vicar's wife takes my part in it. She's given me a key to unlock the door, so at least I need not spend every night a prisoner, and afraid

399

. . . but even so I have sworn to her I will not go out at night any more. I don't like it, but . . . I have sworn it!'

'Then, we won't see each other much more. Not like before. Not if you mean to keep your word,' George says, frowning.

'In a way I do, in a way it doesn't matter any more . . .'

'What do you mean? Come—come and sit down. You look sun struck!' He tows her gently to the shade of the cabin, and they sit on the steps. 'What do you mean, it matters not?'

'George,' Cat says. She looks at him, loves him; puts her hand on the rough skin of his jaw. 'I can't stay there any longer. Even though I can unlock my door at night now . . . I am still a prisoner. I will not tolerate the vicar turning his head away, as though I am some kind of filth! I will not tolerate being told where I must be, and *how* I must be, every sleeping and waking moment of my life! Even the vicar's wife . . . though she thinks to help, still she would have me be a thoughtless drudge. She seeks to govern my thoughts and actions and I *will* . . . *not* . . . *have* . . . *it*! Not any more!' she cries, shaking her head and thumping her bony knees with her hands as each word is bitten off. Her skin tingles where she strikes it, and she likes the feeling.

'So, what are you saying?' George is still frowning, still unsure of her, of himself.

'I mean to leave. I will run away from there. There is only one thing I have to do, and it will be done soon. And then I shall disappear. Like a mist in the morning, like a spoken word. I will slip away from there and none of them will be able to stop

400

me, or know where I've gone. Let them see then how they control me! How they own me! They do *not*! But where I go . . . where I go is up to you, George.'

'Is that so?'

'I will run, and when I do I will run straight to you, if you'll have me. I won't marry you, George, but I will stay with you, and be true to you. But this is the moment—now I must have your answer. And if not . . . if not . . . then I will run all the same, though it would break my heart, George. You would break my heart.'

'I would not,' he says, the words wrung tight, tension shaking them. 'I would not for all the world, and you are mine, wife or no.' He puts his hand behind her head, pressing their foreheads together so tight it half hurts. 'So run, Cat. When you may. I'll be waiting for you.'

Cat hears this promise and she smiles; she smiles and the smile goes right the way through her, like it hasn't since she was a little girl. George kisses her but still she can't stop, and the smile becomes a laugh, which passes to George. A laugh of relief, of simple joy.

'Sweet Jesus, Cat—your kisses are salty today!' George tells her. Her skin is sticky and pale with it.

'Oh, I've been sweating like a pig since dawn first broke!' She wipes her hands over her face again; but her hands are every bit as sticky, and grubby to boot.

'What is this last thing you must do?'

'I . . . can't tell you. I hate to have a secret from you, but while I must return to that house, I must keep it. Once we're away, I will tell you, I promise.'

'Is this where the money is coming from?' His

401

voice is weighted with unease.

'It is. And I've thought long about it, and I can tell you that it breaks no law. Don't ask me any more about it yet, I beg you,' she says, squeezing his hand. George raises their knotted fingers, kisses her delicate knuckles, and nods.

'You would not give yourself to another man, would you, Cat?' he asks softly. She grips his hand, as hard as she may.

'Never, George. I swear it.' Beneath the boat, the water laps with a sound like something softly tearing. In the shade of the trees its surface is black and emerald green, with silver slivers dancing all over it. Cat gazes at it with utter yearning. 'How I long to see the sea again! I saw it once, when I was a child. So vast and open and . . . *beautiful*. I *long* to see it again. Can we? Though we're not to wed, perhaps we could take a trip to the seaside, once I am away? What do you say?'

'We shall go wherever you want to go, Black Cat.' George smiles.

Cat takes a deep, happy breath. 'Let's swim,' she says.

'Swim? In the canal?'

'Why not?'

'It's not that clean, love . . .'

'It's got to be cleaner than me right now.'

'There are crayfish . . . and pike, and eels . . .'

'Bugger the eels!' Cat laughs. 'Are you scared of an eel?'

'No, not scared. Not scared, exactly . . .' George hedges.

'Good. Come on.' She stands, holds out her hand to him. He takes it, allows himself to be towed to the very edge of the deck. The boat dips drunkenly with their weight. 'Ready?'

'Feet first, Cat! It's not that deep. What about your dress?'

'Bugger my dress! They can dismiss me for it, and see how I care!' she shouts; and leaps, holding fast to George's hand. The water is only four feet deep, and she bumps her feet on the bottom, feels them sink into silt and muck. But the cold of the water is like a locked door opening, like the break of dawn. It rushes over her hot skin, through her hair, around every eyelash and into her ears, booming. Her heart opens up and pours itself out, is washed clean until no anger or fear remains. In that one instant, she is free. *For the first time in my life*, she thinks, knotting her limbs around George, wet arms sliding like eels to lock around his waist. She tips back her head and lets the sky reach high above her.

*   *   *

The storm begins with what has become reliable regularity. The heat and humidity build for five or six days, reaching a peak like that day's when the air is so fat and bloated with moisture that it is hard to think, let alone to go about the day. And yet Cat's tread was as light as a child's, as she brought up the supper dishes. Whilst they all wilted—even Robin Durrant, whose chatter was for once subdued—she'd all but skipped about on the balls of her feet, a secretive smile playing at the corners of her mouth when she thought herself unobserved. Hester tries to imagine it is because she has the key to her room, but that alone can't have brought about such a change, can it? She thinks of the girl's shrieks, her crying and her begging, when her bedroom door was locked. Perhaps it is enough for her to have the key.

Hester stands at the parlour window. She has unlatched the shutters which Cat closed earlier, and folds one back to look out. The lights in the room are all off, and Hester is in her dressing gown. She went to bed at her usual hour, and woke again a short while ago. Alone, of course, with the first rumblings of thunder chasing ghoulish flickers of lightning in from the west. It is almost two in the morning, and no light comes from beneath Albert's study door. He is not in the drawing room, nor anywhere in the house. Rain hits the window. A fitful, sparse scattering at first, and then a steady downpour. Water rolls down the glass in an unbroken wave, bounces from the garden pathway, makes a sound like a distant sea. *Where are you, Bertie?* She casts this sad little thought out into the night, with no hope of an answer. She can't remember a time when she felt more alone. Another flash of lightning drenches the room, and thunder chases right after it, making Hester jump in spite of herself. There is a soft chuckle behind her and she gasps, turning quickly to find Robin Durrant walking towards her. He is wearing the same creased and crumpled trousers as he's worn all day, his shirt undone. His chest is smooth and flat, the skin taut over the shadowed striations of his ribs. Dark hair blurs a diamond shape in the centre, reaching down towards his stomach. Hester catches her breath and looks hastily away. This is more of any man other than Albert that she has ever seen. He is broader, darker, more solid looking than her husband. He seems more animal;

invulnerable.

'Does the thunder frighten you?' he asks softly. His friendly, affectionate tone of voice is something she has come to dread.

'No,' she whispers, shaking her head. She takes a step backwards but her legs bump the wide window sill, forcing her to grasp it for balance. There is nowhere for her to go. Robin saunters towards her, and stands too close. He seems to tower, though he isn't that much taller than she. Hester looks at her feet, looks past him across the floor to the open door, and pictures herself walking through it. The scent of him fills her nostrils. Animal again, slightly stale from the heat of the day, but at the same time compelling. She fights the urge to breathe more deeply.

'Do I scare you?' he asks; and Hester says nothing. 'Something must be scaring you, dear Hetty. You're shaking like a leaf.'

'Please . . .' she manages to say, when words are snarled up and caught in her throat, refusing to be spoken. 'Please, leave me alone.'

'Hush now, don't be that way. I suppose you're watching out for Albert?' He looks out at the crashing rain for a moment, then grunts carelessly. 'I wish I could tell you. I know you blame me for this new-found Christian zeal of his, Hetty, but I swear I never suggested it. At least, I never meant to. His understanding of what I've been trying to teach him has gone awry, somewhere.'

'You've driven him half mad!' Hester's voice is choked with emotion.

'Not my doing! Why would I want that? He was proving a most astute pupil, and a useful colleague . . . at first. But don't worry. I think he just needs to

405

sleep. Once I've gone, he'll calm down again, I dare say.'

'You're leaving?' Hester gasps, hope surging through her. Robin smiles. He reaches out and takes Hester's hand, which is quite boneless, and holds it against the skin of his chest. Hester's heart jolts horribly. The world is so altered that nothing makes sense, and she is helpless to act; a mere passenger in a tiny craft, heading for a maelstrom. His skin is hot and dry. Hester can feel the hairs there, sharp against her fingertips.

'Soon, soon. Will you be so very glad to see me go?'

'Yes! Oh, yes!' Hester says, and she begins to cry, helplessly, not trying to hide it. She does not turn her face away, or reach to wipe her eyes. Robin Durrant takes one look at her stricken face and bursts into delighted laughter.

'Hester! Dear girl, why do you fret so? Stop that, you're making yourself ugly. Why do you want me gone so badly? Have I been such an awful house guest?' He cups her face with one hand and rubs his thumb along the line of her cheekbone.

'Because . . . because . . . Bertie loves you so! Far more than he loves me . . . than he has *ever* loved me! With you here I may as well . . . I may as well not exist!'

'No, no! You're quite wrong, Hetty. He *does* love you. The problem lies elsewhere, with Albert. It's not love he feels for me, but something else. Something I dare say he does not even know. Or won't admit to himself.'

Gradually, Hester stops crying. She notices that her hand, though he has released it, still rests on his chest. 'What is it then? What does he feel?' she asks.

Robin takes another step closer, so that when he speaks, his lips brush the skin of her forehead, send shivers tumbling down her spine.

'You're such innocents! You and the vicar. Hard to believe such innocence can last so long into a marriage. Normally by now the innocence is gone, replaced by satisfaction, by knowledge and experience, and then by familiarity and distaste. Not that I can claim to have experienced marriage myself, but I have seen it enough times, in friends and family.' He puts his arms around her loosely, but Hester is caged. The smell of him fills every breath she takes, his flesh so close that her skin flares with heat, as though they are already touching. 'Haven't you experienced anything like this with him? Not even on your wedding night? Has he never touched you, or kissed you?' Robin whispers. Hester can't find her voice to answer him. She shakes her head minutely—though in answer to his question or reaction to his embrace, neither of them can tell. 'Such a dereliction of duty! And such a terrible waste. He denies you one of life's great pleasures, Hester; when you were good enough to save yourself for him.' Robin shakes his head and then presses his lips to her forehead. Hester stands transfixed, entirely trapped between the terrifying excitement and the wrongness of his touch, unable to move or think. She shuts her eyes; Robin kisses her eyelids. 'Shall I show you what he should have done? Hester? You look so pretty with your hair undone like that, and tears on your cheeks. If you were my wife, I wouldn't waste a single moment of time with you . . .' *I am not your wife!* Hester cries silently, but still she does not move, for underneath her disgust at this betrayal of Albert, her fear and confusion, she *does* want to know these things he offers to show her. She is desperate to know. The room is dark, protective. It makes her invisible, makes her disappear.

When he kisses her mouth she sags against him, her legs tingling and weak. She cannot breathe. All strength seeps from her, and though she braces her arms against him, as if to fend him off, her mouth kisses him back, in spite of herself. When he breaks away he is smiling slightly. Had it been his normal smile, she might have acted differently. Had it been a smile of triumph or satisfaction, or a mocking smile, she might have found the resolve to run from him. But it is a soft and tender smile; one of admiration and desire, one that she has so longed to see, albeit on another man's face. The storm lights his face again, gives every inch of him an unearthly glow, so bright that Hester flinches. He is beautiful, it is true. She does not open her eyes again, but lets herself be touched by him, be kissed and held by him. With every movement of his hands and mouth she feels her own rising desire—a longing like an ache, an unbearable ache right at the core of her. Robin opens her robe and pushes her back onto the window sill. The pain as he reaches for this ache makes her shudder and clench her teeth together, but it is wonderful too. A thousand fiery sparks whirl behind her eyes, shoot her thoughts to pieces, set light to every inch of her and leave her to burn. For that short while, she is not herself. She does not even exist.

When she opens her eyes Robin Durrant is pulling up his trousers, buttoning the fly, catching his breath. There is sweat gleaming on his chest now, and on his brow. Hester is on her feet again, still by the window, her heart slowing down, and a cold touch of horror to make her sick just beginning to grow. Between her thighs she is stinging, burning, and something begins to trickle. She touches her fingers to it, finds smears of blood amidst something else, some other stuff she does not know. Robin looks up at her as he tucks his shirt in roughly.

'Go to bed, Hetty. Albert will have to take care of himself tonight,' he says, impatiently. Hester swallows. Her throat is parched, ragged. Slowly, with limbs that do not wish to obey her, she pulls her dressing gown closed, and fumbles for the belt. Staring at him all the while, her eyes wide in her face, mind racing now. Robin sees this expression of hers—of incomprehension, of shock. He rolls his eyes a little, scornfully, and then comes to her, puts his hand to her face again. 'It's all right, Hester. Nobody need ever know. It's quite natural—it's not a crime, you know! Go to bed and sleep. I shan't ever tell a soul, I swear.' He speaks in a bored tone, as if to a child. That is all she is to him, Hester sees. A weakling, a fool to be used to his own ends. Now Hester snatches her face away from him. Now she can move, on numb legs, clumsy and slow. But she can't lay all the blame on him, she knows. She walks from the room, eyes fixed and flat like a somnambulist's. She takes the stairs steadily, quietly, and the burden of her guilt grows heavier with every step.

12

Now that she has made up her mind, has settled things with George, Cat itches with impatience. She longs to be gone, to be away with him, and heading for the coast on a train. Not for half a day, which is all the time off she has in a week; not for one precious full day, which she is granted for each two months she works. But for two days, three, four. However long they want, with the silver-grey sea stretching to the far horizon, and the tang of salt water clinging to their skin. She thought for a while that she should give notice to Hester, give some kind of warning. But then she remembers Hester's broken promise, to send her out to see George, and the motto she embroidered, which hangs on Cat's wall: 'Humility is a servant's true dignity.' *Then I have neither*, she thinks with grim satisfaction. The words repeat themselves in her thoughts, giving her face an expression of disgust, and she hardens her heart against the vicar's wife. Let her find her breakfast table unset one morning; let her be obliged to lift a finger for once. But she finds it hard to stay angry with the woman, as she takes their dinner up to them in the evening. Hester has dark circles under her eyes, red rims around the lids. Her face is drawn, her expression stunned. She looks wholly miserable, and Cat must repress a flicker of unease, the unexpected urge to seek her out, to find out the cause of her dismay.

In the end, she tells herself that she could do nothing to help Hester, even if she knew what troubled her. She is a servant, a non-entity. Not a person, not a friend. The night is sultry again, warm and balmy, and the breeze that blows is so soft it feels like a lover's fingertips, brushing her arms as she stands, and she smokes, and she waits for Robin Durrant to appear. She does not have to wait long. All she need do now, when she wishes to speak to him, is catch his eye at the dinner table. She kicks off her shoes as he walks towards her, feels the warm bricks of the courtyard on the soles of her feet, and the springy tufts of moss between them, like strips of fine carpet. Everything feels more real, now she knows she will be free. Everything is more alive, and brighter.

'Well? How goes it with you, my costly model and muse?' Robin asks, as he lights his own cigarette, pushes back the flap of his jacket and stands with his hand in his pocket, like a schoolboy.

'I'm leaving, Robin. If you want more pictures, it must be soon. Tomorrow, or the day after.'

'What do you mean tomorrow or the day after? The Theosophical Society hasn't decided what to do yet, who to send down . . . it can't be so soon! We'll have to wait a bit longer . . .' He frowns.

'No, I won't wait. I mean it, theosophist. I have plans, and I shan't change them for you, much as I would like to collect my next wage from you. Tomorrow, or the day after,' she insists.

'What do you mean "leaving", anyway? Going where? How do you plan to go anywhere when you're watched all day long, and locked in at night?' he says, petulantly.

'I have my means,' she says, and smiles. In her pocket the skeleton key sits, its weight a constant reassurance.

'You can't go until I'm ready! I thought we had

411

an agreement . . . I thought I told you—'

'Well, I'm tired of being told! What can you do to stop me? Come after me, when my George can knock down any man in a fifty-mile radius? If you try it, I will start talking about these pictures of yours. To anybody who will listen—and I'm sure I could find people who'd be interested to hear.' She leans towards him, takes a slow drag of her cigarette, fixes him with a baleful stare. 'I'm *tired* of being told. By you, by everybody. So now I'm telling you. For the agreed sum of money, I will let you take my picture tomorrow or the next day; and I will keep my mouth shut for ever after. That's the last offer I'll make to you. I'm tired of it *all*.' As she speaks, Cat feels her resolve like a solid shape inside her. She will let *nothing* stand in her way.

Robin glares right back at her for a minute, and then breaks into a wide grin. He laughs softly, pirouettes on his heel with his head thrown back, appealing to the sky at such treatment.

'God! I'm going to miss you, Cat!' he says. Cat blinks, bewildered. 'You truly are a breath of fresh air. It's a shame we've met under such odd circumstances, and you a servant. I think we could have been friends,' he says, still smiling at her.

Cat thinks about this for a moment. 'I very much doubt it,' she says at last. 'You're a liar and a hypocrite.'

'Very well then, Black Cat. You truly are as stubborn as a cat, and as difficult to govern. The day after tomorrow, then. Dawn, at the same place. We shall capture the elemental again, and I shall have to perform some magic when they send down their witness—if they insist on supplying their own film for the camera. Some switching of frames in the dark room—*voilà!*' he cries suddenly, throwing his hands wide like a magician. 'I shall win them over yet, just you watch.' Cat slips her shoes back on, grinds her cigarette out with her toe.

'I won't watch. But you carry on.' She pauses. 'What's wrong with Mrs Canning? What's happened?' she asks, in spite of herself. Robin's smile fades, and an expression flits over his face that Cat can't decipher. Anger? Or guilt?

'Oh, don't worry about Hetty. She'll be fine. A little marital strife, I believe,' he says, in a stilted voice. Cat thinks to press him harder, but thinks again.

'Don't forget to bring the money,' she says, and leaves him there.

Later, once Sophie Bell is safely out of earshot, Cat turns back the lock in her door. She opens it a few inches and waits for her pulse to return to normal, her breathing to grow deeper, more even. Still feeling sick, and with her head aching, she sits on the edge of the bed, uses the night stand for a table, and writes two letters.

Dear Tessy—well, I have come up with a plan, just as I promised. Soon, I will have left this place and gone away with my sweetheart, whose name is George Hobson. If you ask around, someone will know how to find us. I say this because I will write to the mistress here, before I make my escape, and beg her to send for you to replace me. I think she will do as I suggest. I have told her a little of your situation, and how we came to be arrested, and I know she will do the right thing. So expect to hear from her soon, because not this morning but the next, I am leaving with George. I can't tell you the joy and anticipation

I feel, Tess! To be making my own way from now on, and not governed by anybody. I feel as though a new life is about to begin, and one in which at last I can be happy. I'm so excited I can barely keep a straight face as I go about the chores! I hope that you will be more content here than I have been. You always were better than me. The vicar's wife is a good woman, and always tries to be kind. But there are alternatives if you can't settle, Tess! I met a woman at the butcher's shop just the other day who had worked for fifteen years at Cowley Park, which is a huge house near to here. Now she works at the telephone exchange. She is a professional! And out of service. Things are changing, Tess, and only for the better I believe. However you find it here, it will be better by far than Frosham House. I will be in touch, I promise. We will see each other again soon. Look after yourself, and please be strong enough to come here, and take my post.

With my love, your friend, Cat

Mrs Canning—if you are reading this it is because you have sought me out and found me gone. I apologise that I did not give notice, but sometimes a person must follow their heart and their impulses, and strike a blow for what they believe. I can no longer live as a servant, and as a free person I leave this house without a by your leave. One thing I beg of you—please send for Teresa Kemp to be my replacement. She is in the workhouse, as I told you. It is called Frosham House, on Sidall Road in London. She is a good, sweet girl; not at all like me. Her current misfortune is all my doing and none of her own, and she will be a good girl for you, and work hard. *Tell Mrs Bell to be kind to her. I know Sophie has a soft heart behind that sharp tongue of hers, and Tess will have much need of the former when she comes down. She is little more than a child, still.*

I also must tell you another thing. Perhaps you have wondered at my lack of propriety, and my unwillingness to accept a life of servitude. I place the blame for this at my own door, with my own temperament, but the blame also lies with my father. He gave me an education far above my station, and taught me that there was a wide and mysterious world that I would never see. This was a grave injustice on his part. It has caused me always to question my station in life, and when I was told that my blood was to blame—my breeding that is—again he was the sticking point. My father is your uncle— the very Gentleman who sent me to you. My mother worked in his household at Broughton Street when she was younger, and they—at his behest—were lovers, and she became pregnant with me. She was forced to leave her job, of course, but my father looked after her and made sure she was provided for; and when she died I was taken into his household. My mother told me this on her deathbed, and she was a woman who never lied. Perhaps this summer you have come to learn a little more about the nature and behaviour of men, and will not find this too hard to believe. We are cousins, Mrs Canning; and if my mother thought it best that I know the truth about my parentage, nevertheless that knowledge has only ever caused me anguish. I was born neither one thing nor the other, neither gentlewoman nor servant, and so I intend to be neither, from this day onwards. I intend to make my own path.

Robin Durrant is treacherous, and not to be trusted. I think you know this already, but I say again—if you can remove him from your household, do so at once. Perhaps I have no right to offer you advice, but since we are not to meet again, I shall offer it anyway. I know something of your troubles with the vicar. A servant will learn these things, whether they would want to or no. In London there was a gentleman, a friend of my father's, who came to visit from time to time. He only ever brought with him, as his companions, young and beautiful men, whom he kept and spoilt like pets. He found women inferior to men in all regards, and shunned their company, from his life and from his bed. If you come to suspect that your husband may feel this same way, then you will never be happy until you have left him, or accepted him as he is and sought companionship for yourself elsewhere.

Goodbye, and please mind what I have written about Teresa Kemp. You have in her an opportunity to do tremendous good. I have written a letter to her, which I will post myself, telling her to expect to hear from you. This is presumptuous of me, I know, but I trust you to do the right and charitable thing. I wish you well, and I hope you can find it in your heart to wish me the same.

Your cousin,
Catherine Morley

Cat finishes these letters with cramps in her hand, the muscles more used to scrubbing than writing. She seals them into their envelopes, addresses each one, and puts Hester Canning's on the night stand, propped up to be easily visible.

She slips Tess's into her bag, which she has packed with her few possessions, and what money she has saved. Outside the window the moon is mottled and full, as pale as fresh milk. It shines onto a landscape of graphite grey shadows and silvery outlines, and in the perfect quiet and calm, Cat sleeps.

The Rev. Albert Canning—from his journal

TUESDAY, AUGUST 8TH, 1911

This is the time. He has told me to stay away, he feels the time is right and I feel it too. He goes with his camera so I know, I know. He will summon them again, he means to take more pictures. I will go, and I will be there, and I will show that I am worthy since I will not announce myself, I will let him go about his great work all undisturbed, and when the images are captured I will reveal that I was there with him, and this will prove that I am ready, and I am pure, and that the elementals can look into the heart of me and will find that I am all I should be. This night has been long but I have waited it out. And all my nights in the meadows were not wasted. Without the sun's energy the ethereals stay hidden—just as the daisy curls its petals, and shuts its eyes to the darkness, so they sleep. But I have spent long hours, alone and cloaked in darkness, and I have studied my soul and my heart, and I have looked inwards and I have rooted out all lust and material desire, and all the wrong feelings that the devil has sent to torment me of late, and I have scoured myself of it all, and left

417

nothing but the light and pure energy of my astral and ethereal core. I am ready, I know this. I know this. Never at prayer alone have I experienced such vivid dreams and feelings. How dead and cold the stones of my church seem now, when all along the real church was all around me, and I could not see it. Until now! The church of the living light and the living breath and the living spirit of all that is holy and good, lying all around us in its green and golden splendour, and I at last have come to see it and to belong to it. And those of impure heart and those whose minds cannot encompass these mighty truths will be left where they are, lower down, further back, below us on the journey, on the ladder to enlightenment. They have many lives left, many turns of the cycle, to atone for whatever sins and misdeeds have rendered them incapable, in this life, of advancement. Even my wife must atone. Like all women, her heart is full of lust and wanting. Now is the time—this very dawn. I am ready and I will go, and I will see, and all will be complete. Dawn is breaking and the sky is clear, and the sun's holy light begins to touch, to awaken. Soon the dance will begin and I will dance it too, and I will leave this shell of crystallised spirit, and find my true form. I am ready.

1911

Before dawn, Cat opens her eyes. *This is the last time*, she tells herself, and smiles. The last time she will wake up in a servant's bed, the last time she will be in a house where she must labour, and be treated as lesser, and have no freedom. She pauses

418

for a moment, makes note of the feeling of the bumpy mattress, pressing into her spine, and the way the muscles that run from her ribs to her hips are aching, from scrubbing the flagstones of the cellar floors the day before. She makes note of the smell of yeast caught under her fingernails, from taking over the kneading of the bread dough when Sophie Bell got too hot and had a funny turn. She remembers that today she would have had to wash a load of the Cannings' underwear, if she stayed. With all of this absorbed, and studied, and scorned, she rises and washes her face and hands. The water wakes her, makes her shiver. It splatters into the enamel bowl, fills the room with tinny echoes. The whole world seems to hold its breath.

She pauses outside Sophie Bell's room as she passes it. She has not told her she is leaving, and there is a needle of guilt about this, behind her excitement. The woman's loud and heavy breaths sound clearly through the door, and Cat presses her hand briefly to the wood. Too late to do anything about it now. Bidding her a silent farewell, Cat resolves to write to her, once she and George have found rooms somewhere. Hungerford, or Bedwyn. Small towns and villages strung along the canal like beads as it heads west. They can visit, explore, choose. She creeps as silently as she can to the back door, because she knows the vicar no longer takes to his bed. His pillow is smooth every morning, one side of the sheets uncreased. The library door is shut, and though no light comes out from under it, it seems to watch and wait; the silence behind it a watchful one, a poised one. Cat pauses, listens as hard as she can for sounds of movement within. When she walks on again, her heart is thumping. The top step of the cellar stairs creaks, and she freezes. She thinks she hears a footstep, behind that secretive door. The squeak of a chair being risen from. But she won't go back so she rushes on instead, as quietly as she can. Down the cellar steps, through the kitchen and out of the back door. The latch seems thunderous in the silence.

The world outside is still colourless, flat and surreal with that odd pre-dawn glow, neither dark nor light, not day or night. A suspended moment, when what was before has gone, what is to come has not yet begun. Cat walks through this between-time and feels the blood in her veins, cool and vital. The air is damp, and touches her cheeks and hair with moisture. She pauses by the garden gate and looks back at The Rectory with its high walls and shuttered windows. How much like a prison it looks, and she reassures herself that she will never set foot inside it again. She takes a deep breath, hopes that what for her has been a prison, for Tess will be a sanctuary, of a kind at least. A safe haven, a place to heal. She hopes that in bringing Tess here she has begun to atone for all the violence she brought upon her friend.

*   *   *

The force-feeding had a peculiar effect on some of the gaoled suffragettes. Their faces were bruised and cut, they had frequent nose bleeds, and suffered attacks of nerves they couldn't contain; many had chest infections, racking coughs that robbed them of air. But beneath all of that, a few of them began to feel stronger again. The food that was poured into them went some way towards nourishing their bodies, and the dizziness and listlessness dissipated for a while. After three days of the terror and violation of it, Tess, Cat and some others stumbled from their cells, strong enough to stand and desperate to see the sky. Leaning on each other like a pair of elderly widows, the two servants from Broughton Street made their slow way out into the yard. Cat could hardly bring herself to look at the cuts and scabs on Tess's face, the chalky pallor of her skin and the way she shivered constantly, though the day was mild.

'Tess . . . I'm so sorry I got you into all of this,' Cat whispered as they stood in the sunniest corner of the yard. Tess tried to smile but could not manage it. The wall behind them was slick with early morning moisture, dark streaks drenching the cold stones.

'It wasn't your fault, Cat. It was those policemen . . .'

'No—you wouldn't even have been there if it wasn't for me, making you! You'd have been back at the house, safe and sound . . .'

'I'd rather have been out and about with you than stuck in that house, even if it has led us here, Cat, truly I would. You're the best friend I ever had . . .' Tess said, her words broken off by a husky, bubbling cough.

'No, I'm not!' Cat shook her head as angry tears filled her eyes. 'Come off the strike, Tess. Please. There's no need for you to continue with it . . . I'll do it for both of us! Start eating, and soon enough you'll be out. The Gentleman will have you back, I'm sure of it . . .'

'Perhaps he might, if you're there to speak for

me?' Tess said, hope lighting her eyes.

'Of course I'll be there to speak for you! I'll make him keep you on, I promise.'

'But . . . I won't come off the strike. I won't be the only one to give in to them, Cat! And if I know you're doing it too, I can put up with it, really I can.'

'But I can't bear to think of it, Tessy! I can't bear to think of you suffering this treatment, when I am the one responsible!' Anguish reduced Cat's voice to a croak.

'Don't you cry, Cat—that's something I can't bear! I'd rather starve than eat the slops they feed us in here, anyway. God—couldn't you just murder one of Ellen's pies right now? A beef and ale one, with a big puddle of gravy and some potatoes . . .' Tess shut her eyes, dreaming up this feast. Cat's mouth filled with saliva.

'When we get out of here, we'll have one. One of the big ones, cut in half just for us and steaming hot,' she promised.

'A big slice of blue cheese with it too, and almond tarts to follow. That's food worth breaking a hunger strike for—not that horrible soup they give us. It's probably just dirty water—the water The Crow has washed her feet in, most likely!' Tess said, with a delicate grimace that opened up a cut by her mouth. She winced as Cat dabbed gently at the oozing blood with the cuff of her blouse.

'The Crow? Wash her feet? Don't be daft. I heard she hasn't washed them for a decade. I heard those aren't stockings she wears—that's her filthy grey skin!' she said, and Tess found a tiny smile.

'That's disgusting!' she whispered.

'And what's more, it's those feet that have left her stranded, stuck working in this dank and smelly place all her days. She was due to be wed, you see,' Cat went on, improvising.

'The Crow to be wed? I'll never believe it!'

'Oh yes, many years ago, when it's said she still had elegance, even if she was never a beauty. But on the night before the wedding her fiancé paid her a visit, and in the grip of his passionate embrace she forgot herself, cast off her shoes . . . and the smell of her feet killed the poor boy stone dead!' She threw her arms wide and collapsed theatrically onto the cobbles, though it made her head spin. Tess laughed a little, clapping her hands covertly. Then she stopped; her face fell.

Cat looked up and saw the dark-haired wardress standing over her, her arms folded and her eyes shining coldly in the morning light. Cat tried to get to her feet, but dizziness assailed her and she remained on the damp ground, suddenly queasy.

'Heard something funny, have you?' The Crow said to Tess, her voice treacherously light, almost friendly. Mutely, Tess shook her head. Shivers gripped her again, shaking her whole body. 'It sounded like you were laughing. Your friend come up with another funny song or a poem, has she?' Again, Tess shook her head. 'Come now, don't be shy. Let's hear it,' the woman ordered. Tess stayed silent and still, her face drawn and deathly pale. Cat struggled to her feet.

'Leave her alone,' she said to the wardress. 'She wasn't doing anything wrong.'

'I'll be the judge of that. Come on, I want to hear what she said. If you don't tell me, I'll start to think there's some special reason you don't want me to hear,' said The Crow, the words laced with menace. Tess glanced desperately at Cat, and Cat racked her brain for something that might placate the woman.

'I said that . . . ah . . . I said . . .' she floundered. The wardress's mouth twisted to one side, a bitter sneer that made Tess take a step backwards, until her shoulders hit the wall. The Crow closed in on the younger girl, who started to whimper. 'I said that you're a bitter old snake who stinks like corruption! There—now you can punish me for it!' Cat cried.

'Oh, I will,' the wardress said, catching Tess's wrist with her strong, gaunt hands. 'But what's most galling to me right now is not what you said, but that this little bitch laughed at it.' She twisted Tess's arm and dragged her back towards the cell block, and Tess uttered a small cry of pure fear.

'*No!* Leave her alone!' Cat shouted, running after them. The Crow turned and with one flat hand gave Cat a shove that sent her crashing back to the ground. For a minute Cat couldn't get up. She coughed and struggled to find her balance; and when at last she got to her feet, Tess was nowhere in sight.

Cat raced up the stairs and back to the corridor where she and Tess were kept, the exertion making her stumble, and spots dance in front of her eyes. 'What's going on?' another prisoner asked, lips grey in an ashen face. 'The Crow had the cosh in her hand!' The door to Tess's cell was shut, and though she knew there was no point, Cat hammered on it all the same, shouting to be let in until two other wardresses came and took her to her own cell, slamming the door behind her. They

424

cast a look at one another as they did it, in disapproval at the sounds coming from Tess's cell, but they did nothing more. Pressed their lips together and moved away. Numb with horror, stunned by guilt, Cat sat with her back against the wall, listening to the blows, hearing the screams and the sobbing. She thought she might explode into flame, with shame, with rage. But she did not. Shadows closed around her, filled the room, suffocated her, and she knew it would be with her for ever: the feeling of killing an innocent thing; of impotence; of the irrevocability of harm done.

When Tess's door was next opened, Tess did not walk out through it. She was huddled in a far corner with her clothes all torn, blood drying around brand new wounds and a hundred new bruises swelling on her skin. And some essence of her gone; fled from the room. The little sparkle that lit her laugh, the avid look in her eye. Cat stood for a long time at the threshold, staring full face at what had been done, letting herself suffer the consequences of her actions. She told herself then she could never suffer enough.

*　　　*　　　*

But perhaps, she thinks, as she turns her back on The Rectory, perhaps now she has. She has relived it in countless nightmares, and shouldered the crushing weight of blame. She has barely slept, barely eaten. She has scoured her body and her soul. She will see Tess again, in a few weeks, a few months. She will find out if—in spite of her broken promises and the tide of misfortune she let close over their heads—if in spite of it all Tess still loves

425

her, and is still her friend. Somehow in her heart, Cat feels that forgiveness is coming. She sees a figure waiting up ahead. Robin nods, giving her a tight smile as she joins him by the stile.

'Good morning. Are you ready to dance, willow spirit?' he says.

'Have you got my money?' she asks blandly. She will not let him see her joy, her excitement; will keep it all for herself. Robin makes a rueful face, fishes in his pocket for a few folded notes, and a handful of coins. Cat puts them away quickly, safely into her bag.

'Here you go. You'd better dance beautifully, for that wage. I have your disguise here with me.' He pats his leather satchel, and can't keep the excitement from his own voice; nerves wound tight.

'One more time then. Let's get on with it,' Cat says. They cross into the meadow, and make for the spot where the willow tree waits.

And as Cat slips on the floating white dress and the long, trailing platinum hair, she feels watched. Not just by the theosophist, not just by the waiting day as dawn begins. Watched by something else, by someone else. She straightens up, the skin at the back of her neck prickling. She casts her eyes to the horizon and sweeps them along, turning a slow circle. Nobody is in sight. But the grass and plants are long, waist high in some places. Cat stares at it, all around, but can see nothing. No telltale place where the long green stems are broken, the dew knocked from flower heads, apart from where she and Robin just walked. No movement, no twitching of a hidden watcher. But still she feels it, and strains her eyes and ears; a rabbit with the scent of fox on the air. A barn owl ghosts across the

426

meadow, making for the trees to the north on silent white wings.

'What is it? What's wrong?' Robin asks, looking up from his camera as he fiddles with the lenses, checks the range of the shot.

Cat shrugs one shoulder. 'Nothing,' she lies. She folds her dress into a bundle, and stashes it with her bag.

'Ready?' he asks, and she nods.

Cat walks at first along the edge of the stream, stares at the rocks and pebbles and weeds at the bottom of it, just visible beneath the reflected sky. She does not feel like dancing, not like she did before. All the rage that fired her before has gone, and inside she is happier now, has less to fight. She spreads her arms, like a bird's wings, tips her head to the promise of sunrise, and closes her eyes. When she opens them again, she sees him: the unmistakable fair hair and pink face of the vicar; his skinny shoulders, the black cleric's coat with its high, tight collar; soft features framed by whiskers. He is a long way off, and frozen at the sight of her; half crouching as if to hide. Cat's heart leaps into her mouth, her stomach twists. They are discovered, for certain. She wonders if Robin knows anything about him being there—of the vicar being let in on the game. But no, she knows he's not supposed to see this. The vicar is Robin's believer, his advocate. For nobody else could it be more important to maintain the charade. Her throat dry with nerves, Cat draws breath, is about to announce Albert's presence to Robin Durrant. The theosophist is crouching low to the ground, is quite absorbed in his work with no idea of the approaching visitor. Cat can feel Albert's eyes on her, even though he is still too far away for her to make out his features. His stare is tangible, like a touch, like a strong grip that seeks to hold her, possess her.

But then nonchalance fills her, and a touch of mischief. Let the vicar come upon them. What is it to her? She is half curious to see what will happen—to see how Albert Canning will react, and how the theosophist will try to argue out of it. A tiny smile touches her lips, and onwards she goes, not wild like before, but walking steadily. Long strides, pointing her toes. She keeps her arms wide or held back behind her, fingers stretched out. She turns in slow circles, her face to the sky; just fast enough for the dress to swirl, to lift away from her legs, following the movement. And soon she is caught up in it again, this dance of hers; steady and hypnotic this time. Her mind empties and the rhythm captures her, and the sun lights the sky a little more as the seconds tick by, and she forgets about the vicar and the theosophist, and notices only that she is alive. And soon to be free; so soon. Clear lungs, clear head, the clear, resolute beat of her heart.

The vicar stands up from the grass to the west of the willow tree. He has slowly come close to them, low to the ground, concealed by barley, foxgloves and wild irises. Now he stands, right in front of her, so that she stops with a gasp, and lets her arms drop. The theosophist is behind her, lying on the ground. *Will he photograph this?* she wonders. The expression on the vicar's face. For it is quite a picture—pale skin, pale blue eyes so wide they might drop out of his head. His jaw hangs slack, tongue pressing softly behind his teeth. There is spittle on his bottom lip, tiny traces at the corners of his mouth, a little of it shining on his chin. Cat smiles, can't help herself. She wonders whether to make him a bow, to end her performance thus, but something about him stops her. He recognises her, this she sees. And changes are working, behind the shifting muscles and lines of his face. Tiny twitches as the last of thought vanishes from his eyes and leaves nothing behind. An emptiness that suddenly scares her. Cat stops smiling, stands still. Only for a heartbeat, two heartbeats or three. She should move; her muscles begin to tighten. She should step aside, run to meet George and let the two men work this out between themselves; make order of their lies and beliefs and strategies, if they may. In the glare of the vicar's vacant eyes, Cat is suddenly desperate to urinate, and the air seems to trickle from her lungs. But it is too late. The vicar's arm comes up into the air. His binoculars, heavy and black, tremble in the hand at the end of that arm. Cat sees them, high above her head. An odd, unnatural outline against the far sky. Then they fall.

*   *   *

In darkness, Cat can hear voices. They waver and lurch, distorted out of all sense and meaning. In her head is a blinding pain, and even when she thinks she has opened her eyes, still she sees nothing. Her throat is wet, full of a warm liquid; what little air she can snatch must come past this, bubbling slowly, using all of her strength. She tries again to open her eyes, to see. Light fills her head like an explosion; the pain is excruciating. She shuts them again, holds them fast. The ground is swelling underneath her, shifting like water, rising and falling. *The sea?* she thinks, at once happy and uneasy. She can make no sense of it. The voices start again, high and then low, fast and then slow. *Hush,* she thinks. *Too loud.* Gradually, the voices even out, become just one voice, high with fear and disbelief.

'Oh, God—what have you done? What have you *done!*' She knows that voice, struggles to place it. A beautiful face, cruel too; laughing eyes. *Robin.* She tries to ask him what has happened, where she is. Why her head hurts and her eyes are blind and her mouth is full of blood—salty, tinged with iron. 'Albert! You've *killed* her! You've . . . you've killed her! Albert!' More words. Their meaning sifts slowly down to her, through layers of pain and confusion. She is puzzled. *Who is killed? I am not killed!* she says, but the words remain inside her head. She can't make her mouth move, can't make her tongue shape the words. Their disobedience enrages her. She tries to take a deep breath, to steel herself for the effort of moving, of sitting up, but her throat clogs and everything is too heavy, too painful. Her head is made of stone, and slowly crushing itself.

*   *   *

For a while, the voices fall silent. It could be seconds, minutes, years. Cat cannot tell. She drifts, rising and falling. The sun touches her face and she thinks it is the fire she built, to keep her mother warm as she died. The silence booms inside her head, thumping like a vast, vast drum, over and over. It's her heartbeat—the pressure of it in her ears. 'They . . . she . . . she must not be found, Albert. We must say nothing of this! Everything will be ruined . . . Take these, take the dress—Albert! Listen to me! Everything will be destroyed . . . all our work . . . Albert!' The voice starts up again, fast and manic now, full of fear and trembling and wild desperation. Rough hands move her, manhandle her. Hands that jerk with panic. She is jolted about, her hair is pulled. She wants to protest at this, wants to be left alone. Each movement is torture, puts spikes of pain through her skull, worse even than the Holloway feeding tube, forced into her swollen and bloody nose for the tenth day running. She must get to George. He will chase them all away, he will protect her from these hands, these voices; he will help her to sit, to cough and clear her throat. 'Albert! Take these. Oh, sweet Jesus . . . her *face* . . . Albert. Take these—*take these*! Go back to the house and say nothing. Do you hear me? Albert? Say *nothing*!'

* * *

Cat is lifted up. She feels like she's flying, just for a moment, but then she's jolted again and the pain clouds everything. Time has disappeared, no longer has meaning. The voice has a new sound now. Wrenching, coughing; as strangled as she. 'Oh, Cat . . . Cat. Oh, God . . .' He's crying, she realises. *Put me down!* Cat says silently. She is uneasy now. She wants to get to her feet; she wants to open her eyes. The booming in her ears is getting slower, and quieter, and while this should

431

be a relief, it is not. It is not. *George!* she tries. *Help me. Please.* The theosophist's breathing is hard and ragged, the jolting faster and harder. There's a whispering sound, a gentle rushing. *Trees? The canal?* Robin is gasping and sobbing. 'I'm so sorry, Cat!' he says, over and over. 'I'm so sorry.' Now Cat is afraid, horribly afraid. With a violence of will she did not know she possessed, she opens her left eye. Light staggers into it, veers drunkenly into her thoughts. Trees, the canal, the bridge by the edge of the meadow where the lane crosses. How did they get here? A figure, in the distance, so familiar, so beloved. *George!* She screams, without a sound. He is running along the path towards her, fast and desperate. Then she is in the water, feels it closing over her face. For a second it eases the pain, folds her into a cool, green darkness. She does not breathe, no longer seems to need to; she is calm. George is coming. He will help her, protect her, take her up and make good her escape. She waits, and sure enough she feels his arms around her, the familiar heft of them, hard muscles over strong bones. She is lifted up, and the world is once again bright and fierce, spinning. She wishes she could open her eyes and look at him, wishes she could smile. There is a smile in her heart, to know he is holding her. She is safe. The pounding in her ears stutters into silence. She lets it go, and there is nothing else. Not even darkness.

*   *   *

Hester seats herself at her dressing table, stares into the mirror and tries to find some way, with powder and rouge, to mask the corruption of her

432

face. She sees it in the outline of every feature, in every hair of her head. The tiny moist corners of her mouth; the crease of her lower lip into her chin; the space between her brows where a fine line is forming. Traces of the theosophist's adulterous touch are everywhere. She can't think how Albert, how everybody, can't see it too. Except that Albert sees nothing, of course. Nothing but fairies and Robin Durrant. Her eyes are puffy, since she cried again in the night. Hester almost calls for Cat to bring up some slices of cucumber for her eyelids, but she can't bring herself to. Can't face the girl's knowing expression, the way her black eyes see so clearly. She can't help thinking that Cat will see her guilt—recognise it in an instant and pour scorn on her for what she has done. The thought is unbearable. Because Cat warned her, after all—not to trust the man, and to be rid of him if she could. And instead she'd let him take advantage of her, let him take the maidenhead she'd saved for Albert for so long. So very long. Her eyes blur so she can't see to put on make-up. What right has she to hide her ugliness, anyway? The ugliness of what she has done. Hester rubs her eyes viciously, and rises to go downstairs.

As her foot hits the bottom step of the stairs, Hester pauses. She knows at once that something is wrong, something is different. As if a strange smell filled the air, or a clock that should have been ticking had stopped. She pauses and listens, and tries to place the source of the feeling. Mrs Bell is clattering the breakfast things as softly as she can in the kitchen, the sound drifting up through the floorboards. The hall clock's deep tick in fact still plods; the library door is shut; light still pours through the ornate glass above the front door. But not from the dining room or drawing room. These other doorways opening into the hallway are dark, and this is what Hester isn't used to seeing—what she can't remember ever seeing. She peers into each room, her stomach twisting when she looks at the drawing room window. The shutters are still tightly closed. She listens, holding her breath. The silence in the house, aside from the kitchen, is complete. More so than usual, she thinks, but can't be sure. Cat moves on soft feet, just like her namesake. Hester goes to the cellar stairs, and down into the kitchen.

'Good morning, Mrs Bell,' she says, as the housekeeper lifts a steaming kettle from the stove and begins to mash a pot of tea.

'Morning, madam,' Sophie replies, putting down the kettle and wiping her hands on her apron. 'How is the vicar? Is all well?'

'Well, yes—that is, I haven't seen Albert this morning . . . yet. Why do you ask?' Hester frowns slightly. She feels the housekeeper appraising the state of her face—the pallor of it, the purple shadows under her eyes. Hester looks away, ashamed.

'I thought he might have cut himself somehow—when I came down I found this dish towel by the sink, all bloodied.' Sophie points to the stained cloth, in a pail of water by the door. 'I put it in to soak straight away, and Cat can scrub it later, but I can't promise all the stains will come out of it, madam. There was quite a lot of blood on it.'

'Oh! How horrible . . . I do hope . . .' Hester pauses. For some reason, her stomach is fluttering so much that her chest constricts, too tight to

434

speak. She presses her fingers into her diaphragm, steadies herself. 'Sophie,' she says, in a voice that comes out odd and strained. 'The shutters are all still closed upstairs. Where is Cat?'

'Still closed? She's not still in bed, surely—I turned the lock and banged on the door to be sure she was awake. Well over an hour ago.' Sophie scowls.

'But you haven't seen her?'

'No, but where else could she be? I locked the door when we went up, just as I'm supposed to . . .'

They are interrupted by a loud knock on the door. The two women pause, listen for the sound of footsteps going to answer it. There are none. They exchange a glance, and then Sophie begins to undo her kitchen apron.

'No, no. I shall answer it, Mrs Bell. Please don't trouble yourself,' Hester says. She goes up to the hallway, and past the deafening wrongness of the dark front rooms, still shuttered to the bright morning outside. A man in smart uniform is at the door, young and fair, his moustache little more than a reddish blurring of his upper lip. Hester recognises him from church. His cheeks are flushed with excitement.

'Constable Pearce, isn't it?' she says, and her effort to smile produces nothing more than a slight tremble of her mouth.

'Good morning, Mrs Canning, I'm so sorry to bother you. I'm afraid I come with grave news, very grave news indeed. Is your husband at home? I would very much like to speak with him,' the young policeman says, all in a rush.

'I don't . . . that is, he may be in his study, but he is often out at this hour . . . I would have to . . .' She pauses, clasping her hands so tightly in front of her that the muscles begin to cramp. 'What news is it? Please tell me.' Constable Pearce shifts his weight from his left foot to his right, and his eyes fill with uncertainty.

'I would much rather speak to your husband first, Mrs Canning. What I have to say is not suitable—'

'Young man, if you have information regarding a member of my household, then please disclose it at once!' Hester snaps, her heart racing so fast that it shakes her. The policeman flushes an even deeper colour, reluctance written all over him.

'It's your maid, Mrs Canning—Catherine Morley. I'm afraid she's been found dead this morning. *Murdered*, I'm afraid,' he says, not able to keep the thrill from his voice.

'*What?*' Hester whispers. For a second, everything is hung, everything pauses. Time seems to slow, and the halt between the tick and the tock of the clock stretches horribly long, and the air rushes out of Hester's chest and will not return. She blinks and says: 'No, you're quite mistaken.' But even as she speaks, she turns, goes back to the stairs and begins to climb them.

'Mrs Canning?' Constable Pearce calls, uncertainly, still hovering on the threshold, but Hester ignores him. Her walk becomes a run, and then a scramble, up the attic stairs and along the corridor to Cat's door. She throws it open, and in her head she pictures the girl leaning her elbows on the window sill, staring out into the sunshine. So clearly can she see this—short dark hair growing in the shape of a V down the back of a fragile neck—that she manages to be shocked

436

when Cat is not there. The bed is neatly made, and no trace of the girl's possessions is left. Her gaze sweeps the room desperately, as fear pours into her, cold as ice, and her eyes light upon a small white envelope on the wash stand. Downstairs, she hears Sophie Bell begin to wail. Sophie, who never could help but to find things out from people.

An odd silence falls over Hester. The house itself is filled with noise—with footfalls as the policeman walks Sophie Bell back to the kitchens and tries to get a statement from her, and the woman's loud and ugly sobbing all the while. *And she barely seemed to tolerate Cat*, Hester thinks, distantly. She picks up the envelope, which has her name on it, and carefully opens it. Cat's handwriting, which she has never seen before, is elegant and sloping. Far more elegant than a maid's should be. Far more elegant than her own. The words scroll with a gentle rhythm across the paper, and Hester casts her eyes over each of them before realising that she has not made sense of a single one. She slips the letter into her pocket and goes back downstairs on wooden legs, so stiff and unwieldy that she stumbles more than once.

The library door is still shut. If Albert is inside, he has not roused himself to see what is causing all the commotion. From outside comes the sound of a small wagon and pair, driving along the lane and stopping opposite The Rectory. More footsteps, more knocking at the front door. Hester ignores it. She stands in front of the library door, close to it; the grain of the wood in every corner of her vision. Her breathing is quick and shallow, and she can't seem to get enough oxygen. She raises her hand to knock, but stops, cannot bring herself to.

437

Somehow, she knows there is no point. Whether Albert is inside or not, there is no point in knocking. Shivering uncontrollably in the warm air, she turns the handle and steps inside.

The room is in darkness, the heavy velvet curtains pulled close together. She waits just over the threshold for a moment, letting her eyes adjust to the shadows. As footsteps sound in the hallway behind her, she quickly steps forwards and pushes the door gently closed, so as to go unnoticed. The atmosphere inside is heavy and thick, as though many weeks have passed since it was aired. There is a dark shape at the desk, and Hester's heart lurches before she realises it is only Albert's coat, thrown over the back of his chair. *I am afraid of my own husband, now?* she wonders. Her spirit shrinks like a candle caught in a cold draught. On the desk is the Frena camera she had so admired when Robin first arrived, and Albert's journal, not closed and tied as he usually leaves it, but with his pen wedged between pages, as if he had been in the middle of writing when he'd risen and walked away. The room is empty, and Hester's nerves ease a little. She walks forwards, thinking to throw open the curtains and the window, to banish the stifling air, prickly with dust and tainted with secrecy, with Albert's dark fascinations. She hasn't gone three steps when her foot catches on something heavy and she trips, turning her ankle as she fights for balance. She reaches down for the object. Robin Durrant's leather bag. Frowning, Hester picks it up, and the leather strap feels soiled somehow, sticky and damp. She has never seen Robin go out without this bag of his. Hester takes it to the window to cast some light on it, but as she twitches

438

back the curtains, squinting, she drops it in shock. Red smears daub her hands where she has touched it. Smears with the unmistakable, iron scent of blood. Hester gags, her stomach clenching in horror. For a long moment she stands frozen, barely breathing, as icicles of utter dread assail her.

13

2011

Leah waited impatiently while the phone rang, fidgeting with nerves. She was sitting in pale vanilla sunshine outside the library, while Mark read through the newspaper reports about the murder of Catherine Morley. The wooden bench was chilly and damp through her jeans, but the sky overhead had turned a gorgeous china blue. There was a lull in the traffic now that rush hour had passed, and the park across the canal from the library looked a brighter green than it had even two days before. At last there was a crackle and pop at the end of the line, and the receiver was lifted.

'Chris Ward Limited,' croaked a man's voice.

'Oh, hello,' Leah said, taken aback. The voice sounded like raw meat. 'I'm sorry to bother you. I got your name from Kevin Knoll—the caretaker at The Bluecoat School in Thatcham? I understand that you did some restoration work there last year?'

'Yes, that's right,' the man said, then broke off to cough. Leah winced, holding the phone a little further from her ear until the fit passed. She could hear him wheezing, catching his breath. 'I'm afraid I can't come out and give quotes this week at all, love. I'm off sick,' he said.

'I can hear that—you sound awful.' The man chuckled roughly. 'Actually, I don't need a quote. I'm writing an article about The Bluecoat School, and I was wondering if I could ask you a couple of quick questions about the restoration work you did?'

'What kind of questions?' Did she imagine it, or had a hint of defensiveness crept into his voice?

'Well, about what condition the building was in before work started, and how much of the original fabric you were forced to replace—'

'Well, the caretaker and the committee is who you want to ask about that, really. They have all the survey reports and the like,' Chris Ward interrupted her.

'And whether you found anything while you were doing the work? Say, behind the plaster . . . or underneath the floorboards?' Leah pressed.

There was a startled pause at the end of the phone line. A pause loaded with shock and—unmistakably—unease.

'Found anything? No, no. We didn't find anything other than a few dead rats and a whole lot of dust. Sorry not to be more help . . .' he said, with a note of finality in his tone. She pictured him edging the receiver back towards its cradle.

'Hold on—are you sure? Nothing at all? Sometimes the original builders of these ancient buildings left little tokens, or dropped coins find their way through the cracks in the boards . . . you didn't find anything at all?'

'Nothing at all. I'll have to go—this throat of mine. Sorry not to be more help. Bye, now.' He rang off, and Leah smiled slightly into the silent phone. She went back inside to find Mark, who was still staring at the microfiche, fascinated.

'Where have you been?' he asked quietly.

'I had an idea—I got the builder's number from Kevin Knoll and gave him a ring.'

'What builder? Oh—the Bluecoat builder? Did you speak to him?'

'Yes. He says he didn't find anything.' She smiled a tight, excited smile.

'So why do you look so pleased?' he asked, glancing up at her.

'Because he's lying,' Leah told him.

*　　　*　　　*

Chris Ward's business address was, as Leah had expected, a residential house; situated between Newbury and Thatcham. A modern brick building, large and solidly built, with a huge and garish array of children's plastic toys in the front garden. The lawn, in spite of the early season, was immaculate.

'He's not likely to be home on a work day, though, is he?' Mark pointed out, as Leah parked the car in the street and they climbed out.

'He's home. Sick as a dog by the sounds of him.'

'Oh, good. In a weakened state then,' Mark said, wryly. Leah glanced at him and he made a calming gesture with his hands. 'Just . . . go easy. You've got the air of a battleship about you this morning.'

'I will! I mean, I will. I'll be nice.' Leah slowed her striding walk and took a deep breath. 'This from the man who told me to bugger off the first

441

time we met,' she added. Mark smiled amiably, and shrugged.

When Chris Ward opened the door it was only a crack, and his face peered out around it, lined and squinting beneath a thatch of steel-grey hair.

'Don't come too close, I'm infectious. What can I do for you?' he rasped.

'Mr Ward? I'm Leah Hickson—we spoke on the phone a little while ago? About The Bluecoat School,' she introduced herself. 'This is my colleague, Mark Canning.'

'*Canning?*' the builder echoed sharply, before he could stop himself.

'You know the name?' Leah raised her eyebrows. The door wavered, and Chris Ward seemed to think about shutting it. Leah put her hand out to stop him. 'Please! Mr Ward, we've no desire to cause trouble for you or anybody. We won't name you as our source, or anything like that . . . but if we could just see what you found under the floor—'

'I didn't find anything under the bloody floor!'

'I think you did. Please. We just want to see it. We're not trying to take it from you, I swear . . .' The man stared at them for a moment, chewing his lip in consternation. 'It's very, very important,' Leah added. The man nodded, opened the door a little wider and stepped outside.

'I keep it all in the garage,' he muttered.

'It all?' said Mark.

'My collection,' the builder said, uneasily.

*   *   *

The metal garage door opened with an ear-piercing screech, and in the gloom within Leah could make out deep shelves lining the wall all along one side. The shelves were covered in objects, and as Chris Ward flicked on the light switch she saw the oddest collection of things, from muddy boots and glass bottles to rusty shell casings; a Second World War tin helmet to a china doll with one cheek smashed in. Some items were in small sealed fish tanks—improvised glass cases. All were labelled with typed script on neat white cards. The air smelt of old spilled oil, and earth.

'What is all this stuff?' Mark asked, walking slowly along the shelves.

'My collection. I'm . . . something of an amateur archaeologist, I suppose. I do a lot of metal detecting as well—that's how I found all these. Medieval and Roman coins,' Chris Ward said proudly, indicating one of the fish tanks where seven or eight small coins were lovingly arranged on a piece of white cloth. 'And of course, specialising in restoration work, I come across a lot of artefacts in the buildings I work on,' he added, slightly more stiffly.

'And do you tell the owners when you find something?' Leah asked, sternly. Chris Ward pressed his lips together, looked away.

'I used to, back in the beginning. But when I did, they never let me . . .'

'They never let you keep them? You know, that could be construed as theft, Mr Ward.'

Mark shot her a censorious look. 'Thank you so much for showing us all this, though,' he said, pointedly.

Leah peered into a fish tank at a selection of tiny children's shoes; most of them very basic, little more than a curve of leather with a short length of twine to fasten them. 'I bet these came out of thatched roofs? Didn't they?' she asked. The builder nodded reluctantly. 'It's meant to be very bad luck to remove them, you know.'

The man fidgeted awkwardly for a moment. 'Here's the stuff you're after. It was under the east end of the floor. The boards were so loose anybody could have lifted them up—they wouldn't have needed tools or anything. But nobody had, it seems. Not in all that time.'

'Unless whoever did just didn't take what they found,' Leah pointed out.

'Look, young lady—there's a thousand builders who'd have just scraped it up with the rest of the rubbish and carted it off with the spoil, without giving it a second thought, all right? I preserve these old things! I keep them safe!'

'Leah, just button it and come and look at what he found, would you?' Mark suggested.

It was a large leather bag with a long shoulder strap. About eighteen inches by twelve, like an over-sized school satchel, dark with age and as stiff as board. The metal buckles were rusty and pitted with corrosion. Leah ran her fingers along it, frowning. Her hands were where Hester Canning's hands had been. She thought hard, tried to picture her. Hiding this bag in fear, in desperation. Hiding it and never returning to it; but never forgetting it either.

'I left the things inside it, just as I found them. I always try to keep things just as I find them. Open it up. Go on,' Chris Ward urged, clearly still excited by his find.

Leah carefully lifted the flap of the bag, and

found herself holding her breath, expectantly, reverently. She gently removed four objects from inside it, and finally a sheaf of papers so stained and ruined that there was no hope of ever reading what had been written upon them. Leah stared at the objects, and felt a sudden pang of recognition. The three of them stood in silence for a minute, and Leah's mind whirled with questions and answers.

'I've . . . read the journal,' Chris Ward admitted, somewhat hesitantly. 'That's how I knew the name Canning. But it doesn't tell you what the other things are. Or what they mean.'

'I know exactly what they are. I know exactly what they mean,' Leah said quietly.

1911

Hester clenches her hands into fists to hide the bloodstains on them. She can't bear to look at them, can't bear having the stuff on her skin, but there is nothing in the room she can clean them on, not without leaving telltale marks for all to see. She stands stock still and tries to think, struggles to breathe. She thinks and she thinks, but can't find any answers. Nothing that makes sense. A policeman is in the hallway outside. A different one, older. He calls her name repeatedly in a deep and gravelly voice. Feeling like she might be sick, Hester swallows convulsively and goes out into the hall. She shuts the library door behind her.

'Ah, Mrs Canning, please forgive me for intruding into your home. The door was open, and

445

I couldn't rouse a servant to answer it . . .' he says, then seems to realise the implication of his words and colours slightly. Hester feels tears, hot and savage, building up behind her eyes. 'Forgive me,' the man mutters again.

'The vicar isn't at home, I'm afraid.' Hester's voice is tiny and thin. 'And neither is Mr Robin Durrant, our house guest. At this time of day they are often to be found in the water meadows between here and Thatcham, going about their—'

'Oh, we know where Robin Durrant is, don't you worry. He's safely in custody, and guarded by three men.'

'What do you mean? Why is he guarded?'

'Perhaps you'd like to sit down, Mrs Canning? I can see this is all coming as a terrible shock, to the whole household . . .' From downstairs, a fresh storm of pitiful crying erupts from Sophie Bell.

'I do not want to sit down! Why is Robin Durrant guarded by three men?'

'Well, Mrs Canning, it was Robin Durrant that committed the murder. He was seen by two men just after he did it, trying to dispose of the girl's body in the canal. He didn't even try to run away, and he was most dreadfully stained with her blood. Now he's sitting in silence and won't say a word to anybody, not even to deny it. Never a surer sign of guilt, in my experience. It's a terrible business, truly terrible.' The policeman shakes his head. Hester's head fills with a muffled, uneven thumping. Grey shadows swell at the edges of her vision.

'There must be some mistake,' she whispers, leaning against the wall to steady herself.

'Let me help you, madam. Do be seated. I shall

446

find somebody to fetch you a glass of water . . .'

'No, no, do not trouble Sophie. She's too upset,' Hester says, but so quietly that the man doesn't seem to hear her.

'Constable Pearce! Please bring up a glass of water for Mrs Canning!' he bellows down the stairs, the noise crashing through Hester's skull like storm waves. 'Please—can you tell me where I can find the vicar, Mrs Canning? We really must speak with him.' The policeman bends forwards over Hester in a way that makes her dizzy. She doesn't know what to say.

'Church. Try the church,' she manages at last.

'Of course. Foolish of me.' And the man is gone.

*   *   *

Hester has no idea how long she stays sitting on the hard wooden chair in the hallway with a drink of water next to her, untouched. Her throat is parched and aching, but she doesn't dare open her hand to reach for the glass. She knows what she will see, what is on her hands. With a surge of panic she looks at the wall where she'd leant a short while ago, but the paint is clean. The blood had dried sufficiently. She stares at the surface of the water in the glass, so clear and pure, shining with the daylight from the front door, which still sits open, abandoned, creaking occasionally in the breeze. But the library door, at the end of the hall, keeps drawing her eye. It is terrifying; dark, and secretive, and watchful. Hester is sorely tempted to get up, to run out into the sunshine and never come back. *He was most dreadfully stained with her blood* . . . The words echo through her thoughts.

447

Oh, Cat! With a gasp Hester is on her feet, and rushing back through the library door before she can lose her nerve. In the light from the crack in the curtains she'd made earlier, she searches the floor. She finds Albert's binoculars, stuffed hastily into their case but not closed. She looks at them carefully, sees some glistening dark mess all over them. Cautiously, her hands shaking uncontrollably, she draws them out and turns them to the light. The lenses are smashed and fragments of glass are stuck to the metal in a slick of clotted stuff. Glass, and fine black hairs. Hester stares at them with awful, grim recognition. Something falls from inside one of the cylinders, landing with a small sound on the rug. Numbly, Hester bends and picks it up. It is hard between her fingers, both smooth and angular, like a chip of stone, all covered in blood. Hester frowns, rolls it between her fingers to clean it off a little. She studies it again, and then knows it for what it is. A tooth. A human tooth, broken off sharply at its upper end. Hester screams. She drops the binoculars and they land with a thump that shakes the floor.

Her breath comes in ragged gasps, fast and uneven. She waits for the police to come and find her, to burst into the library in search of the source of the scream and the racket she has made; to find her all bloody and wild. In desperation, she again considers fleeing; climbing out through the window and running away as fast as her weak legs will carry her, though she has no idea where she would go. But she knows that if she moves she will faint. It takes long minutes for the panic to loosen its grip on her but after a while it seems that nobody has noticed her cry out. No footsteps approach the

448

library. She shuts her eyes until the tightness in her chest eases and her head is clear enough to allow her to think. Crouching down, Hester lifts the cover of Robin's bag and pulls out a silvery blond wig, a diaphanous white dress. All bloodied and ruined. She knows them at once, having spent enough time studying Robin's pictures to recognise what they are. In that instant she realises: Cat was the elemental. *Oh God, oh God, oh God . . .* Hester has no idea if she has spoken aloud or merely thought this short and desperate prayer. Because if Robin has been arrested, with Cat's body and coming straight from the scene of her killing, then only one other person could have brought these items back to the house. Could have washed their hands in the kitchen sink, and left a stained dish towel behind. *My darling Bertie. What has happened here?*

Hester's mind empties of all thoughts except one—to protect Albert. Carefully, she puts the costume back into Robin's bag, on top of a selection of his correspondence which is soon stained and illegible. The dress fabric feels fine and soft beneath her fingertips. The wig is slippery, alive. Hester shudders, gagging slightly, as if this is Cat's hair, as if it is part of the girl's murdered body. She clenches her teeth, struggles to keep herself steady. Then she puts the binoculars in with the costume, crying now, catching the smell of congealed blood coming from the case. A cloying, feral, butcher's shop smell. Glancing up, she remembers Albert's journal, obviously recently used, and left on the desk. Hester doesn't open it, or read any of the entries. She has no wish to learn anything, to know anything more. She wishes she knew less; far less. She puts the journal into the leather satchel last of all, closes the buckles on this ghastly, incriminating hoard, and stashes it in the footwell of the desk, far out of sight to anyone but a person actively searching. She does all this without soiling her dress, but her hands are red and brown. *Cat's blood. Cat is dead.* Hester's stomach churns. She staggers out of the library and shuts the door, and just makes it to the cloakroom before she is sick.

*   *   *

Later, she goes down to the kitchen to see Sophie Bell. The housekeeper is inconsolable, sitting vast and trembling at the table with the tea leaves turned to bitter mush in the pot, and flies settling unnoticed on the rim of the milk jug.

'Why would anyone kill her? Why would anyone do that to our Cat? And her just a slip of a thing, no real trouble to anybody . . .' she mumbles on and on, hardly seeming to notice Hester, who stands at her shoulder for a while, awkward and silent. When she turns to go she notices the bucket of water in the corner, with the stained cloth still soaking in it. Her stomach gives a nasty jerk, filling her throat with bile again. Without a thought she kneels down, wrings the cloth out and flings it into the stove. The iron door clatters shut behind it, and Hester rises, half afraid to turn back to Mrs Bell. But Sophie still stares straight ahead and has noticed nothing. Hester washes her own hands again and again, but like Lady Macbeth, she is sure a taint is left. For days, the smell of blood clings to the inside of her nose.

450

*　　*　　*

The chief constable's own bloodhounds, Puncher and Hodd, soon find the scene of the murder. A place near a stream where the grass has been crushed by footsteps and the dry summer flowers have shed feathery seeds onto a patch of spilt blood where insects circle and settle to feast. There sits Cat's bag, with all her meagre possessions inside, and her day dress, tucked to one side of it. All this Hester learns at the inquest, which is opened at the parish council house in Thatcham by the coroner for western Berkshire, Mr James Angus Sedgecroft. Mrs Bell sits beside her, eyes shining in a face ablaze with hatred, trained constantly on Robin Durrant. The murder weapon isn't found, but the nearby stream contains many large and jagged flints, and it is assumed that one of these was used to beat the girl's skull in, and was then cast back into the stream to conceal the evidence. Only Professor Palmer, a special medical advisor to the Home Office sent down by Scotland Yard to examine the body and assist Superintendent Holt with the case, remains unconvinced by this explanation. He makes special note of the fury of the attack, and the way it focused on the girl's face, as if to wipe out her very existence. He found fragments of glass in some of Cat Morley's deep wounds, for which no explanation could be found. When Hester hears this she turns as cold as ice, right through to her core. She thinks of the smashed binoculars, and once she has thought of them, she cannot stop thinking of them. Albert's binoculars. The ones he

451

was never without.

*   *   *

That evening, Hester takes the leather bag from the library and walks it all the way to The Bluecoat School. She can think of nowhere else that might be safer, less likely to be searched. Because Professor Palmer has a sharp eye and a puzzled, suspicious expression, and when he came to The Rectory to question the household, she caught those sharp eyes of his roaming the corners of the room. Hunting, hunting. When she spoke to him, her own words rang with dishonesty even when she spoke the truth. Because she was full of lies, full of deception. She felt it oozing from her every pore. The bag cannot stay in the house, and it is too big to put into the stove, to burn as she had the towel. Besides, the binoculars would not burn. There is no way to destroy them. And Hester also feels that she *shouldn't* destroy any of it. Just in case . . . in case some situation arose—something she has not thought of, since her thoughts are so mixed and bewildered—and the contents of the bag were needed. The Bluecoat School is never locked, and as she walks to her customary position at the head of the class the loose floorboards shift and rock beneath her feet, and she falls to her knees, scrabbling at them with her fingernails, weeping with relief as this hiding place presents itself to her.

*   *   *

The inquest lasts three days, and through it all

Robin Durrant says nothing. George speaks to the coroner and jury and tells them how Cat had been planning to run away with him, and how she had loved him, and how whatever the reason she had been in the meadows that morning, it had not been to keep a lover's tryst with Robin Durrant, as the police were suggesting. He is adamant about this, he insists it; but only Hester knows that he is right and not merely blinded by love. She stares at him as he stands and weeps, unashamedly and uncontrollably, and she feels her heart breaking for him. The words hover in her mouth, but will not be spoken. *I know why she was there! I know what Robin Durrant was doing!* But she cannot speak. She cannot speak to anybody. As surely as if a spell has been cast to hold her tongue, it stays still and silent in her mouth. Numb and deadened, like the rest of her. He is handsome, this man of Cat's. He looks strong and honest. He speaks about Cat with such passion and love that Hester feels a stab of misplaced envy. What a joy it must have been, to plan an elopement with a man like George Hobson. But Cat's plans had been interrupted. Horribly, irreversibly interrupted. *She must be furious*, Hester thinks. She shuts her eyes, gripped by the thought. Wherever Cat is now, she must be *furious*.

*　　　*　　　*

When Cat's character is defamed, Mrs Bell demands to speak, and stands up for the girl. She, too, denies that Cat was involved with Robin Durrant in any way, and hints that the theosophist must have coerced her out of her room somehow, must have found some way to unlock her door and force her out into the meadows, since she herself had locked the girl safely in the night before. When she cannot give a rational explanation of this, glances are exchanged and notes taken, and it is assumed that the housekeeper feels guilty about forgetting to lock the door and is trying to cover her mistake. Hester hears all this, and stays silent. She thinks of the skeleton key that she gave to Cat, and she stays silent. She forgets to blink for long, long minutes, until her eyes itch and sting.

Barrett Anders, the dairy man, testifies that he had been coming south in his milk cart, along the lane from the London Road, to make his deliveries in the village, and as he'd neared the bridge he'd seen Robin Durrant crossing the meadow towards the canal with the girl in his arms, all broken and dead, and that he'd knocked the killer down while George Hobson, who had come along the towpath, leapt into the water to pull the girl out, even though she was clearly dead and nothing could be done to help her. Hester tries to shut her mind to it, to the unbearable pain George must have felt, seeing Cat that way. Cat, with scarlet water streaming from her black hair, her thin limbs limp, her little hawk's face a ruin. The images strike her like lashes of a whip. 'Minutes too late to save her, I was,' George moans, his face ravaged, twisted with grief. 'Only minutes.' Robin Durrant is charged with wilful murder and committed for trial at the next Berkshire assizes. He does not react to the verdict. He does not react to anything.

*   *   *

The Sunday after Cat's death, the Reverend Albert Canning gives his sermon as usual, to a packed church that hums with suppressed excitement; illicit, disrespectful excitement that the congregation can't help feeling or showing. They've come to see the Cannings, who have housed a murderer all summer long; whose maid has been smashed to death with a rock; who are at the centre of the biggest scandal the parish has ever known. Hester sits in the front row, where she always sits, her back stiff, her skin burning. The tide of whispers rises, laps the nape of her neck, threatens to close over her head. Albert does not mention Cat in his sermon. Hester listens in dismay, as he does not. He repeats a sermon he gave only three or four weeks before, on the subject of material wealth, staring at the back of the church as though his thoughts are a million miles away; the words bitten off and falling from his mouth like chunks of wood. Solid and dry and dead. As if he no longer believes a single one of them. At home, he sits in the parlour and never asks about his journal, or the leather bag, or his binoculars. He never asks about any of it, and Hester never speaks up. Her Albert has gone, and in his place is this sleeper, this man of ice, this shadowy person who barely speaks and barely eats and only goes out on church business; in his place is a man she doesn't know at all—a shell, a liar. She watches him with a heart full of dread, frightened of him, and of what she has done to protect him. The man is a changeling, he is a stranger. And perhaps, perhaps, he is a killer.

Wednesday, October 15th, 1911

Dear sir,

*Why don't you reply to my letters? I don't know who
else to talk to and I must get out some of my thoughts
or I will run mad. I used to write to my sister, and
there were no secrets between us two, but now I have
things I can't write, even to her; and so I must write
them to you. Why do you not speak out? If what I
think is true, why do you stay silent? Perhaps I know
the reason. To keep your own secret—that of the
elemental, and of the photographs you published. To
keep your name and this place in history that you
have carved for yourself, at whatever cost. But it is a
sorry world we live in if the infamy caused by a lie
should be greater than that of a murder. Do you
really think you have chosen the lesser crime of the
two to be guilty of?*

*I found your bag, which was brought back to the
house. I found what was in it, and Albert's
binoculars. I know your secret. The secret you will go
to gaol to protect. Are you willing to die for it? They
might hang you! And what use is your reputation as a
theosophist when you have lost all standing as a
man? Will your precious Society still have you, when
you are a convicted killer? I think not. I think not. So
why persist in this silence? What good does it do you?
The date of your trial approaches. There isn't much
time. If you are hanged, what then? Is that what you
wish—do you think that even if your life ends now,
your name will live on for ever? That you will always
be the theosophist who captured proof of the
existence of elementals? I tell you now, it is not worth
it. Already there are some who denounce your work,*

*and the pictures you took, and their numbers will
grow. You will be forgotten, as will your work. Speak
out, and there is time to start again! Your father
would rather have a failed theosophist or even a
fraudster for a son than a murderer; I am utterly
convinced of it.*

*At one point I thought you noble, I thought you
sacrificed yourself for Albert. But this was a foolish
thing to think. Why would you? Everything you did
was for yourself, from the moment you arrived at my
home, and turned it upside down. Oh, why did you
come at all! How I wish that you hadn't, and that
still Cat lived, even if she had run off with her
George. She was my cousin, did you know that? She
wrote it to me in a letter, which she meant for me to
find once she had made her escape. Perhaps a while
ago I would not have believed that my uncle would
sire a child with one of his servants, and then place
that child in my household without ever telling me.
Now I think there is nothing men will not do, should
it suit them. There is nothing they will not do.*

*I believe I am with child. The symptoms are
becoming harder and harder to deny. I thought I
should tell you, though I have no idea what you will
make of this news. If it will have any effect on you at
all. I myself am quite destroyed by confusion and joy
and doubt. Joy—how can there be any joy in this
house any more? Ever again? Joy or laughter or
merriment. All I wanted was a child, and now I come
to see how true the adage that we should be careful
what we wish for. Albert is like a ghost. He chills the
room. He chills me. My own husband. I have not
told him about the baby. How can I? Though soon
enough he'll see it. What then? Will I be beaten out
of existence too? Will that be the end of me? This*

cannot go on—we cannot go on like this. Something must change. The truth must come out. I can't carry this burden on my own; it's too much for me. I can feel myself breaking with the strain of it, day by day. I have hidden all the things I found, that evil morning. They remain, and they tell their own story. The truth is waiting for you to speak out, Mr Durrant. If you do, I will help you. I swear it. I will tell them of my part in this, and Albert's, and I will take my due. Perhaps they would be merciful to me, knowing that I acted out of fear, and love for my husband. Perhaps not. Oh, but what then of our child? What would become of him? I do not know what to do. Help me.

Hester Canning

14

2011

Leah spent a week reading the police files on the Cat Morley case, and searching the papers later in 1911 for details of Robin Durrant's trial. She stared at the photograph of him that appeared each time the story was reported; at the elegantly curved top lip that she remembered from the dead soldier, so many miles away in Belgium. It was unsettling to recognise that the two faces, living and dead, were one. He was found guilty of wilful murder; the conclusion that it had been a crime of passion, since Cat's reputation was not good and she was found wearing only her slip. As such, the jury recommended mercy and he was sentenced to life imprisonment rather than hanging. Only one man seemed to have had any doubts in what was otherwise treated as an open and shut case. The Home Office's man, Professor Palmer, noted that there was much less blood staining on Cat's slip than he would have expected had she been wearing only that when she was attacked and killed; and that if their meeting had been a passionate one, a tryst gone awry, then he found it strange that she had arranged to meet her other lover, George Hobson, and to elope with him that same morning. And also that she had removed her dress carefully, and folded it up neatly. Hardly the actions of a couple in the throes of passion. There were also the fragments of glass in the girl's face, which never were accounted for.

Added into the file, like an afterthought, was an extra statement from Mrs Sophie Bell, the cook and housekeeper at The Rectory. Made several weeks after the inquest and shortly before Robin Durrant's trial, Mrs Bell stated that she had found a bloodied towel in the kitchen at The Rectory on the morning of the murder, and that it had subsequently disappeared. Asked why she hadn't reported this before, the woman said she had been too shocked and upset at the time, and had forgotten all about it until later on. She also stated that the vicar and his wife had been most peculiar, and much changed since the killing; although she stressed that they had always been good and kind employers, and that the alteration in them might be purely ascribable to shock. There was a memo from Professor Palmer, suggesting that the statement be included in the trial evidence, and that further investigation be made into The Rectory and its occupants, but this recommendation was not acted upon.

Reading the files, Leah felt a tremendous sense of urgency. She knew where the glass in Cat's face had come from—from the murder weapon, Albert Canning's binoculars. She knew that the reason there hadn't been much blood on Cat's slip was because she'd been dressed as an elemental when she was killed. And she knew why the vicar, whose journal reflected a man rapidly losing his grip on reality, would have lashed out at the girl. He had been duped, surely and completely. Finding this out must have rocked him to his very core, and tipped him over the edge of reason. She knew why Hester Canning, desperate at first to stop any suspicion falling on her husband, had hidden the evidence she'd found at The Rectory on the day of the murder; and why thereafter, as she came to suspect her husband, she had been tortured by guilt and fear. Leah felt like running to somebody in authority with what she knew; telling the police, the press, anybody. As if she could change these events, a hundred years later. As if the real killer could be brought to justice, and Hester not forced to live out her shadowed life with him.

The newspapers, by the time of the trial, had managed to find photographs to go with the story. They printed the Cannings' wedding portrait, taken in 1909. The couple stared serenely from the page, two pairs of pale eyes in soft young faces, the irises so clear that even in black and white, it was obvious that they must have been light blue or green. Hester was smiling slightly, glowing with contentment. The vicar, who was wed in his clerical dress, had an air of mild anxiety and no smile on his lips. Leah stared at the woman's face with a feeling of recognition. And there was a picture of Cat Morley, the murdered housemaid, whose role as the elemental was never publicly discussed, even if there had been those with suspicions at the time. It was a poor shot, taken from a distance at the Cold Ash Holt fête for the coronation in June, 1911. An array of finely dressed ladies, including Hester Canning, had paused in their revelry to have their picture taken. Bunting and parasols, tea tables laid with bright white cloths and three-tiered cake stands. And, behind them, a short, slight girl in a grey dress, with a clean apron tied tightly around her and a soft cotton cap on her head. She was holding a silver teapot, as if paused in the act of filling the china cups laid out in front of her. It was not a good picture, and too distant for her face to be clear. Short locks of black hair came out from under her cap, and her face was set in a scowl which might have been down to the bright sunlight, but might not. Dark brows drawn down in a thin, angular face. *The elemental*, Leah thought, with a pang of anguish for the girl.

The more Leah read, the more Hester's letters made sense; facts and references dropping into place. She began to write her article, which grew and grew, and became as much about depicting the truth that Hester Canning had so longed for as resurrecting the dead girl, whose role in it all had never before been properly understood. And as she stared at the Cannings' faces, and went back to Hester's letters to Robin Durrant, something else became abundantly clear.

461

She was interrupted on Friday afternoon by a phone call from Mark.

'Hello, stranger. Are you ignoring me now that you've got your story, or what?' he said.

Leah smiled, glanced at the clock and realised that her legs were numb, her back aching. 'No! Sorry, Mark. Not at all. I've just been so caught up in filling in all the gaps . . . I have some rather significant news for you, actually. I was saving it until I could give you the finished piece, but perhaps I should tell you sooner.' She stood up from her table in the reading room and stretched.

'What is it?' he asked.

'Oh, it's far too juicy to tell you over the phone. Let's have some lunch at the pub—but first, meet me at the church in Cold Ash Holt. Say, in an hour?'

'All right then.'

'And bring that picture of your grandfather, Thomas.'

*   *   *

The day was mild and blowy, a damp wind nudging at them and trembling the grass as they walked along the rows of gravestones surrounding the church of St Peter. Leah had a bunch of flowers underneath her arm, the cellophane crackling softly. White lilies and pink cherry blossoms; a big, extravagant spray.

'If you're looking for Hester and Albert, they're over there,' Mark said, pointing to an oblong tomb near a vast and brooding yew tree.

'We'll get to them. I'll need a photo of their graves for the article. First there's someone else I want to see.'

'This article of yours is getting pretty chunky. Maybe you should turn it into a book?' he said.

Leah paused, a smile spreading over her face. 'That is an absolutely brilliant idea. Why don't I? I've got enough to write about. Theosophy, a fairy hoax, a murder, a miscarriage of justice . . .'

'Was it a miscarriage, though? After all, it was the theosophist's fault she was killed, from what you've told me.'

'Yes, but the vicar should have faced justice too, for what he did. Not just your great-grandfather,' Leah said, and waited while Mark unpicked this remark.

'What do you mean "the vicar, not just my great-grandfather"? The vicar *was* my great-grandfather,' he said.

Leah shook her head, smiling. 'Nope,' she said. 'What links those two letters Robin Durrant kept? What does Hester mention in both of them?'

'Er . . . doubts and fears, suspicions . . . begging for information . . .'

'But what else?' she pressed. Mark shook his head. 'Her *child*, Mark. She talks about her child in both of them. Firstly that she's about to give birth, and that she thinks it's a boy; secondly at length about him as a toddler.'

'Maybe, but so what? She probably talked about him in the other letters she sent as well.'

'Perhaps, perhaps not. And maybe he didn't mean to lose the others. Why would she mention her child at all, to a man convicted of murder who she's clearly uncomfortable writing to, and when she clearly has more important things to write to him about?'

'I don't know . . . aren't all new mothers a bit obsessed with their kids?' he countered.

Leah took a printed page from her back pocket. 'I found this in the newspaper archive—it's Hester and Albert on their wedding day.'

'Oh, so that's what they looked like. That's great,' Mark said.

'Did you bring the picture of Thomas? Hester's son? Can I see it?' Leah asked. Mark pulled it from his coat pocket and handed it to her. She held the two portraits up side by side. The flimsy printout flapped a little in the breeze. 'What do you notice?'

Mark obediently studied the two pictures for a while, and then shrugged.

'I don't know. What am I supposed to be seeing?'

'The *eyes*, Mark. Any A-level biology student will tell you—it's almost impossible for two blue-eyed people to have a brown-eyed child. Thomas wasn't *Albert's* son. He was Robin Durrant's.'

'My God . . . are you sure?'

'I'm sure. They must have had a fling or something. Something that of course ended badly when the murder and all the rest of it happened. The CWGC can do a DNA test for you, if you like. Your great-grandfather was a theosophist, was convicted of a murder he didn't commit, and was sent to fight in the trenches like a lot of convicts. And he died there, with all of his secrets intact. Until now.'

They walked on for a bit longer, still searching, until Leah's eyes lit upon the name she'd been looking for.

'Here! Here she is,' she said. But her excitement

quickly faded into something more subdued. It was a small gravestone, so weathered and furred with lichen that it was easy to overlook. It sagged sideways with a slightly weary air, and the turf in front of it was tussocked and neglected. Just visible were chiselled words, the name and the epitaph. *Catherine Morley, April 1889—August 1911. Safe in the Arms of the Lord*. 'Her nickname was Black Cat, according to the papers,' Leah said.

'Why?' Mark asked, as they crouched down by the stone. He put out his hand and brushed gritty lichen from her name with his thumb.

'Who knows? Some things are just lost, after so much time. It could have been a slur on her character,' Leah sighed. She put the bouquet of flowers on the grave and they looked out of place, too bright.

'God, she was only twenty-two. So young. You haven't got anything else to spring on me, have you? Cat Morley wasn't my long-lost cousin or something?' Mark smiled.

Leah shook her head. 'No. Nothing like that.'

'Well, you did it.' He patted Cat Morley's stone. 'You found out who the dead soldier was, *and* solved a murder along the way. And you managed to get me out of the house. Thank you, Leah,' he said seriously.

'Don't thank me—thank you for all your help! I couldn't have done it without you,' Leah said, embarrassed.

'Yes, you could.'

'Well. Thank goodness you decided to go for a pint at The Swing Bridge that first evening. I'm not sure I'd have had the guts to knock on your door again, after the reception I got the first time.'

'And I probably wouldn't have answered it if you had. Which would have been a huge mistake,' he said. Leah smiled briefly and looked down at the grave between them. His steady grey gaze was disconcerting, made it hard to think. There was a heavy pause, the wind rustling quietly through the cheery flowers.

'So, when is this meeting with your CWGC . . . contact, then? Where the grand reveal of the soldier's name will be made?' Mark asked, with a note of fake drama, fake lack of interest in his tone. Leah watched him across Cat's grave for a moment, until he looked away across the cemetery and into the black depths of the yew tree.

'Tomorrow. There's a party at his parents' house. I said I'd drop it in then.' She searched around for something else to add, but found nothing.

'A party. Sounds nice. Do you want me drive you? Surrey, you said before, didn't you? It's not far. Then you could have a drink,' he offered casually.

'Oh, that's kind of you, but there's really no need to bother—'

'It's no bother,' he said, quickly.

'It just might be . . . a bit . . . You know,' she said, uncomfortably. She did not want him anywhere near Ryan, she realised. As if Mark might get tainted somehow, stained by her toxic feelings, the poisonous shreds of her past life.

'Awkward?' he suggested. Leah shrugged, unable to meet his eye. She suddenly felt horribly guilty, as though she'd been caught cheating.

'Maybe.'

'Look, I won't come in or anything. I'll just

chauffeur you. By the sounds of it, you'll need a drink when you get there. OK?'

Leah glanced up at him and smiled. 'OK. Thanks.'

* * *

'So, what will you do now?' Mark asked, as they headed east along the M4 the next day. The journey had been odd and uncomfortable; Leah's excitement at showing Ryan what she'd found clashing with the strained silences in the car.

'Go home, I suppose,' she said. 'Back to London to start work on my book. I need to speak to my agent—and start touting for a publisher.' She glanced over at him. Mark nodded, smiled, said nothing. 'What about you?' Leah asked.

'I should think about starting over, I suppose. Get job hunting, stop festering away at Dad's place. Put it on the market, perhaps.' His voice betrayed no real enthusiasm at the prospect.

'Mind if I come back and take some pictures before you do? For my book?'

'You can come back any time you want, Leah,' he said gently, and Leah shifted in her seat, fiddling awkwardly with the file of papers in her lap.

'I hope it won't affect the asking price—me revealing to the world that a murderer, his adulterous accomplice and a theosophical hoaxer once lived there!'

'All publicity is good publicity, right?' Mark laughed. 'I don't think it's very fair to call Hester his adulterous accomplice, mind you.'

'No, it's not. Don't worry—I'll make sure

467

'readers know how much she struggled with it,' Leah assured him. They drove on in silence, and Leah thought of five different conversations to start, abandoning each one in turn.

*　　　*　　　*

'Here—this is the one,' she said, leaning forward in her seat with a sudden storm of nerves cramping her stomach. Mark pulled into a smart, wide tarmac driveway flanked by twin five-bar gates. The house was an immaculate neo-Georgian pile, three storeys high, with a long rank of garages topped by a brass weathercock that gleamed in the sunshine.

'Nice,' Mark remarked. 'Not short of a bob or two, then?'

'Or three, or four,' Leah agreed, neutrally. She unclipped her seat belt, flicked her hair back behind her shoulders and licked her lips nervously. She drew breath to thank Mark for the lift, but he cut her off.

'If you want me to pick you up again later . . .'

'No, no. It's fine. It's a five-minute cab ride to the station, and I'll head back to The Swing Bridge from there. Thanks so much for bringing me, and for . . . all your help, Mark. You've been fantastic.'

'Perhaps not quite fantastic enough,' he said quietly.

Leah swallowed, pretended not to hear the remark, not to understand what he was asking. Her heart was high in her throat.

'Well, I'll be back, anyway. Before too long—I'll need to get into the Newbury police files again, and the newspaper archives . . .'

'Sure.' He looked away, rubbing one hand along his jaw. 'Look, are you sure you don't want me to wait for a while? I don't mind. It might be . . . a bit difficult in there. With all the family around and everything . . .'

'I'm sure it will be. But I'll be fine, really—don't wait. I don't know how long this will take, and I hate to think of you just sitting around, waiting for me . . .' Leah flushed, the words suddenly seeming to be about something far more important than a lift back to Berkshire. Mark watched her intently, but Leah could find nothing else to say.

'If you're sure,' he said. Leah leant over and kissed him on the cheek. His skin was warm, slightly rough for want of a shave. The smell of him sent an odd pang into the pit of her stomach. Her pulse was speeding, thoughts confused.

'Thanks, Mark. I'll . . . see you soon.' She got out of the car before he could speak again. Her chest felt odd, too tight, and the familiar excited dread at seeing Ryan washed through her. Behind her, she heard Mark turn the car around in the driveway and pull back out into the road. The sound made her pause, turn quickly to catch a glimpse of him. With him gone she felt suddenly naked and vulnerable. She halted on the front step, frozen, uncertain.

Just then the door opened, and Ryan smiled down at her.

'I thought I heard a car. You're bang on time, as ever. Come in. Did you find out who our mystery man is? I'm dying to know,' he said.

'I . . . did,' Leah said, suddenly breathless. Her eyes scoured his face, the familiar, wonderful lines of it. And something seemed different. Something

469

she couldn't put her finger on. He looked unreal, somehow. Counterfeit. His scruffy hair and playful, schoolboy smile too young for him; only skin-deep.

'I'm so glad you've come, Leah,' he said softly, as if sensing her hesitation. He tapped the file she carried with one finger. 'Is this it? What you've found out? Come in, why don't you—don't hang about on the step.' Leah took one heavy step over the threshold, but then stopped again.

'Yes. Yes, it is. Ryan, I . . . I need to talk to you. About what happened in Belgium . . .' she started to say, but suddenly a tumbling female laugh and a flash of chestnut hair further along the hallway stopped her. She saw Ryan's face tighten, the smile grow slightly strained. Saw him watching her carefully.

'Is that Anna?'

'Leah, don't start—'

'Don't start? *Don't start?*' Anger flashed through her like a lightning strike. 'You didn't say she'd be here. I thought she was still in the US?'

'She was—she is. But she was hardly going to miss her father's birthday party, was she?'

'Her *step*-father's birthday party,' Leah corrected. 'Quite an important distinction, wouldn't you say?'

'Not in this instance. Look, Leah. My parents really want to see you. They've missed you—we all have. Won't you just come in and . . . forget about the other stuff? Now is not the time to make a scene.' He used the gently cajoling tone she would once have found impossible to resist. That she had found impossible to resist in his room in Belgium. Now it sounded wheedling, pathetic. He took her hand and ran his thumb over her knuckles. She

470

waited for the burning sensation of his touch, for the shivers it would send flooding out over her skin. They didn't come.

'You're right,' she said, calmly now. She pulled her hand away. 'I've no more scenes to make. Not for you, anyway. You were sleeping with your step-sister behind my back the entire time we were together, and then you bullied me into keeping it secret for you. Into lying to your whole family—who, I might add, I've always liked and respected, and who certainly don't deserve to have a son like you. What kind of arsehole are you, Ryan?' She shook her head, incredulously. Behind them there was movement in the corridor, and the shocked silence of somebody who's heard something they can hardly believe.

'Leah, keep your voice down for fuck's sake!' Ryan hissed furiously.

'Too late, by the looks of it,' she said coldly. 'Goodbye, Ryan. Don't expect to hear from me, and really—*really*—don't contact me again.' She turned her back on him and his incredulous expression, walked down the steps and towards the gate. There she paused, and turned. 'The soldier's name is Robin Durrant. He was a convict. You can trace any remaining relatives from that information, but I doubt there'll be any. And for the rest—you'll have to wait until my book comes out!' she shouted.

She didn't look back again. Her legs felt elastic, stretching into long, purposeful strides as she walked away. She felt desperate, impatient, but as she walked she realised it wasn't Ryan she was desperate to get away from, but somebody else she could not wait to return to. Hoping it wasn't too

471

late, she got her phone out of her bag and started to dial, her fingers clumsy with nervous excitement. She hit the wrong key and had to start again, swearing under her breath. A car horn blared from across the street and startled her. She looked up to see a familiar muddy Renault, parked twenty yards from the house. Mark waved to her from behind the wheel, his eyes anxious but a grin on his face. A wide smile of relief welled up and lit Leah's face, and she waved back. With happiness making her footsteps light, she crossed the road and ran to where he was.

1911

The weather is turning, autumn stealing in with a noticeable chill to the morning air, and touches of bronze, gold and brown on the trees all around. Tess walks along the towpath into Thatcham with two letters of Mrs Canning's to post. She rehearses the directions carefully in her mind, worried about losing her way, about not finding The Rectory again on the way back. She has only been in her new position for a fortnight, and everything is still strange. From the wide open spaces all around, to the quiet and the calm; and the good, hot food after months of the cruelty and deprivations of Holloway and Frosham House. She can't help but eat everything that's put in front of her, and already the hollow between her hip bones is filling out again, her stomach and arms growing rounder. Sophie Bell seems pleased at this. The cook says little, her moon face careworn, but she smiles at

Tess, pats her on the shoulder from time to time, and treats her well. Most of the woman's attention is showered on a little black and white cat, a scrawny stray that appeared at the kitchen door several weeks earlier, and which Sophie has adopted with an almost superstitious devotion. She feeds it cream from a saucer, and saves the kidney trimmings for it when she makes a pudding. But Sophie Bell hasn't given it a name, simply calling it 'cat', so Tess secretly names it Tinker.

Hester Canning seems an odd woman, full of nerves and disquiet, but she is clearly trying to make Tess feel safe, and welcome. She is softly spoken, so different to The Gentleman, and to Mrs Heddingly. To the many and various wardens and masters Tess has suffered of late. Hester Canning speaks and moves as if there is something sleeping in the corner of the room that she fears to wake. She often keeps one hand curled protectively around her midriff, and Tess wonders if she is expecting. She hopes so. A child is what the house needs to brighten it. The vicar is a vague and silent man. He hasn't said two words to Tess; does not seem to have noticed her arrival. Tess doesn't mind this. She has seen much in the past rough months of her life, and she no longer has much trust in men—even a man of the cloth. The household appears to run quite well without any input from him. And all around the house, unmentioned but unavoidable, Cat's absence is felt. The police found her last letter to Tess, in the bag abandoned in the meadows. It found its way to her eventually, after her arrival in Cold Ash Holt and her first learning about her friend's death. A message from beyond the grave—one that made her cry again, when the first storm of grief had scarcely passed. Tess is here because Cat is not. Everybody at The Rectory knows this, and Tess wonders if it will always be thus.

She takes a deep breath, stifles fresh tears at the thought of her murdered friend. She refuses to walk across the blameless meadows where it happened. She takes the longer route, along the lane and then onto the towpath beside the bridge. Nobody suggests that she should do otherwise. If Cat's ghost is anywhere, it is haunting those meadows, angrily lamenting just how close she came to freedom, how close she came to starting her new life. Whatever the reason she met with the theosophist that morning, if she just had not, if she had gone straight to see George, she would be with him now, loving and laughing; radiating that bright strength that had drawn Tess to her like the moon pulling the tide. The injustice of it is so vast and bitter that Tess is too angry with God to say the Lord's Prayer at the end of the church service. Her eyes stay open, her lips sealed. When she reached for the chamber pot one morning soon after her arrival, she found a small brass crucifix tossed underneath the bed. After careful consideration, she left it there. God will have to prove himself to Tess, after what has been done to Cat.

She keeps walking and at last buildings begin to appear further along the canal. She hears voices, laughter and splashing. Pausing nervously, she pulls her shawl tighter around her shoulders and cautiously walks on. By the bridge where she is to take to the road and follow it to the centre of town, a group of boys are bathing, their blazers and straw hats scattering the grassy bank. It's some kind of impromptu swimming gala, the boys let out from school, and a crowd has gathered—men and women and children, hanging from the bridge to watch. Tess joins them, smiling uncertainly, laughing at the boys' antics as they swim a cigarette race—the winner being he who can make it to the far bank and back twice over with his fag still alight, in spite of the hearty splashing all around.

Eventually, Tess turns to walk on into town, but just as she does a steamboat chugs slowly into view from the east. She pauses to watch it, as the boatman whistles a shrill warning through his fingers, and the boys make way for him, scrambling onto the banks to clear a path. The boat is old and battered; wreathed in clouds of steam and smoke. But it has fresh paint, half-finished. The cabin has been done up in Romany colours—greens and reds and yellows. The sides are still faded and flaking, except for the name of the vessel, done neatly in white against a dark blue ground. *Black Cat*. Tess's heart leaps and she runs back to the side of the bridge to see it better. The man at the tiller is weathered and strongly built. He smiles and thanks the boys as he passes, but his eyes are sad. Tess's eyes stay fixed on him, and she has the sensation that she knows him—so powerful that for a second, when he is close, she almost calls out to him. Tess watches until the boat slides out of sight, and suddenly she grows calm. The autumn sun shines softly on her face, and she walks on into Thatcham with a feeling that things will be well. That she will be well. She feels as though a friend is walking beside her.

ACKNOWLEDGEMENTS

My love and thanks to Mum and Dad, Charlie and Luke for all their support, patience and enthusiasm; to my wonderful editor Sara O'Keeffe for all her hard work and vision; and to my equally wonderful agent Nicola Barr for counselling, reading and plain speaking. Finally, my thanks to Ranald Leask at the Commonwealth War Graves Commission for answering my questions relating to its work and processes.

AUTHOR'S NOTE

For a better understanding of theosophy, I have referred extensively to *Theosophy* by Rudolph Steiner (1910); *The Key to Theosophy* by H. P. Blavatsky (1889); and *The Secret Life of Nature* by Peter Tompkins (1997). There is also an excellent overview by John M. Lynch in his introduction to the 2006 Bison edition of *The Coming of the Fairies* by Sir Arthur Conan Doyle. All and any mistakes in the interpretation of theosophy are mine and Robin Durrant's alone.

Robin Durrant's retelling of Geoffrey Hodson's encounter with undines is taken from Hodson's account of the incident, as recounted in *The Secret Life of Nature* (see above)—although this encounter of Hodson's did not actually occur until 1922.

Cat's experience of force-feeding is based upon a report on its use in the *British Medical Journal* from August, 1912, and upon the first-hand account of her own experiences by Mary R. Richardson in *Laugh a Defiance* (1953).

Whilst some of the places and buildings around Thatcham described in *The Unseen* do exist, including The Bluecoat School, and whilst some of the information concerning these places is historically accurate, all storylines and characters linked to them are entirely fictional.

479